The Deep End

ALSO BY JOSEPH HAYES

NOVELS

The Third Day
Don't Go Away Mad
The Hours After Midnight
Bon Voyage (with Marrijane Hayes)
The Desperate Hours

PLAYS

Calculated Risk
The Desperate Hours

THE DEEP END

A NOVEL BY Joseph Hayes

§§ §§ §

NEW YORK / THE VIKING PRESS

First published in 1967 by The Viking Press, Inc.
625 Madison Avenue, New York, N.Y. 10022

Published simultaneously in Canada by
The Macmillan Company of Canada Limited

Library of Congress catalog card number: 66-23824
Printed in U.S.A. by Vail-Ballou Press, Inc., Binghamton, N.Y.

For Marrijane,
who knows that now is eternity

And for Joseph Donnelly,
in memoriam

Now he gave jeer for jeer, and taunted the apes
that jibed him. With the soul of an Atheist, he
wrote down the godliest things; with the feeling
of misery and death in him, he created forms of
gladness and life.

—HERMAN MELVILLE, *Pierre*

Contents

❦ Sunday

I T had been a perfectly ordinary Sunday. I had spent most of it in the country, in the small rustic cottage that had been Lydia's and my weekend retreat until our daughter Anne's marriage a year ago. Now, although Anne and Glenn were occupying it only until Glenn could get established in business in the Newtown area, I couldn't help feeling a stranger there—especially with Lydia away in London. Bluffer in manner, her blond hair somewhat darker in color, and her skin a sunned hue compared to Lydia's paleness—Anne, nevertheless, reminded me too much of her mother and this, together with the sort of bantering affection and playful hints at intimacy that always existed between Anne and Glenn, only made me feel more alone and detached. By five o'clock I had grown so restless and oddly resentful that I had to leave.

I had driven back to the city in the stuttering crawl of traffic on the parkways, and the evening had stretched emptily ahead. In the month Lydia had been away, concentration on the challenge of work had more or less filled the days, but the evenings and weekends had become increasingly oppressive. Curious, really, because while I had known that I would miss Lydia, I had also felt that a slight and brief break in the routine might in fact be good for both of us. But I had not anticipated this feeling of being at loose ends most of the time.

The city streets steamed with heat and humidity. Instead of leaving the car with the doorman at the apartment, I drove it to the garage myself; then on impulse, or because I wasn't quite prepared yet to face those several blank hours before I could get to sleep, I decided to see whatever film was playing around the corner. It turned out to be a Swedish import called *Dear John*: a rather tender and simple story of the growth of love between two lonely people—the loneliness leading first to sex but the relationship then deepening into more tender and more complex feelings and realizations. Nevertheless, there were a number of rather explicit sex scenes and enough nudity to stir a kind of gnawing hunger in me. If Lydia had not been away for so long or if she had been with me, it would have been different. The comments in the lobby would have amused her. It wasn't hard to imagine what she would have said as we walked home, arms loosely linked: *But they miss the whole point. The idiots are going for the wrong reasons. I don't know whether to laugh or cry.*

Since I couldn't go on listening to that soft English accent in my mind—and picturing a few love scenes of our own—I had then dropped into Pat's Pub, which was no more than a dark neighborhood bar owned by an Italian named Pat. I had several tall Scotches, taking my time because I had too much time to kill. I had never been much of a drinker: one before dinner at home, possibly two at a dinner party, a glass of wine with the meal because Lydia enjoyed wine, sometimes a brandy after. But lately I had begun to drink quite a few more and had fallen into the pattern of dropping into Pat's every other evening or so—both habits that I knew would not persist, of course, once Lydia returned.

The whiskies had a pleasant relaxing effect and by the time I was walking to the apartment I found myself trying, for no reason whatever, to recall a poem that began, "We were very gay, we were very merry, / We rode back and forth all night on the ferry." If Lydia were here, she'd know it like a shot, not only the rest of it but who had written it. It somehow reminded me of those first years in New York after the war when we had enjoyed taking the ferry to Staten Island on summer evenings. How long ago was that? Twenty years now. Impossible.

I nodded to the doorman—the Irish one tonight, Terence, not Geoffrey, the Englishman who amused Lydia so much—and Terence was doing a little nodding on his own. I went up alone on the small self-operated elevator and let myself into the apartment, feeling mellow but aware of the hollow loneliness and the faintly erotic disquiet in myself, and knowing that because I had not eaten since lunch in Connecticut a single stiff drink would now put me to sleep quickly. Then another weekend would be over. I was pouring the whisky at the small bar which was built into a corner of the living room and rarely used for anything but flowers and magazines.

"Well, about time—"

When I first heard the voice, I had an odd impression that I had left the television set in the library turned on. But the impression was fleeting.

A young woman—girl, really—was standing in the library door:

slightly off kilter, as if on one foot, one hip thrust sideways, wearing a flimsy sleeveless dress which stopped well above her knees and clung to the slim lines of her body. Head to one side, she seemed to meet my astonished stare, but at the same time her eyes—I could not be sure of the color but they were dark—seemed to be focused beyond me, almost blank. They did not flinch as the silence extended itself between us.

"Don't you know me?" The voice was far from husky but it had an odd depth, a sort of musical resonance in spite of its detachment, and her wide mouth seemed about to twist into a smile.

"I never saw you before in my life," I said, and instantly felt like a fool.

She did smile then, like a mischievous child enjoying some private joke, and uttered a sound that was almost but not quite a giggle. "You saw me," she said.

"I'm afraid you have the wrong apartment."

"Why? Are they all alike?"

"How'd you get in here?" I demanded, satisfied at the brusqueness of my tone but at the same instant sharply conscious of its source: the girl's motionless stance, bare arms, and steady, frank stare all suggested intimacy. "Who the hell are you and what do you want?"

"You saw me," the girl said and, tilting her head to the other side, blew a perfect smoke ring, then watched it with childlike fascination, lips still pursed. And I decided not to answer, to play for time. "I certainly noticed *you*." She began to move then, her walk a graceful, careless slouch, eyes moving up and down my body with frank speculation, her soft dress making a silken sound in the quiet room.

"*Thank* you."

But the heavy irony failed. She stopped moving and puckered her mouth. "You're not the way I imagined you, though—"

"Why should you imagine me at all?"

"Oh, don't be so ugghy—" She flung herself into a heavy chair, lifted her legs over the arm of it—and laughed toward the ceiling. "Why pretend? Why play it phony?"

I felt a prickling of annoyance that threatened to turn into anger. I took a long gulp of drink, then asked, "Where did all this noticing go on?"

"You know—"

"I'm damned if I do!"

She blew more rings, throwing her head back, her long dark hair trailing wildly down behind the chair. I couldn't help noticing that her legs, above high white boots, were the same bronze color as her face.

"Where?" I demanded, hearing the harshness in my tone.

"In Pat's, man." She seemed to have lost interest. "Where else?"

Then I almost laughed, remembering Pat's gleeful, lustful leer: *Havin' a ball, Mr. Wyatt, while the wife izzaway, yeh?* What comes from confiding to a bartender that your English wife's English mother is very old and very ill and as demanding as ever of her daughter.

"No deal," I told the girl. "And tell Pat he's a sonofabitch."

She laughed then. "Tell him yourself." A faint suggestion of mockery—raillery, really—in her tone, as she reached to stub out her cigarette. Then she kicked off her boots and curled herself into lines of catlike almost ecstatic repose, regarding me again through half-closed lids with that oddly personal, sensuous contemplation and a hint of a smile.

"Make yourself at home," I said, conscious again of the awkwardness of the intended irony.

"Thanks."

Aware of her body and of her eyes drifting slowly down mine with candid conjecture. I turned away, gulped the drink, felt it burning all the way down. I felt the anger quicken, struggled with it, recalling all the warnings of a lifetime: from my gentle father, who, in the end, had himself been corroded by an unnatural fury that had bewildered me; from my teachers at school, who had called it *temper*; from my professors at law school, who had warned that it was an attorney's most treacherous and self-defeating trait; from Lydia, who could either ignore it or lightly scoff it into absurdity, often intensifying it in either case. Now I recognized all the storm signals: that slow climbing heat all through me, the involuntary stiffening, the dizzying drain of blood from my head. I took another long swallow to drown the sour taste in my throat.

"She's pretty," the girl said. Then uncertainly: "Sort of. Her face, anyway." When I glanced, I saw she was staring at the portrait of Lydia over the mantel. "How about the rest of her?"

I dared not look at the painting, knowing its every detail: the pale, blond composure, the small near-perfect features, that odd, touching combination of wistfulness, soft humor, and womanly strength in the familiar delicate face. "She's my wife," I said evenly. "And old enough to be your mother. As I am old enough to be your father."

"Only you're not." She giggled. "Not that it'd matter. Is she a bitch?"

"What?"

"Her. Is she a bitch? She reminds me of my mother."

The sour taste turned poisonous, moved from my throat into my mouth. "She is not a bitch." I heard the spaced level words as if they were not mine. "She is not a bitch in any small or large sense, and I am in love with her." I hesitated briefly. "I love her but I am also in love with her."

"Sure," the girl said. There was no mockery in her tone, only a sort of weary acceptance. "Sure. But she's still a bitch."

"You don't even know her," I growled.

"I know my mother."

I heard myself laugh. What the hell kind of a mind was I up against?

Her head turned; her gaze found mine. Her eyes were definitely brown. "You're not so old." She said it gravely. "Bogey was fifty-four when he split."

"Who?" My head had begun to reel. "When he what?"

"Bogey. You know. It's too bad you're not bald. Bald men are sexier."

I involuntarily ran my hand through my stiff crew cut. "Look," I said, and felt the poison recede somewhat, "look, I'll apologize for not being bald if you'll get the hell out of here."

"Bogey was bald. He wore a mat. Everyone knows that." She stretched, both arms above her head, breasts out-thrust. "You don't want me to go."

In that instant I had to break the impulse to pick her up bodily and carry her to the door.

"Is she good in bed?"

The absurdity was overwhelming—the utter ridiculousness of the entire situation! Did this kid think I was going to stand here and discuss—

"You didn't answer my question—"

In my own mind, though, I considered the question. Behind Lydia's somewhat austere composure and simplicity of appearance was womanly warmth and an intensity of feeling that, after twenty years, never failed to astonish and delight me.

Wanting to laugh, in triumph, I said, "Go to hell."

It didn't seem to offend her. She only shrugged. "You haven't offered me a drink."

"That's not the whole story," I said. "You weren't invited here. For a drink or for anything else."

She stood up, tossed her head, black hair spilling and streaming, uttered some incomprehensible sound deep in her throat—contempt? pleasure? what?—and drifted with loose-jointed abandon toward the bar. "You could be sorry."

The anger crackled through me again. All of a sudden the room seemed terribly hot. "Is that a threat?"

"Tough, man," she said. "Go on. It turns me on."

With the drinks roiling the rage in me and with the heat of the room closing in, I had begun to feel that I had somehow stepped over some indefinable, yet very definite, line, or border, and now I was in some strange alien land where, damn it, I didn't even know the language!

"Y'got any root beer? I like root beer with rye." She laughed again: the abrupt burbling of a child amused. "How's that grab you?"

I strode to the bar. "No root beer. No rye. No drink." Then rasping: "Get out!"

Her eyes met mine: amused, but darkening with an odd excitement. "You gonna throw me out?"

"If necessary."

"It might be fun." She leaned toward me. "Go ahead."

"Look," I said then, the control taut all through me, "I don't know what you're up to, but you'd better make up your mind that you're not going to get away with it."

The excitement in her eyes deepened. "You turn me on, man." Then she moved past me, brushing against me so that I could feel the soft thrust of breast under the thin dress. She slouched to the hi-fi set, whistling softly. I stood motionless. Helpless.

An announcer's voice, blurred with static, filled the room. The same news I had heard several times on the car radio: more troops ordered to Vietnam, angry mob attacks civil rights marchers with stones and clubs while state troopers stand by, President Johnson declares—

She twisted the dial and a shrill discordant blare, deafening and repetitious as a jungle beat, burst through the apartment. A quivering intensity was visible in her narrow back as she turned. A dusky intentness lit her eyes, which seemed to fix themselves on me while at the same time they seemed to be gazing either beyond me or into her own mind. Her body began to move, writhing slowly at first, then faster as it caught up to the beat of the music; in a moment she was moving chaotically, every muscle, hair swinging wildly from side to side, legs lifting, arms flailing. I realized that she was moving toward me. The savage, jungle-like throb inundated my mind. She was very close now, her face still filled with that odd, self-absorbed abstraction.

I made up my mind. I crossed to the radio, flipped it off. My head swam slightly in the abrupt silence. Now what? I finished the drink in a single gulp.

"You're turned on." The whisper was soft and knowing—a taunt. A faint, triumphant smile played along her lips. "I can tell." Her eyes, even darker now, were regarding me from beneath lowered lids. "Now what? You gonna tell me how old you are again? Man, what does it count? You turned me on or I wouldn't be here."

She moved closer and somehow I could not step back, or away. Her face, inches from mine, appeared even younger: soft, the skin incredibly clear, richly tanned. And now the teasing humor was in her gaze again, a feminine mocking. I was quivering all over, and helpless. In her eyes was a knowingness older than time. I could feel the perspiration scalding down my spine and I was not breathing.

Then she was kissing me. Her body thrust tightly against mine, straining so that I could feel every line of it down my own. Without decision or will I felt my arms go around her, felt the pliant softness of her lips open under mine, and my mind went blank, impulse taking over, overwhelming thought, restraint. Vaguely I knew that I had to be drunk, had to be, was, but a crazy exultancy exploded in me, too, and I felt myself go taut and hollow at the same time as we stood clinging to each other while the room reeled crazily. This wasn't happening, this couldn't be happening—

She was standing away, breathless, eyes completely dark now, black and burning. But the smile still lurked on her lips: faint, triumphant. Then she turned away, shoeless, loping with frank, girlish expectancy to the stairway leading to the balcony above.

"What's to stop us?" Childishly conspiratorial. Leaning over the railing now, looking down, hair tumbling over her face. "What, man? You want me to stay, don't you?"

"No." It was a growl. "I want you to clear out of here. Now." And it was true, yet not true.

"Don't put me on." She turned. "What's in there?"

It was the guest room. Once, until a year ago, Anne's room. My throat was closed tight.

I saw her open the door. I saw her go in. I saw the door close.

And realized that the whole scene had reached a climax of absurdity, incredibility. What was going on? How had it happened? I didn't even know her name. And then the fury took over. Heat flooded my whole body. The desire remained, sickening and intense, simple animal passion, lust, but the anger was stronger and, as I glanced around the neat familiar room, consciously ignoring Lydia's image above the fireplace, I made up my mind. I must have known all along, even as I was kissing her, that I couldn't go through with it. Hell, it was against my nature, against my whole life, my way of life. Others might think me a fool, especially any man who ever heard of it. Let them. I wasn't drunk enough, or idiot enough, to allow an impulse, an opportunity thrown at me like this by some kooky little bitch, to change my entire—

The door above opened. Light fell across the balcony.

I didn't wait. If I had to throw her out bodily, I'd throw her out. I was mounting the stairs. No little bitch off the street was going to—

She came onto the balcony. She wore only a flowing flimsy negligee. I stopped on the stairs, going slack, holding the banister. Light fell from behind her.

Then I recognized Lydia's negligee. And, feeling the overwhelming fury choking me, I realized with relief that I was safe.

"Take that off." The words were so strangled and slurred that they seemed to erupt in a single distorted animal snarl.

And she was smiling. Enjoying it! But now her smile was ugly, twisted. "The only way it comes off is if you rip it off." A low whisper, roughened by passion—a challenge. "If you're man enough—"

I did not even realize that I had moved until I was on the balcony facing her, swaying slightly. Her face blurred before me.

Then she turned and went into the bedroom. *"If!"*

I followed, blindly. And then it was as if I had no mind of my own, no will. I reached and ripped it off, ferociously, in the grip of hate and anger and a wild lust that left no space in me for rational thought or decision.

Her entire body was the same rich golden color as her face.

It was while I was lying there afterward that panic struck. She lay curled, childlike, defenseless, her back to me.

"Goo'night, Sam—"

Cold disgust. Shame. Guilt. Stabbing remorse. I had to get up, get away. Avoiding the sight of her, I picked up my clothes from the floor and crept, still naked, onto the balcony, closing the bedroom door behind me, and went into my own bedroom, mine and Lydia's. I sat on the edge of the bed and wished I had a cigarette. What now? How to get rid of her? That came first. Now or wait till morning? Would money do it? How much? Christ, how had I let myself in for anything like this?

I heard a sound. It came from below. Had she gone downstairs?

I dressed hastily, drawing on the first shirt my hand fell on, the first pair of slacks, any shoes I could first reach, no socks. Damned if I could go down there in the buff, or even in a robe—no more of that, none, it was over and done with. And the sooner I could get her out—

But there was no one in the living room when I came out onto the balcony. I went down the stairs, hearing more sounds—refrigerator door closing?—from the kitchen. I paused at the bar and then poured myself a drink, without water, without ice, took a long gulp before proceeding through the dining room to the kitchen, glass in hand. Time enough later for the guilt, the pain; time now to get her out, to get it over with once and for all.

But she was not in the kitchen. Standing at the range was a young man: tall, heavy-shouldered, wearing skin-tight white denims, a Basque shirt with violent horizontal stripes, a thick brown beard, and dark glasses. His hair was long and bushy, combed forward so that his forehead was invisible. On one arm, tight around bulging biceps, was a leather thong or strap of some sort. A cigarette dangled from a corner of mouth, and he had a towel tucked into his belt, apron-like.

While I stared, the fury returned. Why hadn't I thought of this? Why the hell hadn't something like this occurred to me?

"Who are you?"

His head turned, tilted, but I could not see his eyes behind the glittering glasses. He dipped his finger into something bubbling in the saucepan, then threw back his head and licked his fingers. He smacked his lips. "It won't be exquisite, dad-baby, y'stock a poor kitchen, but Wilby did his best-best."

"Answer my question."

"Lobster-shrimp goo-goo, with mushrooms." The gaiety behind

the mournful slyness seemed a natural part of the dreamlike atmosphere. "Thought you'd 'preciate a midnight sup-sup after the fun and
games."

He'd been in here all along. I had to clench every nerve to stifle the
wrath that surged like flame through my veins, threatened to erupt
now into actual physical violence at any second. But, damn it, I had
to use my head. The boy was no more than twenty-five, so at least
twenty-five years my junior. He outweighed me by twenty pounds and
appeared to be in excellent physical condition. Violence now would
inevitably cause a public disturbance that I might not be able to explain.

"How many more of you?"

"Just us, pop." He was not looking at me. "Just Jenny'n me'n you
—ain't it jolly?"

"Jolly," I heard myself say. "If I'd known you two gourmets were
coming, I'd have stocked up on Campbell's soups." The lightness in
my own voice surprised me.

Then he did stare at me. His lips twisted pinkly in the lush beard
and the ash fell off his cigarette. "Pop, you're puttin' it on. You ain't
really with it, but y'got a certain potential."

"If that's a compliment, thank you." In spite of my quivering
nerves, the tone was casual. "You're just trying to make me feel
good."

He snorted a laugh, opened the refrigerator door, and pulled out
two trays. "What kinda host y'playin' here, man? How about you
icin' the goddam wine?" He shoved the trays toward me. "I seen it in
the bar. Make it white-white."

Direct orders, even under the discipline of war, had always irked
me. Now his supercilious arrogance sent a shock of wildness through
me and I almost knocked the trays out of his hands. Instead, I said,
"Go to hell," and turned and went into the living room.

Where Jenny was opening cabinet doors in quick nervous movements. She wore the same dress. She straightened, leaving the doors
open, and continued searching for something, not conscious of my
presence. I finished the drink, watching her. Her face looked clenched
now, lips thin, eyes narrowed, and, recalling the wildness of less than
an hour ago, I was startled: the girl wasn't even pretty. She opened
the drawer of the telephone table in the small foyer, rummaged
through it with both hands, uttered a sound that was not quite a
word, then turned without closing it—and saw me.

No recognition in her face. She glared. "Give me a cig for God's sake."

"I don't smoke."

"Jesus, everybody smokes."

"There's not a cigarette in the place. Unless your boy friend in the kitchen has one."

"Boy friend?" She snorted. "Wilby?" She drifted toward me. "Christ what a joint!" The petulance was clear, nasty. She turned on the radio. Music squalled and bellowed again. Then she stood with one arm stretched along the mantel, the other hand on her hip, which was out-thrust, and regarded me. "Well, Sam—"

Was it a question? "My name's not Sam," I said, and stepped to the bar to pour another drink.

"It could be."

"Who the hell's Sam?"

"Oh—oh shit, what a square! Sam's not just anyone you have sex with. He's—like someone you make it with. Like you could be Sam—"

Like hell! I took a drink. The whisky cut, went scalding deep. I almost gagged. Like hell, you bitch. But I said, because it might be useful to know, depending on what their game was: "If I'm Sam, who are you?"

"Jenny."

"Jenny what?"

"Not Jenny what! Jenny who!" It was the young man coming through the dining room. What had he said his name was? Wilby?

Jenny tittered. "What's on second."

Wilby stepped lightly to kneel on the floor at the enormous glass-topped cocktail table. "What?"

"What's on second, Who's on third."

"All squares off for Times Square!" Wilby shouted.

"Gimme a cig."

He tossed a package toward her. It fell to the floor. "That your belly I hear growlin', dad?" He was clearing the table, his actions quick and almost birdlike in spite of his muscular heaviness. "Where the hell's the wine?"

I decided to have another whisky. Not a good idea in the circumstances, probably—but what, exactly, were the circumstances? All right, I could play their game. Up to a point. I stooped and took out a bottle of wine, placed it on the bar.

Jenny seemed to have lost all interest, now that she had a cigarette between her lips. She was wandering around the room, touching various objects, lightly running her fingers over them: Lydia's collection of miniature ivories, a Ming vase, the pewter Lydia had brought back from England five or six years ago. Curious? Or possessive?

"How'd you get in here?" My voice was normal again: reasonable, curious. But it flickered through my mind that the rational approach might be my undoing. No telling who these strange characters were —hopheads, criminals? Perhaps the only solution was to give in to the gnawing outrage and take savage action now, to hell with the consequences. "Who let you in?"

Wilby picked up a book from the table and examined it. "Don't sweat, pop. Doorman didn't even see me."

"And," Jenny said, beginning to dance alone again, "I told the man I was visiting some cat named Donald Bishop."

"Abbot," I heard myself say, thinking of Donald Abbott, who lived in the duplex below. But how had she come by Donald's name?

"Religious, anyway," the young man sniggered. "See how we protect you, man?" He tossed the book so that it slid against my shoes: *The Green Berets.* "Which one belongs to the Book of the Month culture-club, man? You or the limey wife?"

Every muscle was taut; every muscle had begun to ache. "All right, let's have it. What do you want?"

"Not very polite, is he, Jenny?" The feigned hurt amounted to derision.

But Jenny was dancing, writhing, abstracted, eyes withdrawn.

"What do you want?"

Wilby sat back on his haunches. The table was empty. "Or vicey-versey, dad. What do *you* want? More to the point-point, ain't it? An' we must stick to the point-point, must we not, us attorneys-at-law?" He was fingering a silver lighter I had given Lydia years ago, before both of us had decided to give up smoking. He set it aside with exaggerated care, a small, secret smile twisting his beard. Then he stood up, sighing, shaking his head in mock sadness. "Pop, y'oughtta know better'n to rape my wife."

Whether my shock showed on my face or not, he contemptuously ignored it. Probably savoring it all the more, the bastard. I watched him moving through the dining room toward the kitchen, gliding on rope-soled sandals.

Wife! Revolted, sickened, I could only stare. In spite of his size, he was so obviously, arrogantly what he was—

But when I turned to Jenny, she was dancing and smoking, bare arms making swimming motions in the air, eyes glazed, fixed on nothing. As if I were not even in the room. The whole ridiculous evening was becoming, minute by minute, more grotesque, more unfathomable. Hell, it was *possible* they were married. *Anything* was possible.

Jenny was singing with the music: "I . . . can't get . . . no . . . sat-is-*fac*-tion—"

Aware of the tightening in my scrotum, I realized that I was somehow standing off now and watching, as from a distance—almost as if the scene were being played on a lighted stage and I was in the scene yet in the audience at the same time and could not make up my mind whether the play was outrageously comic, simply absurd, or appallingly sinister.

I saw Jenny, body still undulating, stretch out on her back on the cocktail table with that feline suppleness that gave a certain grace to even the most outlandish movements. Her arms continued to move over her head, face abstracted and unconcerned, and then she lifted both legs, her dress falling, and moved them in the air.

I made up my mind. I walked resolutely to the foyer, picked up the telephone, dialed 0. What I should have done at once, what I should have done an hour ago.

"What're you doing?" It was a hiss that caused me to turn around. She was lying there quietly now, quite still, and her face was clouded with apprehension.

I heard a buzzing at the other end of the line.

"Who are you calling?"—a thin ugliness in her tone, also a warning. She sat up. "I'll—" Then she lifted her voice. "*Wilby!*" A cry for help. "I'll scream the goddam roof off!"

The whirring at the other end continued repetitiously, at spaced intervals, sounding louder than usual in my ear.

"Don't scream, baby." Wilby appeared with a saucepan and a stack of dishes. "Save the scream-screams." His voice was thin and high pitched, but he scarcely glanced in my direction. "Might need 'em later."

"Operator," a crisp voice said in my ear.

"Jus' make sure the fuzz bring the reporters, dad. Jenny-baby, how'd y'like t'be in the *Daily News* tomorrow?"

"This is your operator—"

"Front page or center-fold? *Daily News,* AP, UPI, and I pee on you—"

He slid the steaming pan across the glass surface. It slammed against Jenny's thigh and she leaped up with a gasp.

"You sonofabitch!" she yelped. "You know I got nothing on under." Rubbing her thigh: "You mean sonofabitch!"

"This is your operator," the voice insisted. "May I help you, please?"

"Go ahead, pop." Wilby still did not look in my direction as he produced knives and spoons from his pocket and clattered them onto the table. "Got a dandy-dandy story. Like how you got Jenny sloshed, brought her home from the Pub—"

My mind clogged. "May I help you, please?" I placed my hand over the mouthpiece.

"Like how y'got her in here'n raped her. Like how she called me, come over. Tell the nice lady, man-man. Tell her t'send them cops fast-fast—" He knelt on the floor to arrange the plates and silverware, very meticulously. "Little luck, those London papers'll pick up the story. On accounta the limey wife's fancy family—"

That did it. The rage deepened, hardened, but I replaced the phone in its cradle. I was not breathing.

" 'Course Lydia-Lydia, she wouldn't believe y'raped little Jenny-baby, would she?"

I did not glance at the portrait over his head. "You're damned right she wouldn't," I managed to say.

And Wilby laughed. "Like hell, man!" His laugh was as high-pitched and razor-edged as his voice—a cackle. "Like hell-hell." He sat back on his haunches and turned to me. "Ain't it terrible now, how people always always believe the worst? About somebody else. Disillusioning, ain't it?"

For the first time I recognized something weirdly contradictory about his speech: illiterate, yet—

I glanced toward Jenny. "I doubt anybody'd believe *she* could be raped."

Wilby chuckled. "Y'know what people believe, dad? What they want to believe. Click?"

Jenny was smiling. Without resentment. "I always wanted to be raped." She sounded and looked perfectly innocent—and sincere.

"Like who don't, baby? Fact of life. Click, pop?"

I moved toward them across the room. As Wilby went back to work on the table and Jenny watched, amused. What was I going to do? What *could* I do?

"Pop," Wilby cried, "you ain't even iced the wine yet!" He was pouring the whitish concoction from the pan onto the plates. "Give dad the bottle, Jenny-baby. An' give him the corkscrew, too."

Jenny giggled. "Yeh. I'm all thirst." She picked up the bottle from the bar and extended it. "Oscar's all thirst inside."

And her eyes met mine: playful, taunting.

"Y'gotta feed the little bastard," Wilby said.

Oscar? What the devil did that mean? *Oscar inside—*

Then, reaching for the bottle, I was tempted—in a reckless rush of panic—to grab it by the neck and bring it smashing down over Wilby's head as he knelt on the floor.

Jenny must have sensed the impulse. "Wilby—" she said quietly.

He stood up, whirling around at the same time. Jauntily he stepped toward me. Reached. Took the bottle from my hand. Then he extended his other hand to the bar, picked up the silver corkscrew, and, with calculated disdain, turned his back, placing the bottle between his knees as he began to work on it. "Tough, man, tough, ain't he, Jenny?"

"Maybe he is." Her tone and gaze were questioning, tinged with uncertainty and a kind of animal admiration. "Sam's got all kindsa surprises—"

The cork made a sucking sound, then popped. Wilby straightened to face me then, with his pink-in-beard grin, head tilted. "Paternity, paternity, who'll join my fraternity?"

For the first time I felt a cold sickle of fear probe the flames that were threatening to consume everything inside me. I took a deep drink. I had never had much respect for men who tried to solve their problems with liquor, but I had no space for surprise at myself now. Hazily conscious that the idea was preposterous, I had the hope that somehow the whisky might clear my head.

When I had drained the glass, I faced them again. But they were sitting on the floor, facing each other across the table. Wilby was pouring the pale wine and Jenny was eating as if she had never tasted food before. She looked downright ugly now: sharp-featured, ravenous, a gross child. And I felt a distant relief.

"Boss," Jenny was saying—or some word which sounded like it. She smacked her lips. "Fab gig."

Wilby spoke through his food. "Mushrooms make it. Oscar like it?"

I stood watching, still viewing the scene as from a cloudlike distance. They ate swiftly, with noisy relish and constant motions of hands and spoons and wine glasses. Like a couple of monkeys.

"Damn Oscar," Jenny said. "I already hate the little bastard."

Wilby chortled, spewing wine and creamy food.

My stomach twisted and I went to the thermostat on the wall and turned up the air conditioning. The room was suddenly stifling.

"Mushrooms," Wilby said. "Like the bomb-bomb. What you think of the mushroom bomb, Lieutenant?"

Startled, I turned and went to the bar.

"Y'know, dad here was with the Eighth Air Force, Jenny. Medals to prove it. Reason he won't eat. Nobody in the Eighth ever ate anything but carrots. Made 'em see better at night. Where to drop the bomb-bombs. Click, dad?"

"You did your homework," I said. "How long have you been planning this?"

But I regretted it at once, knowing it would be ignored.

"Y'enjoy the war, pops? Enjoy-enjoy, thou shalt not kill, so get the kicks while the gettin's good. Did you, dad?"

"Nobody enjoys a war," I said, and heard Wilby laugh as I poured another drink. When I looked up, he had stretched out backward, full length on the floor, his sandaled feet propped on the table, and he was chuckling, his whole body rippling with the sound.

"Don't put me on, man. *Nobody enjoys war*! Shit, dad, and double obscenity squared. Look around you." He extended his glass and Jenny filled it. Balancing it precariously, he gazed upward. "You just don't keep your goddam ears open, your goddam eyes. *Nobody enjoys wars*!" He managed to twist onto his side and take a sip, spilling dribbles of wine through his beard and then onto the carpet. "How many parades in New York every year? How many bands, flags, speeches? Where's all them American Legion badges come from?" His voice had taken on, as if in spite of himself, a low dark excitement that I had never heard before. "Y'loved it, dad. Like all the others. Like everybody." Then, still balancing the glass, he came to his feet in a single graceful but violent movement, shouting. "Admit it, you hypocritical sonofabitch, you're like all the rest, you square lying bastard, tell the truth for once in your whole goddam blind fucking life!"

For an instant's shock I was certain I was going to strike. Get it over with. End it.

But I saw him waiting for me to do just that. His anticipation was in his stance, legs planted apart, body tense and quivering. I fought down the rage—again.

When he realized I was not going to move—I wouldn't give him the satisfaction!—he said, "Why won't you admit the truth?" And I heard a startling note of pleading in his tone.

I did not move.

Then, as abruptly as he had exploded, he seemed to wither into his familiar, slack, mocking self. "It's all war, anyways, click, dad?" His tone was light, almost playful again. "Streets. Living rooms. Country clubs. Bedrooms." He snorted and slouched away. "Bedrooms, most-most, click? Nature of the beast. Who y'trying to put on, dad? Yourself, maybe-maybe?"

I took an involuntary step toward him. "Listen, you bastard," I said. "Listen, sometimes force is necessary. Sometimes force is the only thing some kinds of people understand."

Silence. Wilby didn't move. I could sense, rather than see, Jenny straightening, watching.

"Is that a threat, pops?" Wilby's voice was thin, careless—almost amused.

"You're damn right that's a threat," I said.

"You better cool it, man. I don't go for threats."

"Neither do I."

Again silence.

Then Wilby sniggered. "Y'know, dad, I'm probably the only legitimate bastard you ever called a bastard. Me, I'm legitimately illegitimate! How's that grab you?"

I held every muscle rigid to keep from moving. "You've had your fun here. The game's over."

Wilby reached with his glass, and Jenny poured again. "Y'get the impression, Jenny, pop here don't enjoy our company? Wouldn't eat with us. Insults us—"

"Where we gonna go then?" Jenny asked—and I could not be certain whether there was mockery in her plaintiveness. "Where?"

"Ask the man-man, Jenny."

She twisted about on the floor and looked up at me. "Where? We got no pad. Where?"

"I've already told you where to go," I said.

"Didn't y'think lawyers were reasonable men, Jenny-baby?"

"I've been reasonable long enough. Much too long. I happen to know the law. I know what you can do and say, but I also know it's my word against yours."

"And you're respected, square—"

"I have a damned good reputation for telling the truth, yes."

Wilby began walking an imaginary tightwire down the carpet, balancing himself with arms outstretched. "Is law real, dad?"

"Real?"

"Real. You heard me. Is law real?"

"I don't intend to discuss law with you—"

"Reality, then. How about discussing reality? Is reality real? Does it actually exist-exist? Or do we imagine it and that's the only way it exists?" He twirled about on one leg. "Me, for instance, pops? Am I real to you?"

"You must be," I said, "because I'm damned if I could make you up."

"Oh, nice-nice! Listen to the man, Jenny! He's almost in, this square." He made an imaginary leap from the wire and took an exaggerated circus bow, and Jenny applauded. "You might make it yet, pop."

This time I took several steps before I could stop myself.

Wilby backed away. "I'll tell my cousin," he warned, pretending to cower.

"Your cousin won't listen," Jenny said, her eyes on me. "When has your cousin ever listened?"

"Pop don't know who my cousin is." Wilby gazed at the ceiling once, then lowered his head solemnly. "You call him God. That's my cousin. My deaf-dumb-blind all-powerful cousin who runs the stupid show yet doesn't exist, even in my mind."

"You're crazy," I said without thought.

His head came up then. He stiffened. "Watch your language, man." It was not his voice. It was a level whisper and simply not his voice at all.

"I can prove it's not my child." It seemed very important suddenly to hang on to reason, not to strike, not to allow this mad nightmare to explode into the brute ferocity that I could feel building volcanically inside. "I can prove I never saw either one of you until tonight."

Wilby turned to Jenny. "Baby, didn't you tell me dad was the one?"

"Sure," Jenny said and stood up. "I told you."

"I'd hate to make a mistake," Wilby said. "Wouldn't be fair to pop here."

It was like talking into the wind. Nevertheless, I said, "There are tests. Blood tests. Legalities."

Wilby threw himself full length onto the sofa, sighed, closed his eyes. "Y'got any blood, dad? Y'actually got any of that red stuff inside?" He threw out his arm, the wine glass in his hand. "Pour me another, man. I feel pregnant."

Before I knew I had moved, I kicked the glass from his hand. It sailed across the room, struck the brick of the fireplace, and shattered.

"Nebraska U.," Wilby said lazily. "All-American."

My fury, I realized, was directed as much at myself as at Wilby or Jenny: what the hell was I doing? Knowing I was innocent, I was assuming the law—reason—was on my side automatically. How many times had I warned clients against just such thinking, or feeling?

"Y'want to wake the neighbors?" Wilby clicked his tongue, then yawned. "What *will* they think?"

"Wilby—or whatever your name is—don't push too far." Now *my* voice was unrecognizable.

"Or what? Full center spread, *Daily News,* London papers please copy?"

I turned to Jenny, looked her up and down. "I don't believe she's pregnant."

At once Jenny thrust out her stomach, arching her back, and began to waddle around the room on flat ducklike feet, toes turned outward: a spontaneous, cruel, and contemptuous parody of every woman who had ever carried a child. Wilby whooped and rolled over, beating the sofa with his fists.

"I don't believe it," I said and went to pour another drink, ignoring them both.

"Tell y'what, dad," Wilby cried as Jenny plopped into a chair. "Y'don't believe Jenny'n me, y'get some pill-pusher in here, any old penicillin-jabber y'want to call, y'let him tell you about little Oscar."

At once I thought of Arnold Wilder: the heavy, sympathetic, knowing face with the jocular-sad eyes. Twenty years ago he had delivered Anne.

Another door closed. Another risk I didn't dare take. Even if the little bitch was not actually pregnant, Arnold, who loved Lydia as if she were a daughter, would naturally assume, as would any other doctor—

"You're right this time, dad. That's just what the doc's gonna think."

It was as if he had read my mind.

I took a long swallow, then a deep breath.

"All right," I said. "The game's over. How much?"

"What game, pop? How much what?"

"How much, damn it!"

"Jenny, listen to the man foam. He thinks we're playin' games. Y'think he talks about bread?"

"Money. How much do you think you can take me for?"

Wilby shrugged and studied the books in the case behind the sofa. "How much y'got?"

"I warned you before: don't push too far."

"Bread don't interest us, dad." He reached and pulled down a book. "Who reads this trash? Y'wouldn't happen t'have any Nietzsche 'round here, would you? Or maybe Kierkegaard. Y'ever dig that crumb-bun, man?"

I pushed away my surprise. Again. "If not money, then what?"

"Y'got a straight-straight mind, pop. I admire."

"I don't give a damn what you admire. If it's not money you're after—"

"You heard Jenny while ago. We got no pad. We got no place to park our weary asses."

"What are you hiding from?"

Wilby glanced up at me over the rim of the book. "Y'got one of them hackneyed minds, after all, don't you? Pop, y'disappoint me. Y'been watching that late-late show again?"

I tried to take another deep breath, but it wasn't very deep. Before I could decide how to handle it, I had to know—

"How long?"

Wilby returned to his reading. "When's Oscar due, Jenny-babe?"

"Hum?" Curled into the chair now, she seemed to be somewhere else, not even listening.

"When's Oscar claw his way outta the goddam womb? Concentrate, y'little bitch." He said it as casually as if he were asking for a cigarette.

"Up you," Jenny said in precisely the same tone, blowing a smoke ring.

I stood rooted, packed through with hate, uncertainty, frustration. "How long?" It was a throttled shout.

"Y'can't hurry nature, pops. How's seven months grab you?"

"You are insane, aren't you?"

Wilby lowered the book. He was very quiet for a long moment, eyes hidden behind those damned dark glasses. Finally he said, "Dad, I thought I warned you. Y'don't listen good, do you?"

"Neither do you. How'd you like to go back?"

It was a risk, but a suspicion had taken root in my mind and I had to explore it to the end.

"Whatever hospital you escaped from," I said.

Wilby remained quite still, impassive.

But, to my surprise, Jenny snickered. "He didn't escape. He just walked away. They couldn't stand him any more."

"Jenny—" Wilby said.

"Yeh?"

"How'd you like to get clouted? Right here in front of the man?"

"He wouldn't let you." I could feel her eyes on me, although I was still watching Wilby, measuring him, waiting. "Would you, Sam?"—a high wavering note leaped into the demand.

To hell with her. My hunch about Wilby had been right. I could feel the throbbing ridges of muscle along my legs and arms, the terrible shaking deep inside under the hardness of my stomach, and in my veins the blood beating, even in my fingertips.

"My wife's coming home," I said.

Wilby sat up then. Jenny turned off the blasting music, and in the sudden silence I could hear the silken rustle of dress as she moved closer.

"Is she?" Wilby asked languidly. "When?"

"This week," I said.

"Y'don't know when you're licked, d'you?"

"So . . . if you're not out of here, I have no choice but to have you arrested and sent to prison, regardless of the consequences to me. Can you understand that?"

"Prison?" Jenny asked.

"Y'tryin' to scare little Jenny, man?"

"Prison?" Jenny said again. "Wilby, what—"

"*Prison,*" I said. "Both of you!"

"For what, dad? What'd we do?"

"Trespassing," I said. "Illegal entry. Blackmail."

"Blackmail?"

"It's your word against mine," I said.

"And who's gonna believe us?"

"Exactly." My control was reaching a thin taut edge of uncertainty. "You said yourself people are going to believe what they want to believe. Well, when they look at you two—"

"Click, dad. Y'want to risk it?"

"Do you?"

"If y'don't take risks, how're y'gonna know you're alive?"

"I'm telling you: I won't allow my wife to walk in here and find you two."

"Why?" Jenny demanded swiftly. "Ain't we good enough—"

But Wilby cut her short with a single sharp gesture. He sat up then. "D'you mean to stand there and tell me—a man like you, respected, attorney-at-law, all-American Eighth Air Force, all that crap—you mean t'tell me you'd *lie?*"

It was uncanny, the way he could strike at a weak point. From childhood I had had an exaggerated, almost absurd hatred of lies, all lies, no matter how trivial, no matter how justified.

"I only ask, pop, 'cause you ain't what I'd call an accomplished liar." He was grinning again. "Y'see, Jenny and me, we just spent a dull afternoon here reading the limey's letters. According to which, she don't know when the old lady will either get better or konk off. According to which, she misses you, man, how she misses you, so many ways she does miss you. Think that's what got Jenny in heat 'round here. Y'got a real hot prick, don't you, prick?"

It was then that I swung. Without thought, without warning. I heard my glass as it hit the floor, felt my fist brushing against the bristling beard as it only grazed his face, saw his face close for an instant, smelled rancid breath, then felt my hand plunge into the deep upholstery. At the same instant that my wrist twisted, pain exploded in my groin. My mind blanked—went utterly black. And then I was writhing helplessly on the sofa, gasping for breath that wouldn't come, sick all through, weak, trying not to grasp myself, tasting the acrid gall in my mouth. The room reeled. The pain shattered up through me, shot down my legs, knotted in my stomach. I could not straighten up.

And there was Wilby's face, hovering in the dimness that had turned red but kept threatening to go dark again. "Sorry, pop, sorry, my knee musta got in the way of your balls, or vicey-versey—"

I stifled a groan: *damned* if I would cry out!

"Y'want me to rub it?"

I twisted away, knowing I was going to be sick now.

"Or maybe Jenny could rub it, man—"

Wilby had removed his glasses and I could see his eyes for the first time: bright, yet a depthless blue. His face looked naked and strange, floating above me.

And even then I realized that this was what he had been trying to goad me into.

"Wilby," Jenny said, "what are you trying to do?"

I closed my eyes but I could hear Wilby's voice, childlike now, almost whining: "Everybody's against me. I coulda used judo. Or karate. Way it is in the jungle, dad. Y'live in a jungle, y'gotta survive. Man, I could just's easy killed you." Then, in a mockery of defensiveness: "Jenny, I coulda ruined the man for life."

It had been, I knew, a damn-fool thing to have tried: half-drunk, at my age, to attempt brute force against a hood like this! When, except for a little boxing in college, I hadn't even had a fight since childhood.

The grinding pain retreated only very slightly, but enough so that I could breathe again. I opened my eyes.

I saw Jenny. Her body seemed to be straining forward, straining with a strange, sensuous excitement; her eyes were bright, they glittered, and her nostrils dilated. At once, as if instinctively, I knew what had stirred her feelings: the ferocity and cruelty, my pain. Violence. Revulsion mixed with the pain. Dark depths opening.

The telephone rang.

Wilby glanced toward the foyer. But Jenny continued to stare at me with sensual fascination.

It rang again.

Then Wilby said, "It won't be for me, dad. I didn't tell a soul where I was comin'."

Jenny whispered, in uncertainty, for reassurance: "Wilby, you gonna let—"

The phone shrilled again.

"Shut up!" Wilby snapped then. "Y'able to talk, pop, or you want people asking questions why you're not home this time-a-night?"

I met his flat inscrutable gaze. I managed to stand up.

A glimmer of sadistic pleasure came into his eyes.

Bent over slightly, I crossed the room. It was my chance.

"Guts, Jenny. Cool. See: the man has blood, after all."

"I see," Jenny said softly.

The pain spread as I sat down at the telephone in the small foyer, my back turned to the living room. Whoever it was, I would ask for the police and then, using the telephone itself as a weapon to hold the bastard off, perhaps to kill him—

Another ring—which I cut off by picking up the phone.

"Hello."

"So you are home!"

Anne. I could picture her at the telephone in the timbered cottage, impatient and concerned. I could picture her girlish face, less defined than Lydia's but suggesting the same gentleness and vulnerability.

"Daddy? Are you there? Hello!"

It was my chance.

"Yes, Anne," I said. "I'm here."

"Are you *sure*?"

It was my chance and with a jolt I knew I couldn't take it. Not yet anyway, not until I knew what everything really added up to. I was now prepared to take the consequences. But the bastard had meant everything he said. I couldn't put Lydia and Anne through it: it was as simple and final as that. Not only the scandal, but the doubts, suspicions, the personal pain and public shame. Could not.

"Daddy?"

Conscious of the waiting silence behind me, I said, "I just came in a few minutes ago." Had I ever lied to her before? "I . . . decided to take in a movie."

"Have you eaten?"

"Yes." Another lie.

Her voice took on its teasing tone. "I know what you ate. One of those dreadful frozen things. Or a sandwich. You do realize, don't you, that you promised to phone as soon as you arrived in the city?"

"Anne, what could possibly happen to—" Then my irritated voice broke off, and behind me Wilby started to whistle under his breath. "What could possibly happen to me in seventy miles?"

"Ha! Read the statistics."

Her foolish devotion touched me, warmed me: a split second's reassurance, a momentary emergence from nightmare. "I'm fine, dear."

"We-ell, I must say you don't *sound* fine. Whatever's happened to your voice?"

Wilby's whistle grew louder. What was he trying to do—make certain Anne would hear him?

I cleared my throat—and the pain, concentrated again now, threatened to spread. "I think," I said, "I've been invaded by a germ. Bugs of some sort."

Wilby stopped whistling, snorted, and Jenny giggled.

"Probably only a summer cold. Well, take care of yourself, Daddy. I feel so helpless, way up here and Mummy gone—"

"Anne," I said tensely, realizing my hands were wet with perspiration. "Anne, you must get over the idea your father's a doddering old man—"

"I don't have any such idea!" she protested. "I think you're the most handsome, youngest man I—" Then she broke off. "Next to Glenn, of course."

"Tell Glenn hello, Anne. It's late and this is costing you kids money."

"Daddy! Have you been drinking? I mean: I know you don't, normally, but—"

"All right," I growled, knowing that at least I was now telling the truth, "all right, I've had a few. They won't kill me."

Anne laughed. Her laugh was not quite so deep or spontaneous as her mother's, but it sounded young and happy and relieved. "But I think it's *delightful*! I don't blame you. I only wish it made you . . . gayer somehow."

I took a deep breath which seemed to penetrate the pain like the blade of a knife. "I'm gay," I said. "And sleepy. How do you expect a man to sound this time of night?"

"We-ell, you don't have to bark. It's only because I—" I heard her sigh. "Good night then, Daddy."

"Good night, Anne."

I replaced the phone but did not—for the moment could not—stand up and turn. I needed a cigarette. Not wanted, *needed*—worse than at any time since I had given them up four years ago. I wiped the perspiration from my face with a folded handkerchief, then rubbed the palms of my hands. The handkerchief came away wringing wet.

"Gay, are you, pop?" Wilby called. "I never would've guessed!"

I heard Jenny laugh—not a snigger this time but a deep-throated, womanly laugh. "He's not gay. Not *him!*"

"Hell, baby-baby, everybody's gay."

"That's what you always say. I—"

"You're ignorant, baby-baby, you don't study. There's some AC in every DC and vicey-versey, click, dad?" His voice was approaching: the lilting tone, the viperish tongue. "Even pop here, straight as he is, he's not *all* male-male. But he's what they call the decent type. Gotta protect the family in the cave, click, dad?"

I stood up and faced him. His bright, cold eyes looked bland, innocent, but his face wore a smirk and his stance was contemptuous.

"I'm trying to protect them," I said. "But I can only do that up to a certain point. After that point, it won't matter."

"Yourself, dad—that's who you're trying to protect. Y'don't want sweet little Shakespearean Anne thinking the old man's a roué. Ruin her image of you." Wilby laughed. "Oedipus-oedipus, daddy-o. Click, pop?"

The suggestion was more revolting than any he had made all evening. But it was then that I recalled that the last time I had been drunk—one of the very few times in an entire life—had been the night of Anne's wedding a year ago. What had Lydia said the next morning that had annoyed and puzzled me? Something about not being particularly surprised—

"Not everybody has your mind," I said. "Thank God."

"Leave my cousin out of this. Sees evil, hears evil, does evil. Only he ain't gonna help at-all, at-all, cause he just don't give a shit about his lost little sheep like you and me."

Shakespearean Anne, Oedipus, the word "roué," all this talk about God: was it possible that I was making some fatal error in thinking of him as just some hood off the streets, some dirty-necked beatnik? No ordinary criminal could possibly have planned this—whatever it turned out to be—with such uncanny certainty of how I would react.

While I studied him, wondering, he belched. Then he swiveled about and strolled into the living room. Jenny, kneeling on the seat of the chair and looking at him over the back of it, laughed—so he belched again, more loudly this time.

"Annie and Glenn!" He hooted. "Glenn! Baby, how's that for a name? *Glenn!* Ain't a glen where the fairies abide?" And as he passed he slapped Jenny on the buttocks, a resounding whack as if against bare skin. She yelped, then spit a word that I couldn't comprehend, twisted to sit, muttering. Wilby began improvising dance steps, assuming burlesqued ballet poses as he talked—while my rebelling mind continued to try to sort out the incongruities and contradictions. "Little house-house in the sub-suburbs, where the *real* people live, Jenny, salt of the earth, real, like in the movies. Cardboard cottage, papier-mâché walls, with split-level beds and toilets that don't go whoosh when you flush because nobody ever has to shit in the suburbs."

I passed between them, went to the bar. Not a good idea, but to hell with it. As I walked, I realized that the pain had somewhat receded, but I could feel the sweat cold down my spine. Jenny's eyes followed me, but she was listening to Wilby—and the enigma of their relationship struck again.

"Glenn-Glenn catches the seven-oh-seven, and his briefcase is shinier than his face and ten times as full as his brain, and he goes into the office to pinch the secretaries, while little Shakespearean Anne rolls back on *her* side of the split-level bed and hopes someone will, for my cousin's sweet merciless sake, rape her good before *he* comes back after jacking off on the New Haven six-oh-six."

I drank. Was he still trying to goad me? Or was he performing for Jenny's amusement? Or his own? The apartment—no, not the apartment, my whole damned life!—was contaminated. By filth. Infection. Corrosion. I could almost smell the stench in my nostrils.

Wilby struck a climactic pose, arms delicately over his head, mouth grinning, eyes blank.

I had to get it over with. Yet it seemed important to know.

"How'd you happen to choose me?"

Perhaps it was the casualness of my tone that surprised him. He dropped the pose. "Who knows, dad? Fate. Luck. Or the fine Italian hand of my cousin up there." He dropped to the floor, sprawled on his back, arms outflung. Was the travesty of crucifixion intentional or accidental? "Y'think my cousin's a guinea, dad? Catholics probably do. But then you ain't Catholic."

I reached and took a cigarette from a pack lying on the bar. "You know all about me, don't you?"

"Sure, man. Had a Dun and Bradstreet run on you."

Possibly. Whether that was true or not, I knew, of course, that in time we would get around to money again, regardless of his denials. I felt strangely calm as I lit the cigarette.

"But why me? In a city of nine million."

"Accident," Wilby said softly, a speculative wonder creeping into his tone as I drew the harsh, bitter, unfamiliar smoke deep into my lungs. "Like everything. Chance. Chaos. Y'follow me, man? Click?"

"Click," I said—and saw him sit up.

His head tilted—surprise? "You're puttin' me on," he said.

"Sure."

"Y'believe that? That nobody's home upstairs?"

I considered. Although I rarely went to church—only, usually, when the impulse struck Lydia, and more to please her than for any personal reason—I had carried from childhood the idea that there was some vast pattern with some superior being of some sort who had designed it for some reason: yes. It had never seemed very important, however—not since my father's death, at any rate. But I was damned if I'd—

"I couldn't possibly believe in some superior intelligence and still believe in you," I said, and realized that, with the drinking, a curious sense of detachment had set in, somewhat bewildering but rather satisfying.

Wilby didn't reply for a long moment. Then he lay back again and threw his arm over his eyes. "Happened be in airport, old John F. airport, day the limey wife took off. Happened be sayin' bye-bye to sweet fellow I know, on his way to Iraq for State Department. *Happened* see the farewell-good-by, very touching, coupla squares kissing in public, very polite kiss, cool, man, so happened get idea: how much those two got theirselves fooled?" His tone was softly speculative, but there was no way of knowing whether he was lying or not. "Got theirselves'n *each other* fooled."

"If," I said, "we didn't love each other, you wouldn't have gotten away with as much as you have so far tonight."

"If y'*did* love each other, man, you wouldn't have gotten away with's much as *you* have tonight. Click?"

Jenny tittered. I did not glance toward her. What had happened between Jenny and me had nothing to do with love. Yet—

"Love," Jenny said, but she was staring off when I looked at her. Blowing smoke rings. As if she had spoken, if she was even aware that she had, to herself.

"Pop—" Wilby sounded hurt, miffed. "Pop, jus' what've we got away with? Y'gonna tell me y'begrudge us that lousy canned fish, that bottle flat Rhine wine?"

Had Wilby told the truth? Had he seen Lydia and me in the airport? Or had it begun, as Jenny had suggested, when she saw me in Pat's Pub?

Suddenly Wilby leaped up, snapped his sunglasses over his eyes, and almost ran to the foyer.

"Nothing against the company, dad, Christ, it's boresville, I gotta split!" And he began to comb his beard in front of the mirror.

Split? I glanced at Jenny. Her face was a bit blurred now.

"What the hell does he mean?"

"He's going cruising," she said.

That helped. Oh hell yes, that helped a lot. Whatever cruising meant! I moved across the living room to the foyer. The floor seemed to tilt, but only slightly.

"Where do you think you're going?"

Wilby was intent on combing his hair now, drawing it forward, down over his forehead in rhythmical crackling strokes. He looked at me in the mirror.

"Got to find the charlie, dad. Want to go cruisin' with me? Or y'rather stay with Jenny-baby?"

What did charlie mean? Dope, perhaps?

"Seven months is out," I said then, and heard the slur in my words. "Even you must know that."

Wilby did not miss a stroke. "Make a deal with you, man. One night only. That grab you?"

One night. Relief beckoned.

Then, behind me, I heard Jenny stand up. I heard her say, "You hate me, don't you?" Her voice, however, was not angry, not resentful—rather, husky with some sort of excitement, anticipation.

"Now, Jenny-baby," Wilby purred, "dad here don't hate us. He loathes us, despises—"

"Yes," she said breathlessly, and I turned about. Her eyes were on me, pointed and black now, glittering again with that strange hunger I had seen there earlier, after the violence.

My contempt deepened into a sickening disgust. She must have seen it on my face because she smiled faintly, a peculiar triumph and satisfaction in her eyes; and then she began to glide, as if hypnotized, toward the stairway. I could sense Wilby studying me as I watched her go up the stairs and into the guest room and close the door.

I faced Wilby again. "One night," I said, "then what?"

Wilby blew on the comb, then shoved it into a pocket. "Tell you at breakfast, dad."

The room was swirling slowly, the floor lifting and falling in waves. "You'll tell me now."

"Or what?" He was poised lightly on the balls of his feet. "Or what-what?"

"Or," I said, "when you come back here, you're going to find the place ransacked and all my valuables missing. And I am going to be waiting for you with a gun." I heard myself as from an echoing distance and with muted astonishment. "I'll say I caught you burglarizing the apartment and I had to shoot you."

He didn't move. "You couldn't do it, pop."

"There's one way for you to find out."

Silence. My eyes were fixed on the dark glasses. They glittered opaquely, revealed nothing. The silence extended itself into an eternity. But I did not breathe. It was like standing on the deck of a ship that silently heaved in a rough, uncertain sea.

"What about Jenny?" he asked at last.

"If she's still here, I'll kill her, too, and say she's your accomplice. But she won't be. I can make sure of that. She's too scared of going to prison."

Another silence. Wilby's head tilted as he studied me.

"Y'don't miss nothin', d'you?" he said then. "Y'know, this caper's got kicks. I picked you for a vegetable." He sighed. "Y'want me t'lay it on you—it's gonna cost you three thousand."

Three thousand. This time the relief closed over me like a cloud. Hastily my mind calculated: ten thousand in the savings bank, more than a hundred thousand in investments, at least four or five in the joint checking account. It would be worth three thousand to get rid of them.

"Won't break you, man. I seen your checkbooks."

"I'll give it to you now," I said. If he had my check in his pocket, it could substantiate my charge of extortion—even if it might also, in a showdown, lend credence to his claim that I had paid off because of Jenny's pregnancy. I was crossing to the library, aware of my unsteady step, when his voice stopped me.

"No check." And then when I turned slowly, my head swimming: "Not that I don't trust you, man—"

"I couldn't stop payment," I said, the anger returning hotly all at once. "It incriminates me as much as it does you!"

"Sorry, pop. Cash-cash. Nothin' larger than fifties." He turned to the door. "Tomorrow. Only not before noon, click, 'cause Jenny and me, we're late sleepers." Then with his hand on the knob, he grinned. "Jenny's waitin'. That bitch, she's gotta have it or, man, she flips."

Then he was gone.

I looked over the room. Then up to the balcony. Door closed. *Was* she waiting?

I moved, unsteadily, to the bar. It would be a long wait.

Another drink. Then what?

I was splashing whisky into a glass when the door opened above and she appeared. She had removed the dress. As she had said earlier, she wore nothing underneath.

"Hasn't he gone?" she asked.

Without replying I took a long swallow. But I could not take my eyes from her.

"What're you waiting for?" Her tone was petulant again, demanding and puzzled.

A good question. Three thousand dollars. What was I waiting for? Hatred coursed through me, more poisonous and pernicious than the whisky in my blood.

"How much of it do you get?" I demanded, my voice unrecognizable, blunt and cruel and ugly.

She moved to the railing. "How much what?"

"Of the three—" I had difficulty with the word. "Of the three . . . thousand—"

At once her face contorted and her voice dropped into a rasping snarl. "I don't put out for bread!" The cry seemed ripped from her, violent and genuine. "Who says I put out for bread?"

"If bread's money," I said, very slowly, "if bread means . . . money—"

"You bastard! I don't care what Wilby told you, that bastard, that cock-sucking sonofabitch, I don't put out for bread!"

In that instant I enjoyed my bitter triumph. "Three thousand. Three thousand for one . . . goddamned night!"

She was running down the stairs then, eyes wild, body swift and glowing and slim and soft and young and vibrant with fury and desire. "Lies, lies, you bastard, you—" But, across the bar from me, she stopped, and I saw a new expression leap into her face: a sly and knowing and satisfied pleasure. "Oh, how you hate me, don't you?"

And I realized, with a sharp and bewildered intensity, that in some horrible and twisted way she was pleased; even that she intended to incite my loathing, that her own lust somehow was intensified by it, possibly even fed on my animosity and disgust.

I must be drunk. Really drunk. This is impossible.

But then I watched as she stepped closer, and her eyes flared with a cruel and animal-like hostility that I had never seen in a woman's face before. She struck out, swiftly, one bare arm darting into my vision a split second before her palm stung my face a jarring flat blow.

All the pent-up rancor and frustration and venom of the evening burst free in some upheaval so unexpected and overwhelming and total that I had no control. All reason, decision, hesitation, disintegrated.

In the same instant I was around the bar, moving in a blind senseless fury of sensation, and I grabbed her, brutally, uncaring, the first touch of her flesh breaking all restraint, and I threw her to the floor, where she lay staring up at me, a scornful mirth still in her dark eyes, and then, when I was ready, I pumped my hatred and contempt into her in a paroxysm of obscene delight, of lustful drunken physical ecstasy.

Darkness. How long had I been sleeping?

"Sam—"

I recognized the voice—soft now, gentle. And I longed for sleep again: darkness, blankness, oblivion.

"You awake, Sam?"

The taste in my mouth was bitter and my mind was still fogged. I was in a bed. How had I come upstairs? When?

"Sam—"

"My name's not Sam," I heard myself say thickly.

"You're *my* Sam. You really are, now."

How could I have come upstairs without even being able to remember? But we were not in my bed, mine and Lydia's. At least that, at least. My mind flinched from the idea.

"Sam—"

She moved. Then she was lying on top of me, her flesh soft, incredibly hot. Her hair spilled over my face.

Three thousand dollars. One thousand a crack. Expensive whore. Might as well get my money's worth.

The thought was not mine. A stranger's. Not mine at all—whoever I was.

Then all thought was gone again.

When I woke next time, the room was filled with gray light. She lay sprawled in the dimness, body and face slack, mouth open. I felt no desire. Only the clutch of cold disgust. Only shame. And my head was full to bursting—with pain, with a swelling vagueness, dizziness.

I needed a cigarette. Again.

With consciousness the inevitable questions stabbed. Had I had a choice? Hell, I had built a life, a career, on the assumption that everyone, always, had a free choice. How could there be law unless—

God, I needed a cigarette!

Then, from below, I heard a key turning in the front door. Lydia? The door opened. My heart swelled, then stopped altogether.

Panic catapulted me to the door.

Below, the living room was still lighted. And Wilby was staggering from foyer to library. Drunk? Or worse? What did it matter? It was not Lydia. How could I have imagined it might be?

Sagging against the door, I watched as Wilby entered the library. *Got to find the charlie, dad.* Had he found it? And what the hell was the charlie? He slammed the door behind him.

How had Wilby obtained a key to the apartment?

I stepped along the balcony to the other bedroom. Mine and Lydia's. Without turning on a light I found a robe in the closet. No cigarettes here: Lydia had stopped smoking when I had.

Lydia. Must not think of Lydia. Cannot. Do not dare.

In bare feet I went down the stairs. My steps were unsteady, my legs ached, and I balanced myself by holding to the banister. No longer drunk, but I had been. Explained all of it. Could happen to anybody. If I had not had so many drinks when I was not accustomed to them—

The living room reminded me of towns I had flown over during the war: ravaged. In those days I had needed cigarettes this way. Before a mission, but especially after.

Actually the room looked not much worse than it did after a party when I would persuade Lydia to leave the debris till morning—either because I sensed she was too tired or because I wanted to make love to her.

What was it Lydia had said about her father once? *He used to apologize for being weak, as if being weak were an excuse in itself. As if desiring every female on three continents were some sort of disease over which he had no control—*

I picked up a crumpled package from the floor. It looked empty but my fingers, which were shaking, untwisted the paper and exposed a single gnarled cigarette. After lighting it with the silver lighter, I drew the bitter smoke deep into my lungs. It made me go weak, almost sick. I saw the white boots on the floor.

I needed a shower.

After making love to Lydia, I did not feel that I needed a shower. After making love to Lydia, I felt whole. Renewed. Now I stood there feeling empty, spent, nauseous.

If making love is only what the films and novels make it out to be these days, some kind of sensation, like ski-jumping or eating a fine French dinner or—

Lydia again: her voice as clear in my mind as if she were here. And I had to do something, anything, to escape it.

I went up the stairs, carefully closing the guest-room door without looking in, and then into the bathroom adjoining my own bedroom.

In the early sunlight falling through the translucent window I studied my face in the mirror. Familiar, yet this morning the face of a stranger. The hazel-colored eyes stared back: normally clear and friendly but reserved, they now looked bloodshot and bleakly hostile and bewildered. The splotches of ruddy color, usually high on each cheek, had paled. Otherwise, the face looked as it always did: square and blunt-featured, hair cropped short, mahogany-red with a spattering of gray at each temple. A typical face, neither handsome nor ugly; like my stocky but firm-muscled body, it normally did not suggest fifty years.

I turned away, mouth twisting slightly in self-contempt. I entered the shower stall, slid the door, then turned on the cold water. Full blast. My heart stopped, the breath left me in a single deep gasp, my flesh quivered with shock under the piercing merciless needles. But I forced myself to stand straight and unflinching under the fierce stabbing punishment. My mind, however, refused to clear.

The water on my back probed the tiny fingernail-scratches which stung like razor-cuts. The pain was somehow satisfying.

Married twenty-one years. Almost every other man I knew—if you could believe them and if you could believe the so-called statistics—

had had at least one affair. Took them casually, too, without all this shriveling guilt. If you could believe that, too. Boasted of them, laughed, mocked them. Still, it had been a matter of pride with me: one couple in a hundred, perhaps in thousands. Not pride alone: wonder, too. Wonder that I had not felt the need.

Then, with shocking clarity, it came to me: Wilby had intended just this. Not only that Jenny and I should sleep together—he had known in his cynical way that this was inevitable and I had not proved him wrong—but that I should feel as I now felt! Had it all been part of his game?

If y'did love each other, y'wouldn't have gotten away with what you did tonight. Click?

Was that, then, also part of some diabolical scheme on his part— to make sure that he tarnished, and if possible destroyed, the fine and, until now, decent love in which he did not, or could not, believe? For the first time, perhaps because I was sober now, I began to wonder whether that contamination was not as important to him as the money. Possibly more so. Perhaps the money was only an excuse for whatever other destruction he could—

In that brief overpowering instant I actually—and for the first time—wanted to kill him. I had never experienced the impulse before. Never. Not even during the war when I had killed. And, shattered by it in the narrow shower stall, I could only wonder whether that instinct, like the one that had driven me to those three violent orgasms of loveless animal sex, was not some vestigial part of the nature of every man.

The glass door slid open.

"Me, too," she said, and stepped in.

She made a sound, half squeal, half howl, as the water struck. She stared up at me, shivering, shuddering, hair streaming dark and wet over her body. "How can you stand it, Sam?" she asked, voice quivering.

"For God's sake," I said, feeling ridiculous and angry and antagonistic all at the same time, "for God's sake, stop calling me Sam!"

Her teeth were chattering, her lips blue. "You look like you could kill me."

Then, when I did not answer, she stepped against me under the icy spray.

"Will you? Now? Kill me, Sam. Standing up—"

Monday

B Y the time I was in the taxi on the way to the office, I had clenched my mind against the day ahead—and against the memory of the night just passed. I had left the apartment without waking either of them, but I had taken sly advantage of their sleeping by setting up the tape-recorder, which was concealed behind cabinet doors in the hi-fi set, so that when I returned a cautious flip of one switch would set it in motion and, with luck and some conniving, I might have a record of the transaction with the cash. Just in case. Of what? Just in case Wilby should try to carry it further. I had hailed the cab myself around the corner, avoiding the doorman—Geoffrey this morning—because it had occurred to me that he just might be smarter than either Wilby or Jenny realized; also, I suspected, now that I came to think of it, that Geoffrey in particular had been observing me just a bit too closely since Lydia had gone. *He reminds me of an old maid in a small English village,* Lydia had once said. *How he must miss his crumpets!*

The streets were a riot of summer colors, and rather frantic. Even this early, shortly after nine, the leather seat of the taxi was burning, scorching air beat through the open windows, the smoke of the driver's cigar was sickening, and before we had traveled three blocks I was damp with perspiration. It was as if all my senses had been sharpened, brought to pulsing life. My head rocked mercilessly with every swerve and jolt and stop of the cab and my whole body, especially my legs, ached and throbbed.

While Lydia's face hovered before me and her voice haunted my mind. *With me, it's all or nothing, I'm awfully afraid.* How many years ago had she said that? Or had she in fact said it at all? *I know I may be demanding too much, but I do.* Yes, she'd said it. Years ago. England. The room in Bartleck we'd shared. *Blame Father if you like. The daughter of an international philanderer—or is the Yank word "playboy"?—is likely to go one way or the other, I suppose. Well, darling, I've gone the other. And you, lad, are trapped. For life. All or nothing.*

And so it has been, Lydia. By mutual consent—no, not consent, damn it, by mutual volition, *desire*. Until now.

Ravenous, I had not eaten. In the apartment the thought of food had revolted me. Now I decided to have a cup of the weak, pale coffee that Phoebe offered every morning in the office and that I invariably refused. If we ever reached the office!

If Lydia ever learned, she would never forgive. Could not. It was as simple and fundamental as that and I must have known it, without being conscious of it, all along. But, damn it, she should not have gone!

So now it's Lydia's fault!

No. But a whole month!

Would you prefer that her mother had died?

Of course not. But Lydia had never been really fond of her mother. Always joking about what a cold, domineering woman she had always been. *Which would explain Father. If Father didn't explain Mother. Or if anyone is ever responsible for anyone else—which I do not believe.*

Lydia always held everyone strictly accountable. Including herself. Including me.

The taxi finally came to a stop.

I resolutely passed the magazine- and cigar-stand in the lobby, determined not to have another cigarette, although the yearning went deeper than my parched mouth and shallow lungs. Damned if I was going to go through those weeks—no, months—of torture shedding the habit when this was over. Today. *This afternoon!*

The elevator was packed. The trick now was not to look back on the night. Not to look back, period. Whatever I had done, it had been the action of a stranger. A stranger, perhaps, who had lived inside me, granted, but a stranger nonetheless. Not my fundamental self. But did I know that fundamental self, really? Did he in actuality exist or had I only imagined him? Was he real? What *was* real?

Phoebe's "Good morning, Mr. Wyatt!" was as bright and pleasant as ever, and somehow oddly reassuring, but at once I saw—or imagined I saw—a flicker in her eyes when she got a better look at me. "Mr. Welch is waiting," she said.

Damn. Carefully not glancing into the waiting room, I went to my own office. I should have gone straight to the bank.

Phoebe had followed—a habit of hers which had not annoyed me before. "Would you like some coffee, Mr. Wyatt?"

I sat behind my desk and looked up at her. Her flecked gray eyes were quietly impersonal. It was as if I had never really seen her before, although she had worked for me for three years. In her mid-thirties, possibly even early forties, she nevertheless suggested youth and femininity: sharpness of features offset by a softness of the face's contours, severity of dyed blond hair-do compensated for by a full but not corpulent body. "Thank you, Phoebe," I said. "I would. And I can't see Mr. Welch this morning. Make up something."

"You mean you want me to lie?"

There it was again: even Phoebe recognized my reluctance to lie. "It's done all the time, Phoebe. By all the best people."

"Of course. He saw you come in, though. Shall I say you're ill?"

I looked ill: that's what she meant. Ill or hung over, or both—so it wouldn't be far from the truth. I glanced at my watch. "I'll see him," I said. "But give me a minute. And I'll have the coffee."

She withdrew with only the faintest suggestion of surprise on her face. Ever-efficient Phoebe. Divorced years ago, she had told me when applying for the job. Why hadn't I asked her for a cigarette? Why hadn't I sent her down for a pack? The office was stifling. I got up and twisted the thermostat, glanced at the reading. Seventy degrees. Impossible! Where the hell was Welch? I had to get to the bank.

I was about to press the button on the office intercom when Phoebe ushered him in, asking whether he would like a cup of coffee. Colin Welch thanked her profusely, as if she had offered him exoneration for what he had done, and then Phoebe was gone, Colin Welch and I were shaking hands, and he was sitting down across from me, lighting a cigarette.

"I'm sorry I'm in such a rush," I said, "but we'll dispense with the preliminaries. What I'd like for you to do is to tell me the whole story, as you remember it, beginning an hour before you got behind the wheel of the car. I'll try not to interrupt but after you've finished I'll have some questions. Is that agreeable?"

"You're the lawyer," Colin Welch said with a feeble attempt at joviality. Then he cleared his throat and began to talk.

I made a few notes as he spoke, watching his pencil-thin mustache twitching, listening to the small, precise voice detailing, with the inevitable excursions into irrelevancies, what had happened. The case was distasteful in itself, as most hit-and-run cases are likely to be, but

Mr. Welch was insured by a company we represented. How could you have respect, or even much sympathy, for a man who could strike another man on a dark street at night, even if the victim stepped off the curb illegally—and this had definitely not been established—and then drive away, aware of what he had done? It was Mr. Welch's contention, repeated unnervingly, that he had not once seen the victim, even fleetingly.

"There was this terrific *thump* against the front of the car. I'll never forget that sound as long as I live!"

"And then?" I prompted. My patience was wearing thinner.

"And then—well, I guess I just hit the accelerator."

"You *guess*?" The room was filled with smoke.

I waited. Mr. Welch's small face trembled, his chin shaking, and he took a deep breath that sounded like a shudder. "I *did* hit the accelerator," he said firmly.

He had then driven to his home, had watched television all night without telling his wife. He named the late movies and sheepishly admitted, as if it had significance, that he had drunk himself into a stupor.

"But you had not had a single drink before the accident?"

"I told you that!" He was almost whining. "I already said that. How many times do I have to—"

I stood up and began to pace. The office was like a steam bath! "Mr. Welch, I can only help you if you tell me the exact truth, the absolute truth, in every smallest detail. Do you understand that?" Pacing was a habit I had consciously conquered early in my career, having discovered that it made nervous clients more apprehensive; but I continued, legs aching. "This is a complicated case, as I'm sure you know."

"What are you implying? That I lied? What do you mean?"

"I am not implying anything. I am trying to save you more grief. There are criminal charges pending, as well as the lawsuit. If you don't tell me the complete truth, it is likely to come out anyway, at a later date and much more to your detriment. Possibly even in the courtroom. I cannot fight your case, or even assess it, unless there is total understanding between us."

"I thought you were on my side," Mr. Welch said.

Is law real, dad?

I gritted my teeth. The smoke was tantalizing in my nostrils. How could I explain that it was my job to take the facts of the case, all of

them, and to arrange them into a pattern that might lead, with luck
and much hard work, to the exoneration of my client?

"It's not as if it was manslaughter or something," Mr. Welch was
saying. "He's going to get well. I mean: even if he's crippled, he's not
going to die."

"May I have a cigarette?" I asked abruptly.

Mr. Welch began to fumble. "Certainly, certainly."

Phoebe tapped on the door and entered with a tray as I was lighting up. She stared, trying to conceal her surprise, then disappeared.
The cigarette tasted less bitter than those I had smoked last night. In
fact, no cigarette had ever tasted quite so good!

As Mr. Welch poured cream, he clattered the pitcher against the
edge of the cup. "After all, there's another way to look at it, isn't
there? Maybe *he* had been drinking. *That* ever occur to you?"

"It did," I assured him, exhaling the smoke. "Let's hope we can
establish it."

"Oh, it's easy to blame. But how do you know?" He gulped the hot
coffee. "How does anyone know how he'll act till he's in a situation?"

All my easy distaste withered away. "That's true," I said con-
tritely, suddenly overwhelmed by a strangling compassion. Then I
stepped from behind to place a hand on the narrow, bony shoulder,
which was quivering. "It's true: no one ever does really know. And
that's what I'll make every effort to make clear."

I picked up and drank the weak, thin coffee without tasting it. I
could feel the sweat on my forehead.

"Still," Mr. Welch went on, "still, I did do it, didn't I?"

I looked at him. Yes, he had done it. Regardless of any excuses,
pressures, regardless of anything. Regardless of whether he had or
had not been drinking.

"I'll try to tell the exact truth," Mr. Welch promised. "I'll try. Only
sometimes even that's hard, isn't it?"

"Yes," I said, knowing. "Yes, it often is."

"Mrs. Welch is so disturbed. I don't know what's going to happen.
She even blames me for not telling her, like I betrayed her some way.
And sometimes, you know, when she looks at me, I feel she kind of
. . . can't understand. Or maybe hates me for it." He set down his
cup. "Anything else, Mr. Wyatt?"

"Not today, no. Try not to worry too much. I think we can make a
good case. After we do some investigating, we'll talk again. At
length."

He stood up. "Thanks, Mr. Wyatt. Investigating? What kind of investigating? The other fellow, you mean?"

"Yes," I lied. Then I said, "I'm sorry."

He nodded, blinked, and went out.

I slumped into my chair. *Reality then. How about discussing reality? Does it actually exist-exist? Or do we imagine it—* The cigarette burned my fingers and I dropped it onto the carpet.

"Lunch today?"

It was Henry. He had come in, as usual, unannounced. He stood towering in the door as I stooped to pick up the cigarette.

"My God, you look like the wrath of somebody or other, I forget his name. Burning it at both ends, Adam?"

I managed a smile. At once I felt better. It was a way Henry had: not charm exactly but a restrained heartiness. His tall, big-boned frame and rugged, hawklike features, under bushy brows and an almost totally bald pate, exuded good will and, more, competence. I understood, for the first time really, why his clients placed such mindless confidence in him. Perhaps—although I had never thought it out—this was why I had stayed in New York after the war to go into partnership with him. Rather than, as I had planned all through the war, return to Nebraska. *But darling, I'm willing,* Lydia had said. *Don't stay in the East because of me. If Fort Perry, Nebraska, can put up with me, I can certainly survive Fort Perry. If you're there.* In that instant I knew that Henry could help. Somehow. There had to be a way out of this, possibly even without paying the three thousand. And if there was a way, Henry would find it.

"How about lunch?"

"Sorry, Henry. Have an appointment." Another lie—and for no reason. Especially if I was going to tell him, to ask his advice.

"Not according to Phoebe's pad you don't." He was grinning, obviously amused at my discomfort.

"It's personal," I said. And wondered: why was I hesitating, why not tell him, *now*?

"Ohhh—" Henry said and nodded. "Well, in that case—" He turned in a broad swinging motion, arms extended. "Far be it from me—"

Instant anger struck, intense and, I knew, irrational—but uncontrollable. "Don't jump to conclusions," I said. "We're not all like you."

The motion stopped. Henry paused, his arms dropped, he stared.

Then his long craggy face twisted into a frown. "Hey," he said. "Hey now, just because I'm an old divorced adulterer—"

I stood up and he broke off speaking. I brushed past him without a word and went stiffly into the outer office.

"Phoebe," I said, "does it seem hot in here to you?"

"Not to me," she said. "But then I don't have to wear as much as you men do."

You know I got nothing on under. You mean sonofabitch!

"My office is like a furnace," I said, moving to the corridor. "Get somebody up here to do something about it before I get back!"

On the crowded elevator, I stared straight ahead. Let them talk about me, both of them, Phoebe and Henry; let them conjecture. Hangover? What? Henry would conclude, naturally—being Henry, having himself been divorced because Charlene could no longer bear his repeated infidelities—that there was another woman involved. Well, wasn't there? No. Not in that sense.

This time I didn't pass the cigar-stand without buying cigarettes. Lighting one in the door, suspended between the air-conditioned lobby and the blast of humid heat outside, I felt like a criminal. Lydia would be so damned disappointed. The irony struck. Lydia. I walked into the torrid street. Lydia would be disappointed because I was *smoking* again. It was funny, really. Hilarious.

Oh, Henry, Lydia had once said—when? where?—*Henry's the kind of man, I'm afraid, who wants what he can't have and can't be happy with what he can have. So far as I'm concerned, Charlene's perfectly justified. Although I've never been fond of Charlene and maybe I'm talking like the universal woman, or wife.*

My legs threatened to give way, the blood draining. For an instant I thought I would certainly fall.

But, damn it, wasn't I doing it all for her? For her and for Anne. No. Why then? Because of last night. Because of that bitch of a girl and my own primeval lust, atavistic sexual hunger, carried out in rage, in aggression. Not love. Not love, Lydia. Please believe, please understand. *I'll try to tell the exact truth. Only sometimes even that's hard, isn't it?*

The bank was an echoing arched vault of stone—and imperceptibly cooler than the street. Until I was writing at one of the high glass shelves, it had not occurred to me that there might be anything unusual in cashing a check for three thousand dollars. After all, the money was mine, wasn't it? But when the young teller's bland face looked up through the grille, I wished I had withdrawn it from the savings account instead.

"How would you like this, Mr. Wyatt?"

Cash-cash. Nothing larger than fifties.

"Fifties," I said, tempted to wipe my brow and feeling the eyes of the uniformed guard behind me. When I left, would the transaction be reported to some officious vice-president? Or possibly to Internal Revenue? Cash, in a world geared to records and government-supervised accounts, might arouse suspicion.

"There you are, sir. Don't spend it all in one place."

I placed the packet of bills in the inner pocket of my jacket and turned away with what I knew was an insipid smile. One place—one night. Expensive whore. I was on the street before I realized I had not counted it. Probably broke the most sacrosanct rule in the damned bank. Probably make them more suspicious than ever!

It was fourteen minutes until eleven when the taxi stopped in front of the building. I had had a run-down, player by player, on why the Yankees were not winning this season, from a cabbie who twice had had Mickey Mantle in this very cab. *Is reality real? Or do we imagine it and that's the only reason it exists?*

"I guess if you ain't a fan, it don't mean nothing to you," the driver said as he counted his tip. "You look more like the football type. So long, pal."

Geoffrey was holding the door. Grandly, as usual. At once subservient and condescending. He carefully guarded whatever surprise he might have felt at my return this time of day. Lydia had once whispered, gaily: *Aren't you ever tempted to reach up and rip off an epaulet? Just for the bloody hell of it!*

"Humid, isn't it, sir?" Geoffrey asked in his clipped English accent. Geoffrey was infallible about the weather. "And they say it's likely to get worse before—"

I could feel his eyes on me as I walked to the elevator, pressed the seventh-floor button, and waited until the door slid into place before turning around. Let him conjecture. It would soon be over.

For all I knew, Geoffrey was in on it. How did Wilby get his key? It was probably a racket they worked all over the city. Cut the doorman in for a percentage! *Got to find the charlie, dad.* I had read somewhere that addicts would go to any length to get money for drugs. How many other men had they victimized this way? By the time the elevator stopped, I was convinced, without a doubt, that Geoffrey was working with them. Then what about Pat, the bartender? He put them onto me in the first place, that's all. He was part of it, too. He'll get his cut. Three thousand'll go a long way.

In the corridor I could hear the music as the door opened again. If you could call it music. It reminded me of those backwoods tent services I'd heard years ago when I was in Officers' Training in Georgia: the same insistent repetitive beat, primitive, with a suggestion of some explosive wildness underneath. When I let myself in with my key, the din was deafening.

The living room, littered, was deserted. Turning off the radio, I had to choke down a ridiculous, unlikely hope. I stood listening. No sound. I was moving toward the library when I felt heat from the terrace. The terrace doors were wide open. Small wonder the place was roasting! I went to close them and saw Jenny.

She was lying on a huge towel in the sun on the floor of the terrace. She was lying on her stomach and she wore nothing. The tawny slenderness, the rounded flesh—my heart jolted, the hollow tightening returned. The bitch. I glanced up. She was in full view of—how many windows above, how many other terraces across the street?

"What the hell do you think you're doing?"

She rolled onto her back. Her face looked pleased. "Hi."

I turned away. "Get in here," I barked. Then I called, "Wilby!" Then, the wrath churning hotly, I shouted: "*Wilby!*"

I crossed to the library. Wilby was stretched out on the leather couch, one leg thrown over the back of it. He was reading a book, still wearing the dark glasses. Obviously he had slept in his clothes.

"Wilby—or whatever the hell your name is—I've got the money. Take your wife—or whoever she is—and clear out. Now."

No reply.

I turned. Jenny was standing in the door, the towel half-draped around her.

"You want us to go, Sam?" she asked, with a puzzlement that sounded genuinely surprised and disappointed—even innocent. "Honest?"

I couldn't look at her. "I carried out my part of the bargain," I said, turning again to Wilby and taking the crisp bills from my pocket.

"Respectable. Honorable." Today Wilby's voice lacked the ironic high pitch, the mocking gaiety and pleasure; it was low, harsh. He continued to read. "Thought I told you not before noon. Y'don't listen good, d'you, lover-boy?"

"I'm through taking orders."

"L'me alone. Can't y'see I'm readin'?"

"Sam—" Jenny said.

I refused to face her again, refused to reply. I threw the packet of money onto the cobbler's bench. "Count it."

"I can smell it," Wilby said, in that same detached guttural snarl. "I can smell the filthy stuff!" Then he sat up with startling suddenness. "Smell it, *smell* it! What you'll do for that stuff, hah, for that green shit!"

The contrast to last night's mood bewildered me, stopped me for a moment.

"Jenny," he said, glancing in her direction once, "cousin-sake, don't be a cow! Get upstairs, drape the nipples."

Behind me Jenny uttered an extended hiss: at once contempt, defiance, and disgust.

I couldn't resist saying, "You'll do quite a few things for money yourself."

"Not for me." Wilby stood up. "All for Jenny. Click, baby?" His body today looked tense and tight.

"Get outta my face," she muttered.

"Upstairs!" he growled. "Now."

"Stop buggin' me, I said!" But I could hear her voice receding. "Screw you, mama Hitler!"

"So," Wilby said, as he picked up the money, "so you're through takin' orders, lover-boy? Y'don't like my playin' my cousin here?" He stalked past me. "One little slip, one little sin and it's hellfire for all time, man, *eternity!*" I turned to watch him prowl into the living room as the guest-room door above slammed with the explosive violence of a shotgun blast. "An' nobody knows how long eternity is, click? 'Cause eternity's outside the human imagination—longer'n the human mind can imagine. It's forever, man!" He was pacing up and down, every step taut and rigid, in measured strides, with the controlled desperation of a jungle cat in an iron cage. "Now I ask you, man—what kind of merciful, loving sonofabitch of a God could threaten a man with something like that?"

Careful, I warned myself, and went into the living room. What was coming now? Where would this mood lead? I'd almost forgotten the tape-recorder. I strolled casually to the bar. "Farewell drink?" I asked.

Wilby continued to pace in a straight line. "Old-fashioned." He snorted a mirthless laugh. "Think y'can manage that, mine host?"

"For you—anything." But I had learned that to demand a direct answer to a direct question was hopeless and only edged me closer to that dangerous precipice of helpless and self-defeating fury. So I had decided—without conscious thought, really—to play his game.

Meanwhile, though, I waited for Wilby to turn his back and move in the opposite direction; then, with one hand I set down a glass on the bar, hard, and with the other managed to turn on the tape-recorder switch. There was a very faint and distant whirring behind the cabinet doors but Wilby did not break the rhythm of his tiger-like pacing. I mixed the old-fashioned.

"You didn't count the money," I said.

The packet was still in his hand. He shoved it into his pocket without missing a step. "Proves how I trust you, dad."

"It's more than I can say about you." I poured myself a weak highball; somehow I was certain I would need it. "You know, of course, that once you accepted that three thousand dollars, you were guilty of extortion."

"Extortion-abortion," Wilby said, "just so you gave the bitch a roll."

Abortion. I paused and stared, listening to the whir of the recording device.

"I got the full report, lover-boy. Four times in one night. Wonder why she calls you Sam!"

My mind flinched from the picture of the two of them at breakfast discussing the night. *Standing up in the shower, too!* A couple of monkeys giggling together. The idea was absurd and disgusting.

"Abortion," I said, "is legally considered murder. Once that happens, you will be as guilty as the doctor."

Wilby stopped and turned at the far end of the room. "And *you*, dad. Legal mind like you must know about aidin' and abettin', all that fettuccini. Didn't I thank you for the bread, lover-boy? Couldn't afford it otherwise, man."

I lifted my glass, drank deeply. Wilby made a flat and ugly sound that was probably intended to be a laugh. The whisky scorched all the way down.

"Doin' it all for *your* sake, dad. Y'ought t'thank me, y'know."

"You're her husband," I said, for the tape-recorder, but the hopelessness had settled in beneath the numbing shock.

"Y'think Oscar's mine?" Wilby asked. "We wouldn't want another little bastard like *me* messin' up the premises, would we, dad?" He came to the bar, picked up the glass. "Y'think if Oscar was mine, I could let the doc-doc do it?" For the first time today a faint shadow of his familiar, mocking self returned as he sipped. "What kinda father y'think I'm not?"

I was no longer capable of surprise. Perhaps, it occurred to me, perhaps in some part of my mind I had known all along why they needed the money, what lay behind the whole caper.

"When?" was all I could then manage to say.

"Doc-doc says tomorrow. Three o'clock."

So there it was. So that was it. Tomorrow.

"We kinda grown accustomed to the pad, like the song says, man. Why should you have all the goodies?"

"Perhaps," I said numbly, "perhaps because I worked for them."

Wilby took a long swig of his drink, otherwise unmoving. Then: "Me, now, I didn't. Only I got 'em anyways. Now ain't that a ball-crusher, lover-boy?" He seemed to lose interest. "We split tomorrow, pop. One more night—Jenny's idea. Then poof—we evaporate. Y'got my promise." He strolled into the library.

I stood a long moment wondering where the hot fury had gone and when, if ever, it would return, wondering when the shock would actually reach me and what I would do then. The purring machine behind the cabinet door had recorded every word—and almost every word had incriminated me as much as, if not more than, Wilby. I finished my drink in one long draught, flipped off the tape-recorder, and walked—racking aches and pains a part of every move now—to the library door.

"I'd be a fool to believe you," I said.

"Y'got some choice? Get outta my face. I'm readin'."

Still the rage did not return—and now I needed it. He was lying face down on the couch, head propped in his hands above the book.

"Where will you go, afterward? Tomorrow?"

"Maybe the Waldorf, dad. I got the price. Now split."

"You're not coming back here."

"Y'got my word." He rolled over and took off his glasses and proceeded to clean them on his shirt. His face was wan, despite the beard, and the bright blue eyes looked withdrawn and weak. "Been readin' about them Middle-Age tortures, man. Y'read it? Them castrated monks and popes—what they did to those nubile maidens they called heretics. All for the greater glory of my cousin up there. Some, course, preferred nubile *boy* heretics. Heretics-for-kicks." He replaced the glasses on his face. "Like Vietnam. Y'read that *Green Berets* book-a-the-month, dad? What them good civilized South Viets do after our good loyal draftees turn prisoners over to 'em? All for the greater glory of status-quo-quo and Secretary McNamara."

I had waited, scarcely listening: the twists and turns of his mind did not interest me now. But his fascination with pain and torture only reflected the sadistic pleasure he was taking in what he was doing—as if he could avenge himself for what he considered wrong by inflicting this torment on me. And I knew, too, that at least part of that satisfaction came from his knowledge that I *knew* what he was doing.

"You're going to tell one lie too many," I warned him, "and at that point—"

"Man-man," he interrupted, "if I tell one lie too many, they'll make me President. Y'really think I'm presidential timber, pop?" He put his head back and stared at the ceiling. "Pop, you'n me, we both hate lies—click? Only I been studyin' the papers; I learned from experts. Like Ike—y'know about them U-2s. An' Adlai at the UN tellin' the world—literary-literary, that Adlai—he don't know nothin' about no Bay of Pigs. An' Kennedy—say three Hail Marys, penance-penance—Kennedy on television lying through his Back Bay accent. An' Johnson—hell, man, that cat, he's goin' down in the history books. They're gonna make that cat Saint Lyndon if he keeps tellin' 'em!" He rolled onto his side. "Where was you, pop, when all *that* lyin' was goin' on? D'you send a wire to your fast-buck congressman, your crooked senator? D'ya try to bid for their ears against the monopolists, the gun-makers, the airplane stockholders? Them ears cost bread, man!"

I took a deep breath and heard the shudder in it. "You're leaving tomorrow because—"

"Because," Wilby cut in, "because, man, y'want one more night with Jenny. Click?"

Was it true?

"You're leaving tomorrow," I continued, "because if you don't, it's all over. I'm lost then but so are you. I'm finished if you're arrested and start telling *your* lies, but you and Jenny-baby are going to prison. A man can take just so much."

"Prison," Wilby said. "I might enjoy-enjoy, lover-boy. That ever cross that straight mind a-yours?"

"You might," I said, revolted, "but Jenny-baby wouldn't."

"Wilby—" It was Jenny's voice behind me—a whisper. "Wilby, what does he mean?"

Wilby sat up. "He's trying to snow us, baby."

Jenny was standing with one hip thrust sideways; she was wearing a fringed top-piece and tight white slacks so low on her hips that her flesh was bare from below her navel to the bulge of breasts above.

I felt nothing. If anything, more repugnance, intensified revulsion. Then why postpone the showdown until tomorrow? Why not now, to-day? Because I had to find a way to act.

"But—but what have we *done*?" Jenny asked plaintively. I saw fear gather in her face, saw it with satisfaction, *pleasure*. Her words trembled with uncertainty, tinged by indignation. "We didn't *do* anything!"

"Extortion," I said harshly. "Five to ten years."

She stepped closer. "Sam . . . you wouldn't do that to me."

I grunted a laugh. It was hilarious, really—her outrage, her appeal-ing to me.

"Put it on ice!" Wilby shoved me aside from behind, roughly, then faced Jenny, his back to me. "No, baby, he wouldn't do nothin'! An' I'll tell you why. 'Cause we got the bread now and that means we can buy us one of them shyster bastards! Y'got no bread, y'go up. Or the chair." He whirled to face me, shoulders stiff, beard leaping. "Y'never hear of no rich man goin' to the chair, d'you? Well, d'you? Hell no, man, cause they can hire them a front, click, pop, *click*?"

It was, like almost everything he said, a distortion of reality and truth; but, also like almost everything he said, it had a knife-edge of accuracy in it. Nevertheless, I refused to reply.

"Justice, man. You twist the truth for your side, I twist the truth for my side—equals Justice! Flaming sword. *Balls*!"

"But Wilby," Jenny said, "are you sure? You promised nothing could—"

But he could not be stopped now. He whipped about, brushed past Jenny, strode into the living room again, slamming the book to the floor. "Like them M.D. bastards. Y'got the price, we save your life!

Otherwise, *die*! Human life is precious. For a price! Ask the AMA! Hypocritical oath!"

Jenny frowned, helplessly, eyes still blurred with fear—but now I could not be sure whether the fear stemmed from what I had threatened or from Wilby's black dangerous mood.

In the living room he was sloshing whisky into his old-fashioned glass, the bottle clinking against the rim. "Go ahead, pop. You *try*!" Now a certain dark jubilation had come into his tone. "I *hope* you try! 'Cause that's gonna be one sweet hell of a trial. Y'know how people love crime, *all* people! Romance, man! That trial's gonna be front-page stuff. I might even shave the brush for it. 'Cause them ignorant jury-bastards, they got the idea only queers got beards, an' wouldn't want 'em thinking your husband was a queer, would you, Jenny?" As Jenny came into the living room, he snorted an empty laugh. "Baby, y'seen me act. Y'know I *got* it!"

I reached the door as Jenny said, skeptically, "Yeh. Last time they sent you to the nutclub."

I halted, listening.

"Nobody *sent* me anywhere!" Wilby shouted, and the outrage was naked, direct. "Nobody *ever* sends me anywhere! Y'stay outta this. This is strictly between lover-boy and me."

"Yeh, but—"

Wilby moved in a long, swift stride and, in an action so fast that I could scarcely see his arm move or even believe what was happening, he slapped her across the face—an open-handed but jolting blow that resounded through the room. Jenny's head twisted, her body staggered sideways, and then, blinking, stunned, her face began to crumble as the intense white print of Wilby's hand turned a sullen red. I felt no impulse to intervene. If anything—although my mind recoiled from the admission—the violence released some small portion of the tension in me. But only for a moment. Then, watching Jenny sink to the sofa, not quite weeping, although tears welled into her eyes, but whimpering like a hurt bewildered animal, I felt the briefest and most distant flutter of compassion; consciously I steeled myself against it as I saw Wilby move toward me, walking like a prizefighter on the balls of his feet, arms dangling.

"Well, Sam?" Having tasted blood, he was thirsting for more. "Well, lover-boy?"

When I refused to reply—I was damned if I'd give him the satisfaction, although I felt my own body tense against possible attack—

he went on. "Don't try that again, pop. Click? Nothin's gonna happen to Jenny. Just don't try to get in between. Click?"

It was strange to face him without feeling any fear and without feeling the rage that I kept expecting to erupt. He must have sensed this himself because I saw his eyes narrow.

"They didn't *send* me, dad. I chose to go. I *decided.* I gave such a great performance that courtroom, that judge was convinced I needed psychiatric assistance leading toward rehabilitation. Y'heard those fancy words before? I foxed 'em, click? Pretty soon, instead of stewin' in a lousy cell, I'm helpin' the white-coats. Helpin' 'em—they *loved* me!" The harsh bitterness had become a growl. "Helped 'em kill the looneys. *Kill*! Old looney wets his pants too often, takes a swing at an orderly, old woman dirties hers, cusses 'em out—white coats beat 'em up, worse, leave 'em by a window, winter, pneumonia, official record clear, too bad." He had begun to shout again. "That's what's happenin', man! I seen it. I *know*! What y'doin' about that dignity of precious human life, pop? I'm askin' you. You're sittin' on your fat asses like the Krauts outside Auschwitz, that's what, like the good, solid, church-goin' hymn-singers on the outskirts of Buchenwald wonderin' what that funny smell is!"

He paused, breathing hard now, and slapped his glasses over his eyes. Jenny's sobs had subsided. Wilby's breathing was the only movement, only sound in the room. I thought my silence was working on his nerves so I simply stood and gazed into the glittering, dark obscurity of his glasses.

"Y'get any ideas sendin' me back, man—*forget* 'em! They don't want me. No room at the inn and *Adeste fideles* to you! Not enough beds so they let me walk away, *saw* me, borderline case, not dangerous, *auf Wiedersehen*, make room for one more! They got 'em lined up at the gates beggin' to get in!" He took a single step, so that he was very close. As he spoke now, I could smell his breath and see the black snaggle-ends of teeth in the back of his mouth. "Y'just take care now, dad. Y'leave Jenny alone. Click?"

I was too appalled to speak then. And a suspicion slithered into my mind: was it possible that he had struck Jenny—it had been, after all, a wanton and gratuitous cruelty—not because of what she had said, or to quell her terror of prison, but because he had had earlier what he called a *full report* on last night? Was it possible that Wilby, in some contradictory and obscure sick way, was jealous of me?

"Y'give up talkin', Sam?" he demanded loudly. "Y'give up talkin'? It ain't even Lent!"

"I'm only listening," I said, certain now that my quiet detachment was driving him on and aware, too, that he probably knew it was a stratagem on my part.

"Jus' don't try it again," he said in a hoarse whisper.

"You don't know what I'll try," I said. "You'll never know what I'm doing. Or trying."

Silence. Even his heavy breathing was gone.

After letting it sink in, I said, "I paid my money for this freak-show."

"Y'got your money's worth last night," Wilby said and whirled away, striding to the sofa to look down at Jenny. "Way I heard it. What y'crabbin' about, *Sam*? Y'got another night now, don't you?"

Jenny stiffened. She looked from Wilby to me. Her eyes widened.

"Money's worth?" She stood up. "Money?"

I ignored them both and went to the foyer.

"Bread!" Wilby said, viciously. "Three thousand."

"I don't put out for money!" Jenny cried. It was almost a scream. Her body was crouched, catlike, eyes narrowed to red, ugly, slits, face contorting. Then she sprang, suddenly, claws bared, long nails flashing.

Wilby grabbed her wrists, threw her down to the sofa; she rose and sprang again. He tossed her as if she were not alive, hard, and she uttered an obscenity lost in a cry of pain as he twisted her wrists.

Then, when he finally released her, she was crying, head down between her knees, face hidden. Sobbing.

I knew then that I was going to be sick.

"Nothin' to what the old man used to do, is it, baby? With a belt. Across your back. With the blouse off!"

Jenny sobbed more loudly, murmuring incoherently.

"Wilby—" I said.

"Y'talkin' to me, lover?"

"*You* listen now. This is the deal—"

"I got you where the hair's shortest, so y'wanna talk deals."

"Listen," I said, without raising my voice. "We're in this together. Till tomorrow. If anything goes wrong—"

"No threats, man."

"Neither of you leaves the apartment. For any reason. You'll let the phone ring unless I'm here. The curtains stay closed, at all times. No music. And the terrace is out of bounds."

Wilby cocked his head to one side. "Y'makin' like my cousin, man? I don't take orders."

"If—"

"Don't *if* me!"

"*If* you're discovered here, either one of you, it's over. For me but for you, too. *Both* of you."

I saw Jenny's head lift; her cheeks were streaked with tears, eyes baffled and mean. And there was a single trickle of blood at one corner of her mouth.

"Man," Wilby said—and his voice was low and level—"man, you don't bug me. Not a little. 'Cause me, I enjoy takin' chances. Enjoy-enjoy. Only one commandment I don't break: *your* commandment, you squares' eleventh commandment. Thou shalt not get caught."

I turned to the door.

But Wilby said, "Where's that gun, lover-boy?" Then as I hesitated: "That gun you was gonna bring back today, remember? Gonna ransack the joint 'n kill us both."

Abruptly then, as if all the mounting wildness of the morning had finally exploded inside him, he began to move. I could only watch helplessly. He overturned a chair, he swept everything off the surface of the cocktail table onto the carpet with a tremendous clatter; then he whipped about and, with one arm, cleared the top of the bar, glasses and bottles and decanters smashing and spilling and splintering.

He was muttering but I could only distinguish a few words. "Bombs away! . . . Thou shalt not . . . hypocritical oath . . ."

When he stopped, the room was a shambles. Wilby stood panting, facing me at a distance, across the devastation. Jenny, silent now, was huddled into a corner of the sofa, and I saw the terror in her eyes.

But I myself had moved into some area beyond astonishment, even beyond fear or fury. My stomach was quaking and I knew that, soon, it would turn completely and I would only add to the desolation. I knew, too, that I had to act. Now. Today. It could not go on until tomorrow.

"Well, dad? Y'got that gun now? Now's your chance—"

It could not go on until tomorrow because the boy was definitely psycho. Or if not, at least teetering on the brink.

"Y'couldn't do it, though, lover. Too civilized. That it? Human life too precious? Even mine? Precious, ha! Bombs away, look out below, I got me a medal coming!"

But if he was teetering on the brink—

"Y'couldn't do it, man, even if you had a gun. But I could. One kick I never had. *I* could!"

I turned to the door and went out, my mind made up.

The elevator was empty—and incredibly, oppressively hot. Suffocating. My stomach turned over then and I began to gag. I had to lean against the wall.

When the elevator stopped on the main floor, I stepped off, weakly, and, instead of going toward the entrance, I hurried down the hall to a door leading into the basement. Dampness struck—and the thousand overwhelming stenches of trash, refuse, oil, garbage. I managed to make it, on collapsing legs, to a large tin container before I vomited. My stomach was empty, but it was five full minutes before I could stop retching.

On the way back to the office—where else was there to go?—my ribs ached mercilessly and every muscle in my body throbbed with agony while a single question quivered in my reeling mind: if he really was on the brink of madness—after all, he had admitted having been hospitalized—what would happen if he were to go completely berserk before tomorrow?

I could not take that chance.

After buying another pack of cigarettes and going up in the elevator, I passed Phoebe in the outer office, saw her open her mouth as if to speak, hurried into my office, and was about to take a deep breath.

"Do you keep all your clients waiting like this?"

It took a long moment for the shock to reach me. It was Anne. She was rising from behind my desk, coming around it to kiss me on the cheek.

"It's like the South Pole in here! And yugh, your face is wet. Why Daddy, you look ghastly!"

At once I made up my mind to carry it off. "Thank you, daughter," I said. "Those are just the words every father hopes to hear. And to what do I owe this honor?"

She stood gazing at me, her candid blue eyes puzzled, yet amused. She wore a light summer frock, sleeveless, and her face looked incredibly young. She picked up her purse from the desk.

"You owe this honor," she said, "to the simple fact that yesterday you invited me to lunch today. Obviously, you've forgotten—or you wouldn't fall back on such absurd clichés. If you've changed your mind—"

"Not at all," I said, suddenly overwhelmed by an emotion too complex to define. "I'm very glad to see you."

As I walked to the door, she took my arm, pleased again, smiling. "Only let's get out of here before I freeze! In the country I swelter and now—"

"Damned air conditioner's broken," I said.

But Phoebe, as we passed through the outer office, lifted her voice: "The engineer checked it, Mr. Wyatt. He says it's working perfectly. Good-by, Mrs. Spangler."

"Good-by—" and I detected an odd note, almost a question, in Anne's voice.

In the elevator Anne said, "I've been shopping but I couldn't afford anything I wanted."

Anne's frankness always astonished me. Especially in public places. While she had always possessed Lydia's forthrightness, she had never, even as she grew older, developed Lydia's fine sense of place and proportion and reticence.

When we were on the street, I asked, "What was it you couldn't afford, dear?" I had begun to feel refreshed already: it was an effect Anne invariably had on me. For a while now, perhaps everything could be just as it had always been: relaxed, casual, but with that pleasant sense of promise in the atmosphere.

"Oh no, I won't tell you, Daddy. Because then you'll buy it and send it up to the country, and then Glenn and I will quarrel and it's much too hot to quarrel. You're smoking again."

"It appears so, doesn't it?"

"You weren't smoking yesterday."

"Look, Anne," I said, hearing the sharp note of irritation, "it's hardly a federal case, is it?" What was she trying to make of it? "And why should Glenn object if I buy you something when I can afford it?"

"And he can't. Daddy, you're making me feel like the gold-digger Glenn accuses me of being. But only when we quarrel. Did you and Mother quarrel often the first year?"

At once my mind began swinging dangerously backward to a time I really didn't wish to remember, dared not remember now! London. The war. Lydia.

"Not that I recall."

The curtness was a rebuff, and I could feel Anne stiffen, holding my arm. She had always been like this, since childhood: the most casual slight struck with the pain of a blow. While intensely aware of what might hurt someone else—a rare human quality which Lydia had once described as *a curse and a blessing rolled into one*—Anne herself, behind that rather fashionably bluff manner, was so quiveringly sensitive that it was difficult to imagine her quarreling with anyone, even Glenn. As a child she had even refused to defend herself, retreating to her room alone, at once contrite and injured at even a hint of parental rebuke—an action which had always made Lydia and me feel guilty ourselves. Not that I was particularly surprised at what she had just revealed: I had had misgivings about Glenn all along. Damn the current fashion, Anne had simply been too young to marry! And Glenn, with that eternal smile always ready to flash into boyish brilliance, was such a child himself—how could he possibly take care of her? Walking the crowded street, jostled, with her arm through mine, I realized that, until now, these thoughts—or fears— had been submerged in my consciousness. Why should they erupt now, today, of all times?

The restaurant was crowded, loud. And I had not reserved a table.

"Two minutes, please, Mr. Wyatt," the maître de said, consulting his list again in surprise, and Anne released my arm.

"You really did forget, didn't you?"

This time there was accusation behind the hurt and bewilderment. And I realized, in another strange flash of lucidity, that my relationship with Anne had always had a sort of courtship aspect to it. *Oedipus, Oedipus, daddy-o*— Untrue, damn him, untrue. The sick sadistic bastard had to put a dark significance to everything, had to see the world in his own twisted way.

We pushed through a waiting group with mumbled apologies and followed the maître de to a corner table. When we were seated across from each other and after I had ordered my Scotch and Anne's daiquiri, her mood seemed to change—as if she were attempting to throw off her sense of having been slighted, summoning her normal gaiety. She related an amusing story, to which I half listened, about a chauffeured Cadillac, a state trooper, and a motorcycle rider who had tried to flirt with her on the Merritt Parkway, and by the time the drinks had arrived, she was chuckling in that girlish way of hers. She lifted her glass in a mock toast, as usual, and clicked it against mine, then sipped, smiling at me over the rim. I took a long swallow and felt it reaching deep: satisfying, bracing. I was feeling a great deal better, much more myself.

"I'll bet," Anne said, glancing over my shoulder, "I'll bet no one here could even guess I'm your daughter. I mean: you look so young and—say, you are hung, aren't you? I don't think I've ever seen you hung before." She leaned across the table. "What do you suppose these people think? That I'm your—"

"I don't give a damn what these people think!"

I saw her sit back, frowning. Because I couldn't bear to look at her, I took another long drink and realized the glass was almost empty. Still, I had to say something.

"Who gives a damn about these people? The place is run by gangsters. And as far as I know, it caters to them."

"Then," Anne asked solemnly, eyes on me, "then why do you come here? Why do all these people? If everyone knows."

Y'know how people love crime. All people. Romance, man!

"Because," I said, wondering if, after all, my answer made much sense, "because they serve some of the best Italian food in New York." I motioned to the waiter and drained my glass.

"If you're going to have another, so am I."

It was not like Anne. She always claimed that two made her head swim and a third made her downright dizzy. She had once said she never took a fourth, ever, because Glenn didn't like it if she did. Why should I recall all this now? I nodded to the waiter and made a gesture that included both glasses; he withdrew, saying something in an accent too thick for me to penetrate.

"I take it then," Anne said—and I recognized that characteristic persistence in her eyes, so that I guessed what she was going to ask— "I take it then that you and Mummy didn't quarrel—?"

My mind veered toward London again: the hurried meetings in blacked-out pubs, the gutted buildings along which we walked in darkness, the wail of sirens and the whining of the bombs, the small beamed room at the inn near the base. "We didn't have too much opportunity," I said. "Until after the war. We saw so little of each other."

"You make it sound as though you've been quarreling ever since."

It was not quite a question and she let it hang there between us.

But she knew. Anne had to know that Lydia refused to quarrel over inconsequentials, such as when I'd lose my temper over trivia, and that I refused to quarrel over . . . all the things that, I suddenly knew, Lydia wished we had quarreled about. Such as what? Hadn't I asked her that once? *Oh, I don't really know, darling. It's only that we never seem to discuss anything really important or vital, so how could we possibly argue in any really meaningful way?* Like so many of Lydia's remarks, especially during the past year, it had puzzled me at the time and it puzzled me even more now, remembering. I looked up to find Anne's eyes on me.

"Was Mummy a virgin when you were married?"

In spite of all the language I had heard last night and this morning, I felt a tremor down my body, odd yet familiar, familiar because Anne had always enjoyed trying to shock me. I heard her laugh now.

"Take another stiff one before you answer me," she teased.

I set down my glass and stared across at her. The amusement went from her eyes, slowly. She knew it was not something I would discuss. The truth was that Lydia had been very young, even younger than Anne now—and a virgin, yes, when we first made love, a month or two before we were married. Both Lydia and I had always been gratified by the fact.

"Well, anyway," Anne said finally, "what matters is that Glenn believes I was."

"And," I asked, slightly surprised at the casual politeness of my tone because for some mysterious reason I didn't really wish to hear her answer, "and were you?"

"As it happens—no."

Then before I even had time to react—had I known all along, did it really matter?—Anne rushed on. "Oh, Daddy, I couldn't tell him. It didn't seem important—to either of us. But when he asked, I lied. And that's what I think maybe *is* important. To him. That I lied. And I keep remembering what Mummy always said—about sex and love being one thing, or that they should be, and about marriages having a better chance, just from a practical standpoint, if I could understand how the two go together. But—oh, Daddy, everything's against that today. Everything. If only people could get married when they're children. Like in India. Do you understand?"

Did I understand? What? That sex and love should be one? That in Lydia's mind they had to be one?

"Daddy, what is it? What did I say?"

Fortunately menus appeared. And for a few moments, while we ordered, I thought perhaps she was not going to push on with it.

"Look, Daddy, *osso buco*! They must have known we were coming!"

I nodded to the waiter and said, "Two. With green salad, your dressing. Wine, Anne?"

"You'll get me squiffed. Another daiquiri, I think." Then, when the waiter withdrew, she fixed her gaze on me again. "Well, what should I do? What would *you* want *your* wife to do? Tell the truth? If I don't, it's the same as living a lie, isn't it?"

There it was again: truth. No matter how many wiles you used to keep the truth back, even if you succeeded, was it possible to suppress it completely? Or even if you succeeded, could you go on living a lie afterward?

I shook my head. "I don't know, Anne," I said.

I saw the disappointment cloud her eyes. I couldn't help it. I had no answer. I had failed her—and knew it.

She sat back and then, when the drinks arrived, she drank half of hers straight off. "You *were* sozzled last night on the phone, weren't you?"

"What of it?"

"Well, no need to snap my head off. Nothing's wrong with it. That's my . . . point. I think it's probably good for you. Considering—"

"Considering what?"

"Oh, Daddy—"

"Considering what, Anne?"

"Considering, I suppose, how long Mummy's been away—" She hesitated a split second, then asked, "By the way, how's Phoebe?"

"Phoebe?"

"I mean: is her work satisfactory?"

Then all at once I understood. I recalled that odd note in Anne's voice when she said good-by to Phoebe a while ago. Phoebe, of all people. The idea was ludicrous. I could feel the whisky drifting through my veins. I heard a hollow laugh and knew it must be mine.

"Is that so amusing?"

"Anne," I said, still smiling, "Anne, Phoebe's work is quite satisfactory. And I am not carrying on with my secretary."

"Whoever in the world suggested such a thing?"

It was exactly the sort of evasion, or denial, that Lydia would never indulge in. Not that Lydia had ever really been suspicious. Strange that it should be Anne and not Lydia who—

The food arrived and, looking at it, I felt my stomach turn over. I held up my glass, the waiter nodded, and then Anne held up hers, and he nodded again.

"You're not going to get ahead of me," she said.

Anne ate in silence, while I could only stare at my food, the smells somewhat threatening. Too much was happening too fast. And I knew that I had not really reassured her, or convinced her. But what more could I say?

Aware that my guilt was pushing me, I felt myself retreating into irritation. What right had Anne to suspect, or for that matter, what business was it of hers?

". . . can't really say how I feel about it. I'm sure the President must know what he's doing, but he hasn't made it clear and it just doesn't seem to make much sense, does it?"

"I'm sorry," I said, as the drinks arrived. "I'm sorry, Anne, I must have been thinking about something else."

"Yes. You must have." She was staring at me with those candid clear blue eyes—more suspicious than ever. "I said, Daddy, that Glenn has been drafted. And he'll probably be sent to Vietnam. Glenn and I know two fellows who've been killed already. Surely there must be some good reason for it all. There has to be, or the world just doesn't make sense."

Y'read that Green Berets *book-a-the-month, dad? What them good civilized South Viets do after our loyal draftees turn prisoners over to 'em?*

"The idea, as I understand it, is to stop Communism from spreading." Was I speaking to Anne or answering Wilby? "The alternative to fighting now seems to be fighting, on a much larger scale, later."

"Oh Daddy, *really*—"

And at once I was reminded of Lydia again: *Sometimes I envy you, Adam—the way you can so blithely take on the accepted position on almost any issue.*

"Really *what*?" I demanded of Anne.

"Never mind."

One of Lydia's tricks, or habits—withdrawing with a smile or a joke. And annoying as hell! Especially when she would hint later that *I* was the one who cut off intelligent discussion by simply adopting an attitude and then not exploring the possibilities. As if I were the village idiot, incapable of abstract thought, or individual ideas.

But suddenly now the war, if it was a war, was no longer photographs and maps in a newspaper and casualty statistics, all rather blurred and distant and unreal.

"I'm sorry, Anne. About Glenn. Honestly."

Anne shook her head. "It's not just Glenn." And a feverish troubled note came into her voice: "Who elected *us* to police the world? If the United Nations had a hand in it or if some of the other really civilized countries in Europe were willing to do more than support us with words—can they all be wrong and only we're right? Who, after all, are we to run the show? And as far as I can make out, we're only building up more hate for ourselves, and all white men everywhere. How's that going to stop Communism or anything else?"

As I listened, startled, I saw Wilby's face, not Anne's. "Damn it, Anne, you sound like some wild-eyed beatnik!"

She frowned. Then she shrugged. "Well, I'm not picketing and Glenn's not burning his draft card, but a lot of us are—" Then she picked up her glass again. "What it comes down to, for me, is what am I going to do. Follow him to some training camp somewhere or—"

"Or what, Anne?"

"Or come back home and take my old room and just wait it out, I guess."

As her voice drifted off, nostalgia made me go faint and hollow. Anne home again, in her own room. Then the picture of her room now, today and last night, flickered in my mind—and for an instant I was certain I *was* going to be sick again, that I would have to stand up and leave the table.

". . . after only one year. I mean: it's hard to imagine being home again and I don't know how Glenn would feel about it. He keeps saying I'm a big girl now, it's my decision, but—"

"But what do *you* want to do, Anne?" It was important. I found myself waiting for her answer. Somehow it was vitally important.

She was frowning. "I . . . I miss being home. My old room. Everything. Sometimes. But—"

"But?"

"But Glenn says that if married people are separated any more than absolutely necessary, it means . . . it usually means something's gone wrong somewhere."

Gone wrong? Was she implying, was Glenn, damn him, implying that because Lydia was away—

"Sam!"

My body stiffened. My heart crashed to a full stop.

"There you are, Sam!"

The voice came from behind me. Not Jenny's voice—it didn't *sound* like Jenny's voice. Still, I could not turn.

"I'm late. Sorry, sorry, apologies, Sam."

I had to turn then. A short, dark man in a black silk suit was holding a chair, while a plump little woman with high silver-blond hair kissed him on the cheek, then sat down.

I went slack with relief. I could feel the perspiration on my forehead, could feel it running behind my neck and down my back. Anne's eyes were on me: puzzled, frowning.

During the rest of the meal, which I did not eat—a fact on which Anne did not even comment—we chatted about nothings, like strangers: the drought, the brown lawns in the country, and the water restrictions in the city; Glenn's luck in selling a large group-insurance policy last week.

Anne refused coffee. "I warned you," she said—and her voice was not thick but rather high and bell-like—"I warned you I'd get sozzled! But, you know, I *like* it."

Then, while I was waiting for the check, she said, "Daddy, I doubt, don't you, I doubt we would have talked this way—it's the first time, really, isn't it—*this* way—if you hadn't plied me with alcohol."

"It's a father's duty," I managed to say and heard her laugh while I signed the check.

But, just as I had begun to feel I might have pulled it off, as I was about to stand up, my muscles protesting in terrible twinges, Anne reached across the table and placed her hand over mine. "What is it? Can't you tell me? *I* told *you*. Why won't you tell me, darling?"

"Tell you what, Anne?"

She pulled back her hand and reached for her purse. Her manner was brisk again, casual and bluff, but her eyes were dark with disappointment, failure, even pain.

"You always have allowed your imagination to work overtime," I said, but my voice was choked. "I've been working like the devil, that's all. And I'll admit it, perhaps drinking a bit too much."

"Yesterday you wouldn't have a single highball, even before lunch."

"Oh, Anne, for God's sake, take my word for something! Have I ever lied to you, damn it?"

She stood up. "No," she said. "Never before . . . that I know of at least. Thanks for the lunch, Daddy. I honestly did enjoy it." She was moving around the table. "In some ways."

On the street—which was sizzling and so brilliant that the reflected sun stabbed at my eyes—I tried to put her into a cab but she insisted on walking. "You really can't window-shop from a taxi." She kissed me on the cheek and I watched her slim form retreating down the block, weaving delicately through the crowd, back firm and slightly stiff, but her step uncertain. For an instant I was tempted to follow.

And all my firm determination to end it today—get them out at any cost, despite any risk—withered away. Only one more day. *Doc-doc says tomorrow. Three o'clock.* How could I reasonably, possibly chance the scandal, exposure, when I had to endure only one more night? *Y'got another night now, don't you*? Not my reason, no, not my reason, to hell with the little bitch! My reason was clear and simple. If the whole thing exploded in public now, Anne would be as wounded as Lydia. And Anne would not then, *could* not, come home.

I hailed a taxi and asked the driver to take me to Foley Square. Again the seat of the taxi was blistering hot and the tiny scratches down my back made it impossible for me to sit back without wincing. A long shot, oh God what a long shot this was! But the best my mind could devise.

While I talked, Stanley Ephron sat listening, one hand shading his sharp dark eyes from the sunlight that fell in slats over my shoulders. A short swarthy man, he always wore a troubled expression. He did not interrupt or grow impatient. I concentrated as best I could—the office was a caldron, although Ephron didn't seem to notice—leaving nothing out, no detail that seemed even potentially relevant. With one exception, I told the total truth, wondering as I spoke whether that quick shrewd mind—I had dealt with Stanley Ephron before in other circumstances—would cut through the truth and fix itself on that single lie at the heart of the matter.

When I finished, my mouth was parched. Stanley Ephron tapped his fingers on the top of his desk, took a deep sigh, then finally said, "The man's on a spot, isn't he?" Something in the tiredness of his voice, something in the distant softness of his tone gave me hope:

was it possible he really comprehended? Even cared? "Yes sir, Mr. Wyatt, on a spot. A tart and a fag. Jesus! And just what are you asking me, Mr. Wyatt? What you should advise this client of yours?"

Listening carefully, alert, I could detect no quotation marks around the word "client." I felt a surge of relief: he had not cut through to the lie.

"No," I said. "I'm asking what the police—this office—can do to help him."

Stanley Ephron's gaze moved from me around the office that, compared to my own, seemed small, somewhat disordered, old, slightly musty. "Mr. Wyatt, I'm only one overworked assistant DA. And, incidentally, a busy man." He sighed again. "Certainly we can help the poor slob. I can send a squad to his home with orders to arrest. All I need's a signed complaint."

The hope faded; the relief died. "You don't understand. He . . . my client has a wife. Children."

"He should've thought of them before he got mixed up in this."

"You didn't hear me! He *is* thinking of them. He didn't—"

"Mr. Wyatt, with your experience of law and human nature, do you actually believe this poor slob didn't pick up the girl?"

Ain't it terrible now, how people always believe the worst? About somebody else.

"Yes," I said hopelessly. "Yes, I do believe him."

He was staring at me. "Well, that's your privilege. And your problem if you swallow it. It doesn't change the facts, though—what either one of us happens to believe." He stood up and hunched his small shoulders; a certain coldness seemed to come into his manner —impatience, perhaps. "*My* problem, Mr. Wyatt, is that these people, slime like those two, are taking over the city. Hell, maybe the world. I deal with them every day. Now. I can move in, arrest on any number of charges, *with* a complaint, bring them to trial—"

"Can't you see—"

"I listened to *you*, Mr. Wyatt. Now, please, *you* listen to *me*? You got a duty here, too. This, I got to admit, is a new wrinkle on top of an old wrinkle." He shook his lean small head. "What'll they think of next? Your duty is to advise your client to get out of that place, get out and stay. Then you give me your client's name, address, and the names of the other two if you know them—do you?"

"He . . . they wouldn't give their names."

Stanley Ephron placed a small fist in a small palm, noiselessly, and said, "We'll get them fast enough. All right, what's your client's name then?"

I hesitated. Then in a bleak voice I said, "I don't know."

Stanley Ephron regarded me a long silent moment. Then he started toward the door. "His funeral." But he seemed to change his mind, turned, came to where I sat. "Goddammit, don't you see? If those two are wanted for anything, *anything,* this client of yours—whose name you just forgot—is guilty of harboring. If there's an abortion —that is, if there's any *need* for an abortion and they do go through with it on his dough, he's also guilty. If they're junkies and have any of the stuff on the premises, he's guilty of maintaining a place where narcotics are used." He had begun to lean down; now he straightened and stood teetering back and forth. "Hell, Wyatt, what am I doing, reading the law to you? Your client can be guilty and so, by God, can you! You know your duty! Now." He sat down behind the scarred cluttered desk, elbowed things aside and picked up a pen. "Now, Mr. Wyatt."

We split tomorrow, pop. One more night—Jenny's idea. Then poof—we evaporate. Y'got my promise.

Stanley Ephron waited a moment, then slammed down the pen, which rolled, then clattered to the floor. "Christ, Wyatt, is this guy a friend of yours?"

"No," I said slowly. "Well, in a way. Only—"

"Only?"

"I saw him. He looks like hell. He's already—"

"It's *nothing.* Nothing to the way he'll look when they're through with him. Three thousand, *hell!* They'll wring him dry. I'll lay bets. Take pleasure in wringing him dry. I tell you, I deal with this scum every day. If we don't stop them, every move, if we don't find some way—"

I stood up. He stopped talking. "Look, Mr. Ephron," I said, "my client doesn't want to break the law—"

"Only one way to not break the law—that's not to break the law."

"He's trying to save something that's important to him. All he's asking—"

"You think they'll stop once they've squeezed—"

"All he's asking is that you—"

"They'll move down the block, into the next apartment even—"

"He's asking you to do whatever you can do without publicity, without—"

"He's in no position to ask, to—"

"I *told* you that. Didn't you even *listen*? I *told* you what he's afraid of!"

Stanley Ephron leaned back in the swivel chair. It groaned. "I listened." He sounded weary now. "I heard. Only we can't do it that way. Not today." His voice held an ancient sadness, as of a man tiredly trying to hold back a flood even while knowing that sooner or later, with or without him, the dam will crumble against the accumulated weight of evil and destruction. "Nobody wants to see him crucified by the damned scandal-mongers. To sell their cheap newspapers, for Christ sake! But there are constitutional guarantees. You know that. Freedom of press—" He was not arguing now, or even attempting to reason—only flatly stating what he knew, much as it troubled or bewildered him. "Now this new Supreme Court ruling. They're bright men. Me, I'm a constitutionalist myself. Morally, maybe they're right. Protect the innocent. But you know what's going to happen. Even if we could keep the newsboys off it—and it's possible we might, for a while anyway—this kid's going to get a lawyer. Money or no money, today he'll get one quick and we can't even question him till he does. And the lawyer'll bring in the hounds. The kid wants it, it's good business for the lawyer and for the papers. If your man has any prominence whatever—hell, even if he's only reasonably successful—the papers'll make hay out of it and hash out of him. Nothing I can do to stop it. I could lie to you, make false promises. Why should I? Criminals got their rights, even when you *know* they're guilty of the crime. And this particular hood—look what he dreamed up! He's smart enough to know what rights he's got." He turned away. "I got millions like this to apprehend, try to convict! The city's crawling with them. If I had my way, I'd pick them all up in one night, hold a mass trial and—" He stood up with his back to me. "Not true, Wyatt. Not true. We've all seen enough of that sort of thing in our time, I guess. My own grandfather, two aunts, three uncles—" He came around the desk. The pockets under his eyes were dark and heavy, and he looked sad and angry at the same time. "You tell this client of yours—from me, personal—it can only get worse. And also: if they drive him to something, something worse like taking the law into his own hands, *he'll* be the one who gets the trial. And publicity the like of which he can't imagine now. Now. You tell your . . . client that. From me."

"I'll tell him," I said, hearing the definite pause before the word "client," and went weakly to the door, the frustration and helplessness settling deeper inside.

"You said there's a possibility the kid's psycho."

"A possibility."

"Then—" and again the voice grew harsh—"then how the hell can this guy play ball, make deals, *anything*, with a crazy man? Those sick queers can go off any minute. Then what?"

I only shook my head. "I'll warn my client."

The shrewd eyes probed. I met them without flinching. Then Stanley Ephron said, "You do that, Mr. Wyatt."

"Of course," I said "if he did go off, no one would believe anything he said after that, would they?"

"Possibly not." He waited. I opened the door.

"Trouble with advising your client along those lines"—and he took a breath as I paused in the door—"only trouble there being: who can predict what'll happen if he really blows his hinges? What'll happen to this client of yours then? Hell, it might not matter then what gets into the papers."

I nodded. "Good thought. Thank you."

"By the way, Mr. Wyatt—"

"Yes?"

"You don't look so hot yourself. You take all your cases this personally?"

I went out without answering. I had to. I was shaking all over.

I made it on caving legs down the corridors, through the busy echoing halls, outside, blast of heat, down the hot concrete cliff of steps.

He knew. Or suspected. If he did suspect, what would he do? What was *his* duty now?

Should not have come here.

Would he send a squad to the apartment? Was he looking up my address even now?

A mistake. It takes only one.

But he couldn't do anything without a signed complaint. Legalities. On *my* side this time.

He could send a detective, just to get a look, just to report or possibly throw a scare.

Into a cab. Up the stone canyons throbbing with heat. Uptown again. A riot of sound, speed. Oh God, what a tragic stupid mistake.

And how many others have I made? What am I neglecting, even now? Who? Must concentrate. Monday. Tomorrow they'll be gone. Have to believe that. *Must.* Tomorrow will be Tuesday. Something I'm forgetting about Tuesdays. Know it. Damn the drinks. Foggy mind. Damn Ephron and his suspicions. Tuesday—what the hell am I forgetting? And if Ephron is moving now, does it matter anyway? But tomorrow it could all be over. Or the hell just beginning, really.

"I've a list of calls, Mr. Wyatt."

"Save them, Phoebe. And I won't take any for a while. Have to work on that Markham brief."

Inner office stifling. Had my voice been casual enough? Sounded brusque to me. Jacket off. Behind desk. Inferno in here. Concentrate now. Pass time, work to do; if concentrate will not think ahead, or remember. Scribbled jottings on yellow pad: meaningless. Had they once had a cool logic? On Friday I had felt ready to dictate a rough draft of the brief. Now even the main outline of the case was blurred in my mind. I couldn't go on like this, obviously. Whisky wearing off, anyway. But that damned deadly letdown, lethargy. Depression. Perhaps if I stretched out on the couch, tried to sleep.

Wesley Markham. I had it now. It was all coming back. Knew it would. As a large stockholder, Wesley Markham was bringing suit against the president of a toy-manufacturing corporation on Long Island. We were trying to establish that the president—the son-in-law of the chairman of the board—was using company money for personal and private purposes.

Justice, man. You twist the truth for your side, I twist the truth for mine—equals Justice.

The case was not clear-cut. Such cases never really are. But the company's attorneys would, naturally, slant information to convince, as I would; and out of that, more often than not, a rough kind of justice did emerge. Original premise of the Anglo-Saxon concept of law: was there a better way? In spite of its faults, lapses, it had served, still served, and would serve, damn it, until man was able to devise some other scheme or process better suited to his society. *Flaming sword. Balls!* All right—*not* abstract and perfect justice, but a ramshackle way of survival. Only—who the hell was I arguing with? What did Wilby know about law, or care? I ran down the jotted notes. Our investigation had revealed that the young president was something of a playboy who ignored his job in favor of yachting, women, and in general helling it up; on the other hand—and this was the sticky part that I must be careful to deal with—his contract with the company, approved by majority vote of the stockholders, provided the Bentley he drove and the yacht he sailed, for business and entertainment purposes. Now to prove, item by item (and we had photocopies of night-club checks, gambling bills, even copies of his two last Internal Revenue tax returns) that his personal salary and other income were insufficient to support these sums and also to establish, through the company's books—

But it was too much. Overwhelming. Not today. Impossible.

Tomorrow. Something I was forgetting. Abortion: three o'clock. What else? I looked at my appointment calendar on the desk. Pretrial hearing, Corbin case: three o'clock. Must cancel that out, must get a postponement.

Can't go on like this. Cannot. What will happen if—

Bombs away . . . thou shalt not kill . . . hypocritical oath! All the glasses and bottles smashing, splintering.

Then I had it. Remembering the debris, the havoc of the apartment. Minnie. What was her last name? Dignified, matriarchal Minnie would walk into it tomorrow morning. Tuesday morning, as usual, Tuesdays and Thursdays. She would let herself in with her own key, as usual, and—

How could I have forgotten?

I flipped Phoebe's button.

"Yes, Mr. Wyatt?"

"Do you have Minnie's telephone number?"

"Minnie?"

"I don't know her last name, damn it. The maid who cleans the apartment. Didn't Mrs. Wyatt leave a list of addresses and phone numbers?"

"Oh yes. Just a minute. Here it is—Minnie Roberts. Shall I place the call?"

"No. Bring me the number." Then I added, "Please."

I sat breathing hard, listening to my heart thumping. Damned whisky had worn off at last. I was on top of it again. Had to stay—

The door opened. Phoebe placed a card on the desk. I refused to look up. I could feel her eyes on me. I heard her go out, heard the door close.

I dialed 9 and then the number. A low-keyed exhilaration had set in. I was going to make it, after all. Less than a day to go now, less than twenty-four hours.

A click interrupted the third buzz. "Hallo?" A child's voice, heavy with the accent of the Southern Negro. "Hallo?"

"Mrs. Minnie Roberts, please."

"Who?" I could picture the small dark face straining upward to a wall phone in the dingy Harlem hallway.

"Mrs. Minnie Roberts. Is she there? May I speak with her?"

Silence. Had she hung up?

"Hello, are you there?"

"Who?"

My nerves were tight as wires, straining. "Mrs. Roberts. Minnie."

A giggle. "This ain't Minnie."

I could see the sweat running from my hand onto the telephone. "I want to speak with Mrs. Minnie Roberts. *Please*."

Again, silence. Which could mean anything. With one hand trembling I managed to open a fresh pack of cigarettes. How many had I smoked in one day? Less than one day, really.

When Minnie answered—no mistaking that deep positive voice—I explained that I was not feeling well, that I had decided to stay home from the office and that, while I would be happy to pay her for tomorrow's work, her services would not be needed.

"I be there in a hour," she said.

"No. No, Minnie, I don't need—"

"What you eating?" She accused. "Mrs. hates canned soups."

"Minnie—?"

"Mr. Wyatt, I know what Mrs. want me to do."

"No. I don't want to see anyone. Thanks, but—"

"Does Mrs. know?"

"For God's sake, Minnie—"

"I got her address in England—"

"Minnie, now listen. We don't want to worry Mrs., do we? It's only . . . only a summer cold. I've seen the doctor. He wants me to rest. Do you understand?"

Again, silence.

"Minnie—?"

"Mrs. would want to know, though." Now there was a plea in her tone. "Mrs. . . . . I never seen no woman love a man more."

I could not speak then. I felt myself sagging against the desk. I didn't trust my voice.

"If you say, Mr. Wyatt. Minnie won't come. But—I don't expect to be paid for work not done, thank you all the same. G'by."

Click. The humming line. It was over. One more hole plugged, one more door bolted. But I was limp, shattered, just when I had imagined I was on top of—

I leaped up. Had Phoebe been listening?

I threw open the door. She was sitting behind her desk, sipping from a cardboard container. She stared at me, startled. Her legs were crossed and her dress was high on her thighs. Her blouse was open deeply at the throat. I closed the door without speaking—let her think what she likes!—and leaned against it. Hell of a way to sit around an office. Had she heard? *By the way, how's Phoebe? I mean: is her work satisfactory?* It had seemed ludicrous at the time. What was happening to me, anyway? I had never noticed Phoebe before, not as a woman. She could have come into the office stark naked any day of the week and I probably wouldn't even have seen her!

I went to check the thermometer on the wall. Seventy degrees. Impossible. Whole thing out of whack. No matter what some damn-fool engineer had said. I sat down again. Legs stiff now, tight and painful. Four times in one night. Nightmare.

Is she good in bed?

Lydia?

The simple truth was that I had never thought of Lydia in those terms: rather, I had never thought of her in those terms exclusively. What she and I shared was too much of a single entity, a whole—and satisfactory in the extreme.

You didn't answer my question—

Yes. The answer to that specific and crude question is an unqualified yes. Lydia's passion—possibly because of her composed manner and patrician face—had startled and delighted me at first, years ago. London. It was so utterly natural, without restraint or evasion or any suggestion of prudery or shame; over the years since, it had filled me with a wild satisfaction that had never lost the element of incredulity; and the years—habit and familiarity, her age, mine—had not diminished or subdued it to any appreciable degree. Thinking of Lydia now—her soft womanly beauty and knowing eagerness—I stood up, a familiar shot-away emptiness coming over me. What a hell of a time to remember all that!

And, after all, what a hell of a time for Lydia to be away! Not that she had chosen—

You know Mother, darling. The question is whether she's really all that ill or whether she's only hell-bent to have her own way, as usual. Oh, to have my Lydia back in England now that July is here—

I was pacing again. And smoking.

Glenn says that if married people are separated any more than absolutely necessary, it means . . . it usually means something's gone wrong somewhere.

Nonsense. Youthful idealistic unrealism! Her mother's had pneumonia twice within the year and the woman is more than eighty years old.

But what if that's not the reason, only the excuse?

Excuse for what? For Lydia to get away from me?

She's been more and more restless this past year. Not restless exactly—pensive from time to time, now that I stop to think of it. Sharp-tongued, moody. Even bitter.

Ever since Anne's wedding, really.

If she has, it's only because she senses I've been lonely, missing Anne.

It's the end of something, I admit. An era, perhaps. Or another chapter. But not of the world, darling. After all, we still do have each other. Or . . . or is that enough?

Of course, it's enough! Damn it, Lydia, you've always had some strange feeling about Anne. About Anne and me, really. Even accusing me of spoiling her. I've tried to ignore it. No, I have *ignored* it. But it's as if you've been . . . well, jealous in some way. As if Anne were not my daughter but some strange woman.

I could not go on like this! Damn these insights, or suppositions, or whatever! Distortions of reality, probably. Defense mechanism, to exonerate myself, to excuse what's happened by finding some way to blame Lydia. What a bastard. I put on my jacket. Feather-weight in my hand, it felt leaden on my shoulders.

Too early to leave, though. No need to start the whole office conjecturing, gossiping. *Mr. Wyatt never leaves before five, usually five-thirty, but his wife's been away a month now, you know—*

Could it be possible, though, that Anne and I have been too close? That we're still too close? That in some way we've excluded Lydia?

Oedipus-oedipus, daddy-o—

No, damn it. Bastard has to poison everything comes into his view. Has to mock, distort, destroy—

I opened the door and went out. Let them think what they want!

Ain't it terrible now, how people always always believe the worst?

"Good night, Phoebe," I said, consciously ignoring the knees, the unbuttoned blouse.

"I hope you win," she said.

And I stopped at the hall door. "Win?" I heard myself echo foolishly.

"Squash," Phoebe said, and there was a patient note in her voice —or perhaps I imagined it. "You have just enough time."

"Of course. It's why I'm hurrying."

How quick the lie now. Expert. Donald Abbott. Squash. At the club, every Monday afternoon, four o'clock. Then I was not leaving the office early, was I? Small giddy triumph.

I was stepping onto the elevator—

"Hold it!"

And Henry was beside me, towering, grinning, pulling on his jacket. "Sneaking out early myself. You won't report me to my partner, will you?"

"If you won't report me to mine," I said, recalling our morning conversation. *Don't jump to conclusions. We're not all like you.*

Henry laughed—in such a way that the others in the cubicle began to smile, liking Henry at once, responding to his charm and confidence. "My reason's purely . . . personal. How about yours?"

He was forgiving me; he was telling me to forget the morning. Grateful, I said, "Purely," and he clapped me on the back as we emerged.

On the blistering sidewalk he began waving at all taxis, occupied or not, and again I was tempted: tell him, stop him now, take him to a bar around the corner, pour out the whole truth, unburden.

Henry was muttering. "Only one company has cabs on the street at the rush hour. Off Duty, Inc. Wish to hell I owned stock in it." Then he was facing me. "What do you hear from Lydia?"

The question, as natural as the heat and familiar roar of traffic, startled me. Cautiously: "Her mother's no better, no worse."

"I didn't ask about her mother. God, I remember that icicle. Didn't even melt at her own daughter's nuptials. How's Lydia, the girl herself?"

What was he getting at? What did that mean?

"Her health, you mean? Lydia's never ill."

He stopped waving at the passing cabs. His craggy face stared down at me, at once baffled and amused. "Adam, take the chip off. It doesn't become you. You sore at me for something?"

A taxi came to a halt at the curb. I turned away and began to walk. Foolish. Stupid! What are you angry about now? I heard the cab door slam behind me and when the taxi passed, I saw, but ignored, Henry's face staring back at me through the rear window.

Abruptly then—the thought came smashing at me out of nowhere—I knew why I had not told Henry. This morning or now. I couldn't tell him. Ever. I remembered him drunk on champagne—he had a full head of hair then—at my wedding in London. *To think I introduced you two. You lucky bastard. I ought to hate you.* It was all perfectly clear now. Of course! On some repressed level of consciousness I must have known it all along. What was it Lydia had said? I had remembered it only this morning. *Henry's the kind of man, I'm afraid, who wants what he can't have and can't be happy with what he can have.* So Lydia knew, too—had known all along. Then why hadn't she discussed it with me, openly?

Down the blinding sidewalk. Sun shimmering. Exhaust fumes. Faces. Faces. Whole body wet, dripping.

God, I thought Charlene was more sophisticated than that. Imagine a woman demanding a divorce because of that. Can't she comprehend that, to a man, that sort of thing means no more than taking a shower? A man's by nature polygamous.

Is he, Henry? By nature?

Stop-light. WAIT. Bodies close, snatches of conversation. WALK. Women's legs. Girls' legs. Bodies moving under summer dresses. Rarely noticed before.

You're in no condition to play squash. Better that than the apartment. Better that than Wilby's voice, moods, irrational ideas. Are they? Irrational? Are they? Better squash than Jenny, what will Jenny—

More hate than love, Lydia. Understand. No love. Contempt, fury. Please try to understand. Only once, after all, only once in twenty years, and in hate, love's opposite, Lydia, please—

I saw the pillars of the building in the distance. The interminable distance, miles away, *miles*! And I had come only a few blocks; normally a pleasant invigorating walk. Now, with those few yards—not more than a hundred, not longer than a football field—stretching ahead, I was not sure I would make it.

Undercurrents. Henry. Henry and Lydia. Had they always been there or—I missed a step—or was I inventing them? Was it possible I was imagining them? Dangerous, if true. You know how dangerous. Hold on now. Must hang onto reality. The present. Only the present.

Had Ephron sent the police to the apartment? That's the present, isn't it? Had he found a way, without a signed complaint, found some pretext for getting in? It could be over by now, all over, in spite of all my careful painful efforts, evasions, pretenses, lies!

In the locker room—had I even been polite to Roger at the desk? What had I said by way of greeting?—I closed myself into a telephone booth and dialed the apartment. The phone buzzed with spaced abrasive insistence, each buzz rasping every nerve up and down my body. *You'll let the phone ring unless I'm here.* Was Wilby following orders—*Y'makin' like my cousin, man? I don't take orders*—or was he under arrest, even now, asking to see a lawyer, asking to see the press?

No answer.

Spent, drained, I slumped inside the breathless booth and tried to imagine how, how in *hell* it would be possible to play even a single game of squash.

"Where was your control, old man? Your service is shot to hell and you didn't pull off a single half-volley!" Donald was shouting above the sizzle and roar of water from the next shower stall. "For a while I thought that second game was going to a fifteen-ace. Oh, I'm not complaining, never won so handily before. You played like a man demented."

I said nothing. Demented. Perhaps. And now exhausted. Why had I gone through with it? To punish myself? To punish myself *further* —as if physical pain could absolve my sin, shrive my soul, as they believed in the Middle Ages? Not that I, this free twentieth-century man, could possibly believe in that.

Me, too. How can you stand it, Sam? I turned off the water at once and began to towel myself dry, remaining inside the stall for the same reason that I had worn my T-shirt while playing: those nail-scratches down my back. *Will you? Now? Kill me, Sam. Standing up—* Well, no more. Never again. Had I been making certain? Driving my body into exhaustion, hoping for impotence? Damned good reason to play like a man demented.

"I'll order, old man. You could use a double, I do believe," Donald said as he ambled heavily out of the locker room.

In the dim paneled bar later, he sprawled—despite his weight, he always appeared to be luxuriating—and prattled on. The whisky was not bracing. Cold, it tasted strong, bitter.

". . . remember believing, during the depression, that once everyone had at least one car in every garage and a steak on every backyard grille, he'd be free to turn to the better things. A spiritual revolution as well as an economic one. He would, the nice myth had it, live gracefully, devoting himself to matters cultural; art and literature would then flower in the land. My, they do mix a decent Manhattan in this otherwise depressing place. And what have we instead of such flowering in this democracy of the affluent? Two- and three-car garages, at least one motorboat, the more flatulent the better, beer cans littering the roadsides, a crime rate that staggers the imagination, so that even I keep a gun, if not under my pillow, at least within reach, and a poverty of the intellect and spirit that would have shocked even poor old Sinclair Babbitt himself. Corruption on all sides that causes even my not-so-lily-white mind to boggle. How do you account for it, Adam?"

"What amazes me," I said—why, all of a sudden, did he want to discuss corruption, crime?—"is how anyone who can play squash the way you can, can talk like a character out of Henry James."

"Don't flaunt your education, old man. Most impolite. Attorneys are presumed to have none. Henry James, indeed! It happens that my mother, while bulbous with child—me, to be exact—was frightened by a Moroccan-bound set of the old master of the involuted clause signifying little. What are you doing for dinner?"

Lobster-shrimp goo-goo. It won't be exquisite, dad-baby, you stock a poor kitchen but Wilby did his best-best. My mind and stomach revolted. I took a long drink. Might as well sit here lulled by the rhythmical inanities of Donald's chatter.

"It's an absolutely brilliant idea, as most of mine are. Why should you spend a lonely evening alone in your apartment while I spend an equally lonely one down below in mine? Although elegant soirées all over this grimy city are going to absolute pot for lack of my sparkling presence, I'll be magnanimous, dip into one of my several trust funds, and buy you dinner."

A pleasant but deceptive sense of distance, detachment, had settled over me. Why should I go back to be tormented by Wilby's viperish sadism, or disturbed by Jenny's demands, possibly even tempted?

"Anything but lobster or shrimp," I said.

Donald looked momentarily startled. "My dear fellow, I wouldn't presume to order for you. I think you need another highball." A flicker of prankish gaiety appeared in his eyes, which were set deeply in pockets of flesh above and below. "I've heard of a place, but you would have to be willing to take a risk."

"If you don't take risks, how are you going to know you're alive?"

"Now that's amusing. It makes absolutely no sense but it's just reasonably amusing. You won't be offended, will you, at my suggesting you're not your usual self today? In the back of my mind I've been trying to decide whether that represents deterioration or improvement. Oh well, perhaps the evening holds the answer. Ah, observe the frost on the glass! Thank you, Raymond, and my felicitations to the bartender. Instruct him to begin constructing another with his accustomed patience and skill."

The pain was constant now, not throbbing but a steady unremitting anquish of every tissue. Donald seemed hardly to care whether I listened or not. By the time we had finished the third drink, I had begun to consider—in some remote muted part of my mind—the possibility of putting up at the club tonight. Lydia had suggested I might want to stay there while she was gone, but I'd vetoed the idea on the grounds of expense. If I had stayed here the entire time, though, it wouldn't have cost anything remotely comparable to—

"You appear to be ensconced for the night, old man, if not plowed under. Rise up, rise up, we're going to find the charlie."

In spite of the agonizing protest of muscles, I managed to stand. "What the hell is the charlie?"

"My good man, are you totally illiterate? Don't you even read Earl Wilson? The charlie is the *action*. Are you prepared in your soul for a Dionysian revel for two? We'll walk. It's only five or six blocks."

"*You* walk," I said. "I'll take a cab and meet you there."

"Here, here, no need to get abrupt with me. I walk for the good of my figure, you fortunate sonofabitch. Will you whistle or shall I?"

In the taxi he lolled. His eyes, however, followed every pretty woman we passed. Once or twice—without pausing in an involved dissertation on the various forms of snobbism—he even twisted his whole body about to gaze out the rear window. It was, I realized, a habit I had not noticed before, possibly because I usually met him in small social groups or in the somewhat monastic surroundings of the club.

". . . an aristocracy of snobs, of course. Chauffeurs and butlers, for instance, don't hold a candle to doormen. And headwaiters— well, everyone knows they're the *crème de la crème*. But there must be a legitimate, or valid, snobbery, not of wealth, although wealth helps achieve the other, but a snobbery of superior intellect, sensibility—"

Cherubic and innocent, he continued to chatter while his narrow eyes continued to search out, linger on, and probably undress woman after woman, girl after girl. His lips had become moist, and, during the occasional pauses, grossly slack. Why had all this escaped me before? And why should I be aware of it now?

I told the man I was visiting some cat named Donald Bishop. Abbott. . . . Well, religious, anyway. How had she happened to use Donald's name to get past the doorman? Was it purely accidental?

"Here we are, old man. A den of iniquity, let us hope! Harlots? Babylonian whores. Gomorrah without sodomy, let us fervently hope!"

Had Donald picked up Jenny somewhere, perhaps innocently told her about me?

"Keep the change, driver. My mother, rest her immortal soul, died a rich and generous woman. Adam, do you have your passport? I always keep mine up to date so I can pass over foreign borders like these."

The place was dim and had a faintly South Seas décor incongruously and tastelessly mixed with metallic modern. The din was familiar: the jungle beat again but this time mechanically amplified to the final ear-shattering decibel. Three girls, not quite naked, gyrated in separate cages lifted above the room, and two others, behind the bar, wearing costumes suggesting a harem, mixed and shook drinks while their bodies also jerked convulsively. Nightmarish and bizarre, the whole atmosphere was at once amusing, depressing, and ugly. Lust was in the air—in the heavy clouds of smoke, in the head-splitting cacophony, in the abstracted glitter in the men's absent eyes. It was exactly the sort of place that Jenny would frequent.

The head waiter, an Oriental in a ruffled dress-shirt and flaring black tie, did not greet Donald by name, but we were seated at one of the tiny tables alongside the dance floor. On the floor couples faced each other, not touching, most of them not even concentrated on the

partner, every muscle moving and twisting, arms lifted or outstretched, all eyes as abstracted or self-concerned as Donald's as he
now stared or Jenny's when she had danced last night alone. *Dionysian revel,* Donald had said. But if so, where was the primitive joy, the
barbaric exultation? Almost at once Donald's heavy face was covered
with a film of perspiration.

Why had he brought me here? Because he knew? Because, one way
or another, he knew Jenny and he knew what was happening? But
how?

Abruptly, without reaching any sort of climax, the blast and throb
and blare simply stopped. The silence was downright shocking, not
quite sobering.

"Never order mixed drinks in a joint," Donald advised, picking up
a highball that had simply appeared somehow. They knew him here!
He was regarding me. "Well, Adam?"

"Well, what?"

"I assure you I'm not trying to corrupt you, old man. Only thought
you might like to take a peek at the seamier side. People like us, in-
sulated by outworn ideas and outmoded habits, should get shaken up
once in a while. Don't you agree?"

"Is that what you're trying to do?" I asked. "You and Jenny?"

I waited.

Donald set down his glass, wiped his face with a folded white
handkerchief and blinked. "Jenny? I'm awfully afraid that's one of
those enigmatic remarks you seem addicted to today. Should I know
Jenny? Should I want to?"

His eyes looked blandly curious, even amused. Was he lying? Of
course, I couldn't even be sure Jenny was the girl's name. And certainly Donald, rich as he was, could not have any financial interest in
the scheme. But I was in it now, in deep, and something kept urging
me on.

"If you don't know her, you don't," I said. "She claims to know
you."

"Jenny what? Or is it Jenny who?"

Irritated—at him? at myself for even entertaining such a far-
fetched idea?—I said, "What's on second."

"You're terribly witty tonight. You say the most original things just
as if you made them up on the spot."

"Oh, go to hell."

"There you go again. The proper phrase, the *only* phrase, at *precisely* the proper moment!"

His raillery, however—good-natured, friendly, even fond—did not irk me. Not like Wilby's taunts.

"Ah, he smiles. First one today. The patient will indubitably survive!"

"Do we eat here? Is the water safe?"

"Safer than the air, wouldn't you say? My dear fellow, they serve everything from ptomaine to gonorrhea. Speaking of which, I wonder what one does to attract the eye of one of those leggy little waitresses. I suppose whistling's not beyond the—oh, hello there, charmer. May we have a menu, please? Or whatever one calls it. Hm, she didn't seem to appreciate that, did she? Eyes too wide apart, that one, but did you see those legs?"

He had realized his mistake and he was trying to cover up. But I knew he had been here before. I was *positive* now. Yet why should he wish to see me involved? Peculiar human trait: downgrade the other fellow, pull him down to your level, as if that somehow improved *you,* at least in your own eyes. Or, as he himself had suggested, perhaps he'd get his kicks out of seeing me shaken up.

". . . always been an addict myself."

What was he talking about now?

"Since I was four years old, the theater's been a part of my bloodstream."

So he was talking about the theater, not about—

"*They Knew What They Wanted.* I didn't even know what the title meant. And *Rain*—before I even knew what a prostitute was. I could have climbed up on that stage and raped Jeanne Eagels right in front of that matinee crowd of simpering females."

Pop, y'oughta know better'n to rape my wife.

". . . changed, though, have you noticed? What ever happened to that moldy old Greek idea of pity? Compassion. Now the only pity's for self. Contempt and whining and cruelty. Terror, yes, but of a particular variety. Petty and mean. Little, nasty. The snipsnap raspiness of a nest of waspish little homosexuals."

Further proof? Why talk of homosexuals when he never had before? Unless he knows Wilby. No denying that Donald himself often talked like one. And a confirmed bachelor, living alone. Puts on a big show, lusting after waitresses, girls on the street. To cover up?

". . . couldn't conceivably know any more about marriage than, for instance, I do. But I don't pretend to know and of course I can't even write a legible postcard. I find it all amusing, though: that high-minded poetic palaver about the evils of illusion, the necessity for un-varnished truth, the mendacity of the world—when the characters up there on the stage, the so-called men and the so-called women, are pulling a conjurer's stunt in drag. And the playwright's probably sneering up his sleeve in the lobby. Oh well, I suppose they have to pay their psychiatrists' bills some way."

I wasn't following this, or trying to follow it. I was reading between the lines. Was Donald trying to tell me that he actually was a homo-sexual?

". . . but if they are sick, aren't the plays sick too? Then what about all those so-called healthy people who support them by the mil-lions? Maybe that's more of a comment on our whole society than anything the puling little faggot does. You know, I do enjoy the sound of my own melodic voice, but you're allowing me to carry a good thing too far."

The waitress returned, smiled coldly, went away. After watching her—that avid salacious gleam was no cover-up!—Donald studied his menu intently, sighing luxuriously.

I stood up. "Order for me," I said and walked across the dance floor to the foyer.

In my confusion—damned suspicions were almost engulfing me!—I had forgotten the stiffness and pain in my legs. I slid on the wooden floor, almost fell, caught the grinning scorn on several faces, cursed them silently, ignored the head waiter, and found my way into a telephone booth. As soon as I'd dialed the number, the blast of music erupted again. The walls shuddered. The booth quaked, rat-tled.

No answer.

Had Stanley Ephron found a way to arrest, after all? Or were Wilby and Jenny sitting there, eating like monkeys, snickering be-tween themselves.

Click.

And then silence.

I realized I was holding my breath.

"Yeh?"

At first I couldn't be certain it was Wilby's voice.

"Yeh?"

This time I detected—and only hoped I was not imagining it—a note of cautious urgency. I said nothing. I knew now what I needed to know. How could I have hoped for anything else?

"No tricks now—"

Still I said nothing. Waited. The music shook the floor under my feet.

"No tricks now. Listen, dad, don't try to be funny-funny, you be sorry-sorry. I know you're on there, you bastard!"

The rasping uncertainty, even possibly fear, was clear now—and had a music of its own. I leaned against the vibrating glass of the booth and reveled in the sound of Wilby's angry anxiety quivering on the edge of panic.

"Lover-boy, you better get your cock back here. Jenny's waiting an' you don't know Jenny when she's got to have it. She won't wait forever."

Still I did not reply. The silence hummed, stretched until I thought momentarily that he had hung up.

Then he was shouting: "Up your ass, you fink sonofabitch!" As I held the phone away from my numbed ear, my head reeling now, his tone changed to a parody of politeness: "Yes, sir, this is the Adam Wyatt residence. But I'm sorry to say Mr. Wyatt isn't here. He left the same message for anyone who phoned. He's out with three broads fucking himself into a heart attack. Good-by."

The phone cracked in my ear as he slammed it down.

What was I doing? What had I accomplished? I came out of the booth, wiping my face. It was dripping now. All I had learned was that they were still there and that Wilby was unnerved by my absence—as I had intended this morning. *You don't know what I'll try. You'll never know what I'm doing.* I had also learned, though, that Wilby was capable of taking any chances, saying anything when rattled.

And I had learned that Jenny was waiting.

The dancers were on the floor again. The girls were shaking and gyrating and writhing, possibly not even the same girls. A fresh drink at my place. Donald impervious, enthralled. As soon as I sat down, food appeared. And Donald turned and began to eat with the same voluptuous self-indulgence and concentration with which he had been watching the go-go girls. I tasted nothing, had no idea what I was eating. Let Wilby fret and snarl. Let Jenny wait—a long, long wait tonight, you little bitch. But what had Wilby said? *She won't wait for-*

ever. What if she decided to leave? And what if Wilby, furious at me, let her go? One of the two doormen and how many others in the building would see her?

Over the shrieking clamor I shouted, "Thanks for dinner, Donald. I'm going."

I watched him heave a heavy sigh as he dabbed delicately at his thick, moist lips. "For God's sake, stop being so precipitous, will you? Do I have to remind you that you're my guest?"

That did it. I was on my feet in an instant, a glass went over on the table, exasperation coursing like gall through me. "I said thanks."

Then I was stalking off, around the edge of the floor to the foyer where a crowd waited now. I pushed through them blindly. On to the street. Where a weary reluctance slowed my step. I couldn't go back there. Could not. Could not face it all again. One more night. Too much. Dark outside now. Still hot. What a damn-fool way to have behaved! If Donald hadn't been suspicious before—and if he wasn't a part of the whole damned sadistic scheme!—he would most certainly wonder now. Might even drop by later—to confirm his suspicions. Then what? I was walking. Looking back over the endless eternal day—which was still not over. The way I snapped at everyone: Henry, Phoebe, even Anne. Certain they all knew, or were surmising. Well, damn it, they did assume the worst, didn't they? Even Anne. Just as Wilby had predicted. The bastard knew: you had to grant that. *You just don't keep your goddam ears open, your goddam eyes!*

A taxi drew up alongside, slowed. I stopped—realizing that I had been walking stiff-legged with each step shooting pain upward into my groin—and I had opened the door before I saw Donald.

"Demented is indeed the word," he said. "Oh, get in, get in." And when I was beside him on the seat: "I don't mind paying for the meal—it was vile garbage anyway—and I don't even object to playing nursemaid if you're as crocked as you appear to be. But I have begun to wonder whether poor Lydia shouldn't be informed."

"Of what?"

"There you go again. Old man, even to a mind as normally insensitive as mine, you—"

"If you tell Lydia anything—anything!—you'll regret it."

At this Donald blinked. He pursed his lips. Then he said, "Adam, I'm not your enemy."

At once, slumping back, twisting my head away, I was certain that I was going to cry—break down in the back seat of a taxi and weep like a child. I could actually feel the tears burning and stinging in my closed eyes.

Possibly Donald sensed this because he began to chatter again: "They call it progress, of course, tearing down perfectly solid and rather attractive old buildings and putting up these glass-and-steel septic tanks. They wouldn't think of doing the like in Europe where there still some slight respect for—"

How could I conceivably have suspected Donald? It was a dangerous way of thinking. Pretty soon I'll be imagining everyone's against me. Christ. What motive could Donald have? He'd once told me he went down to his office on Wall Street only to keep from wasting away in boredom. Was that it then? Was *that* his reason then? To amuse himself by observing, then threatening to inform Lydia, just to see how I would react? Just to gratify his curiosity, to shatter his own boredom! Like watching a butterfly under the pin or an animal chewing off its own leg in a trap.

". . . least you can do, old fellow, after ruining a perfectly hideous dinner. Brandy, *crème de menthe,* I'll even settle for a spot of Cointreau, any old expensive booze you happen to have stashed."

"Not tonight, Donald." My voice was low, tight.

The taxi had stopped. We were on the sidewalk.

He wants to come in. Wants to see how I'll act.

Neither Geoffrey nor Terence was anywhere in view. No wonder strangers could walk in without being noticed, questioned!

"Adam, please don't be offended now." Donald actually took my arm as we crossed the marble floor toward the elevator. "I honestly don't believe you should be alone tonight."

He condemns himself with every word. He knows I won't be alone.

Avoiding my eyes, he punched a button on the panel, then released my arm. Maybe there's more to it than I had so far imagined. Maybe, in spite of all his talk, he actually is a homo. When Wilby left last night, to find the charlie, had he only gone downstairs to Donald's apartment?

"After all, one cannot evade the obvious amenities and it *is* ridiculously early—"

The elevator came to a halt. At the seventh floor. My floor. Don't panic now! The door slid open.

"Thanks, Donald, again," I said, stepping out and turning at the same time, facing him now and blocking his exit. "Take a raincheck, will you?"

"I'm overcome by such magnanimity—"

But he broke off, tilting his head to listen. Then I heard the music. A guitar. From behind the door. 707. A. Wyatt. I could feel Donald's eyes on me.

"Must have left the radio on this morning," I said, meeting his gaze.

"Indubitably," Donald said.

Fury cracked through me like lightning. I went weak with it, weak and hot. A voice began to sing over the music. Blurred.

"I don't give a goddam what you think!" I cried. "*I don't care!*"

Donald did not blink now. He looked a trifle sad for a moment, then he reached, touched a button. He nodded.

"Who am I to throw the first stone?" Donald asked as the door began to slide and I stepped back. "Or something like that that I read in some book or other. Good night, Adam."

The door was closed. Hum and whir behind it. He was gone.

He was gone but now, if he didn't already know, if he wasn't an integral part of it somehow, he knew more than anyone. Not suspected—*knew*.

Into the apartment. The deep quivering had begun again. Inside a glacier of stillness. Heat gone. Only cold. Blue, intense, frightening in itself.

No one in view. No false hope this time though. Foyer and living room in perfect order: astonishing! Music louder—not the familiar primitive beat, though. A voice, a guitar, to hell with the words. I switched it off, then realized: it was a record, not the radio. One of them had been out of the apartment.

"Welcome, pop. Welcome back to squaresville."

Wilby stood in the door to the terrace—the *open* door. Book in hand. Lounging. He had changed clothes: tight, low-slung slacks, black stripes on yellow, wide belt, black turtle-neck sweater, and high leather boots. All obviously new. He was grinning faintly.

I ignored him, returned to the foyer, picked up the mail, riffled through it. Mostly bills, circulars, a card from a friend vacationing in Maine. "Is this all of it?" Very strange.

"What y'expectin', dad, your draft notice?"

"A letter from my wife," I said.

His mood had returned to normal—if any single mood was normal for him. "Y'mean she writes every day? I find that downright tear-jerkin'."

Several wrapped packages were stacked on the step leading down from the foyer into the living room. Possibly both of them, then, had been out.

"Pop, y're late. I'm gonna have to report you to the time clock. Gonna dock your social security, take it outta your Medicare. Thought you'd bug me, didn't you, lover?"

"Did!" Jenny on the balcony: thin, tight turtle-neck sweater, a skirt so short it appeared to be a pair of shorts. "Did. Been bugged all day. Sweat-sweat, let him sweat, Adam—" She came down fast, toward me; changed, in some way different—how? "Sweat runnin' off his balls right now. If he's got any." She came close, placed her hands behind my neck, pulled my head down, kissed me on the lips. All with quick casualness, almost completely sexless—but possessive. "I missed you, too, honey. Only different from the way Wilby did."

I removed her arms. Christ! What next? She frowned up at me, eyes half-smiling, confident.

Wilby chortled. "Y'not talkin' tonight, lover-boy?"

"What do you want to know, exactly?"

My voice was so matter-of-fact, so devoid of either compliance or defiance, so empty, that it took a moment even to recognize it as my own.

"Like where y'been, dad?"

Jenny sniggered. "Thought you wasn't gonna ask."

"Like walking," I said. "Like walking my dog."

Jenny yelped and dashed around me and ran to sit on the foyer step, tearing wildly at the packages. "You didn't tell me they came! You mean bastard!"

"Slut."

"Fag."

"Bitch."

Jenny ripped open a box, strewed tissue, held up a dress, uttered a squeal of sheer delight, hugged it to herself, then tossed it aside, onto the floor, and started ripping at another box.

"Knew y'had to have a dog, dad. Expected parakeets. Or even cats. Knew there had to be a petty-pet in the woodpile."

I walked toward the stairway. "I have two pets," I said. "Although I'm not sure what to call them."

Wilby whooped. "Lover-boy tried a funny! See, Jenny—told you he'd show."

"You're the one who sweated," Jenny said.

As I reached the foot of the stairs, Wilby stepped into my path. "Who got outta the taxi with you?"

I stared stonily into the dark glasses; it was impossible to meet his gaze. I didn't have to consider my replies now; they came naturally, with a level coldness. "No one."

"He's been seeing things all day," Jenny said.

"Shut, slut. Who was it, dad?"

"I told you: no one."

He hesitated. I saw his mouth open in the beard, then close. Then: "Y'don't look so good, man. Bad day?"

"Obviously no worse than yours," I said.

He shouted. "Who, goddamit, *who*?" and tore off his dark glasses.

"Donald Bishop."

I watched relief leap into his bright eyes, then saw him blank it out. Why relief? That it was only a neighbor? Or—was it possible?—relief that he had not actually *imagined* seeing someone get out of the cab with me?

"I'm touched," I said, "that you were watching me from the terrace. Didn't know you missed me so much."

"Who's Donald Bishop?"

"Ask Jenny."

Wilby brushed past me, one shoulder nudging, strode to where Jenny still sat, the last package opened now, in a sea of white tissue and tumbled clothing.

"Jenny—"

"Up you."

"Jenny!"

"I got his name off the mailboxes downstairs. To get past the doorman."

Slowly Wilby turned to face me again.

"His name's really Abbott," I volunteered—and felt the smile on my face. "Religious, though."

Then Wilby's beard twisted into a grin. "Cool tonight, dad. Really jugglin', ain't you? Tricky-tricks. Y'find out what you want to know?"

"I found out," I said. I had learned that, in spite of all my wild and, I knew now, irrational suspicions, Donald's name had been used by chance and he knew nothing of what was going on here—nothing more than I had myself, damn it, revealed a few minutes ago on the elevator.

Wilby retreated behind his glasses again. "Told you last night, dad —all accident."

"That bug you, does it?"

"It don't bug you?"

"I think I accepted that fact of life a long time ago." But was I lying? Or had the idea ever really occurred to me, or troubled me? Did I really accept it even now?

Wilby's grin disappeared. He moved away, began to walk up and down in a straight line. I said nothing. I recalled how Wilby had taken pleasure last night in explaining how he had decided on me at the airport a month ago—by chance, happenstance. Then why should he be so disturbed by the idea?

"I had about enough your tricks, dad," he growled, the façade of casual mockery collapsed now. "Like that phone call."

"What phone call?"

"Don't feed me that crap!"

It was then that I decided to play it out. Or had I decided it when I refused to answer him on the phone? I was far from certain what I could hope to accomplish, but I said, "Are you saying someone phoned here?" I was proud of the feigned trepidation and irritation in my tone. I even took a step. "And you answered it?"

"I'm warnin' you, man—"

"Who was it? What did they want?"

"I could hear you breathin'—

I shrugged and turned to the stairs, shaking my head. "Everybody breathes." Then I added, "If there was a phone call at all—"

Wilby stopped above Jenny. "Jenny, you heard me. Y'heard the goddam phone ring—"

"Me? I was takin' a bath."

"Y'was on the stairs!"

"I didn't hear nothin'."

Wilby spit a word I couldn't understand. Then, whirling, he sprang. He took two or three steps up the stairs, grabbed my shoulder, spun me around. He was close now, breathing hard, his breath foul. "Y'called, tell the truth, y'lyin' bastard, *you called*."

I forced my gaze to remain on the opaque glasses: noncommittal, blank. "You know me," I said. "I often lie."

His mouth opened—the pinkness ugly in the whiskers, the back teeth visible, black and scraggly—and then it closed. I remained perfectly still, my aching legs about to cave, and felt a tremor of cruel satisfaction.

Into the silence Jenny said, "He's been saying somebody was following us all day."

He whipped about again, started down the stairs, stopped. His back was heaving slightly. "Y'gotta spill your guts, get upstairs!"

Jenny stood up, several dresses dangling from her hand. "They're coming to take me away, ha-ha," she said in a singsong voice. "The nice young men in their clean white coats—"

Wilby stood uncertainly, poised. *Those sick queers can go off any minute.* Then what?

Wilby faced me. "Y'got someone tailin' me, dad, you're taking a big chance. Large."

I hesitated—hoping the pause and then my voice would make it sound like a lie, yet aware of the risk I might actually be taking, too. "I don't have the foggiest idea what you're talking about."

"Y'tryin' to say I'm makin' it up, *imagining it.*"

There was always the possibility that Stanley Ephron had put someone on him. But I said, "I don't know *what* you're doing. Do you?"

He took off his glasses again. There was no slyness in his blue bright stare now. In that cold moment he acknowledged—we both acknowledged—that we shared a single opposing purpose: to break the other if possible. Whatever satisfaction he found in my appearance, whatever ravages of the day he had read there with inner gratification, he was not mocking now. And, like him now, I took my own sharp pleasure in the wretched uncertainty, almost panic, lurking in those steady, pale but bright eyes. Again I had the impression, sharper now, that the money—even Jenny—was only a secondary consideration, or motive, for what he was doing and intended to do.

"He's been driving me nuts all day," Jenny said plaintively. "Make him stop it, Adam."

"Stop trying to drive Jenny nuts," I said.

Then Wilby nodded. He even smiled, a bit wanly, as he turned away and went down the steps again, wandered away. "Anything y'say, lover. You're boss-man aroun' here."

"Thank you, honey!" And Jenny was suddenly close, brushing another kiss against my cheek, her breasts soft a moment against my body. Then she continued past me up the stairs.

"Only," Wilby said, "only lemme clue you, man. I know where y'been today." He snorted a laugh. "Y'make a deal with 'em?"

"With whom?" My tone was still steady but at once I thought of Stanley Ephron again.

"The fuzz, dad-baby. That's *whom*. Big shot like you. Respectable. How much'd you pay 'em?"

"Considerably less than three thousand dollars," I lied, wondering: was I taking the wrong tack entirely?

"*Listen*! They tap that phone, bug this joint, tail us, arrest— y'know what's comin'!"

"I know," I said, "and frankly I'm sick of hearing it. Now if you'll excuse me, I am tired and I'm going to bed."

I was halfway up the stairs when the door of the guest room opened and Jenny came out. She wore a white dress, short but not nearly so short as the one she had just taken off, with red panels and wide black lines in a geometrical Mondrian pattern. She stopped.

"Isn't it boss, Adam? Oh honey, isn't it the most?"

I stared up at her, fighting the instantaneous tightening all through my body as the ugly delights of last night streamed, uncontrolled, through my mind. "The most what?"

Dismay leaped into her face; her voice went flat. "You don't like it."

"I like it," I said, "but Halloween's so far away."

Wilby crowed. "They're coming to take *whom* away, ha-ha, ha-ha?"

Jenny looked appalled, a hand flying girlishly to her face; then, hearing Wilby, her chin hardened, eyes darkened.

"It's the latest. *Wait*!"

She flew into the guest room again.

I was damned if I'd wait. I continued up the steps, legs taut and aching murderously, my mind unable to rid itself of those bitter memories of last night, the cruel twisted pleasure of ripping off the negligee in fury—

But she was standing before me again as I reached the balcony, another dress in one hand while the other reached and pulled at a zipper behind. I heard the sound, then saw the dress fall, slip to the floor around her ankles.

"You'll love this one, honey!"

With one hand I took hold of the banister, conscious not only of

her body but of Wilby watching from below. Forcing myself to move
—there was no room to pass by her—I turned and went down the
stairs, stumbling slightly. I heard Wilby utter a jeering sound and saw
him sitting, cross-legged, yoga-fashion, in the center of the glass cocktail table.

"Have a drink, dad. Enjoy the fashion show. You paid for it, take
your kicks."

My back to the balcony, I said to Wilby, "Larceny."

He eyed me with bleak contempt. "Didn't even need to use them
charge plates we found in the limey's drawer. Not if the purchases are
delivered to the same address as the charge. An', man, y'got the right
address. No questions asked and no *larceny*."

I crossed to the bar.

"Build me an old-fashioned, dad!"

Again I was quivering all over. "Build it yourself." When I poured,
the decanter clattered against the glass. My hand was shaking, violently, like that of a man with palsy. It was a straight, stiff drink.

"Adam—" I could hear her steps on the stairs. "Honey—"

I took a long swallow and looked. She was parading down the
room, head lifted in cool disdain, one hand on her hip: a travesty at
once grotesque and funny, made more absurd by her childish serious-
ness. Wanting to laugh, I felt relief. She turned and came back.

"Well, Adam? Well, hon?"

"My name's Sam," I said and took another drink, relieved by the
impulse to laugh out loud.

She halted, staring. Then she threw a questioning glance toward
Wilby, who hooted.

"This cat's rockin' tonight, baby. Hard t'dig tonight, Jenny? Not to
me."

Frowning, Jenny returned to slump down on the step by the boxes.

"Arab countries, y'know what they do to thieves? Cut off their
goddam hands. Try to get away, they cut off a foot. Moral people,
them Ay-rabs." The lilting manner had returned. "Merchants don't
close up shop five times a day for prayers, they haul 'em off to some
crummy jail and thrash hell out of 'em. All for the greater glory of
Allah-Allah. Last summer they stoned a woman to death for adul-
tery. Wonder what they cut off a man, lover, same offense?" He
paused briefly. "Don't y'ever read *Time* for chrissake? How y'expect
to keep abreast with the horror of the world?"

I finished the drink. Jenny sat staring off. It was impossible to know whether she was even listening. She blew one smoke ring after another.

"Just wondered whether y'knew where your tax money's goin', dad, you'n the other suckers. Send a coupla billion, sheiks buy three new Cads and maybe eight'r ten new wives, rest goes to the American oil companies who get a special tax break, click, dad? Y'know what you get, man? You'n the poverty-struck Ay-rabs? The finger. What makes the world go whirl-whirl."

Again the distortions, the exaggerations; but again, though, the annoying irrefutable strain of truth underneath.

"Make him shut up," Jenny moaned. "Oh, please, Adam, make the bastard shut up!"

"Shut up," I said.

Wilby shrugged. "Who wants the truth, click?"

"Shut up, shut up, *shut up!*" She leaped up. "Adam, it's early. Take me out. Dancing. Take me now."

"I've already been dancing tonight," I said.

That stopped her, but not for long. "Dinner, then. I'm goin' nuts, cooped up with this nut all day!"

I glanced at Wilby. The personal hurt was in his eyes again, unmasked. Was that why he wore the dark glasses—not only to protect those pale weak eyes but to conceal those instantaneous flashes of inner pain? I finished my drink in a gulp. Pain, hell—the ruthless vicious bastard only experienced pain when he inflicted it on others, knew it then with pleasure! Still, there was no mistaking that expression, that flinching.

"Dinner, honey, please. One of those places I only read about. Twelve Caesars, the Colony, that Twenty-one Club."

"How about the Playboy Club, lover-boy? Y'got a key stashed away from the wife somewhere? They turned Jenny down, y'know: not enough class even for one of them bunny-bitches."

"That's a lie!" she screeched. "Lie, *lie!* They just hated me. I don't know why, they just hated me! Oh Adam, I know what's the matter. The dress is too short. Is that it?" She stopped, rummaged through the debris, straightened with still another dress in hand. "You'll love this one, Adam, I bought it just for you, it's a *lady's* dress, a real lady!" She stooped, took hold of the hem of the dress she wore, drew it up over her head. "I'll even put on a bra, honey."

I turned away, splashed more whisky into the glass. Wilby whistled lewdly. Damn the bitch! Well, not tonight, Jenny. Not tonight because I'm going to get drunk, blind-drunk, impotent drunk, and then the laugh, Jenny-baby, will be on you. I'm going to get so drunk I'll pass out before I get up those stairs. How does *that* grab *you*?

"Same old story," Wilby sighed. "Love again. Click? Same old kick everytime."

Every time? Then it *was* a scheme, only that. They'd been through it before. And, each time, Jenny imagined she fell in love with the victim, the poor slob, as Stanley Ephron had called me.

"Y'see the apartment, lover-boy? All for you. Worked her fingers to the nub-nub, dishwater hands, the whole bit. All for you and you didn't even notice!"

I had been right from the beginning: the whole thing was a transparent plot and there was to be no abortion tomorrow.

"Adam, honey, you're not looking!"

I looked. The dress she now wore was lovely: subdued in color and design and graceful in length—the sort of classical simplicity that Lydia favored.

"Glurk," Wilby said, "glug and cluck-square, whose funeral, Jenny-baby?"

"It looks," Jenny said, ignoring Wilby and raising her voice, "it looks just like the ones hanging upstairs. Well, Adam?"

I considered. Whatever their relationship, whatever there was between them—and I was damned if I'd try to plumb those depraved and possibly perverted depths!—the one tactic that I had not tried, although Wilby himself had suggested it, was the one that historians claimed had defeated Gaul. Or was it Rome?

"It's beautiful, Jenny," I said, hoping my voice sounded reasonably sincere. "And most becoming."

Her face burst with surprise and pleasure. "Then let's go, Adam. *Any*where!"

"He's puttin' y'on," Wilby said lazily—a warning.

"What do *you* know? He's a man! How would *you* know?" Then to me: "Wherever you say, Adam."

I had to force myself to say, "Not tonight, Jenny. I'm tired." Because I knew that, no matter what was to come tonight or tomorrow, I could not possibly—even to divide and conquer—take her out publicly. "I'm sorry." It sounded gentle, and by now I did not care in the slightest that it was a lie.

Wilby laughed then, stood up, stretched, yawned. "Look't the man,

baby." He laughed—a high cackling laugh, harsh with delight. "He's
beat! Too bad, Jenny, too bad. Lotta good this cat's gonna do you
tonight. After waitin' all day, too."

Another idea cut across my mind. "Perhaps tomorrow night," I
said. "I'll take you out tomorrow night."

She hesitated a moment, then asked, "Promise?"

"I promise," I said, and then I turned to Wilby and waited.

He waited, too: very still, face blank. Then he put on his glasses
again.

"Wilby—"

"Loud and clear, pop—"

"You were right earlier. I did go to the police."

"Knew it, man. Had my report. That secretary of yours—"

Phoebe? I didn't believe it. Inconceivable! But I had to know
something else now, know for certain.

"I made a deal with them—"

"Paid them off—"

"Wilby—" It was Jenny: a frightened whimper.

But Wilby made a sharp downward gesture with his open palm and
she subsided.

"The deal is this: if you're not out of here tomorrow by three
o'clock, both of you, they move in."

"Wilby," Jenny whined, "you promised!"

"*Shut*! Go on, lover. Keep talkin'."

"That's it. Three o'clock."

"Y'know we gotta appointment at three, dad. Doc-doc's. Y'got my
word, don't you?"

"I've got your word," I said, "but Jenny-baby just made a date
with me for tomorrow night."

He stood rocking on the balls of his feet.

"I'm not going to jail," Jenny warned.

"That's right. You ain't. 'Cause pop here, he's outsmartin' hisself
now."

"Why," I asked, fixing my eyes on Jenny, "why are you so scared,
Jenny—if you won't be here anyway?"

"I must've forgot."

"Like hell!" I crossed to her, passing Wilby. "Like hell, Jenny.
Well, let me tell you what they're going to do when they come in.
They're going to put the two of you in the back seat of a car—it's

going to happen so fast only the doorman will even see it—and
they're going to take you all the way across town to another precinct
altogether—"

"Keep tonguin' it, dad—"

"No reporters, no lawyers. And I won't be here."

"Adam, you couldn't let them—" She was on the verge of tears,
flinching back and away.

"And—" I turned to face Wilby—"and you'll get a lawyer, in time,
because that's the law—but not until the police are through with both
of you in the back room."

"Oh God, oh God, Wilby!"

"I already been that route. They done all that before. Y'know
what? I kinda enjoy it."

That stopped me. It was very likely the truth, too. That sick mind:
it was impossible to predict, even to imagine!

Wilby sniggered.

I turned away. Behind the bar I poured another drink, the last in
the decanter, heard the clinking, tried to stop shaking.

"Jenny won't enjoy it. Will you, Jenny?"

She uttered a smothered scream, but Wilby sprang to his feet.

"Y'leave Jenny—"

"Three o'clock tomorrow afternoon," I said, knowing it was hopeless.

Jenny was weeping now, hunched with her head down over her
drawn-up knees, hair streaming to the floor.

"Might still be here, pop. Might, might not. Give y'somethin' to
sweat about tomorrow."

The fury closed in—the choking wildness. I swallowed the whisky,
felt it burning down inside. Then I set down the glass and stooped—if
only I could stop this senseless shaking!—and found a full bottle on a
lower shelf. Bottle in hand, I went to the stairs. I could feel Wilby
watching me. My steps dragged. Jenny's crying was silent now but her
shoulders still trembled. I made it up the stairs in the silence.

On the balcony, though, I felt the fire inside turn cold. It frightened
me. I paused. Now, all of a sudden, I was freezing all over.

"Jenny," I said, and watched her head lift, "Jenny, I can get you
out of this."

"Pop, I warned you!"

"I can get you out of this if there's no abortion."

Wilby moved then. It didn't surprise me. Perhaps, as I saw him coming, I had even hoped it would happen.

"Leave Jenny alone, y'bastard! How many times I—"

He charged up the stairs.

I heard Jenny cry, "How can you—"

But Wilby was close now, coming to a halt below me. I shifted the bottle to my right hand, grasping it by the neck as if it were a club, then braced myself with one hand on the banister. Certain that I was using my last shred of strength, I said, "You keep coming, Wilby-baby, and I'm going to kick you right in the face." I could feel my leg-muscles already measuring the distance as if his head were a football. "Then I'm going to beat you to a pulp with this bottle. *Before* I call the police to pick up Jenny."

"Wilby!" Almost a scream. Then in a whisper of despair: "Wilby, *please!*"

In the intense quivering silence I realized that I was actually hoping he would take a single upward step. My mind seemed ready to explode with the wild savage hope.

He stood off balance, dark glasses glittering, arms dangling loosely, ready. It struck me then that he too might be hoping. *Y'know what? I kinda enjoyed it.*

In a soft voice he said, "Y'know that letter you was expectin' this morning? It come. Only I flushed it down the toilet. After Jenny and me read it."

All doubt was gone now: he was goading me.

"Old lady's improved, as they say, but the limey wife misses you."

I recognized the words: an echo of those that had triggered my abortive violence last night.

". . . oh man, how she misses you. Jenny told me what a cocks'un y'are."

With a ferocious wrenching of will, I said, "Not this time."

He then took a step. I straightened, every nerve and impulse straining toward action. But I had not come this far, gone through this much, only to let him win out now.

No.

Wilby grinned. "Told you, lover. Y'ain't got it in you."

Over his head I could see Jenny's face below: that same dark glimmer of sensual excitement, her own fears forgotten now as she stared up at us, lips thinned, nostrils dilating. Sick. Christ, as sick and twisted as Wilby!

"Now that," Wilby said, "*that* is what I call coolin' it." He shrugged, but I recognized disappointment in his tone. "Admire-admire. Nobody wins, we stomp each other, click?" He pivoted and went down, approaching Jenny on the floor below, his back to me.

Another thought occurred, flickering, desperate, tempting: what if I asked Jenny upstairs now—not that I was very likely capable in my present condition—and at least tried that method of driving a wedge between the two of them? At once, though—before the lure of the thought could take on substance—I rejected it and turned to the bedroom door. It would accomplish nothing, could accomplish nothing —and I was probably lying to myself. Then did I still desire her?

"I'm going to take a bath," Jenny said. "Y'want to watch, Adam?"

Although she spoke to me, she continued to look at Wilby. And I remembered his striking her this morning—for no reason other than the possible one that he might be in some way jealous. . . . *some AC in every DC an' vicey-versey, click?*

"Baby," he mocked now, "y'ever hear of the water shortage? Y'don't know about them lawns in the suburbs going toasty-toasty?"

"What's that to me?"

Wilby laughed, strolling away from her; suddenly he seemed very pleased with himself, almost jubilant. "That's right, baby. What I always taught you. Y'don't use it, some coochy dame down the hall'll give her poodle a shower, click? Like I always taught you."

"You," Jenny said—and her voice was neither bitter nor grateful, hardly audible—"you taught me everything."

"Everything!" Wilby cried and stared up at me. "Like *up* the human race, click, dad?"

"Since you're not really part of it," I said and opened the door to my bedroom.

Wilby whooped, began mixing an old-fashioned at the bar. "Click, lover-boy! We're out. O-u-t. We *opt* out!"

"Small loss," I said and started into the room.

"I'll be waiting!" Jenny called, and as I went into the bedroom, I heard her lift her voice. "How many times tonight, Sam?"

And Wilby whinnied like a horse.

I closed the door, hearing Wilby shout, "Up the human race!"

After locking the door noisily, I leaned against it, listening to the snap and hiss of their voices below.

"Yellow."

"Stuff it, baby, stuff it."

"Yellow pansy!"

"Jenny—" A plea. "Jenny-baby—"

"I wish he'd clobbered you!"

"It's all for you. Everything I'm doin'. All for you."

"Like you taught me everything."

"Well, didn't I?"

"Everything! Yellow cocksucker!"

"You stupid? You *dumb*? Where'd ya be without—"

"Get outta my face!"

"Somebody didn't take care of you, you wouldn't even take your pill!"

"I'm gonna take a bath."

"Y'need it."

"Awrrrrr."

Sitting on the side of the bed, I heard Jenny come upstairs, heard her in the next room, then heard water tumbling into the tub. I could picture her taking off her dress, stepping in. *Y'want to watch, Adam?*

I stood up. My head rocked. The room spun. Almost drunk. Almost, but not quite, not quite, but on the verge. Now I was Sam again. Kooks. Couple of kooks out of some jungle or other—

I went into my bathroom, took a clean glass from the towel cabinet. Then I opened the bottle. *He's beat. Too bad, Jenny, too bad. Lotta good this cat's gonna do you tonight!* How right you are, Wilby—or rather, how right you are going to be proved! *After waitin' all day, too.* Tough, Jenny. Things, as they say, are tough all over.

All of us must overcome temptation every day. But temptation can't exist unless we make a free conscious choice. Father. Words of ministerial wisdom. Wisdom! How did his wisdom sustain *him* when he needed it most? Reason I stopped going to church. Untrue. Then why had I? Because I no longer believed? Or had I ever really thought about it one way or the other? Think now, then. I'd stopped because the goddamned hypocrites had asked Father to resign his pulpit just when he needed their so-called Christian charity and understanding most! Strange thoughts now. Drunken, startling. All laced with hostility. Can't think about all that now: my mother's death, Father's grief—or was it only grief? And if not, what? What had made him do all those wild things, what had turned him into the creature he became? All past now, gone, gone. Haven't thought about all

that in years. No time now to stand trying to unravel the dead past,
let the dead past bury its dead.

I poured the glass half full, then added water. Sipped. Way of dull-
ing the senses. Escape. Like Jenny and sex. All it meant to her. Like
an animal in the field. Physical act. Yet—never satisfied, never fulfilled, no act ever enough.

I sat on the rim of the bathtub.

*If we're really no different from the animals, if we actually do not
have souls*— Had Father really said that? It was his voice in my mind
again, echoing over the years. Yes. He had. Winter's night, silence except for a freezing crackling, in the kitchen of the house in Fort
Perry, after Mother's death—but how had he, a man of God, come to
voice that unspeakable doubt?

Stay with the present. Now. *It's all for you. Everything I'm doin'.
All for you.* That plea in Wilby's voice. Almost as if it were not his
voice at all: naked need, hurt, puzzlement. What was Jenny to him
then? Unimportant now, though. What had Wilby *meant*? That there
was to be an abortion? Tomorrow, three o'clock.

What was to prevent their returning afterward? Or to prevent
Jenny's dying? An illegal operation, performed by some unethical
quack in some dusty hole in the wall.

No way out. *Pop, y'don't know when y're licked, d'you?*

Not licked yet. I stood up. The whisky hot in me. Sheer pain in
every fiber, tendon. Still, I couldn't stay up here alone drinking myself
into a stupor. Not until I'd explored every potentiality.

I was standing, swaying slightly. If I had his name, if he was
wanted for any crime, or if he actually had escaped from some mental
institution somewhere—

Then what? Well, it might be possible to have him arrested on the
street. Ephron would probably cooperate.

Name. ID card. Driver's license. Draft card. If he hasn't burned it.
Trick Jenny into telling me.

I heard the door buzzer sound downstairs. Or had I?

I went into the bedroom. Yes. It sounded again. I stood frozen
there then as an awesome sense of defeat closed over me. It had been
inevitable that sooner or later—

Like a sleepwalker, I moved to the balcony.

Who? Lydia? My heart lurched.

Wilby was lying on his back on the floor in the living room.

If it was Lydia, I'd kill him. If not now, tonight, then tomorrow, some day certainly. *Kill*—

The buzzer persisted.

"Looks like we got company, lover."

Why would Lydia ring? And she would have cabled, or at least would have telephoned from the airport. Coming down the stairs, I was breathing again, but shallowly. The water still gushed noisily beyond the guest-room door. If only Jenny didn't hear.

"Answer it dad. Maybe it's your Avon girl. Maybe your friends the fuzz got their signals crossed."

The very casualness, slowness with which he spoke, stood up: he was probably enjoying his own fear and tension as much as he was savoring mine. I knew him now, the bastard.

He slouched toward the library. "Whoever, let 'em in, click? No jabberin' out there'n the hallway."

I hesitated. Might it be wiser to ignore the buzzer altogether? No, damn it, I had to know, too.

I went to the foyer. Suppose it was Donald, who knew I was home? Or what if Ephron had sent a squad after all?

When I opened the door, the figure of a man was retreating toward the elevator and in that instant I was tempted to close it quickly—but he turned. Short, heavy-set, with a bulging but slack midsection, an ugly, meek face: I had never seen him before.

He removed a straw hat and shuffled toward me. "Mr. Wyatt?" His voice had gravel in it, but it was hesitant. A hand pulled at his small bow-tie. "Mr. Adam Wyatt?"

"Yes." Then, remembering: "Come in."

Brows lifted, he took a few tentative steps, then entered. ". . . talk to you, Mr. Wyatt. Terribly important—sorry—"

He was glancing around: yes, he could very easily be a plain-clothesman. His dark eyes drifted to the glass in my hand—which I had forgotten.

"My name's Corbin, Mr. Wyatt. Leonard Corbin." Then he waited.

Corbin? *Corbin?*

"Mrs. Corbin's husband," he prompted.

"I'm afraid I don't—"

"You're handling our case. That is, you're handling it for our insurance company."

"Normally, Mr. Corbin," I said slowly, stalling, hoping my mind would begin to function properly, "normally I don't practice law in my home." I crossed to place my glass on the bar.

"I know, I know. I ought to apologize. I do apologize, only I'm so upset, what with the hearing coming up tomorrow, them doctors, and someone in your office, a Mr. Gray, I think, said we shouldn't be there, not couldn't exactly but—"

I had it now. The Corbin case. Car insured by a mutual company in the Middle West, which our firm represented only occasionally. Slight accident, Mrs. Corbin driving, probably her negligence but no summons and no serious damage except a possible injury to a passenger in her car at the time, a Mrs. Sloane, who was suing.

"Sit down, Mr. Corbin." Would Wilby believe this or leap to his own conclusions? "Do you have some information I should have before the pretrial hearing tomorrow?"

"Information?" He sat very straight, hat on knee. "Well, no. But I had to get something straight for my own peace of mind. I don't mind admitting I'm not sleeping nights. Mrs. Sloane . . . Lucy . . . she's our friend, our next-door neighbor—that is, she was, our friend, I mean. My wife was doing her a favor because they have the one car and Harold . . . Mr. Sloane drives it to work. Now she claims this whiplash thing. And it just don't seem fair somehow. My wife was just doing her a favor, taxiing her, you might say, *free*."

Now I was convinced: he knew too much about the case, his bewilderment was too ingenuous—this was no plainclothesman.

"Mr. Corbin, everything you say might be and I'm sure is the truth. But the legalities are a bit different. Now, I have two reputable physicians, one of them a highly respected specialist, who have already given depositions, and they both believe that Mrs. Sloane's injury, if there is one at all, is not nearly so serious as she is claiming."

"That ain't it . . . isn't it, exactly. Mrs. Corbin tells me that you or Mr. Gray told her it's all right for Lucy . . . Mrs. Sloane to sue for a hundred thousand when we're only insured for ten thousand."

"I'm sure Mr. Gray didn't say it was all right in the sense of being ethical, but the plaintiff has the right, under law, to sue for as much as she thinks the damages amount to."

"But . . . but not that, either, so much. I understand that. Only —is it true that you or my wife or no one else can tell the jury or the judge how much liability insurance we carry?"

"I'm afraid that's another fact of law that—"

Upstairs, the water was turned off. *I'll be waiting! How many times tonight, Sam?*

Mr. Corbin, absorbed in his own bafflement, said, "But that's just not fair."

Conscious of Wilby listening, I said, "Mr. Corbin, certain precedents and rulings may not seem fair to you, involved in a particular case. But law's a complex arrangement—a ramshackle system if you like, makeshift if you want to look at it that way, certainly imperfect—" Echoes of Professor Kantor. Law school. I glanced toward the balcony: any minute, any second, she might call, come out, dressed or not— "There's no such thing as absolute justice, only ways of approaching it. The most justice for the most people the most often. Do you understand?" My voice was rushing. "All I can say is that we're going to try to win your case and I think we can. Does that answer your question?"

"We-ell, yes and no. What if Mrs. Corbin just happens to forget herself, you might say, and says right on the witness stand how much insurance we got?"

I had to get this over with. Now. "The judge would declare a mistrial and we'd be obliged to start all over again."

"I just don't seem *fair!*"

"Fair-fair?" Wilby's voice—not Jenny's, *Wilby's!* "But then what's fair-fair in this best of all possible worlds?" He was leaning indolently in the library doorway. "You see, Mr. Corbin—oh, what a *sweet* name, is your middle name Monoxide?" He giggled. "You see, sweetie, those laws're passed to protect the insurance companies. If those juries ever learned how much insurance somebody carries, they'd give the insurance companies the finger." He was strolling into the room, one hand delicately on hip, voice dripping honey. "So those darling big companies, they play the odds-odds. Hire lobbies, get the bills passed their way. 'Cause more people're insured for *more,* not less, click, Adam-baby? It's a game-game: checks and balances. Liberty, equality, and screw you, citizen!"

Mr. Corbin was staring. His eyes took in Wilby's clothes, beard, dark glasses, boots.

"Adam-baby, where're your manners? My name's Smith. Wilbur Smith, Mr. Monoxide. I'm kinda Mr. Wyatt's legal adviser." And as Mr. Corbin rose slowly, extending a hand, Wilby cocked his head to one side. "Adviser, only fresh out of napalm, isn't that a weeping shame?" Then, for no reason at all, he appeared to lose his balance, lurched against the astonished Mr. Corbin, who drew back, but not before Wilby had clutched at him with both hands as if to prevent his going down completely. "Oops, oops, and excuse *me*, double oops. You're such a sweet, *fat* little fellow, I guess I just wanted to *hug* you!" He threw himself to the sofa and crossed his legs. "Adam-baby, I'm just *dying* for another of your old-fashioneds." He turned his head to glance up at the balcony again. Hoping she'll come out. Enjoying himself to the hilt! "How about you, Mr. Monoxide? Adam makes just the most delicious old-fashioneds you ever put in that gorgeous *mouth* of yours."

"No . . . No, thank you," Mr. Corbin managed to say, turning to me and dusting off his jacket with both palms. "I didn't know I was—"

"Oh, dearie-dear, don't let me interrupt. Law just fascinates the bejesus out of me. It's such a sucker's game."

Mr. Corbin cleared his throat. "Uh . . . Mrs. Sloane says it's not her idea to sue for so much, but her attorneys told her if you don't sue for more than you expect to get, you don't get enough—"

"Enough for her attorneys," Wilby said, nodding agreeably. "Those precious fellows get half, don't they, Adam-baby?"

Mr. Corbin ignored him. To me he said, "You see, Mr. Wyatt, if we lose—I mean, if it comes to more than the ten I'm insured for, it'll wipe us out. I don't know what we'd do. Start all over again, my age?" He took a deep breath, his pot belly heaving. "Well, I guess that's not so bad. But we got four kids now. And my wife—she'd have to go back to work, like the old days." He was shaking his head forlornly as he turned and shambled toward the foyer. "I don't know. I just don't know. What'd become of them if we lost the house, the car—"

Suddenly then I understood. Completely. He was not thinking of himself. Only of his family. I forgot Wilby, Jenny upstairs. Forgot myself. I followed him to the door.

"I'm going to do my best to see there's *no* judgment whatever, Mr. Corbin. You have my promise. We have a strong case, believe me, very strong. We'll know better when we hear the plaintiff's doctors tomorrow, but meanwhile try not to—"

He whirled about. "Don't tell me not to worry! It's not *your* family, not *your* money, *you*'ll get your fee anyway!" Then, looking into my face, his eyes fluttered and he shook his head. "I didn't mean that. Only—my wife's not well. She's so nervous anyway, that's the reason she was careless driving, I guess. But she's a fine woman, she's worked hard, she takes care of her children and I—" He couldn't say it. He turned to the door. "She's so worked up about this, it's awful. I can't stand to look in her face." Then he seemed to remember his manners. "Good-by, Mr. Smith."

"Bye-bye." Wilby waggled his fingers in the air without rising. "And don't you fret-fret about justice. You'll get it in the *end*."

"Sorry . . . sorry I bust in like this, Mr. Wyatt—" Mr. Corbin extended a hand which was damp when I shook it.

"You have my promise," I said again, knowing it was a slender and possibly futile reassurance in the circumstances.

"Yes . . . well—"

I opened the door for him and he went out, frowning, probably more disturbed than when he had come in. Which was, of course, what Wilby intended. Another meaningless gratuitous cruelty— toward a stranger.

Closing the door, I turned. If I betrayed my anger, which was cold and deep now, it would only gratify Wilby further. I walked to the bar. "Old-fashioned, you said?"

"Smart copper," Wilby said, more his familiar self again. "Not wearin' a gun."

So that was why Wilby had fallen against him. I took down a glass, splashed bitters over two sugar cubes. "He had orders, I guess."

Wilby stood up slowly. "Still tryin' to bug me, dad?"

"Why should I? You're such a *sweet* little thing."

Wilby grunted a laugh. "Either he's a copper or he's on the level. If he's on the level, he got hit where it hurts, click? The old wallet-wallet." He strolled onto the terrace.

I muddled the cubes, then added ice and splashed whisky, wishing it was arsenic. Wilby could never understand the man's fundamental concern for his wife and family, for someone other than himself.

What now? I filled Wilby's glass to the brim, then poured one for myself, adding only a dash of soda. Now, somewhat sobered, I remembered my intention to get—what was Anne's word?—sozzled. That was it. I was going to get sozzled into impotence.

I took the two glasses to the terrace. There was always the chance, too, that if Wilby drank enough, I might learn something I could put to use. His name, for instance. Smith, *hell*!

Wilby was standing at the balustrade, his back to me.

"Well, did Mr. Monoxide get into a police car?" I asked.

Wilby ignored this, turned, reached for his glass.

"Maybe," I said, "Mr. Monoxide's the man who has *not* been following you all day. No white coat."

Wilby seemed to ignore this, too—but I saw his knuckles whiten around the glass. "Y'put poison in this, dad?"

"One way to find out," I sipped my highball.

He laughed again, not moving—was there a waver of uncertainty in his laughter?

"It's only rat-poison," I said. "Harmless to human beings. Do you think you're safe?"

"How about if I made you take a drink of this one first?"

"I never really cared for old-fashioneds."

"Y'think you're buggin' me, don't you?" He went around me, into the living room, stalked to the cocktail table, set down the full glass, then turned to the hi-fi cabinet. He opened the door to reveal the tape-recorder. He reached in and wrenched the reel off the spindle. "Y'just never stop, d'you?" He hurled the spool to the fireplace, then stooped, struck a match, tossed it. When the tape was flaming, he straightened. "Played it back, lover." Now his voice was purring. "I'm doin' you a favor. More stuff on there to get you in trouble than me."

I drank deeply. What had I hoped to do with it anyway? It could only have been useful afterward, perhaps to convince Lydia, or the police. Still, I felt a sinking inside.

Wilby crowed silently, grinning, and returned to the cocktail table. He picked up the glass, quaffed at least half of the drink, opened his mouth wide so that again I caught sight of the ugly teeth; then he belched loudly. "Pop, y'wouldn't know where to hide the body." He smacked his lips. "Only, man, y'used two sugar cubes. I take one." He laughed exultantly. "Tell y'what, man! I know where there's a Happening. Interested?"

"No, thanks. I've got my own Happening."

"Pop, you're a gasser and I love you! A Happening's like this: they get up there on the stage and they do what comes in their minds. Like this cat starts t'play this piano, only it comes to him to break it up with a ax instead, so he does! Then he does this action painting, uses his two palms and maybe his hair or his prick, it occurs to him. Seen a chick once did it with her naked body. After playin' the cello, then she jumps into this oil-drum full of jelly beans. Audience like to tore down the theater!"

"A logical thought, under the circumstances," I said.

While Wilby sipped, grinning, I recalled having read somewhere of a famous painter who had become fashionable and successful by sloshing paint with his bare feet onto a canvas spread out on the floor.

"What's matter, dad? Y'want it to *mean* something? I'll explain what it all means. Concentrate now. *Listen*! It means . . . it don't mean . . . 'cause it can't mean . . . 'cause nothin' does. Y'dig?"

"No," I said—but in a sense I had begun to comprehend. If this could happen, if I could act as I had acted through last night—

"Ahhhh, man, y're hopeless!" He started prowling again, the demons inside gnawing. "*Hopeless*! Y'just ain't with it, you'll never get with it!"

I crossed my legs. "Wilby, why the hell do you talk the way you do when you're capable of speaking perfectly good English?"

He stopped, rose on his toes, stretched his arms, every muscle rippling—obviously a boy who had spent months, perhaps years, developing a physical-culture physique and who now took egoistic, perhaps even erotic, pride in it. And if so, why—if everything was without meaning?

"That bug you, man? Way I talk?"

I was reminded of photographs I had seen of a gang of motorcyclists, toughs who called themselves Hell's Angels: dirty beards, Nazi insignia and helmets, leather jackets, cruel Neanderthal faces. Hadn't one of them been convicted of killing a child in Florida? Was that the idea then—anything to defy, shock? Even killing. Since life itself has no significance anyway—

"The way you talk doesn't bother me," I said mildly. "If anything, it amuses me."

Wilby stopped stretching. "Ahhh, y'square, lyin' bastard, how can I talk to *you*?" He plunged into the library, and in a moment I heard a newscaster's voice, confident and professionally detached: "U.S. casualties described as light—"

Glenn and I know two fellows who've been killed already. Surely there must be some good reason for it or the world just doesn't make sense. Anne's face, her dear face.

The whisky had had a numbing effect. Thank whatever gods may be—for my unconquerable soul? Father again. His favorite poem. How many times had he read it from the pulpit? *If I ever came to believe that we only lived and died like animals in the field, I wouldn't want to go on—* His gray ravaged face in the casket. His face not his face at all after I had flown all the way from England during the war: not Father as I knew him, had remembered him. The whisper in my ear as—how many years ago?—I stood looking down on what had once been my father: *We didn't know how to tell you till you got here, Adam. Reverend Wyatt didn't just die. He . . . he hanged himself. In the woods.*

Now my heart was hammering. I stood up. Why should I remember now? When all this time I'd been able to close out the thought, the question.

I poured another drink, hand trembling. No sound upstairs. Maybe she'd gone to sleep. Slim chance. I considered going into my own bedroom, locking the door. But then who could predict what Jenny might try? The absurd nightmare went on and on and all I could do was to try to insulate myself.

"We blasted be-jesus outta 'em today, pop!" Wilby was back. Wilby always came back. "Teach those little yellow monkeys who runs the world. Teach 'em white man's still got his goddam burden. Who the hell do they think they are, tryin' t'run their own country when Uncle Sammy knows what's best for 'em? Build me another one, man, let's tie one on, as some jerk said! Quarter million *advisers* now, dad. More tons of bombs in one month over there than all over Europe in *your* war! Fryin' them women and kids—so the barbarians won't take over! Old nostalgia get you by the balls once in a while these peace-lovin' days, man?"

"One cube," I said, shaking bitters.

"You're a polite host, dad." He was standing before me now. "Y'answer me a question? Y'ever hear the Constitution United States America? That little scrappa foolscap they got framed somewhere? Says only Congress can declare war."

"Never heard of it," I said and slid his glass across the narrow bar.

He grunted. "Convenient, man, convenient memory. 'Cause I may've missed papers that day but I don't recall no Congress declarin' war, d'you? How about that UN Charter Huntley and Brinkley bleat about? Or them agreements of the Southeast Asia Treaty-O? You're a lawyer, ain't you? What you think of people don't honor their contracts? Like the U. S. of A.?"

I went to sit down as before and he picked up his drink. I could have answered him of course, but I recalled how weak my reply to

Anne had been over the lunch table—something about stopping Communism, or honoring our commitments, repeating what I had heard repeated so often.

"Man—" He was leaning across the bar. "Law-man, logic-man, how'd y'like t'be logical?"

"It might be a distinct relief," I said.

He snorted. "Y'heard of them Geneva accords? One said old Vietnam's gonna have general elections, see who people want. Y'know who stopped them elections, man? Y'read the papers enough to know?"

It was true, of course, that the United States had prevented the elections—knowing that the Communists would probably win. "I only read the sport pages," I said.

"Y'know what we said when we stopped them elections? Said: we didn't sign the agreement."

"Which is true."

"Yeh, yeh, you're with me, man. Same agreement said North is North and South is South an' nobody crosses that seventeenth parallel. Click? Only when the North, kinda sore about no-elections, crosses the line, what happens? We start screamin' they broke the agreements we'd already broke and never signed in the first place!"

Slightly startled, I had to acknowledge that there were a certain number of contradictions involved—not that I was going to admit it to this bastard who fundamentally didn't give a damn anyway!

"Rule Americana!" he shouted, and took a long swig of his old-fashioned. "Pax Americana! With bombers. Escalation-escalation! We'll kill for peace anywhere, says Rusk-Rusk! My cousin's on our side cause Luci-bird got married in the Roman church, click?"

I took a long drink myself. He was getting tight. Or possibly he had swallowed something else while in the library. What? Marijuana? Something stronger? Where would this lead? You pays your nickel and you takes your chances. I was more than a little tight myself.

"Well, man, what's that make me? The James Bond of the Ho Chi Minh empire? Gatling gun in my tiepin, mushroom-bomb in my truss-truss?"

I thought a moment, then looked up at him. "It probably makes you a draft-dodger," I said—and waited, watching him closely.

He yelped. "I didn't burn it, dad. I shoved it up Hershey's ass-hole. Which ain't quite as big as Johnson's mouth."

He was moving again, with a restless vitality, as if simmering with anger. Had I struck pay dirt? A draft-dodger. But what good did the suspicion do when I still didn't have his name?

"Y'ever think, man—what's gonna happen the economy, they ever stop these wars? Been at 'em since about Thirty-nine now, click? Prosperity-prosperity, what's gonna happen your investments, they ever knock off war, dad?"

"I don't have any investments."

Wilby whistled and stopped dead. "No?"

"No."

"About hundred twenty thousand, man, way I figure it. And market going down, too. Neat little nest egg, pop. Merrill-Dow-Jones-Upham and Up You, Incorporated."

I gazed at him through what I knew now was an alcoholic haze, remembering my broker's statements in the desk drawer in the library. I felt a new fear settle through me.

"Only no Syntex, dad. Now that saddens me, 'cause I got word direct from the Vatican the Pope's gonna approve the pill and y'could make a killin' outta the population explosion. Hurray for copulation, down with population, buy Syntex!"

Then, from above and behind, I heard Jenny's voice. "What's going on down there?" Petulant, irritated, sharp. Then I heard her approaching down the stairs, although I did not turn but instead took another long swallow of the highball. She was beside me but I still had not seen her. I could feel her hand running through my hair and caught the scent she was wearing, heavy and cloying.

I felt nothing. Thank God. Not even revulsion. Nothing.

"I've been waiting, honey." A querulous note. "How can you sit down here talking with Wilby when—" Her hand moved to my neck. "Adam-honey—"

I stood up and walked unsteadily to the bar.

As if she had read my mind, Jenny said, in a strident squeal, "You don't want any *more!*" Then a plea: "It's late, honey. Almost midnight."

I picked up the decanter. Later the better. Drunker the better.

Another shrill sound, then: "Bogey's on TV. You bastard!"

She was gone. I had not even looked at her. Wilby stood up from the floor and came to the bar.

"Y'ever think, man"—softly, contemplatively—"human animal's

only one knows he's gonna die someday?" He set his glass on the bar, smiling faintly.

I poured whisky recklessly, both glasses, splashing it, and then I heard a new sound: gunshots and horses' hoofs from the television set. Let the bastard talk. Drinking jog, talking jag—maybe he'd say something. Maybe.

"Only animal, too, thinks there's somethin' comin' after. Yet . . . only animal ever wants his own death." He picked up his glass and drank. "Maybe if he didn't think there was something after, he wouldn't be able t'kill himself."

He set down the glass and wandered off. Aimlessly. Roving around the room.

"God," he said, "is dead." His tone was flat. "Bet y'don't know who said that! Bet y'think it was *Look* magazine, or some ignorant minister wants to make headlines. Nietzsche, man. Y'can't even spell his goddam name!" Then he stopped and, head tilted back, seemed to gaze at the ceiling as he quoted, " 'Man is the cruelest animal. At tragedies, at bullfights, at crucifixions hath he hitherto been happiest on earth; and when he invented hell, behold, that was his heaven on earth.' " He swiveled about, declared, "*Thus Spake Zarathustra!*" Then his lips twisted into a grin. "Only you was reading Ralph Waldo, click, pop?"

It was uncanny. Emerson's *Self-Reliance* had been my father's favorite essay, and he had read it from the pulpit at least once a year instead of a formal sermon.

Suddenly he strode, with renewed ferocity, to the library door and leaned in. "God is dead!" he cried. He whirled about. "God is dead and she sits in there watching Humphrey Bogart playing cowboy!"

The grotesque humor struck me—but also a strange sadness. I had begun to sense a pain, a longing, behind his crude, defiant wildness and incipient violence. A loss. But I was damned if I'd give in to the feeling. To hell with understanding. I couldn't afford the luxury!

Wilby smiled. "Y'think I got rats in the attic? Y'think maybe I slipped a cog?"

Did I? Earlier I had been convinced. "I think," I said quietly, "for one thing, you're crocked."

He shook his head and took off his glasses. " 'Cause I got news for you, dad. Big news." He spoke gently and he looked, in spite of the beard, like a child—a puzzled, pleading boy. "I can't be off my nut 'cause the whole world's off its. How can anybody be bats when everything's bats? Click?" He leaned closer. "Y'know why some gotta be locked up? 'Cause they *know*. They're onto it, see. So y'gotta get 'em outta circulation. Scared you'll start diggin' it yourselves—" All defiance gone, all challenge and mockery. He seemed—was my mind so blurred with whisky that I was imagining it?—to be begging. For what? Understanding? Help? "Y'gotta make sure y'don't start seein' what's real, 'cause if y'ever start really seein' it—"

He broke off. And I finished his sentence aloud. ". . . it hurts."

And saw startlement leap into his eyes, even as I wondered why I had spoken. Was I that drunk? Drunk enough to feel compassion for this cruel, dangerous—

"Y'tryin' t'confuse me, man? Y'tryin' t'say y'get it?"

Was there, after all, a way of reaching him? If he could feel this pain, wasn't there some spark of decency in him that might be fanned?

"What gives in here?" Jenny—in the library door. Wearing a short, loose shift. Barefoot. Hand on hip. Scowling. "So God's dead, so what?"

Wilby's face clouded as he turned slowly. "Pop'n me's talkin','" he warned in a dangerous whisper.

"Talking! I'm going out of my mind!"

"Going out of your what-what?" And I saw his back lift and fall. " 'So God's dead, so what?' " Abruptly his entire manner changed: he was striding again, with a new exultancy. "Who cares? Mouths of bitches!" Then, obviously quoting, he seemed to throw off his own character, to take on another: " 'We'll stay in this room, the three of us, forever and ever—' "

"I'd rather die right now," Jenny said flatly.

Then he was himself again: elated. "*No Exit*! I played it in college."

"Before they kicked you out," Jenny said, not moving.

"Nobody did nothin' like!" Wilby almost shouted. "I chose! Ask Jean-Paul. I *chose*!" Then swaggering toward me. "I was great, dad. I'm a great actor!"

"He stinks," said Jenny.

But I said, "I doubt that."

And Wilby grinned. Well, it was a beginning. But I had an idea that he had told the truth: so far as I could make out, he was always acting, playing out some role of his own creation.

"I got my Equity card, don't I?"

Equity? The actors' union: another mental note.

"Nothin's real," Wilby said jubilantly. "Everybody knows that. What the hell're y'doin' dad? What you're *supposed* to do, click? So you're acting!" And then the transition again: a different voice, a different stance, as if the lights had been turned on and he was on a stage. " 'So this is hell. You remember all we were told about the torture-chambers, the fire and brimstone, the burning marl. Old wives' tales. There's no need for red-hot pokers. Hell is . . . other people!' "

He stopped and let the words hang in the air.

I glanced over his shoulder at the portrait.

He frowned, then whipped about. Finally he said, "Heaven's other people, too?" He sounded baffled, and faced me with incredulity, or reluctance to believe, clear on his naked face. "That what you're thinkin', man?"

"Something like that," I said.

"I'm going to scream," Jenny warned, also staring at the painting. "Her? I'm going to scream if you two don't——"

"Pop and me's talkin'!" Wilby cried. He went to the bar. "I'll mix, pop!"

And the hope flared in me. Suddenly I didn't want the drink.

Jenny passed between us on her way to the stairs. Then, instead of mounting them, she sat on a lower step and stared sullenly away.

I went to sit down, the pain forgotten even as my legs threatened to collapse under me. Was there, after all, a chance, some slight chance?

"Y'go to church, dad?" It was the voice of a boy asking his father a question, casual but not Wilby's jeering voice at all.

"Not any more."

"Why?" Urgency undisguised now. "*Why?*"

And I remembered a line of poetry my father had underlined in red ink, a single line I'd read in one of the books that I had sorted after the funeral: *But who am I, that dare dispute with thee?*

"Well, dad?" Wilby stood before me, a glass in either hand. "Well? Y'ever dope out why y'don't?"

Had I, really? Was it only because of the way the church-going hypocrites had treated Father?

Wilby dropped to the floor, sat cross-legged, and began to speak in a musing soft singsong: "They say now the sun's only a star—came from a hydrogen cloud . . . that was contaminated with the remnants of some other star . . . that exploded four-five billion years ago . . . which means . . . if the life of a star's only ten billion years . . . sun's half dead now." He was not actually looking at me. His eyes, pale and blue, were on me, but unseeing—as if he were staring through me, as if I were space. "And the earth . . . only a tiny chunk of matter . . . floating in space . . . if we knew what space was . . . because we don't even know what time is . . . and nobody home up above . . . nobody looking down . . . only chaos that we have to call a pattern . . . because we have to think we're important . . . clinging to this little cinder as if it was important . . . as if one of us . . . a million of us . . . could be important . . . when it's empty out there . . . in time and space . . . empty—" He lifted his glass. "Drink to that, dad?"

He waited. No mistaking the wretched protest now, the forlorn longing. Surprise held me: imagine it, this ruthless, conniving—

"Bugs you, doesn't it?" I asked, using his language—which I hazily realized he had not been using—and realizing too that my voice was slurred.

"Try again, pop," he said softly.

"Bugs you so much maybe—"

"Yeh?"

"Maybe you give more of a damn than—"

"You trying to say I *care*?"

"Something . . . like that."

He uttered a sound: not quite a laugh. He took a drink. Then in that same soft rhythmical tone: "Saw a train wreck once . . . outside Columbus. Busload school kids. Helped pick up parts of the bodies. . . . Little girl's foot . . . white sock with blood on it . . . moved in my hand . . . *seemed* to move." He stopped, took another swallow. "If he's up there, man, he's a bastard. Click?"

Instead of replying—the picture was appalling as well as revealing—I also sipped at my drink, again hoping for oblivion. *I cannot believe that God is cruel. If I were ever to believe that—* When had my father said that? While Mother lay dying in pain—

Columbus—had Wilby said Columbus? Make another mental note. Keep your wits.

"If he's up there, he's a bastard, like me," Wilby said.

"You!" Jenny shrilled. "You're not a bastard and you know it!" She was standing on the stairs. "Not that way, anyway! You only say that because you *wish* you were, because you hate *him* so much you wish you were!"

Wilby stood up then, slowly, very slowly, as I struggled to clear my mind. What did she mean? That Wilby hated his father? How would *she* know that?

"Jenny," Wilby said with tense laziness, "nobody asked you in this. Pop'n me, we're talkin'. I ain't talked to nobody for years. Maybe ever."

"Talk, talk, *talk*." She ran up the stairs. "Go fuck an ostrich in Central Park!" She screeched, "Don't you wish you could!" The door slammed behind her.

"Well, dad?" Wilby asked.

I struggled to get things into some sort of focus, logical focus. "You can't have it both ways. You can't say he's not up there and at the same time say he's a bastard."

Wilby frowned. Then, abruptly, he drained his glass and threw it to the seat of the sofa, viciously. "Bitch's right!" It was as if some electrical current had been broken. "What good's *talk*?" Then he whipped about, rushed to the terrace, and disappeared.

I started to stand. Could not. Must. Have to. Can't let the current be broken, have to take advantage—

From the open door: " 'I live, I kill, I exercise the rapturous power of a destroyer, compared with which the power of a creator is merest child's play.' " His actor's voice—outside.

Must stand. Legs like molten wax. Staggering to terrace. Room spinning.

" 'And this, *this* is happiness, this and nothing else—' "

Wilby standing on the stone balustrade around terrace. Back to me. Speaking to space: lighted windows across, gray stone—

" '. . . this intolerable release, devastating scorn, blood, hatred all around me; the glorious isolation of a man who all his life long nurses and gloats over the ineffable joy of the unpunished murderer—' "

I stood staring, listening, myself giddy. He pivoted on the narrow rim of stone.

" '. . . the ruthless logic that crushes out human lives, that's crushing yours out so as to perfect at last the utter loneliness that is my heart's desire.' "

"For God's sake," I heard myself mutter.

" 'Caligula! You, too; you, too, are guilty. Then what of it—a little more, a little less? Yet who can condemn me in this world where there is no judge, where nobody is innocent?' "

I felt myself move toward him—lurch. Heard his mocking laugh.

"Grabs you by the balls up here," Wilby said in his own voice. "Vertigo, the doc-doc called it. Think I could hit the awning down there, splash-splash on the doorman?" He swiveled around again: delicate footwork, arms extended for balance. "Guts. It'd take guts t'do it when y'know there's nothin' comin'. Nothin'. Like, man, if I had religion, there's nothin' to it! Even hell's *somethin'*, even hell's better'n *nothing!*" Then he began to walk, arms outstretched, along the narrow stone rim, and a muted terror held me. "Y'want me to go splash-splash, dad? Your chance, man. Good-by, Wilby, good-by!" He turned, standing on one foot for a second or two, and started back toward me. "One shove, dad. Y're not too stoned for that, are you?"

And in that blinding savage instant I felt the impulse. Horrible. Sickening. *Get it over with!*

Wilby laughed. "How come, man? Life too precious? Like that cat Schweitzer says, y'got some kinda reverence for life? Like how many y'kill on the highways, like how many kill theirselves with cigarette-cancer, like how many with pollution, man, like how many with carbines, bang-bang, like how many with whisky, drugs, like how many corpses on TV every night? What difference, man? Precious, *hell!* *Lies!*" He stopped and faced me and dropped his arms. "Y'couldn't do it, man, 'less you was followin' orders'n they give you medals for it. Click?"

He waited. The impulse had withered in me. I felt only a drunken gratitude and wondered dimly whether I had not made a mistake. Civilized man? Fool?

Wilby laughed and swiveled again, contemptuously. "I oughtta piss on the whole goddam world!" He was shouting again. "That's what it is—whole world—yellow piss!"

Murkily I knew I had to act. Had to stop this. Had to.

Wilby pivoted again. "Well, dad? Last chance—"

It was then that I moved. Uncertain, plunging. I grabbed his ankles, shoulder against his shins, hard so that he would fall forward, and he tumbled over my shoulder. I twisted, released him, and he sprawled to the stone floor of the terrace. A wrought-iron chair clattered over.

From the floor: "Nebraska U. All-American. Dad, y'saved my life. Or did you hope I'd go the other way, s'you could tell yourself it was a heroic accident?"

Spent, unable to speak, I turned away.

"Sat out here today," he said, "watchin' 'em go by down there, thinkin'—" Slowly he stood. "Thinkin': how about that flowerpot there? One shove. Take aim. Kyoto or Tokyo or Hiroshima. *Choose.* One head down there. Like that mushroom they dropped month I was born. Hit one head, it's a crime, man, murder. Hit hundred-thousand—*that*'s civilization." He is speaking dreamily—or, drunk now, I hear him as if he were speaking dreamily. "Or maybe better, *not* take aim. Not *choose.* Hit or miss. Like God."

I heard the note of sadness again, and the bitterness penetrated the pall of intoxication.

"Y'shoulda done it, man."

Should I have given in to that atavistic impulse? Self-survival. Survival of the fittest. First law of the jungle.

"Y'standin' there pitying me, pop?"

"Yes." The word was indistinct. "In a way."

"Don't waste it. Y'need it yourself. I don't."

Furiously I faced him. He was close. "You need it," I said, and only hoped he could understand the words. "You've been *begging* for it!"

The dark glasses appeared, obscured his eyes. "I'll tell you why y'didn't do it, man!" His voice was strident—frenzied, furious. "Not pity! Not *me*! What the hell would the neighbors think? What would the police say? That's *why*!"

"Partly."

"What'd you say, pop?"

"Partly, I said. *Partly*."

"Y'tryin' to say you give a shit about me? Y'tryin' t'say that?"

Was I? Or that human life, even his, was precious?

"Liar!" he whispered. "*Liar!* Hypocritical lying bastard!"

"Look," I heard myself saying, the words blurring wearily and drunkenly together, "look, if it's as bad as . . . you say . . . why set out deliberately to make it worse?"

He stood swaying before me. His beard then twisted into that familiar derisive grin. "So that's what you been up to? Y'want Wilby t'fold his tent and steal quietly away?" He brushed past me, pushing me aside, muttering incoherent curses, into the living room.

I follow.

Jenny coming downstairs. Another dress. Brilliant: I cannot make out the colors. Ugly.

"Where hell think you're goin'?" Wilby demands.

"I'm tired of waiting."

"Nowhere, that's where."

She looks at me. "Any old prick in a storm. Isn't that what you always taught me, Wilby? Isn't it?"

Back to the jungle, sliding into the swamp again.

"Look at lover-boy here. Potted, stoned, smashed! Get lover-boy to take pity. Lover-boy's full of pity! Lover-boy has tricks, all sortsa tricks. Lover-boy listens, only he don't hear. He don't hear 'cause he's lookin' out for number one!" Wilby is drawing on a jacket. Plaid. With belt. With epaulets.

"Y'need your rest, baby," Wilby is saying—with concern, with love. Feigned? Mocking? Genuine? "Big day tomorrow, Jenny-baby."

True then? Abortion true? Three o'clock.

Wilby into the foyer. Sitting at table. Taking note paper from drawer.

"Adam?" Jenny asks. Uncertain. "Adam, you're not too bombed, are you? If you're not, I'll—"

Walls tilting in. Jenny's face blurring.

"Listen, pop. I'm writin' a letter. To you. From me. Y'too stoned to hear me? *Listen*! Dear Adam-baby: We have had such a . . . beautiful two weeks together since we met . . . that I can't bear to see it end. You have found a new way of life and I have found my one true love! Signed: Your ever-loving Wilby." He folds paper. "How's that grab you?" He places paper in inner pocket, jacket. "Don't just stand there blinking like a goddam owl. It's addressed to you—full name, this address." He stands. "Now, man—any fuzz down there arrests Wilby, y'got someone hired to do Wilby in, they find this on the body-body." Suddenly screaming: "Y'don't dig anything else, you dig this? Y'listenin' t'me, you stinkin' square lyin' bastard with your tricks?"

I listen. No shock. Not even surprise now. But I dig. If you can't get through one way, you'll get through another. What comes of my trying to understand. What comes of feeling compassion in a jungle. I dig.

Jenny giggles. "Wilby, what will you think of next?"

Wilby to terrace again. Singing. "Cruising tonight, cruising tonight, cruising on the old camp ground!" He looks down. Over balustrade. Anyone watching down there? Anyone to follow? He returns— satisfied? Ever satisfied, ever convinced? "Y'know what that means, dad? Cruising?" Spitting words. "The gay bars. Fags. *Fairies*!" Close now, beard almost touching my face. "How's that grab you, dad?"

"Wilby——" I hear my voice. "Wilby, let's get something straigh——"
Tongue thick.

"Straight, dad?"

"Straight—I'm not your father."

Wilby laughs. But he knows. He knows and I know. Revenge: hit
low and hit hard. Weakest point for any father, where it hurts most:
your son is a homosexual.

Wilby laughs again, goes to foyer. "Looka the man, Jenny. One
touch, he's done. Don't touch, Jenny." Then to me: "You're lucky
you *ain't* my father!"

Door slams. Walls shudder. My head splits.

Wilby gone. If I hadn't been drunk—drunk because I decided to be
drunk, because of Jenny—if I hadn't, though—if I'd been able to explain, to make him see how I felt—almost got through—almost—
irony—Wilby gone—too late now—irony—

Jenny shudders. "Christ! When he gets wild like that—*Christ!*
Scares *me!*" Drifting toward me: scarlet stripes, black hair, face indistinct. "But then . . . how'd you like to be queer, huh?" Closer
now. Too close. That sickening scent. "He wasn't always, though."

How she know? Or remember? Happen after married? Changed.
Heard of such. Usually older men, though—

"Adam . . . what do you do . . . evenings?" Now what? What
she asking? "With her, I mean? What can you *do* around here?"

Her? Lydia? *Lydia!* Nostalgia again. Worse: longing. Yearning, an
ache, anguish. What do we do? Nothing. And everything. Live. Give
ten years now for one evening, any single empty, glorious, happy evening! Christ . . . what do we *do?* We love. Not make love. Love.
And make love, too. Yes.

"Don't you get bored?"

Bored? Possibly. In the past. But never again.

"You did plenty of talking with Wilby." Petulant, thin-voiced. Stay
away. Too close. "Or is she too good to talk about? Too holy?" Stay
away. If you touch me, I'll— "You think she's so holy-pure, what
about them letters?" Shrill, loud: "Not the nicey-nice parts, the lies
—but *between* the lines, between the lies!"

What letters? What's the bitch saying?

"You think she's any different than anybody else?" Face close,
contorting, ugly. "*You!* She any different than *you?*"

Hate. Taste it now. Bitter. *Bitch!*

"What do you think she's doing over there? I know her kind."

Whirls to face portrait, eyes slits. Spitting: "Nicey-nice. 'Your skirt's too short, Jenny.'" Mimicking: "'Yes, mama.' 'Sweater's too tight, Jenny!' 'Yes, mama.' 'Behave like a lady, Jenny, not like a little tramp.' 'Yes, mama, like a lady, like you!'" Hissing now: "Like her, like *her*!" Facing me, screeching, wild jungle-bird: "I found her in bed with the plumber! When I was ten! When I was ten and didn't even know what a plumber's helper was!"

Too much. Reeling. Grotesque. Unreal. Too much, it has to stop. I walk to library. Stagger, almost go over, stand, walk again. Room blurs, rocks. Television still on. Commercial: woman taking a shower. Stops perspiration longer. *Is anything real, dad?* Women, sex—to sell . . . anything. I begin ransack room. Stumbling, lurching. His clothes. Women not people, only things, to be fondled, give men pleasure, sell cigarettes, sell Cadillacs, sell, sell. His pockets. Nothing. *But oh hell, Father, everything's against that today. Everything.* Anne. Anne, darling. I switch off television. Stand staring: all a blur. What if he's wanted? By Army. Police. Hospital. Actors Equity. Every pocket empty. No shave kit in sight. Now sure could see if—

"Smells like Wilby in here, don't it?" She in doorway. Watching? "Ugh-yugh-ugh. Same smell since he was a kid."

A kid? Had she known him then?

"You a burglar or something, honey?"

She changed again. Never know. Sounds amused. Can't see her. Glad. I search under leather cushions of couch. Damn kid doesn't even own a tooth-brush! Those black teeth—

"I know what you're doing, Adam." Husky voice now: I recognize. Too bad, Jenny, too bad. "You're trying to torture me, aren't you? Making me wait." She laughs. A woman's laugh now. "I like being tortured . . . this way, Sam. By you. Because I love you." Love? She's as crazy as her husband. "You saw how I cleaned up here. And I said I was taking a bath when you called and bugged Wilby on the phone. I'm on *your* side, honey. I knew it was you all the time." A girlish giggle. "Oh, Adam-honey, I've always wanted to be in love." Closer. Stay away! "You're bombed, aren't you? You want me to cook you up something? Like . . . you want coffee? Before or after? We got all night, honey. Anything you want." Nothing in the world, nothing. Hopeless. "Honey, you ever been to the Riviera? The French Riviera?" Yes—once, after the war, on our way to the States. Lydia on the white beach. "Adam, would you take me there?" Grip of revulsion. Trying to look at her. Tottering. She comes into focus: face, body, legs. No lust. Not the faintest glimmer of lust in me. Still, if there was some way to drive a wedge between the two. "It don't matter that you're potted, honey. I know what to do." Her voice, stance: her desire like a current in the small room. How could I drive a wedge if I didn't— "Come on, honey, come on, Adam, upstairs now. Or here. Here if you want. Like last night." *But temptation can't exist unless we make a free conscious choice*— Father again. Leave me alone, Father. Leave me alone now.

"Guhtahell."

I pass her, holding myself upright. Weaving against her. Softness of breast. Last night. Never again, Jenny. Once, no more. Ever.

"Adam—"

Legs collapsing across living room. How many hundred miles to the stairs?

"Adam, I know what you've been looking for. You want to know Wilby's name, don't you?"

That stops me. I brace myself against end of sofa. Cling to it. Wait.

"I'll tell you . . . after."

I see her now: body quivering under thin dress. One more drink maybe. Then, impossible—

"Now." To bar again.

"What you say, honey?"

"Tell me now."

"Oh, Adam, not another—"

"*Now!*"

I pour drink. Insurance.

"Is it a deal?"

A deal? Why not? "Deal."

"Birchard. Wilbur Birchard."

Birchard. And Columbus. And Actors Equity. Could be enough. I take drink, gag, drink again.

"And mine's Mrs. Birchard." Snickers, coming closer. "And now that we've been introduced—"

I force whisky down. Rancid. Almost retch.

But I move. Past her. To stairs. They float above me.

She laughs. "Your room tonight, Adam. *Her* bed."

Revulsion deepens. I am going to be sick. Stairs waver under my feet. Like walking on water, climbing.

"Adam-honey, let me help."

Clinging to banister. She is below: misty, a bright shadow moving in the cloudy room. I reach balcony. Like deck of ship, tilting. I go into bedroom. I close door. Lock it. Darkness.

I lean against it. Waiting. Knowing. And feel a cruel triumph, pride.

". . . promised! *Deal*! You lied!" She is coming up. "Open the door!" Outside it now, turning the knob, rattling it. "You bastard! You lying bastard!" Knocking on door, behind my head: wild, furious. Her outrage amusing, really. Downright hilarious. *They* left the apartment, went out on the terrace, played that damned music, answered the phone, broke every rule I laid down, and now— "You made a deal! I'll scream! I mean it, I'll *scream*!" The doorman downstairs, Donald in the apartment below, neighbors— "I'll scream! I'll —oh, you doublecrossing drunken—" Then silence. Only her breathing behind me, through the door. "Adam-honey—" Different voice: a child's, faint, almost whimpering: "Tomorrow, honey, I might not even be alive." There: spoken. The unspeakable possibility. Tomorrow. Three o'clock. "You ever think of that, honey?" Yes. *Yes*! "Unlock the door, please. I know you're bombed. I forgive you, only please—" One more night: what the hell difference? Only hang a man once. No. "Adam? Honey, can you hear me?"

I stumble to bed. Body caving at last. *I am the captain of my soul.* Fall across bed. Nothing to be proud of. Sick. Drunk. Dead drunk. Coward. But I chose. Didn't I make a free conscious choice, Father? Eyes closed. Darkness deepens. I ache for blankness. Oblivion. Have name anyway. Birchard. What started out to get. Have bastard's name—

"You don't have to move, honey . . . it's only me . . . foolish, foolish man, you can't sleep with your clothes on . . . no, don't move, not yet, honey, just sit up a little, there . . . oh Sam you're so hot, you got a fever . . . you didn't really think you could keep me out . . . not after last night . . . remember, Sam, *remember* . . . he taught me once, Wilby taught me, almost any lock . . . tuh-tuh-tuh . . . kitchen knife, easy . . . no, no, just lie back now . . . know you didn't mean it . . . booze talking . . . there, see, you're not too sloshed, you *see* . . . knew it, *knew* it . . . only fagged out . . . way Wilby treats you . . . no, don't pull away, not now . . . I waited, only you, waited . . . be soon, soon . . . oh, like *this* . . . now . . . *this* . . . you like *this* . . . kiss me, *too*, you bastard . . . *why* won't you *kiss* me . . . oh Sam, I *love* . . . you

can *hate* . . . I don't *care* . . . you *hate* . . . I *love* . . . you
hate . . . *I love* . . . you HATE . . . Awrrrrrr—

"You awake? Almost light outside. You're awake now, I know you
are, I can tell . . . way you breathe. Wilby came in while ago.
. . . Shh, don't talk. I'll whisper. . . . Glad you're awake, honey,
thought you never would . . . I hardly slept at all. . . . Why are
you so—Sam, you're not still bombed, you can't be, here, no, like
this, like this, what're you doing, what's the matter with you, it's been
hours, Sam, you're my Sam, you can, you can, wake up. I know
you're not sleeping—oh, honey, what's happened to you, you can't be
sloshed now . . . you can't just lay there, you want me to turn on
the light, there, now open your eyes, look at me, look, Sam, oh Christ
what are you pulling, it's a trick. . . . I said open your eyes, goddam
you. . . . you're trying to bug me, you hate me but don't hang me
up like this, oh you bastard, you're doing this on purpose, you're trying to—you can, Sam, you *can*, remember last night, oh, you bastard, you're doing this on purpose, maybe you're not, though, maybe
—you can't, can you, that's all, you just *can't*, you bastard old man
you, you sonofabitch, maybe you can't help it but I don't have to take
this, I don't have to stay here, oh you are a bastard, old man, not
even a man, not even a man, I'm not gonna stay here, *you're not even
a man!*"

❧ Tuesday

AFTER an instant's paralyzed confusion, I was awake. At once I longed for oblivion. But light struck, the present impinged, the past—last night, oh God!—struck a staggering blow, and I lay drained and consumed. Panic—no, terror!—gnawed at my heart, my bowels. When I tried to sit up, my whole being rejected the impulse. I lay motionless, flesh sagging, head heavy, muscles slack. Unconsciousness, a deep black well, lay tantalizingly just beyond reach. I closed my eyes. The light, filtering through the heavy curtains, was dim, I knew, but it probed my lids with a merciless brilliance.

Consciousness, all the thousand cruel prods of awareness, refused to retreat. I remembered. I remembered her purring voice, the touch of her hands, the hot softness of her body, my own body's weary, slow, reluctant response in the darkness, mind drunkenly blanked, will gone, the animal's ultimate, natural, uncontrollable arousal and climax. Irony that what I had plotted to avoid by drinking, I had been helpless to prevent *because* of drinking. Then—how much later had it been?—the different helplessness, sober, while she purred again, tried every knowing female wile, grew peevish, then irascible, while I lay limp and experienced a surprised and perverse satisfaction, revenge, listening to her surly pleas as she turned vindictive, hissing, then away from the bed, shrill. *Oh you are a bastard, old man, not even a man, not even a man—*

I sat up then. My head cracked. I could hear it: a distinct *crack* that threatened to split my skull down the middle. Last night's triumph was gone: could she be right, could the bitch be right? Swaying, I stood a few moments until the cloud around me steadied, settled. My bed. Mine and Lydia's. Jenny had her way even in that. I tottered to the bathroom, hoping for yesterday's nausea, feeling instead only the stomach's wretched emptiness and the mind's blank acceptance: you failed. Like some ancient black pall of anguish, guilt closed over me. Your one chance, your only real test of integrity, strength—and the animal reflexes took over.

I love, you hate, I love. Suddenly I was bent over the toilet bowl, not vomiting, retching drily over and over, until my ribs closed over my lungs like a vice. Love. Even her using the word was a violation. Profanity. My hate was so consuming, so abysmal, that I had to force my body to straighten.

I shaved automatically, trying to avoid that gray and haggard ghost in the mirror, my hand shaking so uncontrollably that I nicked my face in three places and had to use a styptic pencil to stanch the bleeding. Then I showered. The savage needles of coldness failed to penetrate, failed to shrive the mind of the guilt that burned like acid. I felt empty, yet filled with a forlorn and aching disgust.

I dressed then, selecting clothes at random, fumbling with buttons, trembling hands fighting the immense and cruel puzzle of shoelaces, whole body quivering.

With effort I made it to the balcony where my shoe caught an object on the floor and sent it sliding to the stairs, where it tumbled down and came to a spinning stop on the carpet below. The silver table knife she had used to slide open the lock.

As I passed the other bedroom door, I wondered whether she had carried out her threat: *I'm not gonna stay here.* Had she gone out to find some other faceless male mechanism to give her the release she could never find, and was she now sleeping the peaceful sleep of the uncaring and amoral behind the door?

Legs failing, I went down the stairs, crossed the littered room to the library. Wilby lay stretched out on the leather couch on his back: snoring loudly in a broken rhythm, mouth open, black teeth exposed in the gape of beard, no glasses. The air held an indefinable faint stench: urine, semen, what? His new jacket lay in a heap on the floor. Cautiously, I picked it up.

The letter was not in the inside pocket where he had thrust it last night. Nor was it in the other pockets. *You have found a new life and I have found my one true love.* The revulsion in me mingled with the smell of the room. What had he done with the letter?

I expected fury, but it was as though the frustration had plunged deeper in me, located itself at some subterranean and mysterious level too fathomless for any feeling so commonplace as anger. Everything he had suggested about the letter was, of course, accurate. Reading it, any average person—or policeman, or reporter, or newspaper-reader —would leap to the obvious and inescapable conclusion. Was there nothing that mind of his was not capable of?

"Warned you, didn't I, lover-boy?" His voice was blurred. With

sleep? With a hangover to equal my own? "Stay off my personal be-
longin's . . . 'cause they're personal. Click?" His eyes remained
closed. "In my hip pocket, man. Safe."

"Wilby—" My tongue was thick, my mouth parched and stiff.

"Y're comin' in loud and clear, dad. Too loud."

"When the operation's over this afternoon—"

"Abortion, lover. Y'still scared t'use the honest word?"

"When it's over, you phone my office—"

"Jenny, she's gonna be touched, man."

"The number's in the drawer of the telephone table."

"Y'got my word—"

"Use the name Smith, as you did last night."

"Get outta my face." He rolled onto his side, facing me, and
opened his eyes.

"If I'm not there, leave word with my secretary."

"Phoebe, y'mean? Good old Phoebe Waldron?"

How did he know her name? *Had my report*, he had said last night.
That secretary of yours—

"Dad, honest t'God, man, y'look kinda shot t'be goin' down there
to see justice is done today."

"Do you understand?"

"That Jenny, she takes it outta a man. Burns it out, click?"

"Do you understand?"

"Click, dad. Just the way y'*didn't* understand me last night."

I turned away. I had to assume that there was actually to be an
abortion and that they would leave. I had to hold onto that supposi-
tion, accurate or not, to get through the day.

"Scared she's gonna die, lover?"

In a second's irrational recklessness, I didn't give a damn. I even
hoped she'd die! But I hesitated in the living room. If that happened,
of course, sooner or later, whether Wilby directed the course of
events or not, the death would be traced back to me.

"Lover—"

I could hear the springs of the couch as he sat up. "One thing
more, now that y'woke me—"

"I'm late now," I said.

"Call 'em off." His voice was very low: dull and morose behind
me. "An' don't lie now, dad. It's too late. Nobody blames you, usin'
'em if y'could. But y'can't, click? So call 'em off. 'Cause we're splittin'
today, anyways."

I turned to look at him leaning in the library door. "Call off whom?"

"If y'don't call off the fat bastard, if he keeps trailin' me today—" His voice was rising and I savored the sound. I was like him now. "An' don't tell me I'm makin' it up! I ain't ready for no funny-house, dad. Y'just like t'think I am."

"You've given me plenty of reason to think so," I said, intensely aware of precisely what I was doing—and enjoying it.

"Lover-man, I got news for you. Big news, so concentrate—"

I turned the knob. He had not been able to conceal his sullen, bitter fear. If I could get away now, I could leave him wondering what I was doing, wondering whether he was only imagining the fat man.

"Y'don't listen, y'be sorry-sorry—"

I paused with the door half open.

"Big news. Jenny-baby, she ain't even eighteen yet."

My hand froze on the knob. I heard him snigger, heard it as if he had bellowed.

"Where I come from, they call that statutory rape. These parts, rape in the second degree, click, law-man? It don't matter whether the female consents or don't. Click?"

Click.

Poised in the door, clutching the knob, I said nothing. Again.

"So call 'em off."

Then, somehow, I found my voice. "How can I call off someone who doesn't exist except in your mind?"

I slammed the door behind me.

As I summoned the elevator, I remembered Stanley Ephron: how could I be so sure? What if he had seen through my lies and then put a man on the case?

But even if he had, Wilby couldn't know it. Whether the fat man was real or a figment of Wilby's somewhat disoriented mind, the trick in either case was to make Wilby think he was imaginary. I stepped onto the elevator. If his mind was in fact disoriented, it might then be possible to—

But did I have that right?

No. Not if, when I returned, they had gone.

As I emerged from the elevator, I wondered where—even now, even *now!*—the rage had gone. Where was the anger that had sustained me up to now? Had some sort of freakish but debilitating comprehension set in? Those strange moments of insight and compassion last night: were those glimmers of human understanding in reality a corruption of my own will? And had he planned it so? Even as he had talked—begging me to *listen,* to *understand!*—had some detached conniving part of his mind been aware that, if he could rouse comprehension, or pity, he could then—

"Good morning, Mr. Wyatt. Taxi, sir?"

"Please."

But Geoffrey—uniform sharply creased, ascot neatly folded, buttons polished—did not lift the whistle to his lips. Instead, he stood on the curb facing me. "Bit late this morning, aren't you, sir? How are your cousins enjoying New York?"

Cousins? I had to look up slightly to determine the expression on the long, lean, English face: deferential, carefully polite, even smiling.

"Lot of that type in London these days, I'm told," he said.

Geoffrey was in on it! No doubt now. While there was no hint of question or accusation in his gray eyes, he stood there refusing to summon a cab.

"She's a particularly attractive morsel, isn't she?"

He couldn't have been more obvious had he used an obscene word. Condescending bastard had made it perfectly clear. Either he was in on it from the start and would get his cut or he was building to a separate pay-off for himself.

An empty cab appeared, and I whistled.

"No need for that, sir," Geoffrey said, sounding almost comically injured as the taxi swerved to a stop in front of me. He opened the door. "Is Mrs. Wyatt coming home soon?"

In the cab I said, through the window, "None of your goddamned business." And I closed the door myself, with a bang, realizing that it was the second door I had closed in the same way within three or four minutes.

Then, ignoring Geoffrey's shocked and puzzled face, I gave the driver my office address and sat back.

"Them doormen," the driver said; "cockiest sonsabitches this town."

I was quivering all over. Had I only imagined that Geoffrey was building up to a shakedown, or that he had helped Wilby and Jenny in? My head was splitting.

". . . more dough on tips than I see in a month. Yah mind I ask yah something? How much yah tip that Cossack every month?"

"Shut up and drive."

I closed my eyes. Let him stare at me in the rear-view mirror. I was trying to recall when I had ever felt this way before. Once, seventeen or so, in Fort Perry: staggering into the house, my father's face a blur but his voice gentle as he put me to bed: *I'm certainly glad your mother's not alive to see this.* But he had been smiling when he said it. How could I have forgotten that smile when it was the only time he had ever smiled after Mother's death? Every swerve of the cab slammed the rock in my head from one side of my skull to the other. Then there was the hangover the day I'd passed the final law exam and been accepted into the Air Force on the same day: excited, frightened, celebrating also the simple fact that I did not have to return to Fort Perry. And to Father. *I know why you're doing this, son. I know I've failed you.* And I had not denied it. Something in me had not allowed me to speak the comforting words, to tell the lie. Then there was that hangover in London, after that long drinking-bout with Henry—whom I'd called Hank in those years before he married a Philadelphia girl who insisted the name wouldn't do. Three times before, and now. And, I told myself, never again. I vowed, regardless of what was to come today, not to have a single drink. The vow every alcoholic, or incipient alcoholic, makes to himself every morning after? Was it possible? Yes—because now, in spite of the wracking pain and the bloodless enervation, I knew, with a terrible certainty, that one drink, one before going into the office, only one would allow me to face the day.

But I did not tell the driver to stop. I still had that much control.

I still had that much control but I could feel a giddy impulse to laughter stealing through me. *It don't matter whether the female consents or don't. Click?* Jenny last night banging on the door. Imagine Jenny not consenting, imagine it, just try to imagine Jenny not consenting!

The cab came to a jolting stop. As I paid the sullen driver, overtipping as a kind of apology, I caught sight of a young man—brown hair over both ears, untrimmed goatee, dirty sneakers, no jacket, no tie—lounging against the wall of the building. I passed him, went in, waited for the elevator—and then he was beside me. About Wilby's age. Looking blandly uninterested. But why had he been waiting out there? In the elevator he kept his eyes fixed on the ceiling. He also stepped off on the nineteenth floor, and when I entered the office, I turned my head to see him wandering—rather too aimlessly—down the corridor, then disappearing around a corner. Was there a whole gang of them? Was it some big operation and had they, up to now, only been playing with me? *Three thousand, hell! They'll wring him dry. I'll lay bets. Take pleasure in wringing him dry.*

"Good morning!"

Phoebe. *Knew it, dad. Had my report. That secretary of yours—* "Good morning, Phoebe," I said and went into my own office.

She followed. "Coffee?"

I probably did look as though I needed it. "No, thank you. I want to make a call. A private call."

"Well, of course—"

"And Phoebe—"

"Yes?"

"I'd appreciate your not following me into my office every morning. I'm quite capable of hanging up my own jacket. And I'll buzz when I need you."

After the first surprise, her eyes turned to dark pinpoints of hurt, not quite resentment. "Yes, Mr. Wyatt."

I sat down, dialed 9, then the number. Phoebe had followed me into the office every morning for—how long?—at least three years. *Phoebe, you mean? Good old Phoebe Waldron.* Wilby's lies, more lies—all calculated to infect, weaken, pollute. But how had Wilby learned Phoebe's name?

"Ephron."

"Mr. Ephron, it's Adam Wyatt."

"Oh yes, Mr. Wyatt. How are you this morning?"

He knows! If he didn't know, why would he ask how *I* am?

"Fine. I'm fine, thank you. How're *you*?"

"Busy as hell, since you ask. Listen, Mr. Wyatt, I been thinking about that case of yours. Have you convinced your client to let the police take over? I'll do all I can for him personally."

"He's a . . . stubborn man." Yet, as I leaned back and swiveled my chair about to gaze out the window at the familiar façade across the street—windows, people moving, desks, typewriters—exhaustion took over: a weight so heavy that it seemed to crush from above the drag from below. How simple, how easy, how final it would be to shift that immense load into Ephron's capable, ruthless, yet gentle hands.

"Did your client see the morning papers?"

I straightened, the taut wires of muscle and tendon at once cramping and contracting as my heart constricted. "What?"

"Here, I'll read you the headlines. 'Sniper Kills Fifteen, Wounds Thirty-three.' Some kid in Texas. Certain kind of mind. Made me think of your boy. You never know when it's going to happen."

I glanced at my watch: 10:13. Only a few more hours. Even now it was possible that I would never see Wilby again. I couldn't go this far only to give in now and risk everything.

"I have some information for you," I said, mouth parched, tongue swollen.

"What kind of information?"

"A name—"

"I can hardly hear you, Mr. Wyatt. Whose name? Your client's?"

"No. The boy's."

I heard him sigh. "You refuse to take my advice, now you want help. Okay, Mr. Wyatt, although I don't see what good—"

"Then I'll tell you, goddammit! I'm not asking favors, Ephron. It's your job to protect the citizens of this borough and—"

Ephron's voice interrupted, crackling. "Don't tell me my job! I can't protect or help people who refuse to live by the rules. If I was doing my job, you'd be here in my office now, on an official summons, giving me your client's name and address, so I could make an arrest! Because you know and I know a crime is being committed—several crimes!—and my job's to see that perpetrators of crime are arrested, prosecuted, and if possible convicted! So don't tell me my job, I'm a busy man—" Then he broke off. In another tone—tired, accepting—he said, "Okay, what's the hood's name for what good it'll do?"

"Sorry, Stan," I said.

"So am I," he growled.

"And I realize it *is* a favor—"

"You should. What's the thinking behind this?"

"If he should be wanted for anything, some other crime, and if he could be arrested on the street away from my . . . my client's apartment, there'd be no need for my man to press charges. And who'd give a damn where the kid's been hiding? Who'd even listen to his story?"

Silence. Then Stanley Ephron laughed. "Okay, give me the name."

"Birchard. Wilbur Birchard."

"How do you spell it?"

"I don't know."

"That helps."

"We . . . we have reason to think he comes from Columbus."

"Ohio?"

"We . . . don't know."

"That helps, too. How many towns in this country do you think are named after its discoverer?"

"I . . . we also think he escaped . . . or at least was confined to a mental institution at one time. *After* some sort of trial."

"Oh, you're helping, you're helping, it should be *easy!*"

"Possibly he's wanted for dodging the draft."

"That's federal. Your office can handle that with Selective Service."

"He might or might not be a member of Actors Equity?"

Ephron laughed again—as I had intended he should. "That may be a crime but it's not one I can prosecute. Well, Adam, you damn well been working. Now tell me something's none of my business: why do you want to pursue this now? Didn't you tell me yesterday they're clearing out after the abortion this afternoon?"

"That—" My throat clogged. "That's what my client wants to believe."

"Only *you* don't?"

"All I'm trying to do is plug holes. In case."

Ephron laughed again. "I'm due in court. I'll call you back on this if we locate anything. And Adam—"

"Yes?" What now? He's known all along that I've been lying! He already has a detective watching Wilby. "What?"

"If I ever get in a bind and need a lawyer, you got yourself another client. So long."

Slowly I replaced the phone. What had he meant by that? That now I'd given myself away completely? What would he do? What would he do now? *Because you know and I know a crime's being committed, several crimes—*

Several crimes. *Jenny-baby, she ain't even eighteen.*

Now, of course, working with legal logic, he would have Wilby and Jenny followed this afternoon. Why? To prevent still another crime? Or to let it be committed, arrest them in the act, make a big arrest, newspapers, television interviews, a feather in his own political cap!

And that letter. Christ, how could I have forgotten the letter? If Wilby were arrested, for anything, *anything,* arrested and searched! Why the hell hadn't I let well enough alone? *Why,* at least until I knew whether or not they were leaving this afternoon?

It was then—as I looked at my watch again: only 10:21—that it came to me that if one of Ephron's men was in fact following Wilby, then Wilby was not nearly so far along that road to derangement as I had been assuming. Was that also part of his plot, then? To feign his psychological condition as he had done before—when he had, by his own admission, escaped prison by getting himself committed to a mental institution? Was he, with cunning and insight and personal satisfaction, leading me down a dead-end road, actually trying to make me conclude that there might be some way to push him over the brink so that, just when I thought I had succeeded, he could stand off and roar with laughter at my condition, mine, not his, *mine?*

As I sat there, my mind roaring in circles, I could feel—or at least I could imagine—the taut, twisted wires of nerves beginning to un-ravel. Like a rope giving way—a rope, perhaps, that holds a ship to dock in a hurricane until the wind rises too high, until it is impossible for that twisted hemp to secure anything, anything, against such a screeching howling violence. I knew that I could not let this happen, yet I was helpless to do more than sit and realize it was taking place.

I could phone the apartment. As I had done yesterday. Say noth-ing. Listen to that wrath turn into fear. Let *his* nerves tighten, disin-tegrate. Drive him along the road that now, damn it, I was not even sure he was traveling!

Instead of reaching for the telephone, I picked up a yellow pad from the desk. How could I know? What if I failed to take advantage of every smallest opportunity? Or what if I took action with a view to one potential only to discover that I had read its consequences incor-rectly? Afterward then—if there was to be an afterward at all—I would find myself staring back into an abyss of my own making. I looked now at the scribbled notes on the ruled legal pad and forced my mind to try to reconstruct the broad outlines of the Markham case so that I could dictate the first draft of the brief. The ache in my head had concentrated itself into a persistent, pitiless throb and the rock had fixed itself dead-center. The scribble blurred before me. Some-thing about a stockholders' suit, Long Island factory, nepotism, mis-appropriation of company funds.

No good, no good: I couldn't even read my own writing. Nevertheless, it had to be done. I turned on the dictating-machine. But its whirring caused a roar in my head—unendurable, *deafening*!

I switched it off. But the roaring persisted.

To hell with the Markham case. Usually . . . what did I usually do first thing in the morning? The mail. Of course. Phoebe had opened most of it, and it was stacked in two neat piles. On top of one was a small gray envelope, unopened, with air-mail markings on its edges and the word PERSONAL printed boldly across it.

My blood stopped, the roar went hollow. Lydia never addressed her letters to the office.

I ripped open the envelope, remembering the futile lie of yesterday: that I had received a letter at the office saying that Lydia was coming home. What a cruel trick if that lie turned out to be the truth! The paper shook crisply in my hand, shook so much that I had to unfold the two thin pages and spread them out flat on the desk top in order to make out the words.

I scanned the first page, my eyes darting down Lydia's precise, slanted handwriting: . . . *in terms of health, much improved . . . doubt, sadly, she'll ever change otherwise . . . poor old girl, honestly think she'd like to hold me here forever . . . not that she's particularly fond of my company, either . . . did try theatre a few times . . . I know absurd no longer means ridiculous in the theatre . . . all such silly worthless creatures in the modern view . . . a certain boredom—*

Nothing important. Thank God. Nothing vital. If she were coming, she would have begun with the news.

I love you, Lydia. Forgive me. Can you ever forgive me?

No. Never.

I took a deep breath and went on reading, more slowly now, faintly relieved: *The weather's been sticky but there's a natural nostalgia in me for London, of course, and I've spent exciting hours in the Tate and the National and whipped up to Stratford for one night—*

With whom? The thought struck, probed; the knife turned in me. With whom, Lydia? Why don't you say?

What do you think she's doing over there in London? You think she's any different than anybody else? You think she's any different than you?

Remorse broke like a wave over me. For a second the room dimmed in my sight. How could I doubt Lydia? I was hollow all through. Christ, had they brought me to this? To doubt, to suspect Lydia? Revulsion choked me—revulsion at myself.

Angry—at them, at myself—I picked up the second sheet. My eyes cleared. I read: *I know you'll be surprised to receive this at the office. The truth is that I suspect that Minnie, dear old thing that she otherwise is, reads our mail, and I know how careless you are with letters—*

I stiffened. Why should it matter whether Minnie—

I don't know quite how to say this, darling. You may or may not have guessed that when I left I did so with misgivings—

Someone has phoned her. Panic crashed through me, took my breath. Minnie? *Mrs. would want to know. I got her address in England.*

Madness! The letter had to be posted last week. I talked with Minnie yesterday morning. Madness even to imagine it. I was breathing again.

. . . and yet with a certain—now please don't get your wind up, try to understand—with a curious hope, too. Hope that perhaps I would be able to arrive at a certain—I suppose perspective's the word—about myself, about you, about us.

Perspective? Lydia, what are you talking about? Perspective about us? Panic turned to a cold gripping dread.

And I do honestly think I have. Or that I'm on my way. One reaches a time of life, I think, when the graceful and civilized thing to do is to demand—of everyone and everything—including oneself, as well as those you love—and to settle for—whatever one has.

Lydia, this isn't you. What are you saying? What the hell are you *saying*?

I love you, darling, and I miss you, and I know that you love me and that you miss me. I'm awfully afraid that's the only perspective open to us—and we'd jolly well better make friends with it. In truth, Adam, I've begun to feel a trifle old this past month, for the first time. No, this past year. But I suppose one makes friends with that, too.

Not old, Lydia, not you, ever—

Good night, Adam—and if you cannot understand, forgive. Love.

Understand? No. Stunned, I sat staring at the paper. While a fierce protest rose inside, volcanic, overwhelming. And memories flooded my mind: Lydia almost drunkenly gay, and without having had a single drink: *Of course I'm ready to go upstairs. Procrastination is next to uncleanliness, isn't it?* Or intense, whispering: *I love you, Adam,*

*you know that, don't you, do you love me, Adam, do you know me
and love me?*

I struck the top of the desk with my fist and felt the pain in flesh, in
bone, felt it travel up my arm even before I heard the sound reverberating through the office. Yes, *love*, you can't doubt that, Lydia. You
don't need any perspective to know that! Surely, Lydia, surely you
must know I love you! You can't doubt—

1 heard a sound in the room. A muted strangled moan. And realized it had come from me.

I sank to the chair and lowered my head. Over the letter. Closing
my eyes.

*Glenn says that if married people are separated any more than ab-
solutely necessary, it means . . . it usually means something's gone
wrong somewhere—*

"Believe it or not, it's eleven."

I lifted my head. Lee Gray had come in. Without knocking. He
was letting himself down into a chair, puffing at his pipe.

It was a second or two before I spoke. "Didn't anyone ever teach
you to knock before barging into a private office?"

He hesitated, bracing himself with his arms, then slid down onto
his spine and threw one leg over the arm of the chair, blinking behind
his thick horn-rimmed glasses. "Sorry. Didn't know the ground-rules
had changed. We did have an appointment at eleven. To discuss the
Corbin pretrial. Ask Phoebe."

I sank down in the chair very slowly, to keep my expanding skull
from exploding. I didn't have to ask Phoebe. What was happening to
my memory?

"I must have forgotten," I said.

He waved a long slender hand and opened one of the folders he carried. "Someone did teach me manners once, though. Not my parents,
however. I grew up in an orphanage."

"Sorry, Lee."

Strange that I hadn't known that. Strange that Lee Gray had been
an associate in the firm for almost five years and I knew so little
about him. I had always appreciated his ability, aware in a disinter-
ested way of a strain of youthful ruthlessness in his direct and intelligent approach to legal matters, but I had never been fond of him. In
his early thirties, tall and thin, he had a precise way of speaking—as
if he had taken elocution lessons too seriously or had been over-
trained in some college speech department—that clashed with his

rather exaggerated casualness of manner. He always had a black pipe between his teeth or in hand, and in a few seconds the office filled with blue smoke and a fragrance more of spices than tobacco, sickeningly sweet.

Leaning back, I felt a momentary relief. My mind, if I could control it at all, was forced to concentrate on something that would keep my eyes from the hands on my watch.

"Before we get into the Corbin matter, I thought you might be interested in what I've turned up on the Colin Welch case."

Colin Welch? Yes, the perplexed, frightened little man involved in the hit-and-run incident. "Don't keep me in suspense, Lee." My voice, at any rate, sounded almost natural in my ears.

"This fellow Higgins, the plaintiff, who claims our Mr. Welch should have seen him stepping from the curb and should have had his car under control—well, this fellow Higgins was in no condition to see a car turning the corner because this fellow Higgins had been drinking."

What a crime. Drinking. Imagine. "It was what we were hoping for, wasn't it? How many?"

"I think I even have a witness who will—"

"How many drinks?"

Lee Gray shifted in his chair. "Let's say that point remains open. Let's just say this witness I've located was in the same gin-mill with the plaintiff half an hour before the accident and that, beyond that, he's . . . well, open to influence." He smiled—something, I realized, which Lee Gray rarely did.

"What sort of influence?"

"Oh, I'm not suggesting anything illegal, even unethical. Only a little verbal suggestion. To the best of his recollection *now*, he saw Higgins drink two beers. The bartender refuses to get involved. But I think our witness's memory can be jogged by a little conversation. He's not exactly a stable type, our witness."

"In fact," I said, "he had been hoisting a few himself that night. Click?"

"Click?" he echoed, puzzled.

"Hadn't he?" I barked.

"It's a safe bet. But as I said, the bartender won't get involved, so who's to say how many?"

"In other words you're not suggesting anything unethical or illegal; you're simply suggesting subornation of perjury."

"Perjury? Have you been listening, Adam? If I can help this man to remember more clearly what he saw the plaintiff drinking, and how many, we have a chance to win this case. What's unethical about that?"

Justice, man. You twist the truth for your side, I twist the truth for mine—equals Justice.

"Do you have a cigarette?" I asked.

"No, sorry. If you have a pipe, I do have tobacco."

Tobacco? The smoke was cloying—almost overpowering. I shook my head, wishing the tightness in my chest would loosen.

"What about our own client?" I asked. "Had he been drinking?"

"What'd he tell *you*?"

"Look, don't get cagey with me. We're supposed to be on the same team! Welch told me he hadn't had a single drink before the accident, then he went home and drank all night."

"Well, he's sort of changed his mind. He'd had three vodkas at a friend's apartment before the incident and unfortunately the friend's been contacted by the attorneys for Higgins."

"So you *advised* Welch to change his mind."

"Naturally. I couldn't let our own client get tripped up on the stand."

"Naturally."

"Anyway, since both of them had had a few, it does muddy up the waters."

"Muddies up the waters in the name of justice."

Lee Gray was frowning. He even removed his glasses and polished them. "I fail to see what you're getting at, Adam. But I do know how important winning this case is to the firm. There's a possible judgment of three hundred thousand dollars at stake. Not out of Mr. Welch's pocket, of course, but from the insurance company, which, after all, is the client we represent. Henry and I would both like to keep that account."

Lee Gray was not only being directly and purposefully impertinent, he was talking as if he were a partner. A suspicion flared in my mind: did he expect to be made a partner?

"Thank you," I said, "for explaining the facts of my business to me."

He replaced his glasses. "Adam, it appears to me, if you don't mind a fellow my age saying so, that you've been working too hard. My wife and little one are up on the Cape. Why don't you and I go out on the town one of these nights?" Then he smiled a second time. "Maybe even find us a little amiable female companionship."

He knew. I was certain of it at once. How the hell could *he* know?

I looked at my watch: 11:07. Seven minutes? It had seemed at least half an hour! At *least*!

"What about the hearing?"

"No need to snap my head off." He went through some papers with his fingers; they crackled in the silence. Finally he said, "It was only an idea, after all. I wasn't suggesting we go out and rape some poor innocent child."

"Let's get to the Corbin case." I did not mention Mr. Corbin's visit last night. I had begun to sweat again. I could feel the beads of it on my forehead, the wetness in my armpits.

"All we can hope for this afternoon is to learn how strong this Mrs. Steele's . . . no, here it is . . . Mrs. *Sloane's,* the injured woman . . . all we can hope is to learn how strong her physician's testimony will be . . . with a view, I should imagine, toward advising our client to try to settle out of court for some reasonable sum if that testimony appears to be too convincing. To a jury, of course."

I'm going to do my best to see there's no judgment whatever, Mr. Corbin. You have my promise.

"The Corbins," I said, "are insured only to the extent of ten thousand dollars. They'd have a right to refuse to make a settlement in any amount that exceeds that figure."

"The Corbins," Lee Gray said, "are not our clients."

"I know that, damn it, stop telling me what I know!"

"If we could get a settlement in the neighborhood of even twenty-five thousand, the Corbins would lose only fifteen thousand."

"*Only*? Fifteen thousand dollars would wipe the Corbin family out!"

"Of course we'd try for something under the ten, to save the company—"

"I'm telling you we can win this case. I don't give a damn what some physician testifies to in a pretrial hearing *or* in the courtroom! We've had the plaintiff examined by reputable doctors!"

"Reputable?" Lee Gray was emptying his pipe into a tray. "Henry warned me you have a tendency to be a little rough on doctors."

"I've learned—and you should as well—that so-called expert medical testimony tends to be inconclusive. Especially in an area as nebulous as whiplash injuries. In the end, it often comes down to the veracity of the patient, or plaintiff, and I'm inclined to mistrust a woman who sues a neighbor after the neighbor does her a favor, and sues for an amount that she knows damn well is not covered by insurance."

"Really? It's done all the time."

"So's murder."

Lee Gray sucked at his pipe. "Can't blame a person for trying, can you? That's the game. The plaintiff's only grabbing her opportunity while the grabbing's good."

"She's not going to get away with it."

Lee Gray went back to work on his pipe: knocking, scraping, blowing. And my head expanded, threatened to burst open.

"Well," he said, as if to pacify me, "well, all I know is that we'd better get out of it as cheaply as we can—for the company. That's our job."

Justice! Flaming sword. Balls!

I stood up. "I've a job for *you*. Take this name. Birchard. Wilbur Birchard. He's in his early twenties, possibly older. I want to know whether he's wanted by the police, FBI, anyone, for anything, anywhere. If so, what? Also whether he escaped from any place— especially hospitals for the insane, probably a state hospital somewhere. The New York metropolitan area is covered, so forget that." I stood resting on my fists on the desk top, astonished at the crisp, even tone of my voice and the precision with which my mind at last seemed to be working again. "Start with the states that have a Columbus in them, any state, but northern ones first. Then the rest of the country."

Lee Gray clutched his empty pipe between his teeth and stared up at me across the desk. "The rest of the country?"

It flashed through my mind that he might also determine whether what was termed second-degree rape in New York was called statutory rape in Columbus, Ohio. And if not, in what city named Columbus *was* it called that? But I dismissed the thought: no use rousing his suspicions, too.

"Check Selective Service first. The *whole* country."

He whistled between his teeth, pipe in hand. Then he rose to his feet. "Are you saying we've exhausted our discussion of the Corbin hearing this afternoon?"

"I'm saying this is what I want done. You have more than three hours before the hearing."

"Well . . . well, I guess that puts Lee Gray in his place. I also take it you don't intend to fill me in on the new case."

"That's as good a way to take it as the next."

He didn't move. "Sounds more like a criminal investigation than anything this firm would—"

"We've wasted enough time."

He studied me through his glasses. I met his gaze. *Cool, man, cool.* Then he almost, but not quite, shrugged, gathered up his papers, shoved them under his arm, and started out.

"One more thing—" And when he paused at the door: "See whether Wilbur Birchard is or ever has been a member of Actors Equity. Start there because it might give you a lead as to where he comes from."

"You're the boss," Lee Gray said with crisp resentment and went out.

Three hours. Then what? I went to the windows, stared blindly. The hearing. The operation. Abortion. *It don't matter whether the female consents or don't.* Not one, two crimes. Who was I to judge anyone else?

Lee Gray, for instance. In his own way wasn't Lee Gray, for all his narrow lapels, his gray neatness and conventional good manners, as amoral, as fundamentally detached and uncaring and selfish, as Jenny? In his own way, as ruthless as Wilby? More to it than that, even. Bearded, dirty, sadistic, even mentally twisted by ordinary standards, Wilby was even now more inextricably involved in the rest of the world, in the world itself, than Lee Gray would ever be. Even Wilby's protests, his defiance and anger and passionate desire to opt out, as he had said—even those revealed more of a sense of justice, of what it might or should be, than Lee Gray, having gone through law school, could ever comprehend.

A knock.

I did not move. I couldn't see anyone now, talk with anyone.

The knock repeated. What next? *Open the door! You bastard. You lying bastard! I'll scream!*

"It's I, Mr. Wyatt. Phoebe."

Not Jenny. Phoebe—who had presumably never learned to pry open a lock with a table knife.

"Come in."

Door opening behind me, closing.

"Mr. Wyatt—I didn't use the intercom because—" Yes, Phoebe—*because?*

"Is there anything I can do?"

"Such as?"

"I don't know. *Anything.* Aspirin?"

"Yes, please." Why hadn't I thought of the obvious?

Movement behind me now: swish of skirt, muted click of heels on carpet. "Mr. Wyatt, everyone ties one on once in a while, as they used to say in Portland." Clink of glass and then the gurgle of water being poured from the cork-covered decanter. Phoebe's voice softly, falsely teasing: "Why don't you take the rest of the day off? See a ballgame. After all, everyone else in the office does occasionally and you never—"

I turned. Mature eyes, woman's eyes, clouded with concern. Smile carefully casual, fixed. I said nothing.

"It seems to be our way, doesn't it? I was reading an article in the *Times* on Sunday. Tranquillizers and alcohol seem to be the American way."

I took the aspirins. Two. Her hand was cool, almost cold to the touch. Then the glass.

"It's always been like that, though. Even the Indians, and natives all over the world—everybody finds a way to get through, I suppose. Hashish and opium and all sorts of plants and roots and seeds. Even cactus." A shrug. "Why shouldn't we have our ways?"

The cold water failed to reach the heat inside. The aspirins stuck in my throat, turned bitter, dissolved.

Phoebe smiled. It was an empty smile. And oddly forlorn. I realized that I knew nothing about her really. *Phoebe, y'mean? Good old Phoebe Waldron.* How could Wilby possibly know her name?

"I'm a walking drugstore, Mr. Wyatt. I have tranquillizers in my purse. Or sleeping pills. I overheard you say once that you had never taken a sleeping pill in your life, but there are times—" Her voice drifted away.

"No, thanks, Phoebe." I handed her the glass. "Do you happen to have a cigarette, though? I seem to be out."

"I meant to tell you. There's a carton in the top drawer of your desk."

Phoebe wouldn't have anything to do with people like Wilby and Jenny. What could she possibly gain?

"Are you sure there's nothing I can do, Mr. Wyatt?"

I shook my head. Nothing except explain to me how Wilby could know your damned name!

"Mr. Brant said he's walking and he'll meet you there."

I must have frowned. My sluggish mind again refused to function. "Walking? Meet me where?"

"Lunch, Adam. It's on your appointment pad."

Adam. Phoebe had never called me Adam before. Was she even aware of it now?

"It's almost twelve, Mr. Wyatt."

I nodded.

What's going on? What's happening?

"How I envy you well-balanced idiots without ulcers. Although," Henry was saying as his eyes roamed the dark-paneled men's grille, "although I have heard it said that an ulcer's proof positive of superior sensitivity."

Was he consciously avoiding my eyes as I sat down. Why?

"I ordered one for each of us. Strictly against Arnold's orders, but what isn't?"

I stared at the pale liquid, the crystal floating ice.

"Well, it *is* what you drink, isn't it? As if I didn't know. One before lunch every day. And, to look at you, God knows how many after dinner."

"I think I'm catching a summer cold," I said dully, staring still, because I had to say something. Did I want to drink it? Yes. Did I dare drink it?

I lifted my eyes from the glass: no, couldn't get started this early. None today. Already decided.

Henry sipped his Scotch and water. "When did you go back on the cancer-sticks?"

I was looking at him: what was he trying to find out? Shaggy brows, bald head, craggy features. When had he become bald? Had his hair gone so slowly that, at each stage, the change was unremarkable? Like the stages of our relationship, indistinct but definite and hardly recognized over the years?

". . . on a contingency basis, like an attorney, only strictly *sub rosa*—"

"I beg your pardon—"

"I was only wondering what sort of arrangement physicians like that do make in a case like this. Beyond the normal fee we legally pay for their time, of course. Have you ever been approached?"

"I've never asked a doctor to stretch his opinion in favor of my client," I said.

The hearing. Three o'clock. *Doc-doc says tomorrow. Three o'clock.* I decided to have the drink, after all.

"Probably get it in cash, too. MDs have got it made. Did you ever think of the dough we could salt away if we ever got paid in simple, old-fashioned coin of the realm? Oh there you are, Ralph. Don't stand there with your pencil poised just because I ordered a Scotch for a change. You know damn well what I do *not* want so bring it to me. Three soft-boiled eggs, dammit! My advice to you, Adam: never develop an ulcer because to cure it they fill you up with enough cholesterol to make *sure* you get a heart attack."

I ordered ham and eggs. "I've had no breakfast."

It was a slip. I saw the bushy brows go up.

And when the waiter had gone, Henry leaned back. "Adam, why don't you level with me?"

The question had been inevitable. And again I was tempted. Why not? Why did I hesitate?

"If there's anything I can do. Like cosign a note for half-a-million."

These parts, rape in the second-degree. Click, law-man? Henry might even have an idea how to handle that.

". . . last of a rare breed. I know you, Adam. Whatever it is you're involved in, you'll put yourself through the tortures of the damned. Probably that minister father of yours is to blame. Whatever, you're taking it all harder than anyone else in the world would."

What could Henry do that I wasn't doing? It was too late now, anyway. Henry might even feel obliged to try to stop the abortion. Or he'd insist on having them arrested. Or he'd telephone Lydia.

The thought startled me. Why should I even imagine he would think of calling Lydia in London?

"I told you," I said tartly. "I'm catching a cold."

"Well, let's put it another way. This *cold* of yours is causing some pretty strange behavior. Forget about taking my head off yesterday. But antagonizing Lee over nothing at all—"

"He didn't waste any time, did he?"

"He walked here with me from the office. On some wild-goose chase you'd put him on." Then he waited but, finishing the drink, I did not reply. "Lee's a valuable man, Adam. Hell, you know how hard it is to get a really first-rate associate these days. All the competition from the big flashy firms. Then to break him in to our way of doing things—"

"It's true, then—"

"What's true?"

"He practically considers himself a partner now."

"Adam—"

"You and he have discussed it."

"Adam, Lee's been with us five years."

"Discussed it behind my back!"

"Oh for God's sake, man, relax! Nobody's doing anything behind—"

"You did discuss it with him! You've just admitted that. Without even consulting me!"

"Why are you getting so excited? It came up in the most informal way imaginable. The boy naturally wonders what his future with the firm—"

"There are two partners in the firm!"

"I was going to broach the subject to you, but I've been too damn busy and so have you. That's the reason we need someone. It's too much for two men to handle now. Lee's willing to put up his pro rata share of actual working capital with three years to pay."

"Most informal way imaginable, *hell!*"

Henry gritted his teeth. "Adam, you're not doing my ulcer a damn bit of good." Then he leaned over the table. "Look at you. You're overworked, you—"

"I thought you'd decided I was overdoing the sex-bit! Isn't that what was bugging you yesterday?"

"*Sex-bit?*" He sat back, frowning, puzzled. "*Bugging?* Where are you picking up this hip lingo?"

"Answer my question!"

"Relax, relax—"

"And stop telling me to relax! I'm relaxed. I need another Scotch."

"Adam, let's try to keep our voices down. Agreed? Now listen to me: something's amiss and, dammit, I'm through asking what. If you're not going to tell me, you're not. But we do have an organization to hold together. I'm not referring to Lee alone. There's Phoebe, too."

"Phoebe?"

"The woman came to me almost in tears."

"Whole goddamned office is jumping with gossip, isn't it?"

"Jumping. More hip talk. No, not gossip, you blind fool. Don't you know the woman fancies herself in love with you? Maybe *is* in love with you!"

In love with me? Preposterous. Preposterous, but if true, it might explain why she'd cooperate with Wilby. The whisky taste turned rancid in my mouth.

"*Now,*" Henry asked, "now what's going through that mind of yours?"

"I'm going to give Phoebe her notice this afternoon."

"Why?"

"Because I can't trust her any more, that's why!"

"Why, Adam? Because she worships you?"

Worship, hell! I was going to fire her, get her out today, because she had been willing to go to these lengths, any lengths! Why? Why, to break down my resistance. If possible to break up my marriage! Why else should she cooperate with Wilby and Jenny? Not for any share in the loot—no, Phoebe had her own personal erotic reasons. More corruption. More devious depravity! Wilby was right, after all. If you look, it's everywhere.

The food arrived. I gave Ralph my glass. I sat staring at the ham and eggs. My stomach was twisting. If I touched them I'd be sick. Right here, on the spot.

"Eat," Henry said, as if he had read my mind. "If you didn't have any breakfast, eat."

Where was that drink?

"Look, friend, you're going to develop something worse than my ulcer if you don't at least—"

"Haven't I been chastised enough? What else have I done wrong?"

Henry paused with his spoon near his lips. Then he put it down and his lips thinned. "Adam, one more question."

"Shoot."

"Damned if I wouldn't *like* to!"

"Shoot your question!"

"Why don't you pack up, chuck everything, and fly over to London? Surprise Lydia."

Lydia. Can't think of Lydia. Cannot—

What were they doing with my drink, aging the Scotch?

"The service around here is getting even worse," I said.

"I'll cover for you at the office. Lee's up on your cases—"

"No!"

"Well, I was also thinking of Lydia," Henry said.

"Yes." Yes, he was, wasn't he? He was always thinking of Lydia —now that I came to think of him thinking of Lydia. "Yes, you are, aren't you?"

He shot me an odd, penetrating look. Cautious. Wary—very wary. Then he resumed eating.

The highball arrived. I gulped it, aware of the shuddering emptiness, not only in my stomach but all the way down deep in my body.

Sixteen minutes after one now. Were they still in the apartment? Did they ever intend to leave the apartment?

"You'll probably slit my throat," Henry said, wiping his lips with his napkin, "but I've one more suggestion. Make an appointment with Arnold. Just . . . talk things over."

And again that kind ironic face flashed in my mind: the man who had delivered Anne, who had loved Lydia from the start. *Young man, that girl of yours is a real woman. She'll never be able to bear another child, but she'll be able to take that, too. Shall I tell her or will you?* How long ago it seemed. Almost another life. How distant and painfully precious. *Well, if that's the way it is, darling, that's the way it is. We do have a lovely daughter, don't we?* Yes, Lydia had taken even that. Better than I had, actually, because I had never stopped wanting a son.

". . . call for you and make an appointment?"

Arnold Wilder's face alone revealed his instinctive knowledge and acceptance of human nature in all its aspects. The idea was tempting: to talk, to unburden.

"Well, Adam? The fact is: whether we men want to admit it or not, there is a kind of male climacteric that most of us have to face at one stage or—"

Then I was laughing. I heard myself laughing. A low, suppressed chuckle at first, threatening—

"I'm damned if I see why that's particularly amusing. It's a fact of life."

"Not fact, *change* of life!" The laughter erupted, grew louder. All I could do was listen to it.

I heard Henry say, "My God, Adam, people are looking. Get hold of yourself!"

But it was no good. His scowl was funny, too. I sensed the turning heads, saw a waiter stop dead with a loaded tray: they all seemed very funny all of a sudden and there was nothing I could do about the laughing.

"All right," Henry growled, "all right, we're going to Arnold's now!"

And somehow that did it. The laughter dribbled off into short heaving sighs, died down, became inaudible.

"I'm not going anywhere with you," I finally heard myself whisper and knew that now I was glaring.

Henry was glancing around the room with a false, chagrined smile, then he made a scribbling motion in the air in the direction of our waiter, and said, "If you're determined not to eat anyway, might as well get the hell out of here." Behind the anger was bafflement. Then, as if forcing casualness into his tone, he asked, "By the way, Adam, what's the case you assigned Lee this morning? He mentioned a name I didn't recognize."

"So you got the full report," I said, recognizing again one of Wilby's favorite phrases.

"Sounds fascinating. Insane asylums, draft-dodging, Actors Equity—"

Abruptly I was standing. My knee caught the table leg. Dishes, cups, glasses rattled.

"None of your goddamned business," I said, voice low. "I know all about you. You and Lydia."

Henry's frown deepened and that wariness flickered into his gaze again. "Lydia?"

"Stop pretending," I said, and knew that what I was saying was true, absolutely true! "You know you've been in love with Lydia for years. Ever since you met her. Before I knew her. Who do you think you're conning? Don't think I don't know why you're asking all these questions. You can't wait to let Lydia know!"

"Know what?"

"You think I'd tell you?" I was leaning over the table, bracing myself on my fists, only listening with wonder to what I would say next. "If you phone Lydia, I'm going to knock the hell out of you. Click?"

Rage entered his face. Almost automatically he started to stand up and—cold all over again, taut and ready—I knew that if he did, I would hit him. I *needed* to hit him, someone, *anyone*!

Then—either because he sensed this or because he found some cautious inner control of his own—he slowly sank back. Shaking his head.

"Arnold Wilder, Adam. A favor to me. Please."

But I only turned and walked away. I could feel the eyes on me. The weakness was gone. I strode toward the door, past the head waiter with his empty, pacifying smile, and went out to the street.

I walked. Remembering.

Henry, cocktail glass in hand, gazing over the heads to where Lydia stood talking to someone. How many times had I seen this without knowing, recognizing, acknowledging? *One thing about Lydia: most women, even happily married ones, so-called, can't look at a man without flirting. Or without letting their eyes drift down him in that speculative way. But not Lydia.* Why had Henry said that? When? The Columbia-Navy game: refilling Lydia's coffee cup over and over. Always lighting her cigarettes whenever the three of us were together. And after the wedding in London, drunk on the best champagne we could get, which was not good: *To think I introduced you two. You lucky bastard. I hope you'll both be happy but I ought to hate you.* Then hadn't he? Over the years? Hated and resented and envied—while I had been too blind to see it!

I was walking, fast, along the crowded sidewalk. It was all clear now, of course—including why I had not confided in Henry yesterday, or at lunch today. In some obscure way I must have known all along. Known yet refused to acknowledge.

Or was I now only turning my own frustration and confusion and pain—guilt, admit it, say it, guilt!—onto others? The way Wilby did!

I slowed, going faint. What about Lydia then?

Lydia and Henry?

Depths opening into bottomless depths.

A man's shoulder struck. I reeled. He muttered an obscenity.

What's the matter with you? You know better than that. Lydia? Well, what did that letter mean? That she'd been unhappy, unsatisfied. That she still was! Lydia and Henry? Behind my back. Because I was blind.

Get hold of yourself. You can't be that far gone!

I am the captain of my soul. Father, from the pulpit. Easy to quote, isn't it, Father? *I am the master of my fate.* But were you the master of your fate? Wandering those hills night and day, plunging blindly down the streets, oblivious, eyes glazed, shutting me out, shutting everyone out, quoting poetry and scripture, finally shouting curses. At what? *We didn't know how to tell you until you got here, Adam. Reverend Wyatt didn't just die. He hanged himself. In the woods.* Were you the captain of *your* ship, Father? Were you, damn you, *were* you?

"Mr. Wyatt!"

It was Phoebe. On the street. Staring. Aghast.

"Here, let me take your arm, Mr. Wyatt. Let's go up to the—"

Staring faces. Hostile. Grinning. The way they stood on Main Street in Fort Perry and grinned at Father, and at me trying to help him, lead him—

"You'll be all right once we get inside. This heat!"

I wrenched myself away, stumbled backward, stood swaying and faint. If she thought I didn't know what she was up to! *Don't you know the woman fancies herself in love with you?* Love, hell. Lust. Something I understood: lust.

Legs shaking violently, I stumbled away. To the familiar revolving door, made it through, seeing Phoebe's appalled face in my mind. Then into the elevator.

There he was again. He stepped in after me: long hair over ears, goatee, dirty sneakers, no tie. He had followed me into the elevator this morning. He stared straight ahead, eyes half closed. Phony beatnik bastard! If he got off on the nineteenth floor again—

He did.

I turned, blocking his way, facing him at close range.

"What do you want?" I demanded.

"Me?" Eyes already sullen; a whine of feigned innocence. "Me, Mistah?"

"You."

"From you, Mistah?" He looked me up and down with cold insolence. "Nuttin'. Whazzamattah wit' yah, yah some kinda nut'r sumpin'?"

He stepped around me and retreated down the corridor, glancing back over his shoulder. He didn't fool me—so that's how Wilby knew where I had been yesterday! He'd had me followed. But if so, what about Phoebe? As he turned a corner down the hall, the young man hesitated only long enough to lift one finger in a lewd, contemptuous gesture. Of course, I was certain then. Just like Wilby. Same ilk. Crawled out from under the same rock.

I went into the outer office. Empty. Into my own. The room was cool now, chilled. But I was hot. My whole body. Nerves jangling, head giddy and light, pains forgotten in a delirium of incandescent dizziness. And only a few minutes ago, in the restaurant, I had been cold.

The buzzer sounded. Abrasive. I leaned over the desk and pressed the button.

"Yes?"

"Mr. Wyatt, may I come in?"

She must have come up at once.

"What is it, Phoebe?"

"I have something for you."

I took a shallow breath, supporting myself against the desk. "Come in."

I waited. Damned if I'd sit down now, reveal I didn't have the strength to stand. Let her come. I was onto her. I had her number.

She stood there then, glass of water in one hand, other fist closed. A damned attractive woman: solid feminine body, good legs, soft face. Then why didn't I feel anything?

"More aspirin?"

"Tranquillizers. Would you take them please? For me?" Crispness gone from her tone: soft now, imploring, womanly.

For her? Why should I?

"Almost everyone uses them today." She extended her bare arm, opened her hand. "But I already said that, didn't I?"

"Do you take many of them?"

"One a day at least. Sometimes more. No—*often* quite a few more."

"Why? Is your work that difficult?"

"No," she said. "My work is not difficult at all. I enjoy it very much."

"Then?"

"Take them, please."

I did. Then the glass. It shook, water dribbling over my hand. I swallowed the two capsules, drained the glass. Now what? And on an empty stomach, after two drinks—

"Do you really want to know why I take them, or were you only making conversation?"

I set the glass on the desk—with some difficulty and a clicking sound just before I released it. "Of course I want to know," I lied.

"They help kill loneliness," Phoebe said, without moving, speaking very slowly, very carefully. "A little, anyway."

The telephone rang. At once, automatically, Phoebe was herself again: the polite, efficient secretary who knew her job and did it excellently. "Excuse me. I had our calls switched in here." She passed close to pick up the telephone; she wore a faint scent that suggested fields and clouds and fresh air. As I moved toward the couch—I had to sit now, simply had to sit down!—I heard her ask, "Dr. Who's office?"

I went stiff, remained standing. Jenny! Something had gone wrong!

"Oh, ye-es?"

But it was too early. Only one-forty.

Through a hollowness in my ears I heard: "Mr. Wyatt's tied up just now. This is Miss Waldron, his secretary. May I—"

But I had moved without knowing, had whipped about, had stepped in, now was taking, almost wrenching, the phone from her hand.

"This is Adam Wyatt. What is it?"

An unfamiliar female voice said, "Oh, Mr. Wyatt. This is Dr. Wilder's office. Dr. Wilder wanted me to tell you that, since it's you and since it appears to be urgent, he'll wait here and see you after hours. Six o'clock be all right?"

Arnold Wilder. It took a moment for it to penetrate. Henry.

"No, it isn't," I said curtly. "Impossible. Some other time. Tell Dr. Wilder I'll call when I need him. I'll call *myself*." I replaced the phone, it missed the cradle, clattered to the desk, and I went around the desk to sit, abruptly going slack, while Phoebe stepped in and picked it up, and as I closed my eyes I heard it being set in its cradle.

Henry. Damn him!

"Why don't you stretch out on the couch, Adam?"

Adam again. I opened my eyes. Phoebe stood looking down on me: was the concern in her eyes genuine or calculating?

"Wilby," I said, "sends his regards."

"Wilby?"

"Jenny, too."

Frowning. "Wilby? Wilbur Birchard?"

So there it was. True, confirmed—all my suspicions!

"Yes," I said faintly. "Wilbur Birchard."

"I'm afraid I don't know anyone named that. Or anyone named Jenny except for a classmate of mine back in Portland more years ago than I like to remember."

More lies. Clever. One to cover the other. "Then how did you put the two together just now—Wilby and Wilbur Birchard? Where'd you hear of Wilbur Birchard anyway?"

"Please, Adam, you're only going to—"

"I asked a question!" It was a smothered shout and it filled the office. "Answer me!"

Phoebe did not move. Her eyes remained fixed on mine. "This morning, just before lunch, when Mr. Gray left your office, he seemed very puzzled and he asked me if I knew of any case involving a Wilbur Birchard. I never even knew there was such a name. And I told him that, so far as I knew, there was no such case here. Naturally, when you said Wilby, I—" She let her voice trail off.

And then for a long moment, while I struggled for control, I was afraid—certain!—that I was going to start laughing again. What she said seemed so logical, so natural.

"Adam—" and there was a new firmness in her tone, in her face— "Adam, I want you to lie down now."

More orders. She *wants*! Everybody giving me orders. Wilby, Jenny, Henry, now Phoebe.

"Why?" I demanded harshly. "Why? So you can lie down with me?"

Her hand rose to her face. Her eyes opened wider. A cleft appeared between her brows. And as I looked at her, I wished I did desire her, wished I could, because if I didn't, it meant that Jenny had been right last night. Whether Phoebe's shock was sincere or feigned, I knew that all I had to do was to change my tone, my approach, and Phoebe would—

But my tone remained hard. "Well, that *is* what you want, isn't it? Isn't it what you've always wanted?"

Panic reached her face then. She darted a glance around the office, avoiding my gaze, then she rushed out, slamming the door.

I sat staring dumbly at it. My blood had slowed. Is that what impotence is—not to lust for, not to desire? Or is it not to be able to consummate? I stood up, weaving, and moved around the desk toward the couch. How should I know what impotence is? I had never thought about it before; had never had to. *Phoebe, y'mean? Good old*

Phoebe Waldron? He knew her name. And he knew more about me than he possibly could without someone's help.

As my knee touched the edge of couch, it was as if all the cruel conflicting pressures of the night and day exploded—a festering abscess finally erupting deep within—and I felt myself give way completely. I toppled face down on the couch. The leather was cool against my burning face. Strangely, there was no regret in me for what I had said. No contrition. Heat closed over me. Hell fire itself, Father? Is this it? Punishment by a just and merciful God: eternity. What is eternity?

I wakened with the taste of gall on my tongue, clogging my throat, and with someone's hand on my shoulder, shaking me gently. I rolled onto my back, muscles protesting, and stared up into Phoebe's face hovering hazily above my own.

"It's time," she was saying, softly, "but you really shouldn't go. I touched your forehead. You're feverish."

Go? What was she talking about? In twenty years I had never before gone to sleep in the office.

"Couldn't you let Mr. Gray take care of it?"

I looked at my watch: 2:41. Why, I'd been asleep almost an hour. I sat up slowly. My blood ran sluggishly, heavy in my veins. And Phoebe's voice reached me from a distance.

"Everyone reacts differently to those pills. I should have warned you. Still, you probably did need the rest, with the hearing coming up."

Hearing? Three o'clock. Corbin case. Had I actually forgotten? I tried to stand—and failed.

Doc-doc says tomorrow. Three o'clock.

"Adam—"

"Yes?" My head was in my hands, leaden and dull, eyes closed.

"I've been thinking about what you said a while ago. What you . . . accused me of. Do you remember?"

No. I had said so many things. It all seemed a long time ago now.

"About wanting to lie down with you." And when I looked up, recalling, her eyes were unflinching and I realized that she had spent the last hour thinking of nothing else. "Well, you were right. It is what I've always wanted. For almost three years. I had no idea you knew."

I had not known—had not even suspected. I stood up. I had not known and I still didn't believe it. Or want to.

"But only if you ever should want me, too," she went on, in the same direct, calm, soft voice. "Can you understand? Only if you ever needed me, too." Her chin was not lifted, but firm, and one hand played with a button on her dress. "You've changed now, but you've always been the kindest man I've ever known. The most considerate and gentle—and I always thought that was because you were so strong. But . . . but you're not strong now. And that doesn't matter to me. It matters only that now maybe you do need me—" It was not a question, but the suggestion hovered in the air between us.

I reached to my tie, but she took a quick step or two, pushed my hands down, and I could feel her hands tightening and straightening it at my throat. Her face was very close now, eyes cast on her job, and I could see the fine lines that had begun to age her face and the roots of her hair near the scalp, a dull gray, where the blond tint had not reached.

All of this could have been happening to someone else altogether.

Then she was talking, again, this time in a whispered excited rush. "Let me tell Mr. Gray to take over. Let me take you home." She lifted her eyes. "I'll take care of you. No demands. Just to be there. You need me. Everyone needs somebody."

It was true. She had hit a nerve. I needed someone.

"Look. Look at you. I don't know what's happening. I don't want to know. Yes, I do, but it's all right, I won't ask. You're burning up. You can't stand straight. Oh, I shouldn't have let you take two of them! With a hangover. Oh, Adam."

I needed someone, and she did *not* know what was happening, she was not in on it, any of it. How could I have imagined that she was?

"Or if you like, we could go to my place. If you'd rather."

Her place? Where I could prove that Jenny had been wrong last night.

"You could sleep the afternoon away."

Sleep. And no imagining what was happening at three o'clock somewhere across town, in some doctor's small office, or in a shabby tenement room.

"Anything, Adam. Anything."

There it was, out in the open: the climax of her plot, the admission of her role in the whole damned thing! I made it to the door without staggering. How could I have forgotten?

Without turning I growled, "I've a job to do."

Her voice followed me. "You shouldn't put yourself through any more."

Possibly she was right. But I was not going to compound the felony, repeat the betrayal with another woman only to prove something.

I halted, turned. She stood in my office door. "I'm expecting a telephone call from a Mr. Smith. Take his message, then phone me at the Sliker and Stewart offices."

I watched her face. It betrayed nothing.

"You want me to interrupt the hearing?"

"Yes. As soon as you get the message."

"If you say so, Mr. Wyatt."

Was it conceivable that Phoebe was not feigning innocence?

"Where's Mr. Gray?"

"He said he'd have a taxi waiting at the door downstairs."

I went out.

Knowing that, even if Phoebe were in reality working with Wilby and Jenny and that if I had allowed myself to fall into her trap—even then, I could never hate Phoebe as I had hated Jenny, as I still hated Jenny. And if ever the flimsy excuse of hate and fury were removed, I would probably not be able to stand up and walk under the mountain of guilt that, even now, dragged my every step and hunched my aching shoulders so that, leaning against the wall of elevator in the crush of strangers, I was certain that my bones were giving way under the immense and unsupportable weight.

"Pretty, isn't she?"

I turned from the rear window of the taxi and faced forward. "Who?"

"The one in yellow," Lee Gray said—with a smirk that reminded me of Wilby's. His voice reached me with a faint hollow echo. "Very nice."

"I detest yellow," I said, and was distantly satisfied by Lee Gray's surprise.

He thought I was pulling Donald Abbott's stunts. Actually, I had been looking back to see whether I could spot the beatnik type with the goatee who had followed me up on the elevator twice.

". . . only thing I've been able to ascertain so far—" His voice seemed remote, dulled to insignificance. "No Wilbur Birchard on the list of Actors Equity."

No surprise. None whatever. Another lie, of course. Almost three o'clock now. Even this fact no longer stretched my mind and nerves to the breaking point. Thank you, Phoebe, thank you for the pills, both of them. If Wilby had lied about Actors Equity, it was more than likely that the whole abortion was fabricated. Nice to think so. If I could only believe it.

". . . started ball rolling in Columbus, Ohio, and with Selective Service, but only a start. There's a Columbus in almost every state."

Out the window the cars and taxis and shoppers and buildings and windows floated by in a dreamlike flow of color and slow motion. If they had invented the abortion to extort the money—and, of course, to terrify and torment me—what then? Would they be gone when I returned?

". . . be so positive we are right."

What had he said? Did it really matter?

If Wilby and Jenny were in the apartment later, I would face it then. Not now. No use anticipating trouble. Not sensible. And later seemed now a long time away.

". . . know I'm sticking my neck out again, but I think you should let me handle this."

Handle what? The abortion? I felt a smile curl my lips. No, the hearing, of course. Handle it, Lee, so that you can report to Henry what a fine job you did when Adam wasn't up to it?

"Not a chance," I said, and my voice also sounded faraway, dim.

"Well, whatever you say. It's on your neck then."

"What isn't?"

Let him chew on that one a while. I saw his face set: sharp profile, youth, no self-doubts, no questionings.

"One thing, though, Adam: we can't be absolutely certain Mrs. Corbin is completely in the right, can we? Or, for that matter, that we have a case we can positively win. I admit Mrs. Corbin did nothing morally wrong, but by her own admission she's a nervous woman and she did not have complete control of the car. She claims the children were wrestling in the rear seat and that they unnerved her. So there's a fair chance they can establish negligence. Which would make her liable. By law."

And it just don't seem fair somehow. My wife was just doing her a favor—

"Is law real?"

The profile turned. Lee Gray's face, slightly blurred, looked stern. "The only question today is whether the plaintiff has sustained enough injury to warrant a jury's awarding her damages."

"That doesn't answer my question," I heard myself say. "Is law real?"

The taxi seemed to drift to a stop along the curb.

"I do want to thank you, Mr. Gray, for reminding me to keep my mind on the point at issue." I climbed out of the cab. "But I was cross-examining expert medical witnesses about whiplash injuries when you were still trying to figure out how a great big stork could deliver a tiny little bee."

The room was so similar to so many others over the years that at first I had the impression that the only difference between this room and all the others I had known—book-lined walls, long conference table down the center—was that this one simply could not be situated on the twenty-third floor but had to be in the hold of a long-submerged ship lying on the bottom of some unknown and mysterious sea. As I assumed my role in the customary and familiar ritual, I felt collected, sure of myself—less mystified than grateful for the impression of being once removed from the empty rites. Introductions, businesslike conviviality masking the acknowledged task of taking an opponent's measure. "How do you do?" "How do you do, Mr. Stewart?" Beefy, dour smile, guarded, half rising. "Nice to meet you." His associate—did he say Thurman? Somewhat younger than Lee Gray, more athletic looking, blond crew-cut hair and steady smile, like Glenn's. Genuine smile? Is Glenn's? Should not think of Anne now. Or anyone. Especially Jenny. Exactly one minute after three. Lee Gray's impressive politeness; no trepidation betrayed, all confidence, gladiator thirsting for battle—yet as I sit, he casts me one of those perplexed, anxious glances. White-faced male stenographer, elderly, hunched over his machine, flexing his fingers, glancing at the clock on the wall. 3:02.

"Witness didn't get scared out, did he?"

After polite listless laughter: "Dr. Harris is a busy man, Mr. Wyatt." Stewart's voice rasps—whisky-voice. Is that a rebuke?

"Who isn't?" Get it settled once and for all. "I'll give him five minutes."

Glances. Stewart clears his throat. Clock clicks once, loudly, as minute-hand leaps forward one minute. 3:03.

Intense heat down here, though. Or—perhaps not in the room. In me. Deep. Solid. Not running, stagnant in my veins. Quiet. Stenographer yawns. Why can't I ever catch their names when they're introduced? Another click, louder this time. Stewart consults his watch regardless. Do they use anesthesia? How long does it take?

"Dr. Harris was due at three o'clock."

Stewart coughs. "You've already granted five minutes. I've already thanked you, I think."

Tough customer? Near sixty, thin gray hair, flowered tie askew, cuffs wrinkled, sweat on face, bulbous pock-marked nose. *Mrs. Sloane says it's not her idea to sue for so much, but her attorneys told her that if you don't sue for more than you expect to get, you don't get enough*— Contingency job. Stewart appears to need it. Where did I hear—when?—that it was only a matter of letting in air? Midwives used to perform it, Europe, Nebraska in old days, probably still.

Another click, then door opens. Lee Gray shuffles papers. Stenographer blows nose. Dr. Harris. Chairs scrape. The ritual repeated: introductions. Tall, distinguished, chalk-striped dark suit, clipped British mustache. No apology. Austere, unsmiling, he takes his seat.

No other preliminaries: Harris knows them all, has been through it all before. Stewart begins. Oath: whole truth, nothing but— Dr. Harris does. Firmly. Crisply. So help him God. Dr. Harris is a man of truth, integrity: observe his cuff links, observe his cravat. The droning questions, clipped answers, all recorded in the click and hum of the small machine while stenographer stares into distance. Degrees. Where? How long ago? Member of—

Dr. Harris would know answer: how long average abortion? Depends somewhat on length of pregnancy. Two months. Oh, not long, not long at all in that case, no danger whatever, that short a time. Relax. Thank you, Dr. Harris.

Stewart's voice leads the witness. Permissible here. No objections. Name of patient, address, age, date of first consultation, subsequent examinations, their nature, findings, inception of complaint, diagnosis.

Lee Gray, slouched, listens with youthful gravity. Seventeen minutes after. Could operation be over? Did it really take place?

Medical terms. The usual. "Would you be kind enough to put that into layman's language for us common folk, Doctor?" Stewart's folksy touch. Smiles.

I was only wondering what kind of arrangement doctors do make in a case like this. Beyond the normal fee we legally pay for their time, of course— Good question, Henry. Shall I ask? Just to hear Stewart's objections? Just to witness the uproar? *Just,* as Lydia would say, *for the bloody hell of it*—

"And your prognosis, Dr. Harris?" Key question.

"In my opinion—" key answer calls for deprecating clearing of throat— "and you understand that I *could* be mistaken"—although I rarely am, gentlemen, rarely, indeed!—"in my opinion this patient has received a painful and permanent injury which may affect her the rest of her life on this earth."

Stewart grunts. Feel like grunting myself. Thurman feeds him another hasty note, Stewart rejects, tosses pad to table, sits back. "Mr. Wyatt."

Almost three-thirty.

More preliminaries. Adam Wyatt of Brant and Wyatt, representing defendant, Mrs. Leonard Corbin. Wyatt with two t's: that is correct. Half an hour. It couldn't take more than half an hour, surely. Dr. Harris prepares in his mind. Room swirls with smoke. My cigarettes, Stewart's cigar, Lee Gray's pipe.

"Dr. Harris?"

"Yes, sir?" Not defensive—cool, faintly disdainful.

One way or the other, if it was performed at all, it's over. Must by now be over.

"Dr. Harris, your testimony now shows that you believe Mrs. Sloane has received an injury that is painful, permanent, and may affect her the rest of her life on earth. Is that correct?"

"I think so, yes."

"If there's any doubt, we can ask Mr.—"

"Elser," Stewart volunteers.

". . . Mr. Elser to read it back to you."

"That's substantially what I said."

"Do you find any contradiction in terms in that testimony, doctor?"

"None whatsoever."

"It just strikes me that if an injury is permanent, it *would* affect her the rest of her life. Not *may* affect her."

"I'm not here to quibble about semantics."

"But just for the record—" and to put you off balance, distinguished sir— "may we have your decision? Is the injury, in your learned opinion, permanent, or may it *not* affect her the rest of her human life, which we all assume she will spend on this earth?"

Dr. Harris turns to Stewart. "Mr. Stewart—"

"Objection," Stewart says, heaving a sigh. "Let the record show I object to this line."

"I won't even ask for your reasons, Mr. Stewart."

"I'll tell you my reasons. For the record. This whole manner of interrogation is intended to confuse the witness and becloud the issues."

The clock clicks. Lee Gray slips a note before me: *Good work. Now—X-rays?* I crumple it. Insolence. Why waste paper on the obvious?

"The issue," I say aloud, "has already been sufficiently beclouded by the witness."

"Mr. Wyatt, you know this is no way to—"

"I know that there is some doubt in the doctor's mind as to whether the injury will cause permanent discomfort, let alone inability to carry on a normal life."

"Nothing that he has said so far—"

"My witness, Mr. Stewart, if you please." Stewart subsides: beady little pig eyes. Why doesn't Phoebe call? Told her to interrupt. "Doctor, can these symptoms you so vividly described earlier—I can almost feel them myself—can these symptoms, described *to* you *by* the plaintiff, be substantiated by an objective physical examination?"

"To a certain extent, of course, if you mean by objective—"

"By objective I mean something other than the plaintiff's subjective description and your subjective interpretation."

Lee Gray moves in chair next to me. A warning?

"Subjective? Would you please—"

"Well, an X-ray, for instance, would be *objective*. For example."

Doctor smiles. Condescending now. "Unfortunately nerves cannot be photographed like other—"

"Then a radiological examination cannot confirm this diagnosis? Yes or no?"

"That is not a question to which a yes-or—"

"Yes or no, Dr. Harris?"

"Mr. Stewart, do I—"

"Objection. Mr. Wyatt, I submit that that is not a yes-or-no question!" Hoarse whisky-voice feigning weariness, tolerance.

"Is there bone-damage, Doctor?"

"Not to my—"

"Is there X-ray evidence that a bone is pressing on a nerve?"

"Mr. Wyatt, I've already testified—"

"All of these questions can be answered yes-or-no. *If* such examinations were made."

"Adam!" Lee Gray: let him whisper.

"Objection again."

"Were such examinations made?"

"Naturally they were made. Routinely."

"And?"

"And what?"

Clever. Sparring for time. Very clever. Comes from experience. Take all the time you want, doctor. Three-forty-two. When is that damned door going to open?

"Mr. Wyatt—"

"Yes. Mr. Stewart?"

"Can't we get on with it?"

"I'll reword the question, Mr. Stewart. For the good doctor's benefit. Now that he is ready. And for yours."

"Thank you." Irony heavy in wrong mouth.

"Dr. Harris, can any sort of objective scientific examination of this patient—radiological or neurological—support your diagnosis and prognosis?"

"Well, each physician interprets—"

"That is not my question."

"Let him answer it first!"

"He is not being responsive."

"How do you—"

"Dr. Harris, on what do you base this diagnosis and prognosis other than the patient's recitation of her symptoms and discomfort and your own *subjective* conclusions, which may or may not be accurate, based on that recitation, which may or may not be true?"

Dr. Harris opens mouth, closes it. Lee Gray removes stinking pipe from mouth. Stewart draws himself up in chair, huffing. Thurman waits. Stenographer waits. I wait.

Finally, Stewart: "Mr. Wyatt, your question appears to be based on certain—"

"Does your witness refuse to answer my question?"

"This is not a courtroom, Mr. Wyatt!"

"Do you refuse, Doctor? Let the record show it."

"I did not come here to be badgered."

"Why did you come here, Doctor?" Watch it now, hold it.

"I came here to try to help a patient of mine who has been injured by gross negligence on the part of—" But he breaks off.

Careful now. Easy. Softly, silkenly: "Oh? Do you practice law as well as medicine, Doctor?"

"Not any more than you practice medicine, sir!" Face flushed now, shooting his cuffs, stiff all over. Mustache bristling.

"Would you repeat my question for the witness, please?"

Three-forty-seven. Forty-seven minutes! Caldron inside now. Caldron and steam pressure building.

"Which question is that, Mr. Wyatt?" Feeble, sad voice.

"My last question!" A bark.

"Adam—"

Stenographer runs narrow tape through fingers. Perplexed. "Do you practice law as well as—"

"That's not it."

"Then what? I'm sorry. I—"

They wait. For me. The question. What—? Panic. Then rage. What the hell was the question?

"Mr. Wyatt asked the basis on which Dr. Harris based his diagnosis other than the patient's listing of symptoms." Lee Gray. To the rescue. Sound of trumpets. Flags flying.

"I have it." And the stenographer reads in a flat dull voice.

Then Stewart: "I object to the question."

"On what basis, for God's sake?" Startlement. More glances. Let them stare! "You can't object without—"

"I object on the basis that the question is *iffy*."

"*Iffy!*" It's my voice—laugh or shout? "*Iffy!* There's not an *if* in the whole goddamned question!"

And now Stewart looks like W. C. Fields getting ready to throw a flowerpot at his wife. And I wonder how much longer I can keep from bursting into laughter.

"I still object."

Lee Gray: "Let the record show the objections and let's proceed—"

"Stay out of it. I'm handling this." And I hear my voice rocking wildly around this damned submerged submarine, I know it's too late, too late for anything, control or hope or relief or Jenny to survive or for me ever to be the same again. I hear Lee Gray mumble something, but it's too late for that, too. "I'm asking whether you have any test results that can establish this woman's injury!"

"My ability to diagnose and my integrity as a physician in this city—"

"That is not my question!"

"You are questioning both!"

"And you are badgering my witness!"

"Yes, I *am* questioning both, damn it! Who referred this patient to you?"

"I don't have to sit here and—"

"Mr. Stewart here? Or his partner, Mr. Sliker?"

Doctor stands. Trembling. "Do I have to take this?"

"How many other patients have Mr. Stewart or Mr. Sliker referred to you?"

"For God's sake, Adam, *please!*"

"Answer me, doctor!"

"My witness is not obliged to answer such a question!" Stewart standing now, too. "Such questions have no place in this—"

"How many times, doctor, have you testified in personal-injury cases for Sliker and Stewart, Attorneys-at-Law?"

"Take down every word this maniac says!"

"How many other whiplash cases?"

"Every word!"

"How many other *contingency* cases?"

"I want every word on the record!"

"And what percentage of the judgment do you collect, Doctor, *in the name of justice and your goddamned hypocritical oath?*"

A shout. Ear-shattering. Almost four o'clock. When did I stand up? I can't remember standing up.

"I'd like to request a short recess." Lee Gray's voice. "Ten minutes."

"I'm a busy doctor. No matter what he—"

"Five minutes. I insist. Mr. Wyatt will apologize."

"It's my professional opinion, Mr. Wyatt is not well."

Leaning across the table, no longer shouting, a raucous whisper: "I didn't pay for your professional opinion, Dr. Harris, and I don't want it. Your opinion is no good unless it's paid for. Your opinion is a commodity and you're a disgrace to your goddamned profession."

"How, sir, would you like to be sued for slander?"

"How, sir, would you like to go fuck an ostrich in Central Park?"

I turn away. Did I say that? Was that my voice?

"Ten minutes recess," Stewart croaks behind me.

Lee Gray beside me in the unfamiliar corridor. What time is it? Am I laughing?

"Adam, you must know: you're blowing the case."

No, not laughing. About to cry. *I'm going to do my best to see there's no judgment whatever, Mr. Corbin.*

Taking my arm: "Let me phone Henry."

I jerk it away. "Phone anybody you like! Haven't you and Henry talked enough for one day?"

Leave him. Get away. Weaving down corridor. Around corner. Where am I? Bottom of the sea. No elevators. No way up. Suffocating. Drowning. Why hasn't Phoebe called?

I lean against wall. Alone. Have I ever been so alone?

Alone and going to pieces. That's it. That's what's happening: you're going to pieces. Cannot. Will not. Cannot. Cold fear probing heat inside now: can I stop myself?

Faces pass, stare. Go to hell! All of you, *go to hell!*

Must find elevator. Must get out of this under-water prison. Where is air?

I walk. Not staggering. Know not quite staggering. Around another corner.

"Going down?"

Down? No—up. Have to get up and out! I step inside. Bodies press, faces: worried, haggard, ugly, frowning, lonely. Operator whistles through front teeth. How much of our lives moving vertically? Miles, miles, thousands of miles in a lifetime. Wilby didn't report. Wilby will never. Maybe—I *hope*—I'll never know.

"Excuse me."

Same under-water effect. But drifting in rushing tide of bodies toward street. Walking. How far? How many blocks? Miles? Phone booth on corner. Occupied. Walk again. What if it's not over yet? Another booth. Empty. If only I have a dime. Oh Christ no, not a single dime, not even two nickels. I search pockets. Frantic. Panic shaking me. Not a single dime in all my pockets! A quarter. It glitters. New shining quarter, silver and copper sandwich. Very well, splurge; shoot fifteen cents. Giddy now. Inside booth, airless, trying to breathe. Humming in ears. Numbers blur on dial. Need glasses? Haven't yet. Lucky. Almost fifty. Whirring click, whirring click, over and over, no mistakes now.

"Brant and Wyatt. May I help you?"

"Mr. Wyatt's office."

"One moment, please."

She didn't recognize my voice. I wait. How many years have I been waiting? Outside time and space now—odd sensation. Know it's after four o'clock, know time utmost importance, yet no time now, cannot grasp time. *This time tomorrow I may not be alive.*

"Mr. Wyatt's office."

"Phoebe—" Bleak: a drowning cry. Despair. "Phoebe, why didn't you call me?"

"Adam? . . . Mr. Wyatt, is that you?"

"Why didn't you phone me?"

"But . . . Mr. Smith hasn't called here."

Time. Important. "What time do you have?"

"Ten after four, Mr. Wyatt."

"Thanks." I hang up. Lean against mouthpiece. Cuts into flesh.

He never intended to report. All part of the same vindictive pattern. Planned it this way, plotted it! Cruel, warped, sadistic—

I take down phone. Then dial again. Nothing. Not so much as a hum on the line. Out of order? I strike the black box with my fist.

Of course: didn't deposit a coin. Search again. Change spills from my pocket. I stoop inside the stifling booth, elbows cracking sides of cubicle. On the floor: a single penny, a single quarter. I straighten. I know what I'm doing now. I'm going to be all right now. I know how to do it all.

But after I have done it, I stand holding the instrument against my face, against my ear, listening to the distant buzzing, over and over and over and over. He's there, though. He's sprawled on the living room floor, smoking, beard grinning. *Don't answer it, Jenny. Let lover-boy sweat-sweat.* If Jenny is there.

I let it ring. I can hold out as long as you can, Wilby. You'll see.

The buzzing becomes a part of my brain. Until I can't bear it any more. Until one more buzz, one more single buzz, and I will rip the phone out by its roots, tear down the booth, smash the glass.

I hang up. Turn. Emerge onto the teeming, hot, dirty street, blinded, walking, knowing now, suddenly knowing, positive.

She's dead.

Jenny's dead and now I am accessory to murder. Add another crime to the list.

Faces. Swarms. Thousands. Strangers. Millions of small contained universes. Alone. *Do you really want to know why I take them? They help kill loneliness. A little, anyway.* City full of Phoebes. World.

Where going? Back to apartment? Make sure. What will Wilby do if Jenny's dead? If he's there, there's nothing I can do about it. If she's dead, there's nothing I can do about it. I don't even want to know. The club then? Nearly five now. Buildings exploding with people, erupting like ants . . . *how could give that flowerpot a touch. Not even looking down. Hit somebody. Some ant. Kill. Or miss. Like God.* Ants rushing to bars, clubs, home to the first beer and the first television idiocy of an idiotic evening. Empty, empty. Ways of getting through. The club then? And Donald. Bastard. He fits in somewhere. Somehow. Huge windows: art galleries. Splotches of color, hot and chaotic. *It means it don't mean 'cause it can't mean 'cause nothin' does.* Nothing? If nothing means— *Even the cave at Altamira—that giant bison—you felt some Cro-Magnon was trying to speak across the years, to impose some sort of order.* Lydia. Lydia and Henry. *You think she's any different than anybody else? You? She any different than you?* Torrents of sun down sidewalk. Then a blessed incredible breath of cool air. Under a marquee. I go in.

Inside, I slouch in rear seat, collapsed. On the screen: shrieks of tires, guns exploding, destruction and more chaos, at least a hundred bodies sprawled lifeless at fadeout. *Life too precious? How can it be if there's nobody home upstairs?* Theater crowded. People half in love with death? Fascinated? Knowing it inevitable, anticipate vicariously? Bullet always marked for the man next to you. Plane just ahead, or just behind, not my plane.

Death.

Jenny.

Her life precious?

I stand up. How long have I been sitting here now? An hour? Longer. But time has no meaning.

I search lobby for telephone.

What, after all, is Jenny? A mass of temporary sensations, a haphazard collection of cells, chemicals.

LOUNGE AND TELEPHONES. Arrow pointing up. Can I make it? Mountain of carpeted stairs . . . *clinging to this little cinder as if it was important . . . as if one of us . . . a million of us . . . could be important—* Tight wide belt around chest as I climb. One foot after the other, muscles screaming. Belt tighter and tighter, excruciating, unbearable. Breathless, at Himalayan crest, head reeling, I make it to booth. Hand in pocket. Two dimes. Miracle. Change from box-office. Miracle nevertheless. An omen? Harbinger of luck to come? I dial familiar number.

Office closed. After five. Closed, locked, deserted. Then what am I doing?

"Brant and Wyatt." The familiar voice. "Brant and Wyatt—"

"Phoebe?"

"Adam?"

"Phoebe!" And in that instant I know I am going to collapse, burst into frantic weeping, wild laughter.

"I stayed late on the chance you'd call—"

And I had suspected her.

"Your Mr. Smith did telephone. Shortly before five. Mr. *Wilbur* Smith."

"Yes," I managed to say, faint whisper. Let her put it together now, let her, Wilbur Smith, Wilbur Birchard, I can trust her.

"Mr. Smith—who, incidentally, knew my name, my full name— said to tell you that his wife came through surgery like nothing had happened. Those are his words. I took them down. Like nothing had happened."

Jenny was alive. No relief yet. Only numbness.

"Are you there, Adam?"

"I'm here—" But where is here?

"He also wanted to make sure to tell you that he and his wife are very comfortable at the Waldorf."

Jenny was alive and they were gone. And it was over. Then why no bursting relief, why no silent inner shouts of joy?

"I tried to reach you at the Sliker and Stewart offices, but the hearing was over. Then I tried your home number but there was no answer."

No answer, the apartment empty. Hard to imagine. Impossible to picture.

"I had planned to sleep here on your couch all night if you didn't phone. I knew it must be important. Where are you, dear?" Silence. Then an odd sound. "Wherever you are, I'll come. If you want me to."

"Phoebe, are you crying?"

"No. Yes. I don't know. Do you want me to come?"

Do I? *Everybody needs somebody.* Do I want her to come? No. Wish I did, somehow wish I did, but do not.

"No, Phoebe—" and picture her face wincing, hurt. "No, thank you. I'm . . . I'm going to be all right now. I'm . . . fine." I'm fine because it's over. I don't believe it, but I shall soon. Over. "Thank you for staying on."

"You're welcome, Mr. Wyatt."

Click. Mr. Wyatt again. Did she call me Mr. Wyatt?

I am breathing again. The belt around my chest has snapped. My head is still light, but that's only natural. That's the relief, of course. One thing certain: I may have come close, you may have pushed me all the way, Wilby, but I didn't go to pieces. Only for a few minutes, an hour or two perhaps.

My walk to the stairway now is effortless. Exhilarating, really. Free and flowing, buoyant.

A young couple comes sedately up. We meet. I step aside. The young man steps aside also. I gesture. He glances uncertainly. I recognize the look: he thinks I'm tight. Wrong, young man. Not tight. The opposite. Loose. Free. Then we both step at the same instant and my foot misses, I feel my heel catching a split second on the edge of step, and then I am plunging out into space.

SNIPER'S THIRTEEN HOURS OF MURDER

The headline, an entire front page of the *New York Post*, held only a distant, an unreal sort of terror. The paper lay, face up, on the bar, and all around it, around me, male voices ebbed, surged, crackled, occasionally exploded into laughter. I had been staring at the page for—well, I had lost track of time again. Time enough for three or four tall ones, anyway. Time no longer held any meaning, therefore no urgency. I had just begun to feel—finally—in the last few minutes, a heady sense of liberation. Probably the way a defendant feels just after he's been found not guilty. Or—a more accurate parallel—has been found guilty, guilty indeed, but has been fined only, say, three thousand dollars instead of being sent back to his cell. Or executed.

Looking back at that fall down the carpeted steps in the theater, I could see the comic aspects of it now, in this new perspective. The young woman gasping, the young man rushing down to help, an usher crying out, "Don't touch him, don't move him," and myself slowly rising, wondering why all the alarm, then insisting to everyone—oh, quite a little crowd gathers fast in the event of tragedy, or comedy— that I did not feel a thing, not a thing. Then the manager insisting on having my name and my assuring him that I did not intend to sue, did not believe in suing others over nothing, then making my way un- steadily to the lobby and into the street. By that time the crack my head had taken when it struck the wall as I came tumbling down had begun to throb. It had throbbed in the taxi and because of that throb- bing I had asked the driver to drop me off at Pat's Pub rather than around the corner at the apartment house. There was no reason to hurry home now, plenty of time to put everything into shape, clean out the last vestiges of my visitors—the evidence, in short, yes, to de- stroy the evidence, to call things by their correct names. The filth and the evidence. I couldn't help wondering whether the library in particu- lar could even be purged of Wilby's peculiar stench, but that could be faced later.

Now, seated at the end of the bar, with the pleasant sounds and smoke and conviviality all around me, with three or four, or possibly even five, Scotches numbing the pain in my forehead and in the knots of muscles and bruises all down my body, I let my mind float freely —enjoying it.

At my elbow, a thin man possibly forty, with short-cropped gray- ing hair, glasses, and a lean intellectual face, was saying, "What gets me, though, what really *gets* me, is it makes no *sense.* To hole up there in that tower by himself and then just to take pot-shots at total strangers, for no *reason!*"

His companion beyond him, whom I could not see, said, "Strange things happen in Texas. When I was in the Army—"

"Yeah, but even Kennedy—that makes *some* sense. Oswald might have been nuts but he must have had some grudge and only aimed at one man. This kook—hell, those people didn't even know what it was all about and then they're *dead.*"

But why me? In a city of nine million—

I picked up the paper. In one corner of the front page was a photo- graph of a young, almost boyish face. Half smiling.

Accident. Like everything else. Chance. Y'follow me, man? Click?

Click, Wilby. I didn't follow you then, but I follow you now.

"Pat."

"Yes, sir, Mr. Wyatt. Another double?"

"If it's still for sale."

Pat frowned, then shrugged his bulky shoulders and took my glass. Doubles? Had I been drinking doubles? Well what did it matter to-night?

Even as I watched Pat pour, what I felt was more amusement than resentment. What difference did it make, after all, whether Jenny had spotted me here in Pat's or even whether Pat had put her onto me?

No longer frowning now, Pat set the glass before me. Perspiration dripped off his jowls, summer and winter. "Yah gotta nasty bruise your forehead, Mr. Wyatt."

"I fell down a flight of stairs. You should see my purple ass."

Pat laughed, but uncertainly, and wiped the bar. Probably thought I'd had too many. But my light-headedness had begun with those damned tranquillizers. No, with those two drinks before lunch. Lunch?

"Pat, I'd like two steak sandwiches. On toast."

"Two?"

I turned to the man at my elbow. "I said two. Didn't you distinctly hear me say two?"

"I wasn't listening."

"Itza hell when the wife's away," Pat said. "Reason I keep-a the kitchen going in summertime. Two, medium?"

"Yes, it is hell. Or has been. Thanks to you. Yes, medium, if you please."

Pat shook his head and started to withdraw when a hush fell over the room. I saw Pat's dark eyes staring at something or someone over my shoulder. Then, scowling, he shambled toward the kitchen.

I turned around. A young woman, not more than thirty, was sitting down alone in one of the booths, and it was as if, while continuing to keep up a pretense of chatter and drinking, every man in the room had become acutely aware of her presence. Her hair was very blond, she wore shorts, her legs were full and richly tanned, and her eyes were coldly aloof but slightly angry as she lit a cigarette.

When Pat returned, a voice down the bar asked in a whisper, "What gives here, Pat?"

"Don't-a ask me. Second time here. She might-a be a hooker, but how yah gonna know these days? Might be a housewife lives in the neighborhood."

"Well, you know what they say. No place for the pros these days, with the amateur competition what it is."

"I wish she'd-a stay in her own goddam kitchen."

I glanced around at the men. Similar conjectures seemed to be niggling at every mind. Wife on Long Island, or in the mountains, or Connecticut or Vermont for the summer—it might be mildly interesting to see which good solid respectable businessman and loving husband would leave with her. Meanwhile, on the beaches and at the clubs far away— *You think she's any different than anybody else? You? You think she's any different than you?* Yes, Jenny, yes, I had always believed that. Or had it been only a hope? *Y'gotta make sure y'don't start seein' what's real 'cause if y'ever start seein' it—*

The sandwiches arrived. How long had it been since I'd eaten a meal? Now, at the first bite, I knew that I could not finish even one of them. Instead, I drained my glass. Clicked it on the bar. And Pat took it.

All, all of a piece throughout: / Thy lovers were all untrue— Some poem or other. College English class, probably. What was the rest of it? I hadn't read any poetry since college. *Thy chase had a beast in view—*

And to hell with it.

"Yah don't like the steaks, Mr. Wyatt?"

Where did all this noticing go on?

"I'm not hungry, after all."

"Yah oughtta eat. Yah oughtta."

In Pat's, man. Where else?

He sighed and shook his head again. "Yah heard me tell 'em. I don't know the lady but I wish t'God she'd stay a-home."

"You don't need to play it cagey with me, Pat."

"Cagey?" His thick lips pursed. "Cagey, Mr. Wyatt?"

"I don't hold it against you. Would I come back in here if I held it against you?"

"Mr. Wyatt"—and he leaned close, whispering "—yah think maybe yah had enough? Eat the meat, Mr. Wyatt. Good-a for yah. Protein."

"Pat," I said, "if I can forgive you for taking me on a wild ride to nowhere, you can forgive me for spending more money in this joint."

He didn't move. The frown deepened. He stood back. Then he grinned. "Look-a, Mr. Wyatt. Let's chalk the *whole* business up to some kinda misunderstanding, like they say. Yah come in tomorrow."

I was conscious of a silence down the bar. The bastard wasn't going to get off that lightly. And he wasn't going to convince me, or anyone, that I was drunk. I may have learned, the hard way, some of the satisfactions, or advantages, of drinking, but if I had, it was at least partly Pat's fault!

"What's your usual cut?" I asked.

"My cut?"

"Your divvy. The hooker back there. Or let's take Jenny. What's your percentage?"

"Mr. Wyatt now, yah got somethin' all screwed up. I—"

"Don't get sore, Pat. Don't take umbrage. *I'm* the one who should be sore. I'm the one who paid. I'm just trying to make sure you get your fair share. You can't trust them, you know."

"That kinda talk—" He looked carefully down the bar, then over my shoulder, then lowered his voice. "That kinda talk could get me inna trouble. Lotsa trouble. Honest, I could lose my license."

"Pat, I'm protecting you! Whatever your cut is, the take was three thousand. Two nights. Fifteen hundred per. I thought you should know just in case."

Pat's face was grim now, dark eyes bright: he wiped his face with the bar towel. Then he grinned weakly.

"Why yah notta go home. Sleep it off, huh, Mr. Wyatt? Three thousand! I donna know what you talk about."

"Bread," I said. "I'm talking about extorted bread." I stood up. "How much?"

"Yah pay next-a time, okay?"

"Why, thanks, Pat. Damn nice of you. And don't be offended because I didn't eat the sandwiches. I guess I'm just too disgusted to eat."

He shook his head. "Good-a night, Mr. Wyatt."

"Good night, Pat." You lying, crooked pimp bastard!

But what's a lie? When everything's a lie? Where there is no truth?

I saw the woman again. Girl, really. A young man sat across the table from her and she no longer looked detached or angry—rather, vivacious, laughing, her head thrown back.

She saw my face. Whatever she saw there caused her to stop laughing. She frowned, and then a defensive scowl leaped into her face. The young man looked up just then, saw me, glowered. Her husband? Whose husband?

Behind me I heard a voice say, "Well, better than going home to *Playboy* magazine." And laughter down the bar.

I went out.

All, all of a piece throughout—

The street had cooled somewhat, dusk closing in: those last few minutes of daylight which tonight seemed to hold an ominous ugliness. Like the rest of the world. I walked. *Y'gotta make sure y'don't start seein' what's real, 'cause if y'ever start really seein'—* What had I answered? That it hurts.

Yes. But not simply because I had discovered around me on all sides anything that I had not always known was there. I was viewing it, though, from a different, sharper angle of refraction. And the revulsion was all through me, dragging my steps: a burden that I sensed now would be a part of me forever. Revulsion and guilt.

Curious, though, my mind—in spite of or because of the drinks —was working with a cold lucidity. Out of guilt, not only this sickening disgust that included myself at its core, but also this keener awareness of what, sadly, man is. All men. Everywhere. Always. Of what he is and what he can never become.

Terence was on duty tonight—for God's small gifts, make me eternally grateful—and as he held open the door, his smiling Irish face did not warn me.

"Mr. Wyatt—"

A stranger stood up from the marble bench in the foyer: tall, spare, wearing a fitted dark suit that suggested English tailoring. "May I have a word with you privately, I wonder?"

The crisp English-accented voice, rather than the dignified towering presence, gave me the cue.

"Why, Geoffrey, I didn't recognize you—"

A touch of merry old Blighty. Lydia. *Warms the cockles and cools the nostalgia—* Lydia in London. Theater. Art galleries. Stratford. Alone? Lydia and Henry—

The lean face creased into a smile that was not quite a smile. "I had to talk with you, sir. Reason I stayed on after going off duty, if you know what I mean."

I waited. Let him hang himself by his own words, no help from me. *How are your cousins enjoying New York? Lot of that type in London these days, I'm told.*

"It's about my wife, sir, that I wanted to discuss with you. She's ill, you know."

"No!" I sounded flabbergasted. "I didn't even know you had a wife, Geoffrey."

"Oh yes. Been married just over ten years, sir, if it comes to that. But, you see, she's . . . well, it's difficult to put into words, really."

"Try," I said, knowing, waiting. "Try, Geoffrey."

"A woman, you know—*some* women—when they reach a certain age—we were married late in life, you might say, by American standards—well, her doctors recommend a rest home, if you know what I mean, sir."

"I've heard of rest homes, Geoffrey." Make him spell it out—

"Since there's no one to look after her while I'm here at work. Now, I'm certain you know I don't make a great deal here, even with the tips—and I must say your monthly gratuity has always been more than generous."

"Well, thank you, Geoffrey. I'm sure you're welcome."

"But—"

"Yes, Geoffrey?"

"Well, sir—altogether, it's not enough to afford a . . . rest home for poor Audrey. And I'm sure you know how tight loan money has become the last few weeks."

"Hasn't it, *though*?" I said, and while my words did not even sound like mine, I was not ashamed of myself. Just another case of extortion, the only question now being: how much?

"So I was wondering—that is, it occurred to me—oh, good evening, Mrs. Weiss—it occurred to me you might be willing to help me out a bit. Oh, only as a loan, sir, you understand. With interest, of course. Any amount of interest you care to name. If you get my meaning, sir."

"I think I do, Geoffrey. Yes, I think I get your meaning."

Then, if this suspicion had not been delusion, what of all my other suspicions? It was curious, but now I felt very calm, very certain. No longer any danger of going to pieces.

"I knew you would, Mr. Wyatt. I was thinking of a small sum—small to you, that is."

"Such as, Geoffrey?" The question now was whether Geoffrey was collecting from both ends—a deal with Wilby for a percentage of the three thousand, which he had probably already collected, and now blackmail for whatever more he could bilk me for. "Such as, Geoffrey?"

"Three hundred a month?" Then in a rush: "Oh, it takes more than that for Audrey, of course, but I'll make up the difference somehow."

Where was the fury? The normal expected sense of outrage, shock?

"That's really decent of you, Geoffrey. To make up the difference."

"And I'll keep a strict accounting, of course, so that I can pay you back. With interest."

"When your ship comes in."

"I beg your—"

"When your ship comes in," I repeated—and my voice sounded reckless, even light-hearted. "I wouldn't expect to be repaid until then, naturally."

"That's . . . very understanding of you, Mr. Wyatt. I knew I could trust you to be understanding—just as you can trust me to be discreet."

"Discretion," I said, "is the better part of cupidity, Geoffrey," and I walked toward the elevator.

"Yes, sir—" But it was almost a question.

"Good night, Geoffrey."

"Good night, sir. May I tell Audrey that—"

Turning in the empty elevator, I said, "Geoffrey, you tell Audrey anything that you think is . . . discreet."

I pressed the button. Let him, as Wilby would say, let him sweat. The door closed on his somewhat baffled face. He had not once mentioned Lydia's name, or inquired again when she would return. Finesse—the kind of finesse all well-trained doormen should exhibit at all times. You might say. If you know what I mean.

The first maxim of a successful attorney must always be: never underestimate the cupidity of men. Professor Kantor. When had I thought of him earlier today? Why had I rejected his cynical maxim only to learn now, so many years later, that he had been right? Strange, though, that now—knowing, seeing—I felt no searing anguish, only an accepting sadness and the need for a single stiff nightcap to knock me out completely.

Then I remembered something else Professor Kantor had said. Surprising I hadn't thought of it earlier: *If any of you gentlemen become legislators, I hope you'll get a law passed requiring every female infant's birth date be tattooed on her belly just below the navel at birth.*

I leaned against the wall and allowed the weariness to take over completely. Almost as if I had willed it. Never again to hear Wilby's thin mocking voice. Never again to have to look upon Jenny's taunting tempting body. Yet I felt no profound sense of freedom or finality.

It was over but nothing could ever be quite the same again. Including myself.

The elevator came to a stop, the door slid open, I walked the corridor—and I was standing in front of the familiar door, key in hand, when I heard the first sound.

Not music. A voice.

Behind the door.

Then laughter. Strange, high-pitched, almost hysterical laughter.

I felt no surprise. None. No shock.

Now I knew why the relief had not taken over completely after the phone call to Phoebe, why I had gone to Pat's Pub instead of directly to the apartment. All along the certainty must have been somewhere in my being—my bones rather than my mind. Wilby had lied again. Had even telephoned Phoebe at the office to support the lie, to add to my torment.

Even now my mind flickered with the tempting hope that they had neglected to turn off the radio when they left. I stood quite still, listening. I pushed the faint hope aside. Behind the door the shrill laughter sounded again, going up and down the scale. And another voice cried out, incoherently. Then a low mumbling, as of several voices talking at once.

Still, no surprise, no hate, no fury—only a muted, unreal despair, oddly painless. And with bleak, unreasoning certainty I knew what I had to do.

Without thought, without feeling, I knew exactly how to do it. *. . . a crime rate that staggers the imagination so that even I keep a gun, if not under my pillow, at least within reach—*

I returned to the elevator, pushed the six on the panel, felt myself descending. The sensation, though, was not mine. All of this now was happening to someone else, some stranger.

I had had the impression several times since Sunday night that I had been standing aside, observing myself yet at the same time acting, so in a sense controlling those actions. Now I had moved completely outside myself, so completely that, when the elevator door slid open again, I was only observing: the corridor, the door, the number 607, the name plate reading "D. Abbott."

True, I heard the buzzer inside as I concentrated on my finger on the buzzer button, holding it steadily so that my fingernail whitened as the sound continued, went on and on and on. True, I imagined Donald behind the door—with a woman or a man, for after all it made not the slightest difference one way or the other—and I knew that if he did not open the door, I was going to get inside anyway. What I saw and heard was occurring in some timeless suspended vacuum. Yet I knew I was not drunk. No amount of drinking— swimming in a lake of alcohol, *drowning* in it!—could carry a man to this level of absurd unreality.

I watched this stranger take his finger from the button, I heard the buzzer stop, I saw him take a key from his pocket and insert it in the lock—a logical and admirable but naturally futile act of human intelligence—and then I saw him try the knob before stepping back two paces, and at once I knew that he was going to kick the door because only violence accomplishes in the end what must be accomplished. It seemed only natural, too, that the door did not fly open, or splinter, as it does in motion pictures, when his foot crashed against it; and it seemed equally natural that he should step back and kick again, harder this time, so that the door frame split with a loud reverberation up and down the hall, and the stranger, off balance, plunged into the small foyer, fell to the floor, and then slowly—he was in no hurry, it seemed—picked himself up, looking around. The apartment's geography was identical to the one above; only the furnishings, lush and Victorian, were different. He walked in long strides, but still slowly, to the stairway, mounted to the balcony, entered a bedroom. This room, too, was unoccupied. He went first to the bed, tossed aside the pillows; then he threw himself down across the bed on his back. He extended his right arm until his hand touched several books on a shelf. He sat up, pushed the books to the floor, reached, came up with a gun in his hand, a revolver. He broke it open, seemed satisfied by what he found, snapped it shut. He shoved the gun into the right-hand pocket of his jacket and, about to go out, stopped. A large brown cat stood in the doorway, hostile eyes glaring up at him, one long leg outstretched in front, like an alert and dangerous panther ready to pounce. He shoved the animal aside with one foot, ignoring its spitting, and retraced his steps, onto the balcony, down the stairs, across the living room, and into the outer corridor.

He walked past the elevator, its door now closed, to a half-glass door with a lighted EXIT sign above it at the end of the corridor. His steps slow and muffled on the concrete stairs, he climbed one flight and emerged on the floor above into a hall exactly like the one he had just left below. He made his way, still not hurrying, to the door marked "707 A. Wyatt," and then, without any suggestion of pause or hesitation, he opened it with a key and walked in.

Inside—dimness. Candles waver, flicker—all shapes and sizes, on the floor. Curtains drawn tight across windows, across door to terrace. A ghostlike unreality, weird. Shadows on ceiling, on walls, on stairs. Whole room misty with smoke. Shadows seated on floor in semicircle, faces indistinguishable in eerie candlelight from below: girls with long streaming hair, male faces, some bearded. Impression of Indians squatting around a campfire, smoking—what? A cigarette in a holder is being passed around, is smoked behind cupped hands, then is passed on. Music: guitars being strummed, being beaten. Voice cries, "Hey, you, get offa mah cloud." And heads nod in rhythm with simple, primitive beat. Off to one side a girl's figure stands weaving, hair flopping from side to side, light and shimmering, arms bare, an indistinct figure casting a distorted, spectral shadow onto the wall, dancing somnolently, alone.

The man, who has come in now, stands observing from the foyer. His right hand is in his pocket, but he still seems in no hurry—only quietly curious, as if his mind has been made up and all urgency has been sapped from his body.

In one corner, away from the uncertain spluttering light, two figures lounge, shoulder to shoulder, backs against the wall, slumped, a woman's head resting on a male shoulder. Only the glow of a cigarette being handed from one to the other causes the man to turn his head in that direction. Then, a door on the balcony opens and two indistinct shadows appear; both wear clothes so identical that, in this light, it is impossible to determine whether they are two young men or two young women. But it is a girl's voice, almost lost in the music's throb, that can be heard: ". . . like a thunderstorm . . . like my body's a sponge . . . groovy, can't believe how groovy, wow—" The words run together into a soft happy blur. ". . . always take a shower, always . . . really neat—" They come down the stairway, their figures as hazy as her voice. "Hot is *hot,* cold *cold,* like you can tell them apart at the same time. Like . . . you know . . . a caress. Body just grooves, really."

She does not pause or glance around the room; it may be that she is not seeing at all. She simply sinks to the bottom step and leans her head against the wall, face dimly lighted by the candles now: a young face, eyes half closed, ecstatic. Her dark hair glistens and drips water. Then she giggles, sounding idiotic.

Her companion—who, lighted from one side now, turns out to be a young man, or boy, with a long, pale ascetic face and wearing white slacks and a yellow sweater to match the girl's—stands leaning against the banister. He speaks, softly. "I don' wan' your damn world!"

Someone from the seated circle calls, "Make the acid-heads shut up!"

Murmurs of approval, mutterings. A shifting of positions on the floor. And the music clicks off.

The man stands as if hypnotized, staring. The girl continues to dance, only shuffling her feet, unaware, uncaring, lost in some world of her own. The cigarette moves on. Someone chortles. A male voice whispers. Another giggle.

The man reaches, flips on a light. Shadows vanish. A groan from the circle, a girl's moan, then a male voice crying, "Turn off the lights off!" A shuffling, grumbling. Most words indistinguishable, a few clear: "Kill it, man." . . . "Who's the—" "What's it, a bust?" . . . "Turn the goddam fuckin' lights off!"

Silence. No music for a moment. Then a clicking sound as another record drops.

The couple slouched together in the corner—a heavy-set youngish man with a pointed, Elizabethan, red beard and a sweatered girl with blond hair so short that it appears plastered to her skull—does not move. In the circle a delicate Oriental girl in a short red dress passes the cigarette to the pencil-thin Negro youth next to her and closes her eyes against the light's intrusion. The youth cups his hands around the cigarette, draws deeply, then exhales slowly, with an audible sigh, and a brawny crew-cut man wearing a business suit reaches, takes the holder between his fingers and lifts it to his lips.

Singing now, or bellowing, on the record: ". . . get your kicks on Route Sixty-six, get your kicks on Route Sixty-six—" over and over and over and over—

As if either stunned or intensely interested, the man in the foyer only surveys the phantasmagoric scene, hand still in his pocket. The others either ignore him or remain unaware of his presence. One—a lanky boy with a farmer's lined, lean face and wearing a double-breasted Edwardian jacket—stands up, walks steadily to the foyer, reaches beyond the man without so much as glancing at him, and flips the switch, dimming the room again. Somewhere, someone utters a sigh.

The man steps down into the room then, walks around the seated group, his own shadow bulky and ominous and slow on the wall and ceiling, and moves toward a closed door at the far end of the room. As he passes the couple at the foot of the stairs, the girl is saying, "Everything's so beautiful, I groove on life," and then she laughs softly. The boy standing above her has begun to moan, almost in silence—a low steady sound that could be either anguish or inner pleasure. The dancing girl is standing swaying now, her feet and legs no longer moving at all.

". . . get your kicks . . . Route Sixty-six—"

The man is in another room now, a room lined with books, containing a television set which is silent but lighted, so that the only illumination pours from behind and out of the distorted, diminished human figures on the screen. On the couch a boy with a mop of black, uncombed hair and with sideburns down his pale blue cheeks is on his hands and knees, uttering a guttural sound that slowly, slowly turns into a growl, then into a roar as his head twists to one side. Stretched out on his back on the floor lies a burly young man with a heavy brown beard. He wears dark glasses and his mouth is open in what appears to be silent laughter. In the bluish, unreal light from the television screen his dark back-teeth look black and ugly beyond the red gape of open mouth.

Behind the man, someone slams the door. And in the living room he has just left, a voice cries out, as if in pain, "Don't, don't, don't, oh, please don't!"

The young man on the floor rises to a half-sitting position, but the dark-haired one on the couch only roars more loudly.

"Pop? That you, pop?"

The man standing over him says nothing.

"Get Ramon"—and behind the blurred words there is laughter—"get Ramon, dad, the cat's a lion." He lies back, staring up into the man's face—or possibly not looking at all since his eyes are concealed behind the glasses.

The man takes a single step forward and for an instant it appears that he is going to kick the prone bearded young man in the head. But instead he steps backward and reaches to throw on a light, flooding the small room that is now brilliantly revealed in all its littered ugliness. The man's left hand lifts to his nose as if to close off a stench, but he only rubs it and drops his arm.

Ramon, on the couch, is a dark-skinned youth, either Cuban or Puerto Rican, with a handsome face and dulled dark eyes. Sitting back on his haunches, he stops roaring, growls.

"Ramon thinks he's Mr. Metro of Metro-Goldwyn-and-Ringling Circus." The voice is unconcerned, delighted. "Ain't he the cutest, though?"

The man simply reaches, grasps the back of Ramon's turtle-neck shirt, lifts him up as if he were actually a lion cub, and in this manner carries him to the door, where he drops him to the floor. Ramon's growl has turned into a whimper now as he sits propped against the closed door—which the man now opens. Then, without violence—almost gently—the man pushes the small body through the doorway and into the other room with one foot, prodding him as Ramon begins to crawl, the whimper turning into a prolonged whine.

In the other room the music has stopped momentarily, and protests can be heard from the circle as light falls across the floor. In the light Ramon crawls and then sprawls, lies still, arms outstretched.

Then the music blasts again. Furiously: "Ah jus' wanna make *love* t'you, baby, *love* t'you, baby, *love* t'you, baby, *love* t'you, baby—"

The man closes the door and turns.

"Wilby, where's Jenny?" It is the first time he has spoken, and his voice sounds gritty.

"Them Rolling Stones." The figure on the floor rolls over onto his stomach. "Hear way they rape them lyrics? Word by word. Statutory rape." And he laughs again, soundlessly, shoulders moving. "You hurt Ramon's feelings. And he's such a sweet thing—"

"Where's Jenny?"

"Y'talkin' to me, dad?" Wilby's voice is slow—mild and distant and very slow, like a slurred echo across a canyon. "Y're not com . . . com . . . municatin'."

"You heard me. Where is Jenny?"

"Y'wanna goof-ball, man? Or a spliff?"

"Wilby, you've pushed it just as far as—"

"Dad, y'oughta treat little Ramon gentle-like. He's a poet." He turns onto his back again, places his palms behind his shaggy head. "Wrote . . . lemme see . . . wrote 'Executive Ability in the Bedroom.' A sonnet. An' . . . an' 'How to Become a Sex Fiend Without Leaving the Choirloft.' A . . . pastoral elegy. All in Spanish . . . with French subtitles."

"Get them out of here."

Wilby sits up, hands still locked behind his neck. "Y'don't like my friends, man? Don't . . . approve? Potheads. Queers. Odd . . . balls. Jus' poor little sheep that have lost their—" He chortles, quietly. "One of 'em's even from Yale." Then he sighs. "Jus' playin' their own games, man. Way you play yours. Like Father. Like . . . husband-game. Like . . . bread-winner, suc . . . success." He crosses his legs beneath him, tilts his head to one side, seems to be peering upward. "Like . . . law . . . man. Only they don't buy your games, dad. What's matter that? So . . . they get high. *Hi-i-igh*. Gotta get by, gotta get from womb to . . . nowhere. Click?"

The man stands listening, both arms along his side, like a statue.

Wilby's voice takes on a singsong slow rhythm. "Grass . . . tea . . . goof-balls . . . religion . . . booze . . . God . . . gold watches at sixty-five—" He shrugs. "What's the big diff, man?"

"Where's Jenny?"

"Baby, y'got your needle stuck. Now me, I stick strictly with the pills. Three peps, one goof. Up y'go . . . an' *down* y'go, down, *down*. At . . . same time. Y'rather we get stoned? Like . . . you squares." His voice changes to a high-pitched squeak. "Cocktail hour, wifey, get the brats . . . away! *Out!* Pop's gotta get smashed before supper!" Then it alters again—into a pleased mocking sincerity. "Been watchin' you, man. Hooked. Y're . . . hooked."

"Wilby, I'm not going to ask you again."

The head tilts even farther to one side. "Y'love Jenny, dad?"

The man then mutters something incomprehensible between his teeth. And Wilby's beard grins.

"Y'don't know who y'are, dad. Nobody . . . knows."

A scream cuts through the muted monotonous nerve-wracking beat of music from beyond the door. The man turns. Wilby's head straightens as he listens. And the man opens the door.

The girl with the dark, wet hair who had taken a shower and come down the stairs is stretched out on her back on the floor, body arched, head thrown back, and she is whispering, ". . . wherever I am, it's beautiful. . . . What a beautiful way to—"

And the boy who had accompanied her is now sitting in the group and his mouth is working, chewing. "Stop him," the Oriental girl pleads with no one in particular. "Stop him, he is eating a candle."

"Them acid-heads!" A man's disgusted snarl. "How'd they get in here?"

Another scream—this time from the short-haired girl in the corner, who stands up.

Through the wax he is eating, the boy says, "I am consuming the flame. Light. I am consuming flame. Fire. Life itself. It tastes— nothing ever tasted so—I can taste the *flame*! I can taste *life*!"

And in writhing ecstasy on the floor, alone and unnoticed, the girl breathes, "Who wants children? So . . . beautiful. I don't want to cry. Having children could never mean . . . this . . . this . . . time, time is beautiful, too . . . time—"

The man closes the door. Stands breathing a moment, facing it.

"Now that LSD kick," Wilby says softly, slowly, staring away, "that's one bit I don't dig. Never make that . . . scene again. Tripped out, man . . . freakout . . . worse . . . like—" And the man turns then to look down on him, frowning. "No . . . thank you . . . thank you just the . . . same. Hiroshima, Nagasaki— way . . . it must have been." Wilby's tone and manner hold a dreamy muted terror. "Like I was goin' off it. Like . . . I was gonna flip. Off my . . . nut. *Alllll* the . . . way." Then he looks up. "Dad, there're places in yourself y'never want to go."

"I've been there," the man says.

"Yeah—" And the dreamy quality fades into a questioning satisfaction. "Yeah, y'look it, man. Like . . . you're gonna cop out. You flipped, dad?"

The man's right hand moves: lifts slowly and plunges into his pocket. "I don't know. It doesn't seem to matter." He steps closer again. "Now." And he spaces the words which seem to shudder with an intensity so great that they threaten to erupt into an inhuman howl. "Now . . . what . . . happened . . . to . . . Jenny?" Then they hang quivering in the air.

"Jenny—" Vague: a man waking from a dream, hearing a strange yet somehow familiar name. "Jenny?"

The man stoops down so that his face is almost touching the other's. "Jenny!" he shouts at last. "*Jenny*!"

Wilby removes his glasses. Blinks. Then softly: "Jenny? Why . . . man . . . she's dead."

Only the inhuman throb and clash of music can be heard, a few words: ". . . little by little, . . . *babe* . . . afraid of what I was a-lookin' fah—"

The man slowly straightens.

"Jenny died," Wilby says and lies back on the floor, throwing an arm over his exposed eyes. "This afternoon."

In the next room someone laughs: a quavering peal that seems to go on and on and on.

It is as if the sound brings the man to life. He whirls about, throws open the door again, reaches to a switch on the wall, stands staring in the flooding, brutal light.

"Turn the light *off*!" It is the boy who, a few minutes ago, had been sitting eating the candle. Now he is standing, legs weaving under him, face glistening with sweat, eyes wide, pupils dilated. "Turn it *off*! I'm happy. I'm enjoying life! Get off my back! Wow!" The word is an anguished cry. "*Wow*. Somebody's gonna pay for this bum trip—"

And the girl who had been squirming in ecstasy on the floor now sits against the wall, knees drawn up, cowering, hands clenched into fists over her eyes, mouth agape, whole being tensed in terror, muttering incoherent sounds of which only the word "beautiful" can be distinguished, the word filled with a searing and terrible agony.

The thin Negro youth is dancing now, alone and fast, fascinated by the twitchings of his legs and feet, which are so fast and wild that they can scarcely be seen. No one appears to be watching him. Other smokers on the floor are leaning back and away, sprawled. Ramon is draped over the back of the sofa, head down, apparently unconscious. The couple in the corner is locked in an embrace, the red-bearded boy's arm plunged down the neck of the blond girl's sweater.

"Get out." It is only a strangled whisper, drowned by the wail and screech from the record-player: ". . . walk inside . . . whew, gal . . . whoaaaa gal . . . stole your heart a-*way*—"

When he speaks again, no one hears him. He then strides to the record-player, reaches. There is a screeching sound, a scratching, then several clicks and a whir.

Then silence.

The thin Negro boy, who is close, continues to shuffle his legs loosely, opens his mouth to say, "Hey, wha—?" but then stops.

He stops speaking and moving because the man takes the gun from his pocket, lets it dangle in his lifeless hand as if it is too heavy to lift.

Into the silence he says, "Get the hell out of my house."

There is a high-pitched cry, not quite a scream—the Oriental girl, the blonde in the corner, or one of the other shadowy figures in the now-broken circle?

Then a whisper: "The cat's got a gun!"

Sound and movement. A scramble. The Negro youth backs toward the foyer, eyes wide, hands out in front of him, pink palms up.

The man lifts the gun now. It is pointed straight ahead of him.

Someone moans—the girl hunched and alone against the wall, un-aware, lost in some hallucinatory terror of her own. Her friend stands with his eyes closed, weaving as if about to fall, saying, "If I could only snap my fingers—"

And the Oriental girl stands up, with a calm dignity, speaking in her native tongue as she moves toward the door which the Negro youth has left open. The husky young man in the business suit is standing. "Where'd you get that?" The bare-armed girl who had been dancing earlier takes his hand and draws him toward the foyer, her eyes glinting, fixed as if mesmerized by the gun. The lanky boy in the Edwardian jacket manages to stand up, to back away from the gun, his eyes more troubled than terrified, his thin face pale and set as he backs toward the foyer; misjudging the step behind him, he falls backward. As he scrambles to stand up, he asks, with a broad Mid-western innocence, "You off your rocker, Mister?" And then he dis-appears.

The man moves to the person closest to him: the young man in white slacks and yellow sweater who had taken LSD along with the girl who still sits hunched and unknowing against the wall. The man points the gun directly. And the boy asks him, piteously, "Why can't I snap my fingers? Help me. Will you help me?"

For just a moment the man seems baffled by this. Then he says, "Get her out of here."

As if following an order that could not be disobeyed or ignored, the young man drifts to the girl, kneels beside her, places his cheek against her clenched fists, whispers, "Laurie, let's go home. Laurie—we have to go home now. Will *you* help me?

And the girl lifts her face, tear-stained and contorted. She studies his a long moment, frowning. Then she whispers, "I can see your face. I can see way beyond your face, Peter. In back of your eyes. You. *You.*"

Peter helps her to her feet. Without glancing back at the man or the gun, they go toward the foyer. Peter helps her up the steps and they go out. But Peter's voice floats back. "I hate everything. Everything. I don't want your damn—" The whine drifts away.

Only Ramon and the man remain in the room. Ramon has not moved. The man stalks to the sofa, takes hold of Ramon's shirt again, rolls him onto his back on the seat of the sofa, stands looking down on him with no expression whatever on his drained mask of a face. Ramon opens his dark eyes, a glitter of panic appears in them, he utters a small sound far back in his throat, and then, although he does not seem to move, a knife-blade snaps open in his hand, catching the light.

The man does not flinch, does not betray even surprise. Ramon sits up, murmuring something in Spanish—possibly a curse, possibly a prayer—and backs along the sofa in a seated position until he reaches the far end. His eyes, by now, are savage with fear, murderous with hate.

That man makes no attempt to follow. He only watches.

Ramon leaps to his feet, then crouches; and, crouching, backs toward the foyer. Feeling with his left hand, he locates the telephone table and as he mounts the single step he throws it aside with a crash, then turns and runs out the open door.

The room, except for the man with the gun, is empty.

He stands a long moment without lowering it. Then he looks down at it as though he had never seen it before and as though he might be wondering what it was and how it had come to be in his hand.

Then, his shoulders sagging, he drops his arm. Like a man so tired that every step, every slight quiver of muscle might cause him to collapse at any instant, he trudges to the foyer, stoops to set the telephone table in an upright position, replaces the two parts of telephone on it, then stands, silent and still, as if trying to decide what to do next, or where he might go. He gazes across the desolation of the living room like a man looking back over a battlefield who has forgotten, if he ever knew, what the battle has been fought for.

The door at the end of the room is open. And from the room now comes the sound of a newscaster's voice, brisk and impersonal and enthusiastic, the words indistinct from this distance. As if reminded of something, the man steps down into the living room and he is plodding in a straight slow line when a voice behind causes him to halt and turn.

"Well! It must have been some party!" A large man in a dark suit stands in the door that has remained wide open. He surveys the room, sniffs the smoke-filled air, and his brows lift. "I must say, old fellow, I usually turn down invitations to such gatherings, but I do resent not being asked at least." He shambles into the foyer. "Except for the music it was quiet enough. No complaints on that score, you understand. I'm damned!"

The newcomer's eyes, set between heavy dark pouches in a wide fleshy face, are riveted, unblinking, on the gun. Then, recovering somewhat, he steps down into the room, sniffs again, nods. "Sweet smell, isn't it? Indian hemp. Isn't it marvelous what those savages knew long before we discovered its delights? I've only tried it twice —try everything at least twice has always been my motto—but the odor is unmistakable. How much have you had, old fellow? Not so much, I trust, that you can't discuss this matter intelligently."

"What matter?"

"Oh-oh, I can tell by your voice. Well, Adam, it gets embarrassing. You see, I've summoned the gendarmerie."

To which the man does not reply. He does not move a muscle. He stands staring bleakly as if he has spent his last shred of energy and now can only wait helplessly for what is to come.

"Oh, not about the party. For all I care, as you know, any of my neighbors can disturb my peace, day or night, more power to them. Frankly, I find my peace something I'd like to see shattered for all time. But it seems someone broke into my apartment. All they filched was my revolver. And now, imagine my astonishment to discover it was only you."

The man looks down at the gun again, blankly.

And at that moment, as if some fixed destiny had already predetermined the course of events or some cataclysmic accident were occurring too mysterious and arbitrary for comprehension, a siren sounds on the street below. Distant, but approaching with an eerie inevitability.

"Adam, since it *is* my revolver, I feel free, if not obliged, to ask: why did you want it?"

"Why does anybody want a gun?"

"Well, you needn't sound so superior. Some people have prowlers, burglars. Some need guns to shoot rats, although God forbid in this building—" He starts across the room, and the tone of his voice changes. "Adam, you wouldn't get any damn-fool ideas, would you?"

"I've had a great many damn-fool ideas these past two days. One of them was about you, Donald. And I'm sorry."

"I see. Well, that makes very little sense, if I must say so—not that I don't gracefully accept your apology. But if you've been imbibing what they euphemistically call pot—by whatever means—I don't expect coherency. I am in something of a dilemma, however. What on earth shall I tell them?"

The man, without glancing over his shoulder, reaches and supports himself on the back of the sofa, his shoulders drooping as from some invisible but unsupportable load. "Send the police in here."

"Adam—"

"Will you, Donald?"

"Of course, of course, if you say—"

"Now you're with it, pop!"

The man with the gun still in his hand does not turn, but Donald looks startled as the bearded young man drifts into the room, his manner reflecting the elation in his voice.

"Now we're gonna have it, man. The whole bit! Flashbulbs popping, the whole story." He stands with his legs apart, balanced, glasses in place again; no suggestion of fear in his manner or voice, rather an excited anticipation, almost glee. "Always wanted my picture in the paper."

Below, the siren approaches: louder, shriller.

"Who the hell are you?" Donald demands.

Wilby laughs. "Me? Man, I'm Maya! Y'know what Maya is? The force that gives out with the cosmic illusion that what *seems* real *is* real! Y'ever heard of me?"

"I can't say that I have."

"Or maybe I'm only a tool of karma. That's fate, man." His words tumble together with a nervous exultation. "Only karma's created by the man hisself, click? Why he has to be born and born again and again till he can reach nirvana. Salvation. Till he can break the samsara pattern an' kick the misery an' death bit so he can get with the nirvana. Truth. Y'heard of truth, man?"

"Adam, whoever this—"

Outside, the siren wail trails off into nothingness as the police car comes to a stop in front of the building.

"Moment of truth! *Olé!*"

"Adam, whatever you say—"

A long moment. Silence in the room. Silence below.

"Invite 'em up, dad. Tell 'em all about Jenny. Show 'em my letter-letter!"

"Well, Adam? They're undoubtedly on the elevator by now."

Another moment of silence.

"Well, old man?"

"Can you get rid of them?"

"My dear fellow, I'm a most adept liar. Learned it at my mother's breast, God rest her mendacious soul." He is ambling toward the foyer. "I'll say my black-sheep brother, an impetuous type when in need of a nightcap, dropped by unexpectedly and, not finding me at home, broke down the door." He turns, though, and stares at Wilby. "If you're absolutely sure, Adam—"

"I'm not sure of anything."

"Fifty bucks should square almost anything but murder with any police officer in New York. But I do suggest you open some of the windows, just in case the smell wafts down."

He is gone; the door closes.

Wilby steps lightly to the terrace door and opens it. A slight breeze blows the curtains. The smoke, still hanging, moves in gray billows. Wilby disappears.

The man looks down at the gun again. Then he places it in the same pocket as before. And follows Wilby onto the terrace.

Wilby stands on the balustrade, leaning to look down at the street. "Y'think this is the night, dad?"

The man says nothing.

"The bomb, man. The mushroom! Hello, Lyndon, *good-by*! Could be any night. Click?" He whips about. "Pop, y'don't listen that eleven o'clock news, y'don't keep up on things. We got another moon-shot in the works. Got t'get Old Glory planted up there! Then the Marines, then the missionaries. Get a better bead on the Russkies from up there! Red China, lay down your gun and *turn around*!"

"Wilby—if Jenny's dead—"

"Lover, we're all gonna be dead. What's time?"

"If she's dead—"

"Man, trouble with you is: y'still tryin' make sense outta things. Click?"

At that the man again lapses into silence.

Wilby stretches his arms along balustrade, as if to keep his balance. Grins. "Too much fresh air, too quick. Where's that six-shooter, man?"

No answer.

"First toy ever had. Yours, too, pop? All-American first toy. Thou shalt not kill, but get outta the kitchen and shoot that brat next door!"

Still no answer.

"How 'bout game Russian roulette, dad? One chance in six. I'll even go first."

Silence.

Wilby chuckles. "Y'on one of them talkin' jags of ours, lover-toy?"

The man's hand returns to his pocket. "How did you manage to avoid an autopsy?"

"Them fuzz down there, supposed t'show three this afternoon—"

"Or *was* there an autopsy?"

"Kinda tardy for roll-call, ain't they?"

"*What happened to the body?*"

"Body?" And he stretches to get an even firmer grip, tone somnolent again. "What's a body, man? A body by any other name still stinks. Dust. Chemicals. Eighty-some cents on the market if there was a market. Inflation prices, too." His head goes back and to one side, as if he were stretched on a cross. "Fertilizer, man. More pretty flowers. More vegetables . . . t'keep more people alive . . . so when *they* die, *they* can fertilize for—" He paused. "What they call continuity, man. Immortality. Click? Only keep it secret. Them down there, crowded aroun' the red light that goes flash-flash . . . don't tell 'em our—" Then he swings around, leans far over, shouts, "*You*, down there! You don't *know*! The joke's on *you*!" Then, his body sagging, he asks in a whisper, "What difference? Know or not know. What—" He faces the man again, removes his glasses. His eyes are as bleak as the man's now. "What does anything really matter? Y'get high, y'see, y'don't see, y'live, y'die, y'don't die—" He slumps. "Man, y'want to use that gun, go ahead."

Slowly the man removes his hand from his pocket.

"Jenny's gone. Go ahead."

The man turns away.

"Why not? Why *not*?"

The man does not move.

"Tell y'why, lover!"

Below, the sound of the siren. A faint double whir as the patrol car pulls away.

"Want me t'tell you?"

The siren fades completely.

"Cause y'dig. Y'begin to dig. Click?"

"What I dig . . . is that you're crazy."

"Don't say that! Y'know better! *Don't say it!*"

And the man turns to face him. "*Crazy.*"

Wilby's naked eyes wild now. "You have to say that 'cause y'dig! What does that matter, either? I seen those people. They believe what they believe! Inside. Some of 'em got peace! I tell you, I seen them! They got *peace!*"

"*Where* did you see them?"

Wilby utters a muted cry of despair. "Dad, stop fightin' me, willya? Stop. I know what's buggin' you, man. Y'believe you been fightin' me for that wife of yours. Then what about Jenny? An' y'believe y'been fighting for that daughter up there in the woods. Only y'know, y'*know* if y'could get her in bed, if y'could without—"

The man goes into the living room. Swiftly.

Wilby's voice follows. "It kills you, man, but *you dig!*"

Inside, the man stops, looks up the stairs, a glimmer of panic in his eyes—then he starts toward the foyer, fast.

And a key is inserted in the lock of the front door.

The man halts. Waits.

The key turns, the door opens, and a girl steps in. She wears a short white dress with red rectangles arranged in a geometric pattern and framed in wide black lines. Her hair is long and dark and falls down her back. She carries a small transistor radio which bursts with strident dissonance.

"Christ," she says, "you can smell the stuff a mile away. Stink-*o!*"

Then, as though she is perfectly familiar with the place, she begins to open windows.

When Wilby appears in the terrace door, she says, with a disdainful shrug. "You wonder why I hate the stuff?" She turns to the man. "I tried it once. It made me sick. Yugh. I vomited."

The man turns slowly to Wilby, who has remained motionless.

Now Wilby says, "Pop here's been worryin' about you, Jenny-baby. Y'stayed away so long."

The man again takes the gun from his pocket.

"Pop," Wilby says then, "y'don't listen so good. I told that Phoebe of yours—"

But, staring at the leveled gun, he breaks off as the man begins to move toward him, his face blank.

"Adam," Jenny cries, "what are you doing with that?"

The man reaches Wilby and stops.

"Put that away! Wilby, go to bed. You're high on the grass. I can tell by—"

But neither man so much as glances at her.

"I told old Phoebe, old Phoebe Waldron, Jenny came through like nothin' happened."

The girl sniggers then—from fright or from some inner detached amusement at the grotesque aspects of what she watches. "Like nothing happened because nothing happened. Joke's on you, Adam-honey."

The man, however, does not pull the trigger although his hand on the gun is white. There is no explosion.

But instead—in a movement so slow and calculated and obvious that its intent could be read and avoided if Wilby chose to move—he lifts the heavy black gun and brings the barrel down, without any apparent fury, in a diagonal stroke across Wilby's face.

The heavy beard does not obscure the crushing sound of metal against flesh and bone.

Wilby staggers to one side at first, then stands tottering a brief moment, pale eyes filling with relief and sadness and pain, then wobbles further, finally collapsing to the floor. Only the sound of the girl's radio can be heard: an announcer speaking breathlessly, with empty but assertive enthusiasm, of a record that *this week is in third place*!

Wilby lies limply on his side, eyes closed, huddled in the foetal position, knees drawn up. And the man steps in, straddles the motionless body, and lifts the gun again, higher this time.

Then he stops, with the gun held above his own head.

The girl speaks. "Go on! Go *on*!"

The gun has begun its downward arc when it stops in midair—and the man, still astride the defenseless prone figure, twists his head to look at the girl

She is lifted on her toes, her body straining, trembling with excitement, hands at her mouth, eyes wide—two glinting points. "Well, go *on*! What are you waiting for?" Then a hiss: "*Give it to him!*"

The man's gaze clouds with incredulity, with horror and revulsion.

His shoulders slump. He draws his gaze from the girl, steps to one side and then stands peering down on the apparently lifeless hulk. He watches as blood appears on the beard and seeps through it darkly until one side of it is soaked and matted.

The man's arm dangles, the gun hanging limply in his hand as if at any second it might drop to the carpet.

In long urgent steps, the girl hurries to the stairway, turning off the radio with one hand. "Leave him," she rasps. "Leave him and come on, Adam. Quick. *Now.*"

But the man does not stir. There are two lifeless figures in the room now, as the girl climbs the stairs swiftly.

"I know how mean he is when he's on the stuff." She is on the balcony, leaning down, speaking in a soft rush of sound. "Those pills, worse than pot. Come on, Adam-honey, come *on!*"

And when the man does not reply but only peers up at her with a stunned and appalled but no longer incredulous expression and then shudders, she takes a step down.

"You were too bombed last night, honey. That's all." Her voice is a silken purr, filled with a dark jungle-like promise. "You didn't even hear me when I said I loved you, did you? Do you know, honey, you only kissed me once. One time. I want you to kiss me tonight, Adam."

At this the man's face flinches, but only once, briefly, as if a shadow has moved across his mind.

Then the figure on the floor stirs, groans. The man, still holding the gun slackly in one hand, only watches as the groan turns into a moan. The girl remains tensely on the top step. With eyes half shut, the bearded boy manages to get to his feet, stands swaying, arms dangling apelike, his polished, blue, marble-like eyes squinting around the room without fixing on anyone or anything. Then he lurches once, as if he might fall again, rights himself, hesitates, and stumbles blindly, still moaning softly, toward the door of the room where, earlier, the man had found him. He does not close the door.

"Are you coming, Adam?" Impatience, irritation thinning her voice.

At last he speaks. "No."

The girl comes down two steps. "*Please*, honey?" A soft childish appeal, almost inaudible. "Please—for me."

The man seems to be staring at her, but his eyes are blank, vacant, as he slips the gun into his pocket.

"I'll scream." She still purrs, but when he does not speak or move, her eyes narrow, her chin clenches. "I'll scream so loud they'll—"

She breaks off, though, when the man finally does move. To the terrace door. He opens it wider. Then he faces her without shrugging, with no expression or gesture of any sort. The invitation is clear.

She comes down the stairway. "I'm going," she says, in a hard tone. "I'm going and I'll find somebody, anybody, and we'll come back and you can *watch*!"

When she pauses at the foot of the stairs, the man turns about, crosses to the foyer, up the step, to the front door. He opens it wide and stands aside.

The girl's face contorts as she strides to the foyer. "And if you won't let us in, we'll kick the door, yell, wake the whole goddam place!"

The man does not move. They face each other.

Abruptly then she reaches out both arms, her hands grasping behind his neck, rises on her toes, and kisses him on the mouth, his head gripped. But he twists his head, his hands remove hers, he sidesteps and moves around her and goes down the step.

She is rubbing her wrists. "God damn you," she mutters. "You'll screw me but you won't kiss me!"

Then, with catlike suddenness she springs at him from behind, claws bared, a low hiss deep in her throat. As he whirls about, her right hand slashes out unerringly so that, even though his head ducks swiftly to one side, her fingernails, like long painted talons, rake diagonally down the left side of his face, drawing blood at once. Scarcely seeming to move at all, he grabs her wrists, one in each hand, and with a single twisting motion he throws her aside and to the floor, where she half sits, one leg stretched out in front of her, body tensed, head lifted still, eyes dark and dangerous.

Panting slightly—the only sound in the otherwise silent room—she undergoes a change. Her body relaxes. She smiles, lips twisting, and her whole being now takes on a calculating quietness.

Softly she says, "I *told* you I don't mind if you hate me, honey. I like it."

The man, regarding her with detached scorn, utters a strange sound—more repugnance than loathing.

At this the girl leaps to her feet, eyes never leaving his, and her two hands fly to the neck of her dress. With a ripping sound that fills the room for a second, she tears the dress down the front. Both breasts flash bare for that instant. Then, as she lowers her arms, a faint smile still playing along her lips, the cloth half covers them, leaving a long wide V to the navel.

"I know what's the matter with you," she says, her tone harsh yet somehow amused. "Like last night. You can't get it up, can you?"

Without a word or any change of expression, the man passes her and goes to the stairway.

Now she whips about, her voice rising to hysterical contempt. "You're not even a *man*! Couldn't even give it to Wilby when you had the chance! Couldn't give him what he's been asking for, what he *wants*!" And, at this, the man on the stairway pauses, frowning, without turning his head to look down. "After all the bastard's done to you, a real man would've killed him!"

Into silence and before the man can continue to the balcony above —the sound of the door buzzer.

The man does turn now, but it is the girl who moves—quick and graceless and wild—and leaps up the single step to the foyer to throw open the door.

The heavy-set man who stands there is smiling pleasantly; but when he sees the girl his smile turns into a slack stare that falls from her face down the V of exposed flesh, then up again, slowly, to her face and bright angry eyes. He wets his thick lips with his tongue as his eyes, with bafflement and hesitation in them, scan the room beyond her, locating the man still standing, rigid and quiet, on the stairway.

"Oh, there you are, old fellow. All apologies and all that." But even as he speaks, he brings his gaze back to the girl. "Only wanted to report it cost an even hundred instead of fifty, but the underpaid preservers of law and order have departed. Even the price of corruption is going up, isn't it?" He heaves a heavy sigh as he smiles at the girl. "Well, unfortunately, even if my presence were desired, I cannot stay."

But as he wheels slowly about, reluctance weighing his ponderous body, the girl chirps, "Why not?"

With his hand on the doorknob, poised and frowning, he takes a deep breath and stiffens.

"Why not?" And now her tone has changed: while soft and husky, it is almost playful. "We're not going to bed." She strolls lightly into the living room, toward the bar, without glancing at the man on the stairway. "What *will* you have to drink?"

"Well"—and his eyes follow her—"well, I scarcely think, in the circumstances—" He glances. "Adam?"

"Why not, Donald?" The man's voice is flat and empty. "Why the hell not?"

"Unless," the girl says from behind the bar, "unless you'd rather get a nightcap somewhere else. Someplace that *smells* better."

Donald's gaze has returned to the girl, who moves from behind the bar and stands leaning, slouched, one hand on hip, body thrust at an off-kilter angle. "Adam?"

"It won't take me a minute to change," the girl says, loping to the stairway. Humming, she climbs the stairs, and as she passes the man, she murmurs, but loudly enough to be heard below, "Honey, you ought to know better than to tear off my clothes when we never *do* know who's coming to the door." Then she disappears.

The man on the balcony, his hands clutching the banister as if it might be difficult to remain in an upright position otherwise, says nothing.

Below, Donald clears his throat. "Look here, old fellow, I'm not one to ask questions and all that, but if you have any objections, now's the time to voice them, you know."

"No objections, Donald." His tone is now almost inaudible.

"*Well,* that's a relief." He steps down into the living room and peers up. "I suppose you know your face is bleeding, don't you?"

The man takes a handkerchief from his pocket, automatically, and dabs at the side of his face.

"*She* do that to you?" And in Donald's voice now there is something like quiet horror and sensual fascination. "Little tigress." Then he chuckles nervously. "Uh . . . by the way, do I . . . bring her back here?"

"Ask her."

"Adam, if you don't mind my pointing it out, you may be under the influence of some drug or other but—"

The telephone rings.

At once, but slowly, the man climbs the stairs, crosses the balcony, goes through a door next to the one through which the girl disappeared. And the telephone rings again.

In the bedroom he sits stiffly on the edge of the bed and picks up the telephone, cutting short its third ring.

"Hello."

"Hello? This . . . this is Glenn."

Glenn?

Glenn.

"How are you?"

The voice—polite, familiar—almost knocked me down. It made me reel. I could feel it reverberating through my mind. Glenn— Anne's husband, always smiling. And with it reality came smashing back. It was almost more than I could bear.

"Hello? *Hello?*"

I clutched the phone, faint and giddy: this was happening, actually happening, not to that stranger with the gun whom I had been observing from a distance, but to me, now, me personally, this minute.

". . . calling about Anne, really—"

Anne.

"What?" I had to collect myself, *had* to. "Has something happened to Anne?"

Stranger with the gun. I reached into my pocket. It was there. Like waking from a nightmare, but a nightmare that had actually occurred, and now was continuing.

"What's happened to Anne?" A strangled shout that hurt my throat, filled my brain, burst my skull. "*Tell me, God damn it!*"

"I'm trying to if you'll let me and stop yelling. It's not the greatest tragedy in the world, after all. I told Anne she should tell you herself but she wouldn't do it."

"Tell me *what?*"

"So I made an excuse to drive into Newtown to my office so Anne wouldn't know I'm talking with you—" And as his voice went on— the smiling, crew-cut boy was doing this on purpose, stretching it out, refusing to answer, tormenting me, on *purpose!*—I smelled that sickly-sweet odor from downstairs. In my nostrils, my head. Would that explain the dizziness? Or was I still drunk? Suddenly I longed in panic for that state of cold detachment which I had somehow been jolted out of.

". . . so you can imagine her feelings—"

I was gripping the phone, bending over, doubled up, mouth dry, so dry that I had to force the words through. "Glenn . . . please . . . what are you talking about? *Please.*"

Silence then. The room was spinning, but slowly, so slowly that, when I closed my eyes against it, I had the sensation of floating in a spiral movement.

"What we are talking about"—and his tone was patient, even

patronizing—"what we are talking about is that today is Anne's birthday, as you know. Or was."

Anne's birthday? August 2. August 2, 1946. Twenty years. Too young to be married. Instantly I saw her face in my mind—her pained, wounded, sensitive, lovely face. And inside, somewhere in the utter utter weariness, an ache began.

"You did accept our invitation to dinner tonight—"

I had to say something, though. "Glenn, I forgot. I simply—"

"Oh look, anyone can forget. But you know how Anne is about such things." A certain sharpness, not quite open hostility, had crept into his tone. "If it was anyone but you—even her mother—I doubt it would mean so much to her."

I think you're the most handsome, youngest man I—next to Glenn, of course—

"You may as well know. Anne thinks you've been lying to her. About what, I don't know. But you know how Anne feels about lies. Well, I'm pretty much like that myself. One of the reasons she and I fell in love, I sometimes think. So when you explain this to her, I suggest you simply tell her the truth, whatever it is."

I opened my eyes. The room had stopped spinning. Nausea deep but under control. Does Glenn suspect? Or know? He has guessed. And he's told Anne what he's guessed. Now he wants me to tell her. Even knowing how Anne would feel. He can't love her then. Not if he doesn't give a damn how she'd feel. Anything to come between Anne and me—

"Are you still there?"

"I'm here." I'm onto you, Glenn, and I'm here.

"Look: I don't know what you can do to make it up to her, or to take that look out of her eyes. But . . . all I hope is that you can think of something because it just kills me to see Anne suffer, that's all. I just can't bear it. That's the only reason I called. Good-by, sir."

"Good-by." My voice only a croak. Indistinct. Could he even hear it? I replaced the phone.

"Sir." Never "Dad" or "Father" or "Adam." Once in a while, "sir." He's resented me from the start. Her own father.

I straightened and, without volition, toppled backward across the bed. Did he imagine *I* wanted her to suffer? I closed my eyes against the light, pain knotted in every fiber. Why was I putting myself through this hell? Why else but to keep Anne and Lydia from suffering? Did Glenn think *I* didn't know that look on Anne's face? That I couldn't imagine an even more terrible one on Lydia's?

And now it was not over. Far from over. No abortion, all lies, both still there—

A sound. Somewhere. Then steps on the stairs. Voices: muffled, distant. Jenny and Donald? I strain to listen. Like an animal in its lair: every sound a potential threat. Is this what they've brought me to, then? The prehistoric jungle where every broken twig, the rustle of every leaf means danger. A predatory animal or painted savage moving in for the kill. After all those centuries, have we come no further than this? I heard the front door close. Silence now. The silence of the primordial swamp, the inchoate ooze.

That smell. *If they're junkies and have any of the stuff on the premises, he's guilty of maintaining a place where narcotics are used.* Another crime then. Add another. No abortion: subtract one.

Fire played along my cyclids like summer lightning. A thin red line wavering and hot with some greater, more horrendous and unknowable threat. Of what?

Of going out of my mind.

Face it. How otherwise explain the way I had acted? Standing off and observing my own behavior as if it were not mine at all. As if I were beyond all control, all will.

If they drive him to something, something worse like taking the law into his own hands, he'll be the one who gets the trial—

But I had not pulled the trigger. I had *not* killed. And when Wilby was on the floor, when I had every opportunity—*What are you waiting for?*—I had not. Proves something, doesn't it?

The gun. I sat up and took it out of my pocket. I broke it open, shook out the bullets. Why? Just in case. Next time, if there is a next time, I'll have to stop and think. I slipped the gun into one pocket, then the bullets into the other.

Then I stood up, took off the jacket, threw it over the back of a chair. I was shaking now. I was filled with a deathly stillness. I took off my shoes, turned off the light, and lay face down on the bed.

Had I made a mistake, a fatal error, in not killing him when I had the chance? Civilized scruples in the forest primeval? Was I committing a greater error in not going downstairs and doing it now?

I thought it was hopelessness that was closing over me, but in the last few seconds before I drifted off, as into a dark cloud, I realized gratefully that it was sleep.

. . . a tennis-match. And I am seated high on the umpire's chair, although I know there is no umpire's chair on the court in the grove by the cottage because I built the court myself years ago and there is no reason to have an umpire's chair—the very idea is absurd. Nevertheless, here I sit, and then I realize that, for some equally ridiculous reason, I am wearing a black judicial robe over my tennis shorts and I have to pay close attention to the game because it is set-point and while I know that I have to be objective and impartial, I cannot help it, or blame myself, if I at least hope that Anne will take the point. It is a fast rally, Anne and Glenn both wearing white, Anne's legs flashing brown in the intense sunlight that I realize now is unbearable. She reaches low for a backhand return that goes so deep that Glenn has to drop back fast, but he makes a clean forehand drive which causes Anne to stretch her slim body, graceful and young and beautiful, and for an instant I am certain she can't make the return, but she reaches it, and the ball grazes the top of the net, drops, and, as Glenn rushes, I realize that I cannot hear the pleasant, familiar plop-sound of racquet against ball and the lighter, hushed sound of the ball bouncing on the clay surface. It is as if the game is being played in an eerie, hot silence under a burning, merciless sun. Glenn has to lift the ball high, and I see, with relief, that Anne is dropping back into place and even before her racquet goes up, a small smile playing along her lips, I know she will reach high for an overhead volley shot which ordinarily would explode with sound. She smashes the ball beyond him into the corner where it scarcely bounces, lifting a white dust of chalk. Glenn has stopped running, can only stand and watch it, smiling. Then, strangely, everything changes. A cloud masks the sun, bringing dusk but no relief from the heat, and Anne is coming toward me, her face changed, too, disturbed, covered with tiny, glistening beads of perspiration, eyes clouded with concern and trepidation as she stops and looks up at me, pleading, saying that Glenn will never lose again. I cannot hear her words but I can read her lips, *Glenn, won't do it, again, Father, please, please forgive him*, but I shake my head because it is my duty to pass sentence and I have no choice, I am terribly sorry, the integrity of the bar is at stake, so I look past her toward where Glenn stands idly by, waiting, but still smiling, racquet grasped loosely in hand, and then Anne is weeping, so I look at her again, reading her lips, *You can't do it, Father, it's not fair, there's no such thing as justice, justice is a farce*, but I am rising up in solemn splendor, straightening my robe, precariously standing on the step of the umpire's chair, and I pronounce sentence, but I cannot make out the words, and then I see Anne stepping in closer, but Glenn moves, reaches out with the racquet—which, I see now, has no strings on it —and places the frame gently over Anne's head, drawing her back and away from me, and as she steps slowly backward, her lips say, *Who are you to judge? You have no right to judge anyone, Father, and you know it*, and when they are some distance away she suddenly wriggles clear of the racquet frame and comes running toward me, and I see that her short white tennis dress has become transparent but I cannot find my voice to tell her, and then she is climbing the ladder to where I stand and then she is standing next to me on the dangerously narrow step and she is saying, in silence, *Before we go, kiss me, Father. You never really kiss me any more*, and I draw back but her hands are on both sides of my head, firm and soft, and she is bringing my head down, her own lips slightly parted as mine come closer, and panic stabs through me as our mouths almost touch, panic and a wild, uncontrollable yearning combined with a terrible, overwhelming sense of shame and horror so that I straighten with a jolt and the movement causes the chair and ladder to wobble at first, then to collapse beneath us both, and then Anne is falling backward, with Glenn's smiling face below to catch her while I go plunging down, down, down through space, through the surface of the court as if it doesn't exist and then I am falling faster and faster into some limitless, bottomless abyss, emptiness—

I woke, thrashing about on the bed and groaning. Then, eyes open in the darkness, I lay there shuddering, sweating all over, while a sickening self-loathing took over. As if I had lived the dream. As if I were, in some mysterious way, guilty. Denial quivered hotly in my mind while cold sweat engulfed my whole body. Disgust clogged my blood. And remorse.

I needed a drink. Not one, several—as many as it would take to allow me to sleep. Not to dream, damn it, to *sleep!* I stood up. *I overheard you say once that you never took a sleeping-pill in your life, but there are times—* No use searching through the medicine chest: Lydia never used them either. *You can always make me sleep, darling. In your own way.* I can't go on like this. What time? How many hours till morning? An eternity.

I shambled barefoot to the door, onto the balcony. The sweet smell faint now, stale. The door to the guest room—the guest room, Anne's room, Jenny's room—was open. A light inside. But the room was empty. It could mean anything. Or nothing. Spending the night with Donald? Or has she gone for good and all? *You can't get it up, can you? You're not even a man.*

I started down the stairs. *Dad, there're places in yourself y'never want to go to.* Another of Wilby's truths.

And all of a sudden I remembered the bottle I had taken up to the bedroom—when? Last night, just before that man came in to discuss his case. *How, sir, would you like to go fuck an ostrich in Central Park?* The case I had blown sky-high this afternoon. I turned around and retraced my steps.

The bottle was in the bathroom where I had left it. I poured a glass half full, did not add water, returned to the bedroom, and sat in the chair by the window. But I did not drink at once. The glass was heavy and moist in my hand. I stared out the window. Dimness. Gray façades of buildings across the narrow canyon of street. Only a few windows lighted this late. The night people. Insomniacs. Lonely. Phoebe and her pills. Some blindly, numbly staring at the unrealities on television—drugged. Possibly fortunate. *What does anything really matter? Y'get high, y'see, y'don't see, y'live, y'die, y'don't die—*

I lifted the glass to my lips. *Been watchin' you, man. Hooked. Y're hooked.* I hesitated, the smell of whisky in my nostrils. *Grass . . . tea . . . goof-balls . . . religion . . . booze . . . God . . . gold watches at sixty-five—what's the big diff, man?* None, you bastard. I took an enormous swallow and felt the Scotch cutting deep inside. No difference and if I was hooked, I had no choice anyway.

A man always has a choice, son. Remember that. I've remembered, Father. I've even believed it. *That's what makes him a man. Free will is what distinguishes him from all other of God's creatures—*

God's creatures? I took another long drink. Was Mother one of God's creatures, Father? And when she lay there dying—that cheerful, heavy woman with the sublime, ugly face withering into a gray shadow with that malignant bulge obscenely visible even beneath the covers, while we *heard* her dying day after week after gruesome month, listened to those unspeakable cries that the doctor's drugs and all your prayers and mine could not quell, those inhuman moans night and day and the tears on her sunken cheeks and the silent apologies in her dulled, incredulous, receding eyes—was she one of God's creatures then?

If he's up there, he's a bastard. Click?

What was it you told me, Father? Told me or yourself, or both? *His ways may be inscrutable but he has his reasons. He must have.*

Then what were you doing, Father, that bright, breathless, summer afternoon when I searched for hours and finally found you at her grave, gaunt by then, muttering in silence and shaking your fist at the sky? At what? At him because you had finally come to admit his cruelty? His cruelty or his indifference.

I stood up. It was coming clear. After all this time. But I didn't want it. Not tonight. Didn't need that, too. Damned if I can sit here remembering what I have forgotten, what I have forced myself to forget for years! I drained the glass. Shivering. Maybe another one. Stun the mind into unconsciousness.

In the bathroom I caught a glimpse of my face in the mirror before I could avert my eyes: as haggard and wild as my father's all those times when I led him home, eyes glittering, hair matted, and dark suit covered with dust and brambles. Grief, they said. I poured a full glass of whisky. Grief, they said, Father, was what sent you stomping the hills at all hours, day or night, winter or summer. Grief, I told myself, was what made you ignore me, forget me for days on end, when I needed you, damn it I did need you, I was in my teens, I did need you, any wonder I joined the Air Force after college rather than come back, rather than come back to the town where the solid Christian hypocrites forced you to give up your church, sniggered at you in the street, made gestures at their heads.

I returned to the bedroom, glass in hand, and sat down again at the window. Only a few lights across the street now. Only a few others tracing their lonely ways through their own private hells?

But who am I, that dare dispute with thee— Why had you underlined those words, Father? I wondered when I first discovered them, then forgot. Until now. Forgot because I wanted to forget? Because it was easier? Well, I'm remembering now. I even remember who wrote them. John Donne. I'm remembering now, Father, and I think I know. You roamed those hills, you shook your fist and cursed that sky not out of grief alone, or because you had decided your God was cruel or indifferent, but because you had discovered that that sky was empty.

And I had blamed you. I had needed you, for myself, and had

blamed you and failed you. Do we always have to fail each other? *Always*?

I am the captain of my soul, I am the master of my fate.

Were you? When you threw the rope over the limb? I went there, you know. I went to look at that damned tree after the funeral I'd flown two thousand miles to attend. It was there that I said good-by, Father. And I've wondered only a few times since. Who was the captain of your soul when you made the knot, fixed it around your poor skinny, shrunken neck, did you do it at night, Father, or in blazing sunlight, no one ever knew, climbing up on that old kitchen chair that I had sat on as a child at all those thousands of happy meals, what did you think of in that last minute, or second, before you kicked it away, what went through your mind, her face, her face, Mother's face, as it was when she was dying or when she was young and singing, oh how she could sing, that big-boned Welsh woman, what went through your mind, Father, or were you out of your mind by then, as they claimed, out of your mind or perfectly sane and knowing and choosing?

I was shaking all over. Wringing wet. I set the glass on the floor and stood up in the dimness. It was not until I had thrown myself across the bed that I realized that I was weeping. My face was wet with tears.

They say the sun's only a star . . . came from a hydrogen cloud . . . four-five billion years ago . . . sun's half dead now—

I heard a bus rumble past, down below, on the street. New York. How had I come here? What was I doing in New York?

. . . only chaos that we have to call a pattern . . . because we have to think we're important . . . clinging to this little cinder as if it was important . . . as if one of us . . . a million of us . . . could be important—

In the entire world only my heart seemed alive: palpitating, fluttering. Like a motor silently misfiring. And an appalling sense of inevitability and dread crept over me.

Forgive my trespasses, Father, as I forgive yours. If we cannot pray, let us sleep.

My body seemed to be slowly shriveling, shrinking.

❧ Wednesday

THE street was one which I had walked before. And a siren wailing. And people were running, colliding, picking themselves up, eyes glazed, trying to run again, stumbling blindly on. An old man sat on the curb murmuring a single word: "Beautiful." Over and over. Could it be London? Yes, the buildings were familiar. London. But the people—staggering, running, floating along, faces dazed, stunned—where were they going? And why was I here? London— wasn't that long ago? The buildings remained upright and intact—not like London at all in that respect. Then it was not an air-raid. But what? A car careened down the street, headlights stabbing: onto the curb, into stone steps. And the driver—a young man wearing a yellow sweater and white slacks—climbed out, stared, then burst into hysterical laughter. And others, I noticed now, were huddled on the curbs, helpless to escape whatever disaster was taking place, some giggling, some moaning, while others lay sprawled across the sidewalk, staring with blank, unseeing eyes at the sky, as if the sky were the source of their panic or their pleasure. A bus—yes, a double-decker bus, so it must be London!—roared along, two wheels on the sidewalk, and as I watched, it rolled over the huddled and sprawling people there, and a great scream went up, overwhelming the repeated, insistent ear-piercing siren sound, and then, after it had passed and rumbled down the street, swerving madly from side to side, the light in the sky changed, turned into a brilliant red, flooding the devastation at which, fascinated and horrified, I was somehow obliged to stare. A ferocious, eerie incandescence lighted the chaos. And I saw blood running down the gutter. And all I could feel was sadness. Not horror, only sadness. And then a figure plunged from above, fell from an upper story onto the pavement, twitched, lay still, crumpled, eyes wide and staring, glazed as if in that final moment of plunging he had seen a vision too splendid to imagine, too unutterable to survive. And I could only wonder what weapon had brought about this terrible silent devastation. Not a fire-bomb certainly, or one of the German V-

2s—then what? And why didn't I feel as these others felt, these others scurrying or drifting past with either terror or mystifying enchantment in their faces? Or perhaps I looked to them as they looked to me. I stepped in the path of a young man wearing an Edwardian jacket and boots and I said something which I could not decipher myself, and he only smiled and mumbled, as from some superior height of knowing: "Mushroom, mushroom, naturally." Then he drifted past, mingling with the others. While I walked until the street itself became lost in distance. And a strange silence prevailed. And across the distance I made out a figure approaching, a girl's figure, slim and light-footed, wearing a summer dress that blew in a wind I could not feel, and it was not until she was very close, so close that I was certain I could reach out and touch her, that I realized, sadness gripping my heart suddenly, that it was Lydia Gilmore, my Lydia, still alive after all, not only alive, more, *young,* incredibly young, half smiling, waiting for me to speak or to reach out a hand. And then the light, which had been dimming all along, faded so that her face began to go, and I felt a protest deep within, a silent cry of anguish as we stood close but untouching in this soundless, gray space, her delicate, lovely, young, *young* face peering up at me, not quite pleading, and I ached to hear that soft loved voice, to feel that flesh of face against mine, that flowing hair in my hands, but the gray was darker now as I struggled helplessly to grasp the image, to hold it, the desolation profound, the sadness total as I realized that I could never touch her, hold her, never, not before this light had turned to blackness, not before darkness blotted out . . . everything.

Was it a dream? Only a dream? It lingers in my mind, vivid and terrible and strangely magnificent, more palpable, more real then the darkness of the room. I reach an arm across the bed. Nothing. No one.

And then, while the sadness only intensifies, I know that I am awake. My heart pounding. Had Lydia ever been that young? A girl, a child. The ache deepens, the sadness more profound and engulfing even than in the dream. And memory replaces the dream. London. Sirens beginning to wail, wardens' whistles on the square below. Lydia knocking on the hotel-room door, standing there when I open it, face gay and grave at the same time. *Just in time, aren't I? Impulse. Well, what are you going to do about it? What's a blitz compared to what you're going to do about it?* Had she said that? I'm not still dreaming. And afterward, in bed, in darkness, the walls vibrating: *If I'm going to die, darling, I'd rather be here than any place I can imagine.*

Not dream. Memory. How long ago? Where had those moments gone? Where were they? They can't be *gone.*

Lover, we're all gonna die. What's time? Stay away, Wilby. Leave this alone. My mind struggles to hold the memory. And yearning turns to craving, a desperate wild hunger.

Is all that gone? How old am I? Almost fifty. Impossible. I don't believe it. How many years left then? Twenty, perhaps? And then? Nothingness. Never to see her face again, never to hear that voice, to reach out and touch—

Y'ever think, man—human animal's only one knows it's gonna die someday? Stay away, Wilby, leave me alone, leave *us* alone, stay away!

Nothingness. Such a short time left. With luck, the same number of years as the time between London and now. Only that? Yes, only that. With a great deal of luck.

I lie very still, eyes open and unseeing in the dark room, aware that the dream has faded beyond memory, that the memory has dimmed as well—as we are all fading, drifting hour by implacable hour, second by wasted second, into . . . oblivion.

I feel myself sinking, without protest, in a slow rising sea of unreality. Asleep? Awake? Is there, after all, a difference? Has there ever been?

The sadness fills every pore and crevice of my body and mind, so overpowering that I can feel myself going down, going inexorably under, with an immense, oppressive weight on me, as if the sky itself were bearing down from above and a depthless void were pulling from below. Even my skin is raw. And there is a taste in my mouth: not the metallic taste of hate and frustration that had been a part of me for two days and nights now, but a different taste, as of ashes, of dust. The taste of despair.

A clock glows, I peer at it: a chimerical face reminding me that time, whether minutes or years, is my enemy, robbing me of all that I have and am. Two minutes after three.

In a real dark night of the soul it is always three o'clock in the morning. I heard the words only recently, quoted during a television discussion—and I had not comprehended. Had not even listened attentively enough to hear who had written it. But Lydia had known, had attempted afterward to discuss it with me. Now, though, the rhythmic sorrow touches my own sense of desolation and loss. And I do not want to move, do not have the will to move.

A sound.

At first it seems to be a distant cry, or wail, as of some wild animal across a vast distance, mournful, the howl of a wolf remembered from childhood. And this time I know I am dreaming again although there is only the sound, eerie and unearthly now, no images, no faces. And as it grows in intensity, as it penetrates my head, cutting through my eardrums like a cold knife, I tense, listening, remembering Jenny's threat: *And if you won't let us in, we'll kick the door, yell, wake the whole goddam place!*

I stand up. The caterwauling subsides—from below, definitely *in* the apartment, from below—and now it becomes, in the moment it takes me to make it to the door, only a low moaning. Not Jenny then: there is pain in the sound, fear. Almost at once the shrieking breaks out again: high-pitched, maniacal, and inhuman, from the direction of the library.

Then I am running, past the guest-room door—which, I notice vaguely, remains open, the room still lighted and unoccupied—and down the stairs, while the screaming increases in intensity, in terror. In my mind I can picture Donald sitting up in his bed below—is Jenny still with him?—and Geoffrey seven stories down listening, puzzling, perhaps even making decisons, a passerby on the street halting to stare up. And, crossing the living room, kicking over used candles, a glass or cup or lamp on the floor, I know, even before I reach the library, that now it is all over. The whole nightmare has reached some unexpected yet inevitable and shocking climax. Yet, halting breathless in the library door, I somehow feel no dread or foreboding or relief—only the necessity of cutting off that sound, destroying it, choking it off somehow!

The television glows, imageless and blue, its light dim. Wilby stands on the couch, flattened against the wall, whole body quivering, shrinking and cowering, head to one side, eyes and mouth open wide. One arm is extended in front of him and with the other he is striking at the air around it, striking over and over, striking, it appears, at his own hand, while the shrieks go on and on, interrupted only by quick, short gasps.

Drunk? Hopped up? Those pills? Berserk?

I hear myself shout his name, the sound lost, drowned out, my dry throat aching.

But, perhaps because he senses my presence—although his wide, terrified eyes are blank—he stops screeching long enough to say, in a piteous trembling convulsive cry, "Make it let go, take it away, make it—" And then he is screaming again, head thrown back, eyes closing—a scream so loud and sharp and ear-splitting that, recklessly, all I can do is to step in, reach, grab his arms between my hands, throw him down onto the sofa. When the screaming breaks, turns into incoherent babblings of horror and dread, I stand over him, undecided, until he rises up, whole body lifting in an abrupt spasm, face and beard contorting. Then I reach out, hit him with the palm of my hand, and in a quick reverse action, bring the back of my hand across the other side of his face, harder, crack-*crack*.

His body wilts and then he falls along the sofa, heaving, blubbering incoherently as his hands cover his head. As I watch him cowering, drawing his legs up, whimpering now, it comes to me that this is only another of Wilby's tricks. In a moment now he will sit up, grinning, derisive.

But it does not happen. The whimpering turns into sobs and gasps. And I step back. What next? What now? I half expect to hear the telephone ring, to hear the door buzzer. But in a moment there is only silence, the sobs subsiding into a quiet weeping.

And, myself spent and weak, I feel not revulsion, not hate and fear and repugnance, but a contradictory tug of compassion. I smother it down.

He is quiet now. He finally sits up. His face looks young and helpless, in spite of the beard, and his wet eyes stare blindly, finally focus, blink, focus again.

"What the hell's the matter with you?" I demand in a helpless, harsh whisper.

"Where is it?" His voice is low, a faint echo of the terror that still quivers miserably in his pale eyes. "Where did it go? Where is it?"

"Where is *what*?"

"Don't play, don't play." He is imploring, though, not commanding. "Where did it go?" Then he leaps up, grabs the arm of the couch, pulls it away from the wall. "I'll kill it. Give me the gun. I've got to kill it!" But the floor beneath the couch reveals nothing. He whips violently about, shoves the desk, stares down at the floor. "Where'd it go?" Then he throws over the large chair, up-ends it in a single motion, and stands trembling and breathing hard, bafflement in face and stance. In a quick motion one arm flashes out and he slams the door to the living room.

Then, as if satisfied, relieved, he collapses onto the couch, body racked by shudders, and sweat breaks out across his forehead, erupts into thousands of glistening bubbles beneath his eyes so that, almost in an instant, his beard is darkened with dampness. And I see the moisture soak into and mingle with the clotted blood along the side where I had struck him with the gun—how many hours?

Finally he looks up into my face as if seeing it now for the first time since I came into the room. "Y'did it, didn't you?"

"You had a bad dream," I tell him. "I've had a few myself. Thanks to you."

"Dream?" His tone hardens. "Dream, *shit*! Y'brought that cat in here, didn't you? Y'been against me all the time."

Cat? *Against* him? I feel a laugh move into my throat, but I do not utter it.

"Jenny talked. Jenny told you how I feel about 'em, so y'had to try funny business. *More* funny business! Y'got Jenny against me, too."

Christ, he's even further along the road to unreason than I had dared hope. And what will it mean? Especially when he discovers that Jenny has not come back?

"It's out there now, waitin'. In the other room. Just waitin'."

"There's no cat here." Why should I try reason? Why should I even wish to—

"I'm warnin' you, dad—don't *lie*! Look at my hand. It wouldn't let go, it had its *teeth* in my hand, it had its goddam teeth in my *bone*!" He extends his hand. "Look't them teeth-marks!" He shoves his sleeve up. "Look't them scratches!"

I look. There are no scratches; there are no teeth-marks.

"*You* look," I tell him.

He holds his arm up. He stares at it. "Bastard cat had fangs like a wolf. Look what he did to me. Just *look*!" Then he whines. "I couldn't shake it off. Harder I shook, the tighter it—jaws like a lion—*jaguar*—and all the time it kept starin' in my eyes—like it was fascinated—like it didn't mean to hurt me exactly—like maybe it loved me and was jus' doin' what it had to do—an' I couldn't take my goddam eyes off it—an' it must've been a hour, what time is it, more than a hour, a whole goddam *lifetime*—and it knew, I'm tellin' you, it *knew* what I was thinkin' and I knew what *it* was thinkin'—it was thinkin' I don't want to have to do this, I don't like doin' this to you, but I gotta, I gotta, I don't know why, it's nature, it's fate, I gotta, that's all—an' *I* kept tryin' to make it understand that *I* understood —I didn't blame the goddam thing, I hated it, but I didn't *blame* it 'cause I *understood*—even when I was tryin' t'shake it off—even when I could feel its goddam fangs boring into my *marrow*—an' we jus' stared like that—*stared*—and I could hear myself yellin'—but I think we made *contact*—I think our eyes made *contact*! That's what I'm sayin'! If I see it again, if you got it hid out there, I'll kill it if I can—or it'll kill me—get them goddam fangs into my *heart* next time, jugular *vein*!—but we understand each other even if I kill it or it kills me!"

His voice has risen to a shaking crescendo. It quavers in the stillness now. Quavers there like . . . madness.

Sensing the wretchedness behind the glint in those pale blue eyes, I feel again that thinning of the blood that I know is pity. As possibly he *intended* I feel! And with those suspicions flaring in my mind, I wonder whether—if I can feel this insidious and numbing sympathy, in view of all he has already done and in view of whatever he now plans to do—I am not as close to the brink as he is.

"Y'tryin' t'make me think there ain't any cat, pop?" The question is startling—as if, again, he has looked into my mind. "Like I'm makin' it all up? That it? That what you're hopin'?"

I hesitate, trying to think. If he goes over that brink now—

"Well, dad? Y'think I got what them doctors out there called delusions? That it?"

But it's an opportunity I can't risk ignoring or evading. "There is no cat."

Wilby leaps up. "An' nobody's been watchin' me all day, either? Y'didn't bring no cat in here an' y'didn't put somebody on my tail t'bug me? That what y're sayin', you bastard?"

For an instant I have the impression that he is going to strike, or kick, and I feel my tired body tense, remembering the gun upstairs.

But he frowns, uncertainty leaps again into his eyes, and he slumps to the couch. "Well . . . might not be so bad. I seen 'em, y'know. Both kinds. Some, they got hell inside. Night'n day. Other, though . . . lucky ones . . . they got a kinda peace . . . faces kinda lit up . . . like they moved past Maya . . . like they found . . . nirvana . . . salvation." He pauses again, then looks up, unsmiling, his eyes sad yet somehow hopeful. Y'dig, pop?"

I dig. While he has a terror of madness, some part of him longs for it. As in that theater yesterday I had felt that the audience half longed for the unreal death it sat witnessing on the unreal screen.

"Y'dig, pop?"

Again I feel the need in him to communicate, that lonely necessity to make himself understood. Nevertheless, I cannot give him the satisfaction of knowing that he has infected me further with the deadly poison of comprehension as well as with the possibly more debilitating infection of compassion. I turn to the door.

"Y'let that cat in here again, man, y'gonna be sorry!"

I open the door and step into the dim living room, then turn around.

He closes the door so that only his face appears around it, while his eyes dart in panic around the room. "Listen, man, *listen* now! Y'gotta stay an' talk with me." His voice is as wretched as his face. "Y'leave me alone down here, I'm goin' off that goddam terrace out there. I mean it! Y'gotta believe me!"

And, strangely, I do. He's imposing his will, as he always must, but he is not making an empty threat. Then why not let him jump? Why not *force* him to jump? Then I recall the letter he carries in his pocket, and with the thought all the accumulated fears and dangers of the past two days and nights rise in me again and I glance up at the empty bedroom—has he noticed the open door, the light beyond? Slowly I return to the library, wondering why. What, after all, does anything really matter?

In the library Wilby has righted the chair he overturned. The sense of unreality persists. Wilby does not chortle at his victory; instead says, as he stretches out on the couch, "Thanks, dad." And before I can even feel my amazement, as I sit and rest my head on the back of the chair, my neck aching and stiff, he goes on. "Y'know what Gautama said, don't you? He tried to teach them people along the Ganges to 'overcome rage with kindness.' That what you up to? Kindness. Like them saint-cats? Them holy-holies—"

Wilby's voice holds an unnatural quiet now, a boyish sincerity that. in my own soporific state, I am unable to define or to deal with

"Y'know who Gautama was, pop?"

"I doubt I ever met the gentleman."

"Buddha. Born six hundred years before Jesus H. Christ hisself."

This sounds more natural, more in character. Wilby might be

lonely, or desperate, or both, but he needs an audience, possibly as much as he needs a victim.

Outside the curtains now, there is a very faint suggestion of light. Another day, and what does it hold? I close my eyes. One day closer to . . . nothingness.

Then I hear him move as if he might be sitting up.

"Enlightenment," he says softly, "came to Gautama after a night without sleep under a pipal tree in Bengal—" Then he lifts his voice: "Enlightenment, pop. Ain't it better t'know?"

I do not answer. *Is* there an answer? Once your eyes have been opened to the subterranean horror, can you ever close them, awake or asleep?

"Ain't it better to *know*?" A miserable plaintiveness in his tone, sincerity, a note of urgency—as if the question has haunted him forever and he has always needed to voice it aloud. To a father, perhaps, a father he never had.

"Go to sleep."

"Damn you, God damn you, dad, can't we at least *talk* to one another?"

"If you don't go to sleep, I'm damned if I'm going to stay."

"Y'ready t'curse God to his face now, pop? Y'got sore boils from the sole of your foot unto your crown? Y'sittin' down in ashes scrapin' yourself with a potsherd?"

Book of Job. *Why died I not from the womb? Why did I not give up the ghost when I came out of the belly?* All those Sunday mornings—

"Y'ready to start cursing life, man? Like life was God maybe—"

"No," I said, before I knew I had spoken.

"No?" Wilby is moving, perhaps standing up. "No? Not yet?"

"Not yet."

"Y'remember how Job kicked it, don't you? Only cop-out for that stubborn bastard. Had t'knuckle under, click? 'Behold, I am vile.' Had t'say it!" A new throb comes into his voice. "Had t'get down'n *grovel!* Had t'abhor hisself, way I heard it. Had *t'give up hisself* so God'd forgive *him*. Forgive *him* for askin' a few goddam logical, human *questions*!"

I say nothing. What is there to say? That I have come to understand the roots of his anger and anguish? Or that I am not like Job in that I am *not* innocent?

Drowsily, I hear him begin to pace up and down the small room: four or five strides one way, a second's silence, then four or five steps to the other wall, or window, or door. And his voice changes rhythm, its tempo picks up.

"Y'know what jus' come to me? Listen now, *listen,* you're not asleep! God didn't start it all. Satan did it. That sly cat Lucifer when he stood up to the old man, said I'm's good's you are! 'And there was war in heaven.' Only Satan lost—lost the battle but won the war, been winnin' ever since! So God cast him out. And that's when God found out how much power *he* had. So had t'go on then, click? Couldn't let a place beautiful's hell go to waste, could he? So he got this idea—man! All we are, y'know—*where* we are—mind of God. Or Satan. Only reason he thought of us—had t'have some *inhabitants* down there in hell, had t'fill up the place, didn't he? Maybe even found out he *liked* t'see people suffer. Been enjoyin' hisself ever since. Only when old Adam ate the apple, God gets scared." He is pacing faster and faster and his words begin to run together slightly in his growing excitement. "Gets scared—read it, it's in the goddam Bible!—gets scared Adam'll go *on* eating an' live forever, like God! Gets scared 'cause *now*—" And he stops across the room from me; a wild exaltation comes into his voice. "*Listen,* man! What old white-whiskers was scared of was that Adam'd eat from that tree of knowledge and understand how he'd been *taken*! 'Cause what God wasn't gonna let him find out is that there ain't no such thing as good or evil! Can't be! *Cannot be!*" He moves closer, so close, that I can smell the stench of his body and breath. But I still refuse to open my eyes. His voice drops. "Or—no, not that they don't exist, something bigger than that, something more . . . *uplifting!* That . . . good . . . and . . . evil . . . are . . . *one!*" And there is awe in his tone, as if he has just made, in his mind, some staggering, earth-shattering discovery. "That . . . everything is . . . *one.*" He begins to move again. "Like how can y'push it, how can y'find new crimes, how can there be any such thing as crime when the whole world's a crime? God committed the first one! Listen to me, man, damn you, I'm *talkin'* t'you, *listen*! How y'gonna carry it to the goddam limit, like murder, when everybody's a murderer? Even you, pop! Bombs away! Y'pay taxes, buy napalm, poisons, *chemicals!*" He is moving faster and faster. "Oh God, oh Satan, I see it all now, first time, really *see* it! *Whole!* Good is evil and . . . evil is good . . . an' God and Satan are one! Like Christ hisself said—said he took on the sins of

the world—only didn't mean he *paid* for them—that phony crucifixion bit—meant he *committed* them hisself—*believed* in them
—*took them on!* 'Cause he knew, too! *He knew and I know!*"

His voice has reached a crescendo quavering with exultancy. And
when I open my eyes, he is standing straight, head lifted, eyes glittering, and, at first mesmerized, I can only stare. As a question pushes
to the surface of my numbed mind: had he spoken the gibberish of a
madman or did his words hold some inverted logic beyond my grasp?
Then, when he lowers his eyes to fix them on me, I have to avert mine
because the hard blue intensity of his seems actually to reflect some
mysterious and savage illumination that might have existed before
man or time or creation itself, some light emanating from beyond the
planets or even beyond what we take to be the universe. I feel a
shiver pass down my entire body.

"Y'dig?" he asks softly. "Y'get it?"

And, already in a state of torpid exhaustion, my own mind seems
carried away as if in some unbreakable hypnotic spell: how easy, how
pleasant and seductive, what relief to be able to cross over that line
into some magical area where distinctions blur into nothingness and
there is only freedom and unreality and rapture.

"Well, man? *Well?*" And now I hear a note of personal urgency, as
if he is begging for comprehension and more, as if he is pleading for
approval, like a child. "Answer me, dad. Please." The plaintiveness
holds some strange fear, too, and the use of the word *dad*, without
any suggestion now of mockery or even irony, stirs again that strange,
contradictory compassion that I know is dangerous yet that I seem
unable to repress. And in that unlikely moment, with morning show-
ing at the windows, I actually feel a longing to be able to offer solace.
If he had been able to satisfy that wretched hunger that is now in his
face and voice, that need to talk with a father who might have understood, would he have reached this room, now, in these circumstances? Would his eyes hold now that glint of madness that can no
longer be doubted?

"I understand quite a lot."

It is the best I can do, the words feeble and blurred and woefully
unsatisfactory, and it is not enough. He sees through it at once.

"Like hell," he whispers, sadly. Then with bitterness says it again.
"Like *hell!*" He utters a sound of disgust. "I know what you're
thinkin', dad. Only that's too easy. That's your *out* 'cause y'still can't
get with it. I'm not nuts!" He whirls and throws back the curtains.

Outside, the gray has turned to a faint golden light. Then Wilby stands with his back to me, slumped slightly, and his tone is miserable and dreary. "I know why y'come runnin' down here while ago. I know that, too. Scared the neighbors'd hear me yellin' at that goddam cat. You didn't give a shit about *me*, so don't try to con me!" He turns, fast, snaps, "When y'hit me, it was to shut me up! Click?"

"Yes," I said, and heard him snort another sound. "But—"

"Yeh?"

Can I risk it? If there's any slightest chance to make any sort of contact—

"Yeh, dad?"

"But also because I felt sorry for you."

"Sorry?" A whisper again. "Listen, man, like I told you, I don't need nobody t'feel sorry for me." Then sharply: "Save it! I don't want it! Shove it!" He is breathing hard again. He hunches his heavy shoulders several times, rapidly. His face appears puzzled. Then he steps closer. And when he stops to gaze down on me, he looks forlorn, even baffled. "I don't go for that pity-bit, but since it's you—" His eyes are half closed. "Y'can do anything y'want, man, 'cause I'm in love with you."

It takes a long moment for the significance of his words to penetrate the dark cloud of drowsiness and fatigue that holds me helpless in the chair. Then, even the revulsion refuses to return. No surprise. No shock. Only a feeling of desolate exhaustion.

"Y'hear me? *Love*."

What I hear is myself laughing—a single low burst of sound.

"That funny? Y'call that funny?"

I peer up at him. "Wilby," I hear myself say, wondering whether I am trying to reason or whether I am simply stalling for time, waiting for fury to come. "Wilby, you not only hate me, you hate every damned thing I am and everything I stand for."

Again he nods. "Like I say, man. Love. Love-and-hate." He shrugs, eyes fixed on mine. "Same thing."

I vaguely remember a scene on a London street corner long ago: a burly American sergeant standing over a prone figure in an RAF uniform, sergeant's arms moving like pistons while blood spurted and covered the pavement, and two MPs standing by, only watching, one of them saying to a civilian in a bowler hat, *We'll arrest him soon's he finishes what he's doing. Little fruit asked for it. Made a pass.* Recalling violence, I feel none. I only sit and stare up into the pale, bearded face that now has changed from sadness and tenderness into an expression of stark and knowing smugness, even smiling loftiness.

"Adam—" It is the first time that I can recall his using my name. "Adam . . . Y'ever think about it? Maybe queers're straight an' straights're queer. Maybe normal's ab an' ab's normal. Who's there to say? What's to prove different?"

Nature. But I say nothing, still expecting the repugnance and anger to come. Nature. Life. No gods required to know that.

"Who can say, lover? Maybe we got it mixed up, way back. Accounta that fairy tale 'bout Adam's rib." He smiles. "Your rib, Adam?"

He towers above me, too close for me to stand up, and his breath is fetid.

"Get out of my way."

He remains. He ignores. "Y'read that cat Kinsey, didn't you? More'n fifty per cent admitted, one time or other—"

It is impossible to stand without pushing him back. Nevertheless, I plant my feet.

"Y'ain't lived, Adam, till you tried dessert."

And his beard and lips twist into a wider smile, eyes glinting with such satisfaction that I wonder whether my face could reflect the revulsion that, if I feel it, I am not yet aware of. If he glimpses it, of course, it would only feed that monster gnawing away inside him.

I stand. He does not move back or away.

"Y'gonna sock me, man? Like red-blooded hypocrite?" His tone is soft. " 'Cause if y'do, I'm gonna have t'twist off your balls'n throw 'em out the window."

With the backs of my lower legs I manage to push back the chair slightly. What does he read in my eyes? Contempt, hatred—or that corrosive pity that, even now, I am helpless to smother down completely? Standing on one leg and bending the other at the knee, I push the chair even farther away with the sole of my foot. Then, evading any contact, I move to the door.

"Jenny told me all about last night. How y'couldn't straighten up an' fly right." And as I open the door: "Need a new target, man— that's all."

I go into the living room, recalling his earlier terror and uncertain whether he will follow. And not caring. Because in moving I have discovered that I am sick. Sick all through. I walk to the stairway in the faint sunlight.

From behind he calls, "What y'scared of, man? Scared I'll rape you in your goddam sleep?"

Without pausing, I reply, "I'm not nearly so scared as you are," knowing as I go up the stairs that it is true and that in this alone there is some flicker of hope.

"Methinks," Wilby cries, a jeer in his tone, "methinks the man doth protest too much!"

I pause then. "In other words"—and my voice sounds amused now, and detached—"in other words, if I stay, it will prove I'm a homosexual and if I go it will also prove I'm a homosexual?"

I look down on him standing in the center of the despoiled room. He is clamping his dark glasses over his eyes, his mouth a gaping pink hole in the matted brown beard with the bloodstain down one side of it, his head to one side.

"Listen, lover—I'm givin' you a chance. Last chance. man. Y'can *choose*!"

"Choose what?"

"You'n me, or—"

"Or what?"

He snorts a laugh. "I ain't doped it yet. Nothin' y'could imagine. But it's the whole route, lover. The whole route—"

I continue up the stairs, slowly, my legs wobbling as if at the next step both might cave simultaneously and send me tumbling backward and down. Too worn out, too drained to feel the panic and fright that I somehow know I should feel.

"Before I'm done with you, lover, you're gonna dig! Y're gonna be right down in the bottom. Only place anyone ever understands!" Then he is shouting with fanatical fury, without restraint. "Y're for-gettin' who I am! *I'm* the one who pities! Who needs your stinkin' pity? I'm the one hands out mercy! The one y'better feel sorry for is *you*! An' I'm tellin' you, you'll get no mercy! *None*! *None*!" Then he is screeching, "Lucifer has no mercy! Lucifer is like God! We are one!"

And, with a sensation of relief, I feel all compassion wither in me, all the pity that had been smoldering in my heart goes to ashes, and my heart shrivels. Waiting for hatred to fill the vacuum, I turn to the bedroom door—and see again the open door to the bedroom where Jenny should be sleeping.

I pause. Is it possible that Wilby's so blinded by his sick rage and the wild images of revenge flashing in his disordered mind that he has not yet discovered the empty room?

"Meoww." I have made the sound before the idea has even occurred to me. "Meowwww—"

And behind me, and below, I hear him padding swiftly toward the library, a broken cry of dread in his throat. I turn.

The living room is empty. The door of the library is opening slightly, with caution.

"Adam—"

I step to the railing, grasp it in my hands weakly. "Yes?"

"Y'heard that, didn't you?"

I do not hesitate now. "Heard what?"

His head appears in the crack of door. "Y're lying." But uncertainty trembles in his tone. "Liar! You *heard* it!"

"Pleasant dreams, Wilby."

"Y'hate me or you'd tell me the truth!"

"There is no truth, Wilby. Isn't that what you've been trying to teach me?"

He screeches, "Y'hate me or y'wouldn't have brought that goddam cat in here!"

Is he demanding that I reassure him as to the imaginary cat or is he demanding to know that I hate him because he needs hatred to survive? And if I admit that I hate him, won't he twist that into my admitting that I love him, love and hate being one and the same?

I go into the bedroom, hearing him shriek, "Everybody hates me. Everybody's always hated me!" And I close the door.

He cries hate, yet needs hate, thrives on it, calls it love.

I wait, leaning against the door, until I hear the library door slam shut. Then I return to the balcony and carefully close the door to the other bedroom. With luck Wilby won't realize till noon. Then what? Why, by then Jenny will probably have come back. Yes, and what then?

I fall across the bed again.

I close my eyes. The room glows dimly with the morning sun. Or is it dark with night—since words have no meaning? Love is hate and up is down and God is the devil and good is evil and male is female, and vice versa. *Gentlemen, let me warn you again: develop a respect for words.* Professor Kantor. *Words represent distinctions, concepts, ideas that it took your ancestors a million years to develop.*

To blur those meanings instead of to refine them is a form of evolutionary regression, a betrayal of civilization—

If only I can get an hour's sleep. Half an hour's sleep. Fifteen minutes.

What day it it? Started Sunday night. Three nights. Must be Wednesday. Wednesday, August 3, 1966. Day after Anne's birthday.

Anne. Twenty years—

I roll over, open my eyes. Night almost over. And the night's horrors extending into the day. How many days? How many *more* days? And nights? Will it ever end? There is no end. None.

Lydia—

Wilby downstairs. Alone. His pathetic inner cry: *Love me, help me, why can't you love me, why can't anyone love me, help me, why can't I love myself? All right then, if you can't love me, hate me, I'll accept that, anything's better than nothing, hate me then as I hate myself, just so I can know I'm alive!*

Begging for pity, can't bear it, hates it, kills it before it can take root. Kills it by pitying himself, kills it by interpreting it as weakness, turns it then to his own destructive uses. Thou shalt be corrupted as I am corrupted. If corruption has any meaning. If destruction—

Himself castrated, must emasculate—

She lies on her back on softness—silk? velvet? a cloud?—and I am gazing at her from above her head so that I look over her face, which in slight shadow still appears delicate and lovely and forever young and fresh, and then in slow detail, and with a strange, abstract hunger, down the length of smooth-fleshed body: lifted, swelling breasts with firm, pointed nipples, above rich softness, indentation of waist and flare of hip, for it is a woman's body now, no longer a girl's and all the more beautiful, full-fleshed legs slightly spread, one lying not quite straight, in repose, along the bed—for it must be a bed, after all, a bed with silk sheets perhaps—and the other leg lifted, bent at the knee, arms outstretched at either side, relaxed, palms up, in an attitude of patient, knowing waiting, inviting, the whole reposed figure one woman, familiar, yet forever new, and yet all women, the flesh radiant and lustrous, dazzling, so exquisite that, as I feel the impulse, the necessity, to reach, to disturb, to touch, to possess, and gently to ravish that incredible and somehow hurtful beauty, I long at the same time for the moment to remain as it is, fixed and eternal. But, despite myself, I reach. And as I see my own hand nearing the glow of shoulder, she rolls over and lifts her head to face me. And it is her face, unmistakably her face, of course, but distorted in an expression I have never seen before: a mocking smile of malice and delight. *The joke's on you, honey.* And it is not her voice: although the accent is hers, the tone is scoffing, cruel. And I feel myself cry out, *Lydia, don't call me honey!* but I cannot hear the words now because she is standing, adjusting a wide-brimmed hat on her head, the kind she used to wear, years ago, in London. *You just can't, you bastard old man you—* She swoops down to pick up a purse from a chair in a single motion so lithe and graceful and sensual that my heart clenches and I feel a stab of pain. *I don't have to take this—* Now she is standing by the door, head turning over her shoulder to mock me as she opens it, and outside a figure appears, with sun blinding from behind, the tall figure of a man whose features I cannot see in the glinting light, and as she goes out, wearing only the hat, she whispers, teasing, *I'm only off to a matinee, honey!* but still the words do not come and I watch the door close before I can reach it. Then I throw it open —and outside the sun has gone, vanished as if it had never been, and I stand in the doorway gazing out on a bleak, gray wasteland that stretches to no horizon, on which no figures can be seen, no structures or trees or growth, only an undulating sea of gray, lifeless dust without definition, without end, as if even the sky has gone and only a dusky, glowering light lingers threatening to darken, and as I stare, believing and without shock, I realize that is only a dream, only a dream after all, I'm waking up now, it's fading, has faded, more nightmare than dream—

More nightmare than the one into which I waken. Room light now. Clock: 7:46. Clock my enemy. If time has meaning. Does it?

I stand up, stand up and look down on my crumpled, damp clothes and then realize that I am sweating again. But no longer chilled. I take them off, all of them, and put on another suit, without thought or selection. And without showering. First morning in years. Since childhood probably. Then into the bathroom where I confront my own countenance: flesh pale, eyes blank, dark pockets under each, fine lines deep, deepened, four scratches distinct and fiery red. Atonement, Father. Expiation? Without forgiveness, yours, or mine or Lydia's or—

I throw cold water on my face, then look again. *In truth, Adam, I've begun to feel a trifle old*—How many years left? If any.

I turn away and urinate. *That's what the world is—yellow piss!*

In the bedroom again, I go to the window, gaze out. Windows across. A couple at breakfast; he reads paper. A woman drying gray hair. Boy and girl tussling over—what? toy? schoolbook? Melancholy has stolen over me. A pervasive gloom. As I gaze at palpable solid world. Like returning from—where? The dead? And looking at the familiar and discovering it unbearably strange, and aware now that it can never appear the same, or *be* the same, as it once had seemed because things are only what they seem, unreal and impalpable, and all dissolving and dwindling, invisibly crumbling into nothingness even as I stand stunned and staring.

The sickness of my body, the nausea, has moved deeper. Into my soul? Which I know now does not exist, Father. Into my heart, then? Where decay is already silently and inexorably at work.

Downstairs, the door buzzer sounds.

The day, then, had actually begun. As I turned from the window and crossed the bedroom, I felt no startlement, no terror—only a deepening sense of inevitability and ultimate doom. Despair seemed now, in some strange way, to sustain me as I went down the stairs.

The buzzing came again, insistent. It crossed my mind that Lydia might have taken a night flight from London to surprise me. How Lydia loved surprises! Or Donald might be returning. To report that Jenny had taken up with someone else in some go-go joint during the night? Or it could be Jenny.

An automatic caution stopped me at the door. "Yes?"

"Mr. Wyatt? It's me." Deep-throated woman's voice, familiar. "Yes?"

"*Me*. Minnie. I don't have no key now."

Minnie. Of course. But Minnie came only on Tuesday and Thursday, and hadn't I phoned her?

I glanced over my shoulder, across the littered room: the library door was tightly shut. Against a cat that did not exist. Or possibly, because it was so vivid in his mind, existed more horribly, fang and claw, than if it were now actually lying in wait for him. With an overpowering sense of absurdity and unreality, I opened the door.

The dark face—not brown but black, broad and matriarchal and gently stern—confronted me, head held straight with Minnie's customary pride and dignity. Her large eyes, great circles of white in darkness, regarded me, then traveled over my face—taking note of the scratches?—and returned, troubled, to meet my fixed unblinking gaze. "You goin' to work, your condition?"

"I'm over the worst of it," I said, knowing that in all probability the worst was yet to come.

Then I saw her peer over my shoulder into the living room. "Tk, tk, tk, you menfolk. Leaves you alone and look! Just look, will you?" But her scolding was tinged with womanly amusement and tolerance. "I been frettin' about you an' you jus' lucky I come, you jus' lucky."

She came toward me, barging gently through the door, shaking her head, and I stood aside, having no choice but to stand aside, and then she began to remove her hat, looking over the havoc as if she welcomed the challenge.

Yesterday on the telephone she had said, proudly, that she would not accept money for work not done. But she had come today, hadn't she? Why? She had changed her mind. Fair enough. What's pride compared to coin of the realm?

I reached for my wallet, which I must have mechanically transferred from the other suit when I changed, took it out, started counting out bills. "How much do I owe you for yesterday, Minnie?"

"Yestiddy?" Having stepped down from the foyer, she turned to stare—but she didn't fool me. Clever of her to try. "Mr. Wyatt, I told you—"

"I know what you told me. How much?"

"You jus' lemme tidy up this here—"

"How much, Minnie?"

Her eyes opened wider then, she frowned, and her head tilted to one side. "Mr. Wyatt, you ask me, you got a fever. You got feverish eyes. Mrs. wouldn't want you—"

But she stopped—possibly because she saw my expression change. If it had changed it was because, over her shoulder, I had seen the library door open, slowly, not more than six inches.

Then Minnie swung about, puzzled. The door was no longer moving and Wilby did not appear, not even his face.

But his voice sounded—and this, too, seemed inevitable and ordained, part of the fixed and hopeless pattern of the day. "Who y'talkin' to out there?" His words slurred together. "Chrissake, what gives?"

I saw Minnie's back stiffen. But she did not move.

"I was only talking to the cat," I said.

Silence. Minnie, too, waited.

Then the door burst open, slammed against the wall with such violence that all the pictures, even Lydia's portrait over the fireplace, shook as if they might fall off the walls. Wilby appeared, barefoot, huge, swaggering and grinning. He wore his glasses. He placed his fists on his hips and set his legs apart, staring across the room.

"You lying bastard! Man, y'say somethin', I believe the opposite. This the cat? She don't look like no yellow cat. She looks like a black nigger bear to me."

Minnie gasped. I saw her shoulders lift. And I expected her to turn to me, questioning, even demanding. Instead, though, she said, in a whisper, "That . . . that's him." Then she was pointing at Wilby and crying, "That's him! He's the *one!*"

"Don' make s'much noise, nigger-bitch. Y'wanna wake me up all the way?"

She took several lumbering unfrightened steps toward him. "You did it. I'd know that face anywhere. Them glasses. I'm gonna call the police!" She whirled about then and faced me. "Mr. Wyatt, can I use your phone?"

"What did he do?" I asked, aware that anything was possible.

"What did he *do?*" Minnie, outraged, heaved her shoulders, grasping her purse. "He snatched my pocketbook, that's what he done! Thursday last, after work, I was on my way to the subway and he just bumped onto me so's I like to fell down and when I got righted aroun', he was gone and so was my pocketbook!" She shambled up the step. "That's reason I don' have my key, Mr. Wyatt. That why I had to ring the bell this morning."

"Thought I seen that ugly black face before," Wilby said. "Thought it was in a nightmare, beatin' a drum aroun' some fire'n Africa!"

Minnie snorted and picked up the telephone. "How I dial for them police, Mr. Wyatt?"

I was looking at Wilby, who was now slouching in the door frame. Waiting. Amused. Last Thursday—then how long before had he been watching, learning her pattern, planning? And all along I had been blaming Geoffrey for giving Wilby the key to the apartment.

"How do I dial it, Mr. Wyatt?"

"You don't," I said.

"But he's a thief. He oughtta be arrested. He—"

"The gentleman," I said, "is my guest."

Wilby sniggered.

Minnie studied me, bewildered at first, eyes wide. Then something else entered her face: a knowing, bitter cognizance of depravity and wickedness and the ways of man, forged in a corrupt Southern city or town and honed to a fine edge of perceptivity in the tenements of Harlem. She set down the telephone. She did not nod, but she did twist her head, for a final glance at Wilby, before she passed me and went to the door.

"Minnie. How much money was in your purse?"

The sadness left her face then, and her chin came up, the dark pupils of her eyes pinpointing in circles of intense white. "If you mean you're gonna pay me back what he *stole*"—and she paused—"there wasn't a single red penny in that pocketbook."

She went out and closed the door, softly. *I got her address in England. I never seen no woman love a man more.* But the fear of what Minnie might do now seemed remote, for after all I was helpless to prevent . . . anything. Whatever was to be, would be.

"Y'go for them niggers, dad? I only ask 'cause I know some of your best friends're dinges. Like whose ain't?"

What now? There was a faint smell in the room, at once sweet and rancid, as of crushed and rotting flowers, a smell that even the air-conditioner apparently could not remove completely. The stench of marijuana? Or of corruption itself?

"I askt about boogies, man. Your daughter marry one?" And when I did not reply: "No? 'Cause I feel sorry for anybody has steady diet white meat." Pause. "Me, I can say nigger to their faces, like you can't. 'Cause I slept with more'n you even spoke to." He hitched his belt up and plodded through the dining room as if he, too, shared my exhaustion and lassitude. "My gut's growlin'."

I followed—why?—and as he disappeared into the kitchen I wondered also why, this morning, he was no longer terrified of the cat. Had he exorcised that phantom of terror from his consciousness? How? By conscious rational thought, a return to reality? If so, was last night's seeming madness only the effect of drugs or pills, after all?

In the kitchen he was taking a container of milk from the refrigerator. "Your balls inna uproar this a.m., dad? Bugs you, don't it—what's comin' next?" He picked up a package of dry cereal from the cluttered, stained table, shook a huge amount into a bowl that still held the sodden dregs of some previous breakfast. "Hell, I lived my whole life like that." He sloshed the milk over the flakes, then picked up the sugar bowl in his hand and shook it, the grains falling to bowl, to table, to floor. "Y'feel like eatin' man, it's your house." He sat and began to scoop huge spoonfuls into his mouth, the milk dribbling onto his beard, and in a moment the kitchen filled with the sound of his self-absorbed slurping.

"If I did feel like eating," I said, "I don't now."

"Man, you are playing it cool *this* morning, click?"—and he spewed milk and cereal as he spoke through it.

But I was not playing now, I was only waiting. Because there was nothing else to do.

"My goddam jaw aches, y'know that, y'bastard?"

When he had consumed the last enormous bite, he lifted the bowl to his mouth, tilted it, drinking the milk down noisily. Then he looked up, as if surprised that I still stood there, and he removed his glasses.

"Y'know, you felt sorry for me last night, I feel sorry for you this morning. How's that grab you?"

I did not believe him.

"Sorry, man, sad, 'cause I can see what's goin' on behind them bloodshot eyes of yours."

"That should add to your kick," I said.

Wilby snorted a laugh, brows lifting. "You are with it now, you are . . . *with it*! An' y'got them bloodshot eyes open at last. Rough, ain't it? Real rough to see."

Yes.

"Y're gonna be late for that time clock, man."

"I'm not going to work today."

"That ain't wise." He tilted back on the chair and lit a cigarette. "Dad, that ain't wise. Y'want t'get docked?" He blew smoke, twirled his glasses in his hand. "An' y'want t'put up with our jolly company that much longer? Your choice. 'Cause I worked out a proposition for you this morning. A strictly business proposition."

"That," I said, "is what I've been waiting for ever since you came to the party."

"Oh, cool-cool. Only that's where you're mistook. I'm playin' this concerto strictly by ear now. Started out, we needed a pad. Started out, jus' another caper. Then that Jenny, she took a fancy-fancy t'your cock. An' y'kept bleatin' about the bread. Y'kept *insistin'* that was only reason we made this scene . . . so I decided t'give in t'you. Make y'happy. 'Cause that's the kinda lover I am, lover."

"How much? When? How? And how do I know you'll leave then?"

He shook his head. "Now you, y'got one of them legal, logical minds. Mine, mine's more biblical, y'might say." He threw back his head, closed his eyes. " 'If I have made gold my hope, or have said to the fine gold, thou art my confidence; if I rejoiced because my wealth was great, and because mine hand had gotten much—' " He broke off, eyes still closed.

" 'This also,' " I quoted, " 'were an iniquity to be punished by the judge.' "

Wilby opened his eyes, laughed. "Man, looks like you'n me went same Bible-school, click? Y'dig now, Mister Job?"

"You're the judge, I suppose."

"Click, man, click! I'm the judge and now I'm gonna lay it t'you. Gonna hit y'where y'live!" The legs of the chair came down with a sharp crack. "Right in the wallet-wallet—where y'keep your heart! Where y'keep your soul'n your heart, your core, your goddam life-blood!" I caught a glimpse in his eye of the same fanatical wildness that I had seen last night. "Only this time, Mister Job-man, we're goin' all the way, the whole route. And when I'm finished, you're gonna be broke. Flat. Crushed. An' then, man, y're gonna curse God. *Me.*"

Still, I felt no shock—and no longer even anticipated feeling it. "You're not God," I said. "You simply have delusions of sanity."

He leaped up. "Y're not gonna bug me today! I'm not nuts but before I'm done, y're gonna be!" He extended his hands. "Look! Not a scratch!" He shoved up one sleeve. "Not a goddam mark! I was dreamin' last night! Y'*knew* I was dreamin' but y'let me think—" He broke off, breathing hard, and clamped his dark glasses over his bleak angry eyes. "Now y'listen!" He stalked into the dining room. "*Listen*! Y'go that office yours, y'call that broker-bastard, Dow-Jones-Up You, tell him sell, man, sell!" He whirled about to face me over the dining room table. "Tell him send check, tell him old Phoebe'll pick up check personal, today, today, one hundred twenty thousand! The works, man, the works, click?"

"I suppose I bring it here, give it to you, properly endorsed, and then I am to assume you will leave."

"Pop, don't start outsmartin' yourself again. We been that route. Y'get that bread in your regular checkin' account, 'cause we're gonna keep this transaction strictly legal, kosher-kosher."

"That's going to be a trifle difficult."

Wilby laughed again, but it had a hollow sound. "Told you I'm playin' it by ear! I'll dope out somethin'. Gonna get Jenny-baby what she always wanted. Bread, it don't mean nothin' t'me. Green shit. But that Jenny, she keeps talkin' about Riviera. An' that's where she's goin'. Riviera, clothes, men—anything Jenny wants!" Then he came around the table, came closer, lowered his voice, pink lips grinning. "A cat's gotta take care of his sister, don't he?"

Sister. Wilby was quietly anticipating the surprise that I couldn't feel. Not shock or repugnance or disgust. I could only recall his pleading with her, saying that he had taught her everything, and her contempt for him, and his striking her and my suspicion then that his violence had been triggered by some obscure, perverted sexual jealousy. But it all seemed faraway, long ago. Besides, once you have all but drowned in the depths, you can't be astonished or confounded if the depths turn out to be fathomless.

But I did not want to disappoint Wilby. "Jenny told me she was your sister," I lied.

The grin flickered. Then faded. He made a sound in his throat and strode into the living room. "That bitch-bitch."

Feeling no slight throb of satisfaction, I followed again.

He was waiting for me, legs spread, arms dangling, head shot forward. "Y'made several big mistakes last night, man. Large. Like not finishin' the job when y'had the chance. Like not doin' what Jenny told you."

So he had been conscious lying there on the floor—conscious, listening, quivering inside, waiting for the next blow, or blows. What had he said once about enjoying being beaten up in the back room of a police station? What had he said, too, about his father's being too weak to punish him? Then, last night, had he experienced erotic pleasure in the anticipation of pain? Afterward Jenny had reviled me for not being man enough to give Wilby what he *wanted*. Depths— fathomless. But all part of some bizzare pattern that I might, even yesterday, have thought diseased, revolting, but, after all, rare. Now I was not even appalled.

"Well, pop," Wilby demanded, "why didn't y'do what Jenny told you?"

"Because," I said, lying again, "because I knew it was what you wanted."

When he didn't answer at once, I could only surmise the expression of bafflement in his eyes behind the glasses.

Then he said, "Lyin' again, ain't you? Y'couldn't do it 'cause y'felt sorry for me." He began to shout suddenly: "An' *that* is where y'made your *big* mistake, man! Y'think I give a shit y'wouldn't cooperate-copulate? Hell, I been turned down by *queens*! Real *queens*! Only nobody . . . *nobody's* gonna feel sorry for me. Click? *That*'s why I'm playin' for keeps today, dad. *That*'s why we're going the whole goddam route, pop!"

"Wilby," I said, "before I go, let's get one thing straight. Just one . . . I am not your father."

But I knew that this, too, was hopeless, and I felt the first prickling surprise: why had I tried to voice what I now knew so well—that Wilby was using me to avenge himself on a father who had failed him? Or possibly on a whole world which he believed had failed him. I went to the foyer, knowing that he would stop me.

"Pop—"

I halted at the door.

"Y'got one chance t'cop out."

I waited.

"One."

Still I waited.

"Turn around."

To hell with you.

"Turn *around,* I said!"

I stood there with my back to him.

And then I heard his barefoot approach behind me. "Suicide pact. You'n me. Now."

Slowly then I turned. He was not grinning. His glasses were off. His face was a mask: bleak, wretched. Had I ever seen such naked misery, hopelessness, on a human face? Yet the pity that had died in me early this morning remained quite dead.

"Both of us. Cop out." He reached into a hip pocket and flourished a sheet of paper, which he then unfolded. "My letter to you, man." Then, crumpling the paper in one hand, he struck a match with the other, touched it to the letter, and stood holding it by one corner as it burned. "Token of good faith." He stepped back and dropped the flaming page into the fireplace, where it turned to black ash. Then he tilted his head, the gleeful cruelty and challenge in his eyes again.

"You'n me—off the terrace. Splash-splash." Could he possibly be se-rious? Another melodramatic flourish? He himself might not really know whether he was serious or not. After all, it would end for him a life that, for all its kicks and capers, he found insignificant and full of terrors. And if he could bring me, in this final and irrefutable way, down to his level of meaninglessness and despair, that triumph would prove his principal point.

"How about it man? Before Jenny wakes up. Joke's on her this time—"

Even then I was unable to conjure up even a shadow of the horror and shock that I knew, distantly, that I should feel. Extinction: Wilby's crowning triumph? His own, mine, the world's. A certain warped logic here, too.

The gun. I had left it upstairs in the pocket of the suit I had taken off. How could I have forgotten it? To leave a gun in the apartment with this maniac!

I stepped down from the foyer and crossed to the stairway. How could I be sure he was a maniac? I ignored Wilby and climbed the stairs. How could I even be sure that insanity actually existed? I went into the bedroom, found the crumpled suit on the floor, still damp with last night's sweat, still redolent of the long night's series of sleep-ing and waking nightmares. Had all that been madness—or a revela-tion of reality? I took the gun from the pocket and the bullets from the other and stared down at my two hands holding these implements of death. What might once have seemed beyond imagining, now seemed—in a perishable and transitory world that no longer pos-sessed even the hard certainty of reality, reason, or significance—only the natural and necessary tools for death. But then what meaning, after all, did death possess? I slipped the gun into one pocket and the bullets into another, as before. When, instead, I should load the gun, step onto the balcony, take careful aim, and blast away. Why? To save one hundred and twenty thousand dollars? Would murder then be reasonable, justified—*sane*? I left the bedroom, closing the door.

On the balcony I was aware that Wilby had not moved.

"That's the other way," he said—and the taunting lilt had returned to his voice. "Y'forget y'had it, pop?"

I refused to reply, came down the stairs, and crossed the living room to the foyer. I opened the door.

And he shouted, "Listen man!"

I started out.

"What about the limey wife?"

I halted.

"Y're kinda forgettin' her, ain't you, man? Her and the Shakespearean daughter, Annie-Annie—"

Forgetting Lydia and Anne? Had I?

"It come t'me while y'was upstairs thinkin' 'bout finishin' me off—"

Without turning, I closed the door. The numbness held. Whatever canker was spewing whatever fresh poison through that already diseased mind, my walking out would not evade it.

"Y're listenin' now, ain't you?" His voice, streaked with malice and pleasure, approached. "Like this: y'get any ideas today, like tryin' t'save that bread—life savings, all that fettuccini—y'get any big strong manly ideas, lemme give you somethin' t'think about. *Her.* Her up there over the mantel. An' little Annie married t'that dinge up there Connecticut."

Then I turned. He was on the step, head cocked to one side. A suggestion of grin.

"They can't give me no life sentence, y'know—'cause up to now, up to right now anyways, I ain't killed nobody. That's a kick I'm savin' up." His voice softened, became a purr that was almost sensual. "Prison. State hospital. Two years, five, even ten—it don't matter t'me how long. Then—not you. *Her.* One of them two. You'll never know when, or which one, or *how.*"

My hand did not go into my pocket. I did not even feel the impulse—only a muted surprise that it should be so.

His eyes had turned dreamy, contemplative. "Only . . . not death maybe. Lotsa things worse'n death, I hear tell. Especially for chicks. Y'know me, man: I don't care how I get my kicks. Use your imagination. I'll use mine. Give me somethin' t'think 'bout in that cell—that padded cell y'got all fitted out for me in your mind, click? Give us *both* a way t'pass the time."

My hand was still on the knob, but I felt, finally, a clenching of the muscles in my right arm and shoulder and hand; then I was overwhelmed—*staggered*—by an impulse so stark and savage and absolute that, in the instant, I felt helpless, blinded, knowing that I was going to use the gun now, knowing that nothing could stop me.

Wilby, too, waited.

And in his grin, mocking but somehow empty, and in his pale eyes, sardonic but wretched, I saw into his mind. He wants to die. He has probably wanted to die for years. What better way than to drive me, by whatever scheme or threat or act, to do the rotten job for him? Not only to die at the hands of a male, but to know in the final moment that he has prevailed totally. Because if I kill him, letter in his pocket or not, I am finished. While my body strained with a feral instinct toward murder, my mind was illuminated with such brilliance that I could see the instant in all its aspects, see it whole.

My hand remained on the doorknob.

"An' who knows, lover—maybe by time I'm out, Shakespearean Anne'll have a kid y'wouldn't want t'see anything happen to. Kinda things I got in mind." Then he shook his head, slowly, as with sadness. "Warned you last night. No mercy."

He was goading me. Begging? But it was no good now. The instant had passed.

"Which are you now," I asked, "Satan or God?"

He smiled. "Both. 'Cause like I been tryin' t'explain, they're the same. Remember?"

I remembered. "I'll get the money and bring it back. If you don't get out then—"

"Yeh, man?" he asked lazily. "Yeh?"

"Then," I said, "you might get what you want."

I opened the door again. And then he leaped, his hand clawed my shoulder, talons sinking into flesh, breath close and foul, eyes glinting again. "Y'scared now, pop? Said I was scared last night! *You* scared now?"

The ends of his fingers seemed to crush bone. "Yes," I admitted, vaguely wondering why I was not more terrified, "yes. But not—" echoing my words of the early morning—"not nearly so scared as you are."

His grip fell away. He stood back, frowning, a flicker of bafflement and defeat in his eyes. And I wondered why I felt no triumph or satisfaction. He was breathing hard now and his arms dangled.

"Man," he said in a slow whisper, "man, you're gonna eat the ground. No mercy! You're . . . gonna eat shit."

I opened the door. "Don't forget to feed the cat," I said, and went into the corridor.

Behind me I heard him hurling the door open and then crying down the hall with fanatic ferocity, "You're gonna eat shit! All the days of your life! You're gonna curse the day you was born!"

I passed the elevator, hearing him bawl: "It's you or me now, dad! You or me!"

But his words were meaningless: hadn't I known this for some time now? As I descended the seven flights—one foot after the other in a mechanical unhurrying rhythm resounding in the stairwell—I could only wonder why I was not quaking with apprehension. The incredible viciousness of his threat sent no anger through me. Or even hate. How could this be? It was then that I felt fear. But it was in my mind only—a questioning: why *wasn't* I shaking and furious? There was fear of a kind in that cool thought. Had I myself lost touch with reality? Possibly I had, somewhere through the night, moved across that line that I had always thought of as distinct but which I now knew was wavering and obscure, the line that separated Wilby's mind from my own.

Geoffrey was not on duty at the door. Geoffrey who had not, after all, given Wilby the key. Geoffrey who, nevertheless, was trying to blackmail me. More irony. *All, all of a piece*—

After Terence had whistled me a cab, I climbed in, thanking him, giving the office address, performing mechanically all the ordinary habit-fixed actions of any ordinary day.

In the grip of a lethargy that amounted almost to apathy—shouldn't I make some effort to throw it off?—I sat there knowing what had driven Wilby to what he now planned: *not* my violence with the gun, *not* my repulsion of his perverted advances, but only the civilized and human weakness I had revealed and admitted. Pity—which might generally be considered decency. But in a world turned upside down—

I stared out the window. All those millions of people. Existence. All those millions of automatons moving on their habitual paths, blind and half alive. *I am the master of my fate*. Another of the foolish illusions—perhaps necessary to prop us up, carry us from day to day, year to year—but illusion nonetheless. And what comes when the illusion finally disintegrates? Why, then, of course, one accepts the insubstantiality, the absurdity of . . . everything.

I closed my eyes.

The taxi radio. Symphony, concerto, sonata, fugue? I had no idea. Music. Beautiful. Lydia's kind of music. The kind she always loved. And that I had failed to share with her. Why was I thinking of Lydia in the past tense? And why, in that remote world of more than twenty

years of living together, had I failed to share it with her? Because I
too had been one of those mechanical men, deaf and mute, senses too
absorbed in the moment's petty, delusive urgencies.

In my mind now I looked back on the brief and terrible impulse to
kill, only a matter of minutes ago. Heart hammering, blood pounding,
every juice of body pumping, with that hard brilliant clarity like fire
in my mind—in that instant by the door I had been totally alive. And
what did it prove? That I could only be fully alive now with the intent
to *kill* quivering in me? Another irony, perhaps. Auguring what? A
harbinger of hope: something in me then does remain alive? Or an
omen of some inevitable and ultimate disaster: only savagery can end
this dream?

I wanted a drink. If I was *hooked,* as Wilby put it, what possible
difference could that make, either? What, after all, was alcoholism
but just another way to get through—from nothingness to nothingness?

But having a drink at this time of day was not a part of the pattern
that I now seemed obliged to follow blindly. Like all those others
passing by out there. A pattern reflecting the worn and familiar one,
but with a difference: a knowledge now of its emptiness and futility.

The taxi stopped. I paid—calculating the tip as automatically as I
counted the money. I went inside.

The beatnik with the goatee was nowhere in sight this morning.
Looking around for him had also, apparently, become part of the
routine.

*Three thousand, hell. They'll wring him dry. Take pleasure in
wringing him dry.* You prophesied well, gentle Jewish oracle. But
how could even you have known on Monday, Mr. Ephron, that by
Wednesday morning any help you could offer would only carry me
closer to ultimate disaster? Would in fact seal the bargain with fate.
Limited by your knowledge of the ordinary criminal intelligence, how
could you have foretold that this particular criminal mind was capable of carrying his diabolism to levels beyond the personal and into
the mystical, mythical, legendary? *No mercy. All the days of your
life! You're gonna curse the day you was born!* Then how could any
amount of money—destruction on that superficial level—ever satisfy
the fanatical monster that gnaws away inside him and that he must
turn on others for reasons beyond his comprehension, or anyone's?

What then was the point of altering the day's routine to telephone

Vincent Harkness as soon as I sat behind my desk? What was the
point or hope?

"Adam, how are you? Long time no hear."

"Vincent, I'm selling out."

"Selling—"

"Everything. Today. At once."

"Oh now, look, Adam—I know the market's taken a terrible drub-
bing since May, but it has to recover and your holdings are all solid.
You're not in the high-fliers and glamour-issues where the speculat-
ing's been—"

"Vincent—"

"Johnson's largely responsible and now this damned airline
strike—"

"Vincent, I did not phone you to get a lecture on the current state
of the economy. I called you to instruct you to sell out, everything,
this morning."

"Well . . . I must say you're the last person in the world I expected to panic. Adam, do you realize the losses you'll have to take if
you sell at market today?"

"Losses. That's very funny."

"Well . . . if you have that sort of sense of humor, I suppose.
Most of my clients don't laugh at—"

"It *is* my money, isn't it?"

"Well . . . if you want to take that attitude—"

"And you *will* collect your commission, won't you?"

"My God, Adam!"

"Then kindly do as I tell you."

"Today?"

"Today."

"At market?"

"At market."

"Well . . . it's your loss."

"What isn't?"

"Adam, you don't even sound like yourself."

"When will I have the check?"

"You must know it takes four days—"

"I want it today."

"Today? But that's—"

"This afternoon. Before the banks close."

"Now you're being even more unreasonable. The SEC requires

that four days have to elapse between the date of trade and the settlement. Four *working* days. This is Wednesday; I could have the money for you Tuesday morning, possibly Monday—"

"God damn it, can't you understand? I have to have it today!"

"All *right*! This office will advance it on a straight loan basis and charge interest for the three days. That satisfy you?"

"I'll send my secretary to your office as soon as I hear from you. After lunch. Today."

"Adam, I honestly can't believe this is you."

"That makes two of us. Good-by."

On top of the stack of mail there was a *Memo from the Desk of* LEE GRAY: *No luck re Wilbur Birchard. Confirmed only that he not—repeat not—wanted by Selective Service. No Wilbur Birchard registered in any of fifty states. Columbus, Ohio, eliminated on all counts. Investigation continuing.*

Then I went through the mail because, normally, it was the first thing to do upon arriving. No letter from London. No reason, of course, to expect there might be. Yesterday's letter: *One reaches a time of life, I think, when the graceful and civilized thing to do is to demand less—*

The buzzer sounded. I touched Phoebe's button.

"Yes, Phoebe?"

"May I come in?"

I recalled yesterday morning. Or had it been on Monday that I had given her hell for following me into the office? "Yes, of course, Phoebe."

In only a moment she stood before me, a small tray in her hands. "I thought perhaps you hadn't eaten," she apologized. "You didn't look as if you had when you—" Then she broke off, staring at me. The scratches? My face? She placed the tray on the desk: a steaming container of black coffee and a crisp-looking Danish pastry.

"Well, Phoebe?" And even though I remembered now that my suspicions of her had been only delusions, my voice sounded empty. "Well?" At least, though, I was beyond the point of suspecting everyone, wasn't I? Some improvement, wasn't it?

"Mr. Ephron of the District Attorney's office called before you came in." She was consulting some notes scribbled on her stenographer's notebook—possibly to keep from looking into my face. "He only wanted to report that he's had no luck whatever getting information on that name you gave him yesterday."

"Thank you, Phoebe."

About wanting to lie down with you. Well, it is what I've always wanted— I allowed my eyes to drift down her body: softly curved under the thin dress, rich with maturity but still youthful, legs slim but rounded. And I could not imagine sleeping with her—or wishing to. No temptation whatever, Father. And isn't it better to feel no temptations than to spend a lifetime fighting them? Isn't that some sort of civilized ideal—and therefore itself only an illusion? Wasn't it more likely that I did not desire her, or Jenny, or anyone, because I was now incapable of desire, or of passion? As Jenny had accused, as Wilby had all along hoped.

I became conscious of the silence then. I looked up into her face: quiet and also waiting, eyes questioning and nakedly anxious.

"Also, here's something." She extended a sheet of paper across the desk. "You scribbled the first two lines down on some notepaper yesterday. I thought perhaps you were trying to remember the rest of it."

> *All, all of a piece throughout!*
> *Thy Chase had a Beast in View;*
> *Thy Wars brought nothing about;*
> *Thy Lovers were all untrue.*

When I looked up again, she smiled, faintly. "I get songs in my head sometime. I guess everyone does. And it seems so important to—" The smile faltered. "Anyway, I was never much on poetry, but a nice man at the Public Library helped me and I found it just before they closed last night. It sounds awful till you get to the end."

I read:

> *'Tis well an Old Age is out,*
> *And time to begin a New.*

> –JOHN DRYDEN, 1631–1700

Yesterday those lines had held so much significance; they had summed up the world, hadn't they? In that frenzied time of despondency. But now they struck me as only superficial: what difference did it make if the world was corrupt when even the concept of corruption had no meaning?

"Thank you, Phoebe." It was the best I could do. Distantly aware that I owed her not only gratitude but an apology, it seemed scarcely worth expressing either.

"Adam—" she said, and then corrected herself. "Mr. Wyatt, I'm going down now to buy you a necktie. If you don't want to take calls, I'll speak to whoever's on the switchboard and—"

Necktie? My hand went to my collar. I saw Phoebe turn away—to keep from looking again? I had come to the office without a necktie.

At the door she said, "And I'll get an electric razor, too—unless you planned to go to the barber."

My hand did not lift to my chin and face. I had actually stood in front of the mirror and looked at my face this morning. And I had not shaved.

Something faltered, deep inside—like a motor that, purring with precision and confidence, suddenly begins to stutter and fail. A low-keyed panic took over, quiet and appalling.

At that moment the door opened.

Henry stood in it. He glanced from Phoebe to me, then back again.

Without looking at Henry, troubled eyes averted, Phoebe said, "Excuse me," and as Henry stepped aside, she hurried from the office.

No tie. No shave. Was it possible then that I had been pushed over the emotional brink that had come waveringly into focus for me several times before? Possible that I had already gone over without even being aware of it? That all the calm certainty of the morning had been itself only a symptom, like moving completely outside myself last night and watching while I almost committed murder?

Henry had begun to pace, running his hand over his head in the familiar gesture that invariably betrayed his feelings. Finally, still walking up and down, he said, "I hear you blew the Corbin case yesterday. Really *blew* it!"

"I was fairly certain you'd hear of it." My voice sounded oddly normal and composed. "I was pretty sure our loyal Mr. Gray would delight in giving you what a friend of mine calls *the full report*."

He stopped at the far end of office. "Adam, I can't get it through my head. Did you actually stand up there and tell a reputable physician, a *witness,* to go fuck an ostrich in Central Park?"

"If Mr. Gray quoted those words, I'm sure you can rely on his accuracy."

"Good God! And you canceled out with Arnold yesterday."

"I didn't make the appointment. So you've been discussing me with Arnold, too? I trust you described my symptoms as accurately as Mr. Gray would have."

Henry advanced. "Dammit, Adam, the truth is I don't like those symptoms—which, yes, I damn well *did* try to describe to Arnold Wilder, who is not only a doctor but our mutual and loving friend! Agreed?"

"I don't need a doctor." But was it true?

"And what the sweet bloody hell is going on with Harkness?"

"You've been a busy little fellow this morning, haven't you? How did you know about Harkness? Did Phoebe listen in on my call? Did you ask Phoebe to—"

"Phoebe, *hell!*" Henry growled. He was standing across the desk from me. "Vincent called me. *Reported* you're liquidating your investments. Taking ridiculous losses. He thought maybe I could talk some sense—"

"If he doesn't do as I've instructed—"

Henry towered above me. "Adam, what's up? And you're only wasting time to tell me it's none of my business. It became my business yesterday afternoon when you involved the firm in a possible slander suit and in unethical behavior that will be the talk of the legal community."

"You're not addressing a jury. That's a lovely word. Unethical. It rolls on the tongue."

"Adam, *listen* to me!" He strode away. "If it's dough, alimony for Charlene's free spirit keeps me pretty strapped, but I could raise—"

"As a matter of fact, it *is* dough. Referred to as bread in some circles. Not squares, circles."

Across the room, a look came into his eyes; bafflement, skepticism, concern. "How much?"

"Exactly as much as I have. Give or take a thousand or two."

"I see. You know, you had me frightened yesterday. This morning"—and he was moving to the desk again, frowning—"this morning I'm terrified."

"Of what?" The calmness was so great that even I could scarcely hear the words. "Of what, Henry?"

Very quietly, gently: "Look at you. You've aged ten years. No tie. No shave. You sit there like a goddamned glacier. If you want the truth, I think you're cracking up."

I hit him. The wildness exploded in me again, like a bomb going off inside. And I was standing up, my arm stretched out, and I knew that I had struck only after I saw and heard the blow. It caught him sharply on his pointed chin and I saw disbelief flash into his eyes as he staggered backward. Then, after what seemed a long time, he groped behind him and sank onto the leather couch, hand to his chin. He moved his jaw from side to side, then took out a folded handkerchief and dabbed at his mouth. But there was no blood. Thank God, thank someone, anyone, there was no blood, oh God he must be right, I must be cracking up, he's right, only thank God there's no blood—

"Now that," Henry said, "that is more like it. Friend, you had me scared."

And I knew he had worked—as Wilby had, as Jenny had—to stir this wildness that was now churning all through me again. Had worked to trigger it, but for different reasons.

"I'll say it again and I think now you'll agree: I think you're at least very close to a nervous breakdown, Adam. And I'm not going to stand by and see it happen. Not without a fight."

And that did it. Suddenly I was weeping. I could feel the tears on my cheeks, blinding my eyes, and I felt a shuddering eruption of relief as I sank back into the chair and listened to the low gasps as they turned into sobs that wracked my body. He was right, he knew, I knew, I was beyond help. Wilby had won, it was over. I lowered my head to my arms on the desk and gave in entirely. Wilby had licked me and I hadn't known it, hadn't even recognized it, had been too cowardly to acknowledge it. Sick as he was, he had brought me to his level, lower, and now I had gone under first.

I sensed rather than heard Henry approaching, and could scarcely hear his words over the sobbing. "Adam, get hold of yourself!" But the words meant nothing because I was helpless, shaking all over. "Adam, for God's sake!" But it was gibberish above me. "No, damn it, for your *own* sake, I'm telling you, you've got to get hold," and now I heard the words clearly because the sobs were subsiding slightly. "I'm going to get you the best help I can, but it's up to you," and the voice, very close now, sounded harsh. "It's up to you in the final showdown, it always is," and I felt his hand on my shoulder, "Everybody needs help some time or other, it's nothing to be ashamed of—" and the hand was clutching my shoulder, shaking it, "Dammit, Adam, listen, you've got to stop feeling sorry for yourself!"

And the terror receded. It did not drain out, it remained, oh God, it remained, seething and black, but I felt a hot denial rise like bitter gall in my throat, felt anger quivering deeper in me again—the first anger because I had not struck him in rage, only in alarm, in panic at his words, as he had intended—and I lifted my head. The surface of the desk was wet and the sheet of paper Phoebe had typed was damp and glistening, the words blackened and stark: *All, all of a piece*—

Henry's face was close over the desk and, long arm extended, he still held my shoulder. "Well?" he challenged. "*Well?*"

The denial went cold in me. Died. Is that what I had been doing? Feeling sorry for myself? What I had accused Wilby of.

"After all," Henry was saying then, withdrawing his hand, "after all, Adam, law's based on the assumption of individual responsibility, as you know." He straightened. "It's your job to keep yourself on the track, that's all. Agreed?"

It was then that I knew I was going to tell him. There was something in his face, his manner, his voice, something so strong and reassuring and concerned, that I could only wonder why I had not confided in him before.

"Agreed," I said. "Sit down, Henry. Sit down and I'll try to tell you what's happened." Then I corrected myself. "What's happening."

He slumped into the chair, one hand rubbing at his chin, and his eyes narrowed in a listening attitude that, I realized, was totally unself-conscious on his part yet generated a certain calm confidence.

I began with Sunday night and, possibly confusing the sequence of events from time to time because my mind was not so quick and precise as it normally was and also because some of the events tended to run together in my memory, I described what had occurred. I tried to give Henry a picture of Jenny and Wilby, finding it difficult to make Wilby's personality clear because my own attitude toward him, now, had become even more ambivalent. I concentrated hard on leaving out nothing of significance, knowing that I was almost certainly doing so. I described the sex episodes without giving myself the benefit of any doubt or evasion, no excuse of hate and fury masking lust, and moved on to the threat of second-degree rape charges, Wilby's two propositions that, if accepted, might have altered the picture— homosexual love-making and the suicide pact—and tried to trace last night's madness, both mine and Wilby's, but without the nightmares that, after all, had significance, if any, only to me, and then, with a tightening and coldness of mind and body, told him of Wilby's climactic threat to Lydia and Anne. My own personal confusions, despondencies and conclusions I left to Henry's imagination.

When I had finished and Henry said nothing—he had not moved a muscle or blinked an eye—I felt that oppressive weight lift very slightly, as if, in the simple voicing and exposing, a certain purging had begun.

Finally he spoke. "Eat your breakfast." And as I stared at the pastry and the coffee container: "How long since you ate a meal?"

It was a simple question—but I could not answer it. And then, as if his words had triggered it, hunger struck. Such a gnawing terrible emptiness and weakness and need that I picked up the pastry and tore into it like a man shipwrecked on some desert island finally being offered meat. I drank the coffee and consumed the bun, relishing and savoring every separate taste and drop and crumb. And then realized that I was still ravenous.

"Questions?" Henry asked softly.

I nodded.

He stood up and now began to walk again, in slow long strides, his tone gentle, his questions on target, point by point, as he led me back over the terrain, clarifying time and sequence and event. He was particularly interested in the complex relationship between Wilby and Jenny. Did I believe they were brother and sister? I was inclined to, but I could never be sure. And what of Jenny's age? Could I be legally culpable? I did not know. Was I certain narcotics had been used? Yes. And what of the three thousand dollars? Had I paid it in cash and, if so, did I have at least a cash-check to substantiate my claim? Yes.

Then, when he seemed reasonably satisfied that he had the whole picture, he stopped walking and said, "Birchard's not the name. The girl lied. We're wasting time in that area."

Of course. Obvious. Transparent. After all the other lies, to be gulled by this one. To waste all that energy and time—

"You're right," I said. "I guess I had to grab any straws I could find."

He had been standing straight, legs apart, hand to chin. Now his hand lifted over his face, went flat-palmed over his heavy bald head. "Look. I'm not blaming you. Nobody can *blame* you." He stepped closer, lowering his tone. "You damned fool, you. To try to play it out alone. You poor goddamned beat-up fool."

Pity? Wilby hated it. Yet demanded it. And Henry was right: I *had* been pitying myself. But *his* compassion now was like a healing balm. Something in me seemed, at least momentarily, restored. And I was grateful.

Suddenly he was walking again, his tone changing. "Those god-damned perverts. They keep trying to convince us all they're not sick. I'm up to here with it myself. Hell, pretty soon they'll have the whole world convinced. It's already respectable, even chic in some quarters. Until they admit they're psychologically maimed, and dangerous, until we all admit that basic fact—hell, we're almost as sick and dangerous as they are for playing along." I let him talk, knowing that behind his words he was thinking of something else, exploring practical or possible solutions. "I've always been willing to concede the private acts of consenting adults should be beyond the law. But when I hear something like this—and when I read some of the other things these perverts are capable of—I'm damned if it makes sense to let them run around loose! And why the hell do they always feel it's necessary to corrupt as many others as they can to prove their point? They're a race of *missionaries,* the whole lot of them. I hope you broke his jaw when he propositioned you!"

My confidence withered. Was that a question? I felt a jolt of fury, for which I was vaguely grateful—proof of returning life? "If I had socked him, I would have told you. If anything else, I also would have told you."

He stopped striding, hesitated. Then: "Adam, I've known you for twenty-five years. It would never occur to me to ask that question." He came closer. "But since you brought it up, let's start there. You *assumed* I meant something I didn't intend at all. Probably out of some sort of guilt over the girl. You've been *assuming* a lot of things lately. Agreed? You keep on making those assumptions—world's against you, friends plotting behind your back, doorman trying to blackmail you, secretary giving *reports* to your partner—you keep on *assuming* and acting on those assumptions and, friend, it's not going to matter whether you can pull yourself out of this hole or not. Because by the time you do, *if* you do, you won't be you. You'll just be a shell. Or worse. Lydia will come home and she won't even know you."

Lydia. Lydia and Henry. The hollowness came back. He *would* think of Lydia.

"Do you understand what I'm saying, Adam?"

I understood. And more than he had said. But the fear shouldered out the suspicion in my mind: did he imagine I wasn't aware of the brink, the gaping void?

Abruptly he growled, "Listen! Let's the two of us go up there and knock the shit out of the little cocksucker right now!"

I said nothing. But I comprehended the impulse, the irrational savagery. All I could do now was to sit and wait for Henry's reason to reassert itself, aware though that his outrage was in itself natural and good. Good?

Henry heaved an audible sigh. "Adam, it's out of the question to pay over the money—however he plans you do it. The only hope there, anyway, is that it'll send him off on another caper and he'll forget you. You think that's what *will* happen?"

It's you or me now, dad! You or me!

"I don't know," I said. "But I can't think of any other . . . *assumption* to work on. Can you?"

"You don't even have the right. That money's as much Lydia's as yours, no matter who actually earned it. And you can't pay out her own money to keep her from being hurt, or even in the hope of protecting her life, unless she can share the decision."

Lydia again. Always Lydia. The hollowness deepened. What does he care if Lydia finds out? He knows it would spell the end for Lydia and me. Then—

"Adam, if I were your attorney, I'd have to advise you that the only conceivable way is Ephron's. Sign the damned complaint, throw them both behind bars and take the unpleasant consequences."

Would that spare Lydia? Could he do that to Lydia? Not if he loved her. Not if he was thinking of Lydia instead of himself!

"You're going to make sure Lydia finds out, aren't you?"

Henry's face stiffened. "Watch it, Adam—"

"That's why I didn't tell you before. I knew what you'd advise."

"Hold it now, hold it. There you go again—"

"I shouldn't have told you now—"

He gritted his teeth. "*Christ!*"

I stood up. "If you take it on yourself to phone London—"

"Shut up and *listen!*" His voice low and gruff. "Listen now! All right, you want it, you'll get it. You made a certain accusation yesterday. I understand now how you could get into such a state of mind. *But* . . . but you're making it again. *Now* by God you're going to get the truth and I hope you can take it!"

He paused and my mind retreated, in panic: no, no more truth, I don't want it, I *can't* take it.

"There's nothing between Lydia and me. Nothing. Has never been. Not so much as a glance, a touch—*nothing.*"

He waited, as if to see whether I believed him. Did I?

"Nothing," he went on quietly, "on *her* part. Why the hell do you think I couldn't be true to Charlene? I couldn't stand to see the two women in the same room together." Then his tone hardened again. "Yes, you sonofabitch, I love Lydia. Have for years. Even before you two were married."

So I *had* been right! My suspicions had *not* been delusions!

"Sometimes I've loved her so much, wanted her so much that I've been sick with it. Charlene didn't know and Lydia doesn't know. I've made damned *sure* she doesn't know."

There was relief in knowing that I had not imagined it. At the same time my resentment washed away, turned to compassion: imagine loving Lydia and not having her!

"Lydia knows," I said. And Henry lifted his shaggy brows. *Oh Henry—Henry's the kind of man, I'm afraid, who wants what he can't have and can't be happy with what he can have—* "She's known for some time."

An expression of defeat and sadness entered Henry's eyes. "Well," he said, "now, so do you." Then almost angrily: "You had to kick those ashes yesterday, didn't you? I've been scorched in the fire ever since. Two hours sleep last night!" He took a long single step. "And if I thought I had a chance, even the slightest shadow of a—" But he stopped and shook his head, once. "No, damn it, I wouldn't. Believe that or not, you poor beat-up bastard. I'm on your side. I don't want to see Lydia hurt any more than you do because I love her but I don't want to see you go under, either, because, damn it, I love you, too."

Then he hesitated an instant and whirled away, stood staring out the window.

Believe him? How could I not believe him? I sat down. Was I going to burst into tears again? But no self-pity this time. Or even compassion for Henry. My anguish now, I knew, sprang from an intense knowledge of the moment: that Henry did love me, as I loved him, had always loved him, and that if it had not been for this weird and unlikely thing that had happened, neither of us might ever have spoken or acknowledged that fundamental fact. And our friendship was unlike any that Wilby was capable of imagining: decent and untarnished. Even the embarrassment and self-consciousness between us now was probably, I realized, due to the corroding corruption that Wilby and his kind imposed cynically on any relationship between two men. And there was sadness in this thought, and loss: why should we go on living from day to day, year after year, without ever really exploring or expressing these deep and valid and innocent feelings?

All I could say, even then, was, "Sorry, Hank."

Slowly he turned from the window. Grinned. "Christ, nobody's called me Hank in years. Charlene didn't think it was sufficiently dignified, remember?"

I nodded, remembering: *If Hank's willing to go along with her, I suppose it won't really hurt us to. But I do feel a trifle sorry for him at times, don't you?* And with Lydia's kind words echoing in my mind, I discovered that the hollowness inside had gone.

"All right," Henry said, "all right. Let's say we play it your way. You pay him off. Agreed? Now, to cover, you'll have to raise some dough, fast." He snapped his fingers, moved, picked up my phone. "Phoebe, it's Mr. Brant. Would you step down to my office and ask Louise to make an appointment with Dr. Crittenden for lunch today." He looked at his watch. "One o'clock. Give him time to get into the city. My usual place. . . . Thank you." He replaced the phone and stood frowning. "Now. He cleans you out. Will that be enough for him? Seems we're both missing the main point here, getting mixed up in our own past history. This . . . character hates you, that's clear. Thousands of reasons. You made it, honest man, he hasn't been able to corrupt you, he gets you confused with his own father, you symbolize everything he imagines ever hurt him—now, what makes you think he'll take the money and just fly away? How do we know he won't carry out those threats anyway, especially if he's as far off beam as you think he is?"

It was the question that I had not yet faced. Even in that savage instant when I had been tempted to kill, the threat had not quite penetrated, in all its cruel and horrible implications: *Use your imagination, I'll use mine.*

"If you don't warn Lydia—and Anne, too, of course—either one of them could be a sitting duck. You won't have a second's peace the rest of your life. You'll die a thousand deaths every time you leave Anne in the country, every time Lydia goes marketing, or to the hairdresser's, or to a concert."

The idea—this possible next step in a mind as illogical and warped as Wilby's—had not occurred to me. A measure, again, of my own derangement? *You're gonna eat shit! All the days of your life!* Henry was right.

"Well?" Henry asked.

"Maybe that's the chance I'll have to take," I said.

"Without warning Lydia?"

"I don't know!" I heard the sharp anger. "I don't *know!*"

Henry crashed his fist into his palm. "Sick or not, he doesn't deserve to live in a civilized world! Society can't allow it. It's a luxury we damn well can't afford!" Then he lowered his voice and stared at me, eyes brooding but quiet. "There's only one way. Kill him. Both of them if necessary."

"There's one other." It had come to me even as I spoke: a reasonable solution that my clogged and groping mind had not yet explored.

"Yes, Adam?"

"Get him away from the apartment on some pretext or other—"

"Yes?"

"And, in front of witnesses—"

"Yes?"

"Force him to kill me."

"Adam, for God's sake—"

"Why the hell didn't I think of it before?"

"Adam, listen! What you—"

"I wouldn't even have to pay over the money."

There was no excitement in me, but a kind of release: pushed to extremes, one makes use of extremes. Quite simple and logical.

"Adam, face it: your damned mind is still not working." What did he mean? Why couldn't he see it? "Swing away if you have to, but you're making assumptions again, and dangerous ones. Number one: that he would be arrested, tried, convicted, and executed. You have more faith in law and justice than I do if you think all that's a certainty. If it's not a certainty, what would happen to Anne and Lydia then?"

I shook my head. "It's strictly between him and me," I explained. "Anything he'd do to Lydia or Anne would only be to make *me* suffer, you see. And how can *I* suffer if he's already killed me?" That was simple enough, wasn't it? Any fool could comprehend *that*.

But Henry's fists were on the desk; he was leaning on them, shoul-

ders hunched. "Assumption *number two:* that Lydia could be saved
if you were dead. You're not thinking of Lydia, Adam!"

Not thinking of Lydia? Why else would I do it? In that moment of
wild confusion I had the impression that I was talking to a man who
had lost his reason.

"*Number three:* what about that love note he burned up? You
think he hasn't written another one by now? If your mind were working properly, Adam, you'd know you couldn't put Lydia through that.
That's probably the one thing that could conceivably be worse than
your death—living the rest of her life with that doubt about what you
were. Hell, that could be worse than death for *any* woman!"

The logic and certainty in my mind fragmented. I closed my eyes
and varicolored, odd-shaped bits and pieces, as of a jigsaw puzzle,
moved against my lids, refusing to settle into a pattern. Then they
blurred, lost shape and color, and I stared into blankness.

"The thing I can't comprehend," Henry's voice was saying, "is how
that guy can understand you, or anyone, well enough to do this. But
get that idea out of your mind, Adam. Agreed?"

"Agreed." It was a desolate sound in my ears.

"Adam, I'm no help, am I?" His tone reflected his gloom and I
longed to be able to say, *Yes, Henry, you are a help, have been, are,
because you have forced me to recognize that every decision and
thought from here on must be appraised ruthlessly and coldly in the
light of my distraught and possibly unbalanced intelligence.* But he
snapped his fingers again and went on, "Listen. To deal with a mind
like this, we need someone who—well, I've one more idea. Far-
fetched, maybe, but hell, what isn't today? There's a private investigator I know of, never met him, not one of the reasonably respectable
ones we might use for a legit investigation. But he can operate—for a
price, of course—inside or outside the law. I think his office is somewhere in the neighborhood. Adam, believe me, I wouldn't suggest
anyone like Chenery if I wasn't as stymied as you are. You want me
to phone him?"

"Yes, Hank. Phone him."

He was reaching for the telephone when the buzzer sounded. Automatically I touched the button. "Yes?"

"Mr. Wyatt—Mr. Gray has Mr. Colin Welch in his office and
wants to know whether you'll see him now."

Henry was shaking his head. "Tell him you can't. I'll talk with—"

But I said, "Do you have the necktie and razor?"

"Ye-es—"

"Bring them in, please, as soon as Mr. Brant leaves, and tell Mr. Gray I'll talk with them in fifteen minutes." I pressed the button again and said to Henry, "What the hell am I going to do with myself until Harkness has the money?"

Henry nodded, started to the door, then stopped and turned. "You mentioned a gun. You didn't say where it is now."

"In my pocket."

"I ask because, a short while ago, you suggested doing something that struck me as . . . suicidal. Now you *listen*. You pull a stunt like that, you sonofabitch, and I'll never forgive you. Never. And neither will Lydia."

He stood with his eyes boring into mine. I had not considered it once. Not once.

I shook my head. "Not a chance, Hank," I said.

"And Adam—you've suffered enough for sleeping twice with a whore. You've paid for it. Lydia might not understand, but I do. So for God's sake, take off the sackcloth."

He went out.

My eye fell on the typed sheet of paper on the desk, its edges curled from the dampness of my tears. *All, all of a piece throughout* — Was it possible that *all* was too large and inclusive a word? That *throughout* was too sweeping and final? What of Henry? Of Phoebe?

She was placing an electric shaver on the desk now, and a narrow box which she opened, all in the same efficient motion.

"I hope you approve. It . . . it's the kind you seem to favor."

I gazed at the tie: an offering of love, a token. And, my heart twisting, I thought of her purse, the tranquillizers. *They help kill loneliness. A little, anyway.*

"It's perfect," I said. "Thank you, Phoebe."

She tried to smile. It didn't quite come off. "Do you need a mirror?"

"No, thank you. I think I can manage."

After she had gone, I opened the razor, and with it buzzing and vibrating in my hand as it moved over the stubble, I faced, calmly now, what had to be faced: that the spell of loss and cynicism and despair had somehow been cracked, if not broken, and now, more vulnerable to pain and terror, I had to some extent emerged from that limbo of numbness and apathy that had fallen over me like a pall through the night and morning. And now, for the first time since that moment of primitive instinct at the door when Wilby had spoken the words, the threat tore through my awakened mind: *Not you—her.* And horror struck. *Only . . . not death, maybe. Lotsa things worse'n death, I hear tell. Use your imagination.* And now my imagination flared with pictures so cruel and horrible, so packed with atrocity and bestial cruelty, that my heart jerked violently.

I stood up, yanking the razor cord, my other hand passing over my face automatically, while I stared across the office, where the sun from the windows fell in a brilliant blinding slash. For a moment I was certain that I was going to blank out. I fought the possibility, fought it with such intensity that I could feel tears of helplessness and fury scalding behind my eyes, tears which I refused to allow—no more self-pity, damn it, no more of Wilby's whining!—and then I felt the shaking begin, deep inside at first, and I forced a stiffness into my body so that the volcanic upheaval remained inside, contained.

A tap at the door and Lee Gray was inside: pipe spewing smoke, eyes friendly but cautious behind black-rimmed heavy glasses. "Good morning!" Then he frowned and took the pipe from between his teeth. "You ready for me?"

Ready? As ready as I'll ever be. No.

"Where's Welch?"

"Before he comes in, I wanted to—"

"I don't need any warnings—"

"Not warnings. I just wanted to ask how you were coming along on the Markham brief."

Markham brief?

"If you're having trouble, I'm sort of up on it all and I could lend a hand."

Henry has already talked to him. Henry has told him to play it cozy, be gentle.

"I'll ask when I need a hand."

He was leaning over the desk slightly, blowing the sweet-scented smoke into my face. "You don't want to see Mr. Welch. It's all under control anyway. We've had several long satisfactory conversations."

"Ask Mr. Welch in, please."

Lee Gray shrugged, straightened, clenched the pipe between his teeth, and turned to the door to call, "All right, Mr. Welch; we're ready now."

And Colin Welch entered. At once I saw that he was a changed man; there was a jauntiness in his manner, a confidence, even a certain buoyance, as he shook hands. I recalled—have to concentrate now, time will pass if you concentrate on what's happening here, now—the frightened, slightly shriveled man who had sat in that same chair two days ago. Colin Welch was now smoking also: a dark and large cigar which mixed an acrid stench with the sweetness of Lee Gray's pipe.

"Suppose you tell Mr. Wyatt the conclusions you've reached, Mr. Welch," Lee Gray said and drifted away to perch on a window sill.

"Well." Colin Welch cleared his throat. "Well—" and I watched the pencil-thin mustache leap above his moving mouth—"you see, on Monday when we talked, you said I was to tell the truth, only the truth, and that's what I've been thinking about ever since." Colin Welch sounded downright hearty! He even laughed, apparently at nothing. Then he said, "Say, you know something? Your forgot your tie."

This time my hand did not move. I saw the tie-box open on the desk. If only I could keep from shaking.

"I was about to change when you came in," I lied. I took out the tie, threw it around my neck, and tried to listen to Colin Welch, who sounded absolutely drunk with relief.

". . . so how could I stop? I mean to say, *why* should I even consider stopping the car when I didn't see anything or hear anything or feel anything?"

There was this terrific thump against the front of the car.

"Mr. Welch," I said, looping the tie, "you distinctly told me on Monday—"

"Mr. Gray and I looked at the street at the corner. It has chuckholes. What I felt was a bump—"

I'll never forget that sound as long as I live!

My hands were trembling so that I couldn't finish making the knot. I looked beyond Colin Welch to Lee Gray. Was I going to burst into laughter? Or tears? "I hate to remind you," I said, "since you're feeling so gay this morning, Mr. Welch, that—"

"You have to remember, Adam," Lee Gray said evenly, "that on Monday Mr. Welch was overwrought. As you have been. As you—"

"This does not concern me!" I placed my hands flatly on the desk surface, pressing down until I could feel pain climbing both arms. "We have to stick to the truth."

Truth. *Y'know what people believe, dad? What they want to believe.*

"I'm not lying!" Colin Welch protested, the elation ebbing from his manner. "Mr. Gray—"

Lee Gray stood up. "Of course you're not, Colin. You're remembering accurately, that's all—with perspective."

I suppose perspective's the word—about myself, about you, about us—

"How many vodkas had you had previous to the accident?" I asked, ignoring Lee Gray, pushing the enigma of Lydia from my mind.

Colin Welch was looking at Lee Gray, though—almost pleading. "I just forgot that the other day."

"And you remembered when Mr. Gray reminded you, because he had come across some evidence."

"Look here, I'm not on trial here. You're supposed to be my attorney. Not some kind of judge."

"Yes," Lee Gray said then, "what right have you to judge this man?"

I sat back. It was a good question. All the accumulated guilt returned, intense and enervating and destructive.

"Congratulations," I said to Lee Gray.

"I'm afraid I don't quite understand that, Adam."

"I think you do."

Why should I spell it out? That Colin Welch was also open to verbal influence—enough to change his testimony, distort his memory! Why should I bother? What was the struggle all about anyway? Truth. Wilby was right. Law, truth, the nature of man—right! And to hell with it.

The smoke whirled in clouds, filling my nostrils, filling my head, reaching into my stomach; nausea took over.

"I think you should handle this," I said to Lee Gray, and heard the weariness, the numbed withdrawal in my tone. "I think you're better . . . equipped."

Colin Welch stood up, heaved a deep breath, blew smoke. "Well, I must admit that's a relief to *me!*"

Get out. Both of you. God damn it, get out!

"It was my suggestion in the first place," Lee Gray said, and I heard the scorn, the quiet polite hint that I was either getting old or suffering a nervous breakdown. So Henry had told him everything! Had left the office, had gone directly to this snide, unethical, shrewd boy and betrayed my confidence!

"Mr. Wyatt," Colin Welch said then, and his face and tone were serious, disturbed, "I believe it *would* be best because you confuse me. Mr. Gray doesn't. And, you see, the Mrs. seemed to lose her respect for me. I don't know whether I can explain this, really—or why I even should try. But . . . what she thinks is important to me. You can believe it or not, but I'm one of those men who loves his wife. And what she thinks of me is more important even than what I think of myself. And—well, I just wanted to say it. I don't know whether you can understand." He turned and walked out, with Lee Gray opening the door.

Then, over Colin Welch's shoulder, Lee Gray lifted his eyes, gave an elaborate confidential shrug of ridicule and puzzlement, as if to ask: now what do you make of *that*? Then he followed and closed the door.

And what did I make of it? That Colin Welch, for all his distasteful weakness and his eagerness to distort the truth to his own ends, was more conscious of what he was doing than I had thought. And that he knew his reason: his devotion to his wife. And that he was willing —no, desperate—to tell the lie and live with it. For her sake? For his own? Out of love? Then there was love, after all?

Well, what should I do? Tell the truth? About what, Anne? Oh yes—your virginity when you married. Or lack of it. Her lie to Glenn. *If I don't, it's the same as living a lie, isn't it?* Yes, Anne, but don't you see? You have to be willing to lie—in order to live at all. To survive. Don't you see, dear? You have to live a lie, too, if necessary—if the truth would wound someone you love. But what of the one you love? What if he, or she, would prefer the wound to the lie? In Lydia's case, not prefer—would demand, no matter how painful to herself. How is it that I have not glimpsed this different, this deeper, integrity in her until now?

The buzzer again.

"Yes, Phoebe?"

"Mr. Smith is calling. *Wilbur* Smith." The same Wilbur Smith who had phoned last evening to say his wife had survived the surgery as if it hadn't even taken place.

"Put him on."

Why should Wilby call now? But it came to me even before he spoke.

"Where's Jenny?"

"Jenny who?" I asked. "Jenny Smith or Jenny Birchard?"

"Birchard? Who?"

"Who's on first, Birchard's on second—"

Wilby snarled. "No time your goddam jokes! Jenny ain't in her room!"

"Plenty of time, Wilby," I told him breezily. "Hours to go before I get the bread."

"Y'gonna play it that way, huh? Well, pop, I ain't in no playin' mood, so get off that kick'n start talkin'. Like fast, man!"

I heard the desperation straining his voice. *Jenny-baby, it's all for you. Everything I'm doing. All for you.* Was that how he knew how to get at me? His own feeling for Jenny?

"Y'there, man?" A whisper—with fright in it.

"I'm here." *Here, you bastard. Now it's your turn! Sweat!*

"Man, y'better talk! I mean *talk*!"

"Where do *you* think she might be?" I asked.

A growl. Then: "Y'get her arrested, pop, it's a big mistake. Large."

"What isn't?" A flicker of cruelty—and satisfaction. "Yes, she might be arrested."

"Y'sayin'—" But he stopped himself and I could hear him breathing. "Y'got her stashed away, dad? Want her for yourself?"

Warned you, pop: don't try t'come in between.

"That, too," I said, "is possible."

"You mother-fuckin' bastard!" He was screaming, screeching. "Y'get her back here, see, get her back! 'Cause I'm stayin', I'm stayin' right here till she comes!"

The satisfaction withered, turned to panic. "I'll have the money after lunch."

"Money? Money? Listen, man! I'm stayin'! I'm stayin' forever, y'don't get her back here!"

"Don't forget to feed the goddamned cat!" I heard myself shouting. I was standing, clutching the phone and bellowing. "Stay there'n go nuts all by yourself!"

I threw down the phone with a terrific clatter. And stood trembling violently. *If Satan also be divided against himself, how shall his kingdom stand?* A terrible triumph shook me: he was alone now, like me, and he was staring into the void.

Like me?

Then it occurred to me: Phoebe, suspicious, had listened. I

rounded the desk, fast, strode to the door, and was about to throw it open.

But I stopped myself. *You keep on assuming and acting on those assumptions and . . . you'll just be a shell. . . . Lydia won't even know you.* Hand on knob. *Had* she listened? I had to know!

No. I had to do what Henry had suggested: get hold. I released the knob and leaned against the door. What had I been trying to do? Drive Wilby all the way? Or indulge my own irrational rage and frustration? Which one of us had been edged closer?

Or were we now only two madmen screaming gibberish at each other over the telephone?

Slowly, stunned, I made it back to the desk. The shaking had subsided somewhat. Good omen or another false hope?

Uh . . . by the way, do I bring her back here?

I located Donald's phone number in my private directory, took the phone out of its cradle again, placed it on the desk, my hands surprisingly steady, and with one hand holding the leather book open—to memorize the number was beyond me—I dialed 9 and then the number.

And sat and waited, picking up the phone.

Waited while the distant buzzing repeated itself over and over at nerve-wracking intervals. Waited while my mind flashed pictures: Donald and Jenny in the apartment, staring together at the ringing phone and smiling, sipping brandy, perhaps in bed, probably in bed.

No answer. I swallowed down panic, felt it fluttering all through me. What if this is also an assumption?

I put down the phone and then repeated the procedure, this time dialing his office number from the address book. And sat wondering how my voice would sound, whether it was under control.

"Abbott, McCaslin, and Lynch."

I asked for Donald Abbott and heard a faint tremble behind the words, nothing extreme, only enough to alert me.

"Mr. Abbott's office." A pert bright voice.

"Mr. Abbott, please. Adam Wyatt calling."

"Oh, Mr. Wyatt. I'm sorry: Mr. Abbott isn't in the office today. He telephoned early to say he was ill. If it's urgent, I imagine you can reach him at home. Do you have the number?"

"It's . . . not urgent," I heard my voice say—and the tremble was now quite distinct. "Thank you."

"You're welcome, Mr. Wyatt."

I sat holding the humming phone. Not urgent. Hell no, not in the least urgent. Still, this *one* suspicion had not been imaginary! Not if Donald had stayed home. Small consolation.

Jenny. *Any old prick in a storm. Isn't that what you always taught me, Wilby?* What was Jenny, after all? A creature—amoral, floating through the world on sensation, without reason or will or thought. A body. A bundle of cells, chemical, worthless. Some of last night's despair returned: a quiet gripping sadness. The world was, after all, made up of Jennys, wasn't it? Ninety per cent, probably more. Uncaring, except for self. Worse: incapable of caring. Without even the *concept* of caring. Therefore innocent? His sister. Was even Wilby capable of some kind of love? Then what of Jenny? I had never heard her speak a kind word to him, had never heard a note of softness in her tone—only unveiled, blatant contempt. Innocent? Father had always maintained, *insisted,* that each human being was responsible for any single act, regardless of background or circumstance. The Christian ethic. Then Jenny, amoral, was not innocent. And who could say whether Wilby's love for her—if love was the proper word—might not be based on some need in him for that cruel and consistent derision, revulsion and hate? Perhaps he thrived on her hatred—as *my* hatred had stirred *her* lust.

I have to stop thinking. I must. I don't want to see these things. Cannot go on looking at them this way, or I'll return to that bleak empty world I discovered last night. I can feel myself edging closer to it, the more I learn and discover. The void. The truth? Is the void truth? *Y'gotta make sure y'don't start seein' what's real 'cause if y'ever start really seein' it—*

And only half an hour ago I had felt a healing begin. Or had imagined it.

I stood up. I had to know. I straightened the knot in my tie. Had to know, so would go to Donald's apartment. Only common sense. Reason. If Wilby won't get out, money or no, *without* Jenny, then only one solution: make sure Jenny returns. Make certain he leaves *with* Jenny. How? I went to the door. At least confirm the suspicion that she *is* with Donald.

The buzzer: abrasive, grating my raw nerves. By the time I reached across the desk to touch the button, I was quivering all over again.

"Yes, Phoebe?"

"Mr. Wyatt, there's a Mr. Chenery out here. He doesn't have an appointment, but he says Mr. Brant asked him to drop around as soon as it was convenient for him."

The private investigator. I took a breath, shallow and tight. "Send him in, please." Well, he hadn't wasted any time. Nor had Henry.

I retreated to my chair and as soon as I saw the man who entered, dabbing his forehead with a folded white handkerchief, I was certain I must have made a mistake, perhaps not heard the name correctly. This man was going to try to sell me insurance or to ask for a donation to a charity.

"Muggy, isn't it? Although not as humidified as yesterday." Humidified? His voice was gentle—just this side of inaudible. He extended a hand, which I shook—fleshless, weak, moist. After a faint but remote smile, he began to stroll around the office, examining it in some detail: a slender, rather small man in a pin-striped business suit, with thinning gray hair combed flat across a narrow skull. "I really don't like talking in offices, Mr. Wyatt. There are so many possibilities of being overheard. Are you with me?"

He stopped strolling and regarded me with courteous pale eyes that, behind rimless, almost invisible spectacles, held no slightest suggestion of curiosity or even interest.

"Do you mean you think someone might have a listening device hidden here?" I asked.

He held up a thin long-fingered hand. "Just precautionatory measures," he apologized. "Are you with me?"

Precautionatory measures! Oh hell yes, I was with him. Why not? I was either with him or I'd stepped through the looking glass, like the girl in the story. I was either with him or I had lost my senses entirely. I almost smiled. We went to the door. Passing Phoebe's desk, Chenery was discreetly silent.

I love your smile, darling. I love the way your lips curl up at the corners. Did I ever tell you? Yes, Lydia, you told me. But did I listen? Where was I when you told me?

In the elevator Chenery stared blandly ahead as if secretly pleased with life in general. And in the lobby he asked, "Would you care to have a drink?"

Oh Christ, would I care to have a drink? I'd care to have several drinks, a great many drinks! Hooked? To hell with being hooked or not hooked!

On the sidewalk Chenery said, "I prefer public places for private confrontations."

My mouth desert-dry, my whole body yearning for the calming effect of just one Scotch, just one, I said, "Let's walk," thinking that walking side by side was the best way to have a confrontation, after all. And wondering when I was going to start believing in the reality of this man. In the reality of anything ever again.

Chenery was relieved. "That's an excellent proposition." He fell into step beside me. "Truth is: I don't drink myself. My wife has a thing about it because her father was almost an alcoholic. No, he *was* an alcoholic. And drinking's not conducive to my business. Now. Mr. Brant filled me in on a few of the details. But like I told him, I prefer *not* to know too much. I do know those two have been shacked up there with you since—I believe he said Sunday p.m. last. And Mr. Brant mentioned there had been some threats made—I don't want to know what they are—but that you believe have some substantiality. Now the simplest solution, it almost always is, is to have one or both of them knocked off. Some of my men refuse to kill a woman, but I got a large staff. We could make it look like a gang killing. That way, police are more apt to overlook it. Although the girl's a fly in that particular ointment. *Daily News* makes a big thing of women getting croaked, as you know. Especially if she's sexy, and I gather she is. Now, there's another way. It costs more but sometimes it's worth it. Long haul, it's cleaner, too. We could have the bodies disposed of entirely. These are only suggestions, Mr. Wyatt. I want to do whatever *you* want me to do. He who pays the piper calls the tune. Are you with me?"

Fifth Avenue now. Sun shining. Crowds of people. Tourists in shirtsleeves, cameras strung around necks; women in bright, frilly hats, flowered dresses; children perspiring, asking questions, staring at the skyscrapers. And this pleasant mild-mannered man selling murder as if it were any other marketable commodity like the ones displayed in the elegant windows we were passing.

To kill. Simplest solution. As I had known all along, of course. But no rage or passion now colored my thoughts. Wilby wanted to die—hadn't I decided that? In some mysterious way I felt lulled by Chenery's voice. Wilby wanted to die, Jenny was no longer with him, that particular fly in that particular ointment now removed—

"Now in considering the alternatives, only you can weigh what it would cost against whatever he's blacking you for. If you want to know, I can give you the cost either way, without even asking what he's shaking you for. Now that's about as fair as a man can be, isn't it? Are you with me?"

Was I with him? With anyone? *Is reality real? Does it actually exist-exist?*

"Ah, Rockefeller Center," Chenery said, a note of pleasure distinct in his voice. "Would you believe I haven't been here in . . . well, since before the twins were born." Our walk had slowed to a stroll as we turned in and walked down the plaza where flowers bloomed down the center, and where, down either side, airline companies advertised exotic places with colored photographs in huge windows. "We could arrange that they didn't even know what hit them, or if you have any feelings about it, we could make sure they both knew who was giving them the shuffle just before they got it. And if you're hesitating because of that letter Mr. Brant mentioned, we can make sure we get that first."

"Mr. Chenery," I said—and my voice sounded weak while the longing for a drink became an ache—"Mr. Chenery, I don't want to have anyone killed." But was it, after all, true? Hadn't I realized, today, that it was the only way out now? . . . *two years, five, even ten—it don't matter to me how long—*

"Nobody wants anyone killed," he reassured me. "And I appreciate that most people have compunctions. But I've found from experience sometimes it's the only rational way."

We arrived at the stone railing above the area where, in winter, skaters performed on ice below and where, now, in summer, people sat at tables sipping cool drinks or eating. The colors in the sun were blinding. The dreamlike quality held me in a strange thrall. I remembered Lydia's face, touched with winter, looking down on the skaters.

What if this man is right? What if I pass up this chance?

"I don't mean to say there aren't other methods. We could rough him up, rough up both of them if that'd help. Anything from a few bruises and black eyes to scare hell out of them to a genuine going over or a permanent crippling. Anything in between you're able and willing to pay for."

I leaned against the stone, stared at the man. But his attention was on a small bright-cheeked boy leaning over the parapet, feet off the ground, shouting to his parents, "Look! It's a waterfall! Right in New York!"

Chenery's faint smile turned into a frown as he glanced at the parents. "People who don't take care of their children don't deserve them," he said.

"What else?" I demanded. "What other ideas?"

"Mr. Wyatt," Chenery said, shaking his head, "I don't think you realize. War is war."

It's all war, anyways, click, dad? Streets. Living rooms. Country clubs. Bedrooms.

Christ, hadn't I learned *anything*? What did it take to make me realize what everyone else seemed to take for granted? But what good would it do to have Wilby beaten? Sick bastard would enjoy it. And even if permanently crippled—my mind flinched—Wilby would find his own way.

I turned away. And over the entrance to a building, carved in stone, read: *Wisdom and knowledge shall be the stability of thy time.*

"There's one other road we could travel. Mr. Brant said there was no doubt about him being a pervert. That sets it up. You're in luck there."

Luck? *Luck?* Panic struck. I had to get away, get a drink.

"We get queers in all lines of business. Senators, judges, State Department, everywhere. That makes it simple. Set up the frame, get him arrested—"

"I could have had him *arrested* Sunday night!" I felt my body wobbling and the glare was murderous. "Didn't Mr. Brant *explain*? What do I accomplish by having him *arrested*?"

I moved away. Slowly. Weakly. He didn't understand. No one understood. Possibly even Henry did not believe, could not believe, that Wilby was capable of carrying out any threat, *any*! I began to walk. Where? Anywhere? Wilby was not only capable, but eager! *Y'know me, man: I don't care how I get my kicks.*

But Chenery was alongside again. "If you have any ideas of your own, Mr. Wyatt, I'm willing to listen. After all, way I see it, you're an innocent man and you have your constitutional rights."

It's too late. I'm walking along a perfectly ordinary familiar street I've walked many times before, but it's too late: I've already gone over the brink.

Y'didn't bring no cat in here an' y'didn't put somebody on my tail t'bug me? I slowed down. *Y'think I got what them doctors out there call delusions.* I halted.

"Yes, Mr. Wyatt?"

"Do you have men who can follow him?"

"Mr. Wyatt"—and Chenery sounded dismally disappointed, even personally injured—"Mr. Wyatt, you don't need my organization for that. Any detective agency in town—"

"Can you follow him?"

"Mr. Wyatt, people are looking. Of course I can—"

"I want him followed." But did I? If I shrank from murder, how could I try to drive him into psychosis? Did I even have the right? "And I want to make sure he *knows* he's being followed."

"Knows?"

"You heard me. Are you listening? Do you have men who look like police detectives? Do you have a fat man?"

"I got any kind of man you want. Let's walk along now. People will think we're controversial." And as we walked: "Mr. Wyatt, I can supply any kind of man you want. Any shape, size, color, nationality. And I have anything you might need, any time. Or one of your clients, maybe. Poison, dope, knock-out drops. Any kind of weapon you can name."

"Taxi!" I shouted and a blade turned over in my parched throat. "*Taxi!*"

"Calm down now, Mr. Wyatt. I'll handle everything. A taxi is an excellent idea. Cab!"

Three young men in apparently identical, tight, dark suits, walking arm in arm, came abreast of us, and as Chenery approached the curb, they brushed heedlessly past him, their delicate faces oblivious or contemptuously conscious of what they were doing. Their girlish laughter floated back to us.

"They'll run you off the street," Chenery said, and for the first time his polite voice was roughened by emotion. "They'll push you off the sidewalk."

A taxi stopped. When we were in it, I gave the driver the address and leaned back limply.

"It used to be those sexual deviators kept to themselves, mostly in the Village. Now they're up and down Madison and Fifth thicker than gray flannel suits." Chenery seemed to be talking to himself. "And there are certain bars and even hotels, some of the best—some that used to be called *men's bars*—where you can't even get a peaceful drink at the cocktail hour. They sound like birds getting ready to go south for the winter. I don't know what it's coming to, but what I can't figure is how there can be so many of them when we all know they can't propitiate! I got three sons and the first one that approaches one of *them*—" He did not finish the sentence, but there was no need. "Well," he asked, settling back, "where are we going now?"

"My apartment. Or the building, anyway. He was in there a short time ago. If he hasn't left already, I have an idea he'll be coming out soon. He has a beard, brown, and he's at least six feet tall, husky. Young. Wears way-out clothes—boots or sandals or maybe some fancy outfit, jacket with epaulets on the shoulders—and dark glasses most of the time. Remember: he must get wise to the fact that he's being followed but it can't be obvious, either. Whatever else the bastard is, he's bright. Are *you* with *me,* Mr. Chenery?"

"He who pays the piper—" Chenery was pleasantly relaxed again. "And what about the girl?"

"I'm not sure where she is now, but I have a pretty fair idea. She wears short skirts, kooky clothes, has black hair, long, and she might go out or come in with a man about my age. Heavy-set, lazy-looking, elegant. If you'll wait in the street, I'll find out whether she's inside. If she's not, you'll have to locate her."

After a silence, Chenery said, "Well, you seem to be percolating on all twelve cylinders now, don't you? What's the name?"

"Her first name's Jenny. He calls himself Wilby. That's as much as I know."

"That's pretty slim. You're asking a lot."

"I imagine I also am paying quite a lot."

"Now. No cause to be provocative, Mr. Wyatt. After all, you did get yourself into this fix, didn't you?"

Ain't it terrible now, how people always believe the worst—

"No hard feelings, Mr. Wyatt. I'm willing to do my uttermost." Then he was whispering, leaning close so that the driver could not hear. I could make out only a few words: ". . . not the full-rate . . . one queer more or less . . . die in gutter—"

"What?" I asked. "What?"

Chenery spoke in a slow precise whisper so that the driver could not hear: "I'm saying that I can give you a slow-acting poison you can feed him, maybe in a drink, and then get him out on the street. I'll charge you just what the stuff costs me, because like I say what's one queer more or less. Are you with me?"

Laughter threatened: wild, hysterical. But I choked it down. Knowing that if it threatened I was *not* in control, still teetering on the edge, *not* percolating on all twelve cylinders.

"Stop here," I said, and when the taxi did not slow down I cried, "Driver, *stop the cab!*"

Brakes shrieked. I felt myself being thrown forward and to one side as the cab swerved to the curb. Chenery muttered surprise and the driver cursed.

I opened the door. "The entrance is the first awning around the corner." I climbed out and started walking, wondering whether Wilby was watching from the terrace as I turned the corner.

Was I even now making a mistake? Perhaps the crucial one? Had I passed up my one best chance? *Way it is in the jungle, dad. Y'live in the jungle, y'gotta survive. Man, I could just's easy killed you.* If I knew now that it *was* a jungle, if I really believed it, why had I turned Chenery down? Why, even now, gun in pocket, did I still refuse to kill?

If only Geoffrey was not on duty. Or had it been Terence who had called my cab this morning? I could not remember. How many cylinders then?

"Good morning, Mr. Wyatt." No matter who had been on the front door this morning, it was Geoffrey now. Probably wondering what I was doing here this time of day. Yes, Geoffrey, I have broken the fixed pattern of my life. Twice in one week. Horrors.

He had followed me to the elevator. "Mr. Wyatt, I trust that you didn't take anything amiss that I might have said last night. If you know what I mean, sir."

I was inside the cubicle when I faced him. Was it conceivable that I *had* taken him amiss? After all, Wilby had not obtained the key from Geoffrey but from Minnie.

"I don't think so, Geoffrey," I said in a perfectly pleasant tone. "You expect me to pay you three hundred dollars a month. Blackmail."

"Blackmail?" His elongated English face looked longer than ever. "No, sir, that idea is as foreign to me as—"

"Blackmail, you bastard," I said, in precisely the same polite voice, as if I were only passing the time of day. "You don't have a sick wife. I doubt you have a wife at all. You're taking the main chance. No one can blame anyone for grabbing opportunities as they find them, can one?" I pressed the button: 6, not 7. "But I wouldn't give you the sweat off my balls if you were dying of thirst."

The door cut off my view of Geoffrey's startled face.

Here I was talking like Wilby again. Because he knew and I had learned—what? Reality? Was Chenery real? Like the guards at Buchenwald and Auschwitz going home after a hot day at the ovens to rock their fat little children to sleep. Was Geoffrey real? Geoffrey with the polite manner and the imaginary wife with the imaginary mental illness.

But what then of Henry, Phoebe?

The door slid open. Out of nowhere I felt momentary hope. I still had a chance. I walked along the hall. A chance? To push the stone to the top of the damned hill again, like the the the man in the Greek myth, the man condemned by the gods to keep rolling that stone up the steep hill, over and over, when each time, just before reaching the crest—and peace and rest—it rolled back down so that he was forced wearily and against all hope to begin all over again.

607. D. Abbott.

I buzzed. No answer. No music.

I could hear the buzzing as I leaned against the button, then recalled how, only last evening, I had kicked in this same door, breaking the lock or the frame or possibly both. I pushed against the doorpanel with my hand—and it swung slowly open. The buzzing still echoed in the quiet. Was I acting on still more assumptions, as Henry called them?

No. The floor of Donald's normally overtidy Victorian-looking living room was littered: overflowing ashtrays, cups with lip-smears, odd dishes, glasses of all sizes and kinds. And on the low marble-topped table with scrolled legs stood two open champagne bottles. My eyes traveled to the stairway. At the foot of it, lying in a heap on the floor, was a woman's dress, violently colored. My assumption this time had been valid.

"Donald!" It was not quite a shout as I slammed the door behind me. "Donald!"

I moved to the foyer step. Both bedroom doors off the balcony were closed. Silence, with only my voice echoing, then fading. I went to the foot of the stairs and called again.

I was halfway up the stairs when, very slowly, one door swung slowly open, and I came to a stop.

Donald's tousled head appeared first. "Oh, it's you." Pulling a robe around his heavy, soft body, he emerged without glancing back. "Well, well, don't bother to knock, come right in, as you did last night. Make yourself at home." He peered down on me and ran a hand through his hair. "I trust you've come to pay me the hundred dollars you owe me." He came down the stairs, his bulk carrying me back down before him.

On the bottom step he paused and stared down at the heap of dress. Then he looked up, his normally bland eyes gleaming with caution and annoyance. "What exactly do you want, Adam?"

"To talk to Jenny."

The bulbous lips smiled with tolerance. "My dear fellow, do you imagine that because she and I—" But he knew he couldn't possibly pull it off, so he stopped and asked, flatly, "About what?"

"Is that any of your business?" In that instant, perhaps because of the way he had demanded to know, I began to sense that some new and possibly threatening element had entered the picture.

"Yes," Donald said, "it is."

"I still want to talk to her," I said as I brushed past him and mounted the stairs to the balcony.

"She doesn't want to talk to you, old fellow."

"Jenny!" I barked. "Get out here!"

I heard Donald down below as he moved into the living room and stood staring up. "Your manners recently have left something to be desired, to put it—"

But he broke off because the door opened. Jenny appeared. She wore only the jacket of a pair of Donald's pajamas; below it her legs glimmered brown and rounded in the sunlight. She had Donald's brown Abyssinian cat—I could never think of its name—cuddled in her arms and she was smiling. I felt only a faint distaste, mildly sickening. Her expression was pleased, like the cat's.

"Wilby," I said, "will have the money in a few hours."

Her eyes remained fixed on mine with a knowing satisfied contempt—calculated, whether consciously or not, to stir that ancient male fear which somehow I could no longer feel. Whether I was impotent or not did not seem to matter in the least at the moment.

"One hundred and twenty thousand dollars," I said.

"That," Jenny said, "is a lot of bread."

"You're damned right it is," I said, conscious of Donald listening below. "It's my entire life-savings and probably the biggest blackmail haul you and Wilby-baby have ever made on one sucker."

Jenny glanced beyond me, then advanced so that she could look down on Donald. She made certain her body brushed against mine. I was conscious of its softness but immune, even scornful.

"I don't know what he's talking about, Sam," she said to Donald.

"I'll tell you." I stood at the railing alongside her, looking down on Donald, who was staring up at us, head tilted back. "Her brother—if he is her brother—is wiping me out. Everything I own."

"And . . . are you going to allow him?"

"If I go to the police, he intends to kill Anne or Lydia, or both. Or worse than kill. Of which he is totally capable."

Jenny uttered one of her jungle-like screams and ran down the stairway. "He's lying! Adam's lying, honey!"

"If he is sent to prison," I said, "he says he will simply wait till he gets out."

And at this Donald's face tightened; he frowned, and Jenny stopped to glare up at me.

"You lying sonofabitch! He never said nothin' like that!" Then to Donald: "You don't know him. Adam. You don't know how he can make up lies!"

"Donald," I said, "you met Jenny for the first time last night. Whose word are you going to take?"

It took him a long moment to frame his reply, and in that moment I wondered why I was following Wilby's orders again. Didn't I have a better chance with Wilby if Jenny was *not* in the apartment? Better chance to what? Shoot? Poison? Drive him into total collapse?

"Adam," Donald said at last, "what exactly do you want of Jenny now?"

I gave myself time to answer by going down the stairs. How could I go on functioning on the assumption that once he had the money this afternoon, Wilby would take Jenny and disappear? Wasn't this absurd and unreasonable?

"Well, old fellow?" Donald challenged—and, closer now, I caught on Donald's face a new expression: almost but not quite a reflection of Jenny's contempt.

Jenny was crouched on the love seat, her legs drawn up under her, and she was stroking the large cat in slow sensuous movements of her arm so that now it had begun to purr softly. "He loves me, Sam," she said to Donald. "See how he loves me. Listen, honey! Listen to Cheetah!" The sound had become a steady thrumming and the cat's eyes were half closed. "Just *listen!*" she cried childishly, in delight.

"I told you last night he loved you," Donald chided softly, gazing down on the two of them with possessive benevolence. "Adam will tell you: Cheetah normally won't allow anyone even to touch her. No one but me, of course."

Adam will tell you more: Cheetah is one of the most vicious cats that ever lived.

I remembered Wilby's nightmare. If it had been a nightmare.

Donald's eyes had changed. As if hypnotized by the rhythmical gliding of Jenny's hand over the smooth short fur of the cat, they had narrowed, clouded; his bulbous lips had opened, moist and slack. His whole face now had taken on a look of carnal pleasure that sent a stab of hopelessness through me.

Nevertheless, I said, "Jenny, Wilby needs you." I recalled his voice on the telephone. But futility echoed in my tone. "He's doing all this for you. Riviera, all the clothes you want—"

"Wilby," Jenny said, her voice as contented as the steady thrumming, which was growing louder. "Wilby can go goose a giraffe."

And Donald chuckled quietly.

"After all Wilby's done for you Jenny?" I asked.

"What that bastard did for me!" She leaped up, scooping up the heavy cat in her arms, holding it against her. "What he did *to* me, you mean!" The purring had stopped. Her eyes—and the cat's—glowered. Then a familiar glitter came into her gaze—not this time stirred by violence but unmistakable all the same. She knelt down and began talking in a low, sensuous whisper to the cat as she lowered him to the floor. "No, not you, Cheetah. You can't come. You're too jealous." She straightened then, ignoring me this time, and drifted toward the stairs, her body already beginning to quiver. Donald followed her with eyes which had now become glazed. The cat sat back on its haunches and also watched. "I'll go back, honey. Back to Wilby, I mean. If *you* want me to, Sam." She went up the stairs, touching the banister lightly with her fingers, legs flashing in the sunlight, eyes returning to me although she spoke to Donald. "You come up and tell me what you want me to do, Sam." And I recognized the vengeful cruelty: I had committed the one unpardonable crime in Jenny's book—I had rejected her body. In a voice husky with promise, she said, "Only don't be long, honey. I hate to wait." On the balcony she paused, triumph in her slouch as she looked down on us. "I always wanted someone to love me, Sam. Not hate me." She leaned over the railing, whispered, "Only don't let Cheetah come up. I think he wants to do it himself. Only all he can do is watch." She straightened. "Like Adam."

Then she went into the bedroom and left the door partially open.

Donald continued to stare upward, mesmerized—and I realized that, no matter what I said now, or did, I would be wasting my time.

Cheetah moved to the stairs, large body stretching in slow long strides, lithe and confident, like a tiger or leopard.

"Cheetah," Donald warned, a fond reprimand in his tone. And when the cat stopped, poised, one long leg stretched forward: "Down."

And the cat, without hesitation, turned in smooth grace and retraced its steps, not hurrying. Then it prowled, with feline dignity, to the sofa, and disappeared behind the Victorian fringe.

"Donald," I said, "Donald, for God's sake, you don't even know her."

"I know her." He seemed now to remember my presence. "I know her. She told me all about . . . everything. Did you know what that brother of hers did to her?" He tore his eyes from the door above and regarded me. "Seduced her when she was too young even to know what was happening. Before he turned fag."

Nausea curdled in me. I ignored it. "How can you know her?" I demanded in a harsh whisper. "One night, Donald. *One night!*"

"It was," Donald said simply, "the best night I ever lived."

It was like trying to talk to a man under water. "Donald, believe me, she'll tear you apart."

"How?" He took a cigarette from a carved ivory container and lit it, hand trembling. "How can she?"

That Jenny, she takes it outta a man. Burns it out, click?

"In every way you can imagine," I said—and realized, for the first time, that I was actually thinking of Donald now, not myself. "Money, for one thing."

"I have a great deal of money."

"Every other way, too!"

From above, her voice called, faintly, "Is he still here, Sam?"

"She needs someone," Donald said and picked up a champagne glass that was not quite empty. "The poor child. If you had any idea." He swished the warm wine around in the glass, then drank it, letting it roll voluptuously around his mouth before swallowing. "She needs someone."

And she called again, softly, "Make him go away, Sam. Please—"

Donald set down the glass, took a long draw on the cigarette, and regarded me with curiosity and with the faintest suggestion, again, of Jenny's contempt. "After all, you can't blame Jenny for what happened to *you*."

"Donald," I said, "I admit I have my own motives here. But I *am* thinking of you, too."

"I'm the first one to accept the concept of complex motivation, old fellow. You say she'll destroy me. But I have nothing to be destroyed, you see. My life's pleasant but unrewarding—mostly boredom and, now I know, loneliness. If Jenny can destroy that, more power to her. I've just begun to feel alive."

Alive? Sensation. Sex. Kicks. Is that being alive? I shook my head. But was I certain? Or was I simply clinging to some anachronistic concept from the past, from the time before I had realized that there *are* no values, therefore no way of judging?

"Don't shake your head," Donald said. "What do *you* know?"

"Sam—"

"Don't blame Jenny for what's happened to you," he said coldly. "After all, it's not her fault you picked her up and then met that faggot brother of hers and decided you preferred *him*." Donald swung about and climbed the stairway. "I realize it's one hell of a discovery to have to make about yourself at your time of life, but I fail to see how you can lay the blame on poor Jenny."

Rooted there, I watched him go into the bedroom and close the door. I heard Jenny's voice, soft, the words indistinguishable. Then a giggle. Still, I found that I could not move. And inside the nausea thickened. As it had done—when? Monday?—after Wilby had struck her, with gratuitous pleasure, and I had gone down on the elevator and vomited in the basement. It flickered through my mind then, as I turned to move leadenly to the foyer, that if I could feel this sick, possibly I was still alive, after all. Alive and still capable of shock. Of emotion.

I had almost reached the door. *Look at my hand. It had hold, it had its teeth in my hand, it had its goddam teeth in my bone!*

I listened. Whispers from upstairs now. Behind the door, which was now closed. Donald's subdued laugh.

I turned around and, walking cautiously, approached the sofa, dropped silently to my knees, hearing another giggle from above, pushed aside the fringe.

Cheetah, stretched out, appeared to be asleep. I reached with one hand—and the cat snapped to abrupt life, squirming, then sitting, slashing out with a single almost invisible paw. The claw ripped flesh and I felt instant burning pain before I could withdraw my hand. I muttered a silent curse, sat back on my legs, hearing a tinkle of glass and a snigger from above. Behind the disarrayed fringe I could see Cheetah half sitting in the dimness, tensed, eyes glowing, glaring like a trapped lion's while, pointed teeth bared, he spat—a hissing sound that sent a shiver down me. The paw was lifted slightly, poised for action.

Then, in a single quick action, I lifted myself to my knees, grabbed a pillow off the sofa seat, tossed it to the floor at the far end of the sofa, pushed aside the fringe, saw the cat twist at the sound, momentarily off guard. I reached, fast, with both hands, trapped the large body between my palms, pressing into the fur with every finger as the cat arched its back, squirming furiously, violently. I increased the pressure of my thumbs, hard and brutal on the back of its neck, hearing the hissing as I drew the writhing body out of the cave, seeing the claws thrashing furiously, the head twisting and snapping from side to side, sharp teeth biting down over and over, unable to reach the flesh of my hand.

I stood up. The animal was heavy. There was blood on my hand. Above: no more whispers—only a creaking of bed. I trod carefully to the foyer—although there was no slightest chance that they would hear me now—and left the apartment.

You're gonna eat the ground, Wilby had whispered. *No mercy!* I passed the elevator. The cat had given up the struggle, but I could feel its heart beating wildly, flesh leaping—no more hissing. As I shifted my hold to grasp it by the scruff of its neck, freeing my other hand to open the door to the stairwell, I saw the red slash of flesh along my hand from wrist to thumb. Climbing the concrete stairs to the seventh floor, I reached a decision: no matter what state I find Wilby in, no matter how wretched or forlorn, I'll not allow that corrosive sense of pity to prevent my doing what has to be done. No more compassion or comprehension or hesitation—no mercy! *Y'live in a jungle, y'gotta survive.* I approached the familiar door along the hall. If Jenny is not coming back, there is only one solution: to drive him by whatever means, as far as he can be driven. If he is inside the room, I'll hurl the damned cat into his face and watch him collapse in terror.

But he was not in the room. Not in sight. Now what? I closed the door behind me.

"Out here, dad!"

His voice from the terrace. Terrace door open. He had seen me come into the building.

"Taking my morning con-stitu-tutional, man!" His voice was high-spirited, even playful. "C'mon join me!"

And at once I remembered his dismal voice on the telephone: *She ain't in her room.* His rage and fear and desperation only an hour ago, or less.

I started across the living room, became conscious of the cat dangling from my fist, hesitated. Then I turned about, returned to the foyer, opened the closet door there, dropped the cat to the floor—where it glared up at me—and shut the door on it. An ace in the hole.

Wilby was standing on his head on the stone balustrade—body stiffly balanced, feet high, facing the door, upside down, arms bent in support, hands planted flat on the stone surface. His long hair fell over his face, somewhat obscuring it, and he was not wearing the dark glasses. But what surprised me even more than his precarious and outlandish position was his face: he had removed the beard.

"Join me, pop, plenty room."

In the streaming sunlight I could see his face clearly for the first time. There was a pattern of bluish flesh where the beard had been, surrounded by paleness. And I realized that I must have, unconsciously, pictured his face as lean, possibly even delicate and sensitive behind the mask of beard. Instead, it was the face of so many of the most popular American motion-picture stars: heavy, brute-jawed, essentially animal-like, suggesting physical as well as other cruelties.

He gave a heave and flipped himself over, and then he was standing facing me, upright, face flushed and excited—and the elation in his eyes astonished me. I could see clearly now the diagonal, red-tinged swelling down one cheek. "Where y'been hidin', man?" He sounded friendly and pleased to see me. He smiled—not grinned, smiled. "Been jackin' off down the cellar to screw up guts to come up here?"

I was tempted, for a second, to tell him where I had been, and why. Let him talk to Jenny, do to Donald whatever he would do, and to hell with it. But almost instinctive caution took over. "Were you watching for Jenny?" I asked, knowing.

"Jenny?" And he laughed. "That chick-chick, I swear, man, I thought I taught her better, but never bet on Jenny, never bet a penny on Jenny, stand pat, who was Pat and what does he wear in the pea-green Irish sea?" He pranced past me into the living room, face lit with exuberance, and there he did a cartwheel, came upright, pushed back his hair and regarded me. "Oh Father Job-Job, y'need a drink. Job needs a drink, Job is a Scotchman after all, needs a Scotch drink, but only a little one, teensy one, 'cause he's Scotch, man, real Scotch with the Scotch!"

Was he drunk? High on dope? Or those pills he had mentioned? I glanced at the bar: a decanter glinted and again I felt the longing. Not longing, damn it, *need*!

"Lemme pour y'one, pop, on accounta y'got that look, hook-look, say when, when do we bomb Hanoi, we annoy t'bomb Hanoi, so did it today, listen to the news-news, Job, bombed Hanoi, Haiphong Harbor, historic day, so won't be long now, push the button, who's got the button, ring around the mushroom bush!" He stood before me, glass in hand. Eyes not mocking—only mirthful, jovial. "I ain't had a drip-drop, dad, that what you're thinkin', an' no peps, no grass." Again it was as if he had read my mind. "Take a Scotch from Lucifer, Job? Good what ails them boils on the balls, them burnin' sheep an' the servants all consumed!" And I accepted the glass, noting for the first time that he was dressed in total black: shoes, tight slacks, sweater. "Burn. Y'know that napalm burns till the victim's a bubblin' mass? Messy mass. Solemn papal high mass. No dogs or Buddhists allowed. Dog. God spelled backward. Lazy Dog—new bomb, made USA, ten thousand slivers razor-steel in it, so, patriots and murderers, save . . . your used . . . razor blades! See y'shaved, man. Meant remind you this a.m., slipped my mind. And dad, I do like that tie! Tie slies me!"

When he stopped, standing straight with the excitement seeming to quiver in his eyes and face and stance, I said, "You shaved, too."

And he burst into laughter. He rocked. He roared. And tears began to stream down his face. Between guffaws he said, brokenly, "Man . . . wonder I love you . . . wonder . . . oh pop, you'n me . . . beautiful music . . . only . . . only—" And the laughter ran down, seemed to drain away. "Only, man, y'got that conscience, click, not enough concupiscence, fresh outta concupiscence, how 'bout little *im*potence, important impotence, that Jenny—"

I watched him sit, then spring up as if he could not bear to be still, strut to the bar, splash whisky straight into an old-fashioned glass, lift it, drain it in one long swallow, wait, sigh, belch, then slap his thigh with his palm, hard. "First one of day, burns, ahhhhhhhh—" Then he laughed again, facing me. "Man, owe you apology. Now do hereby, all that shit, hereby and forthwith do apologize. Knew Jenny-chick not with you, Jenny-chick found new prick, click, in the bag-bag till he burns out, like you, Job, burns, burns, like in hell, Lucifer burns, only—" He was moving now, frisking in light steps over the debris, picking his way between bits and pieces and ashtrays and candles like a football player doing a broken-field run in slow motion. "Lucifer burns, only Lucifer *prefers* burn, matter pride, *somebody*'s gotta stand up t'him, him, whim, graybeard, Lucifer's whim, reason shaved beard—" And now he was playing hopscotch. "Lucifer has . . . no beard . . . 'cause . . . beards *singe!*" A final hop, turning fully about in midair. He faced me, legs apart. Smiled. "Father Job! Solemn, by God! In God we trust, Jenny bad penny, always comes back!"

What if he was not high on some narcotic or pill? Or on whisky? What if this unnatural jubilation, like my detachment last night and this morning's apathy, was only some sort of symptom of a deeper disturbance that I couldn't possibly interpret?

"Wilby," I said, "I'll have the money within two hours."

He nodded. "Knew y'would! In Job we trust! Trust you but bust you. An' I got it all doped now, all dope-doped, like hoped, all gonna be on paper, wild caper, man, strictly kosher-kosher, legal-beagle, dog, God spelled backward, only God couldn't dreamed it, took Satan!"

"Well," I said, "since it takes man to carry out Satan's orders, perhaps you'd be kind enough to explain it to me."

Again he roared with laughter. It rocked uproariously around the walls. He threw himself face down on the sofa and beat the cushions with his fists. "That's my old pop! That's the top, pop! Like always! Forever! The more y'change, more y'stay the same." He rolled onto his back, threw one leg over the back of the sofa. "Wanna play the game, d'you? Money-game? Money-game, honey?"

"The banks close at three."

"Job, Job, what you do is: y'put that bread in the bank, your bank, an' then y'make out a check-check, certified—" He broke off, tensing. As at a sound. I had not heard it, but in the silence now I did: a scratching. From the closet in the foyer.

For an instant I was certain Wilby would look up, dash to the foyer, and open the closet door.

Instead, he sat up. "Jenny?" And then with a whoop he bounded to his feet and tore to the foyer.

He threw open the door to the hall. He leaned out.

I strained to hear the sound from the closet again. But could not. Could *he*?

Slowly, frowning, he turned from the door. For the first time today he looked uncertain—bewildered. When he spoke, his tone held that same morose bleakness that I had heard on the telephone. "After all I done for her. Got her away, away from old man." He came down the step, half stumbling. It was as if I were not in the room. "Old man, cold man, beat her, belt, bareback, bareback rider, circus clown, funny man, only way could get it up—" Eyes glazed, he shambled into the room. Then he stopped, stood weaving slightly. He reached blindly for the arm of the sofa, as if for support—and in spite of myself I felt a slow, sickening pity come over me again.

"Wilby," I said, "to whom do I make out the certified check?"

He did not hear. He did not move. What was he thinking of now? What unimaginable memory or fantasy behind those fixed blind eyes?

I raised my voice. "How do I get the money to you?"

"Thinks I can't get along without her. Needs *me*." But it was a bitter whisper. "Dumb. Stupid-stupid. Never knows what I'm talkin' about. Hell, I'm free. Bird in tree. Fly. *Hope* she stays away, hope she *starves,* hope she . . ." But his whisper trailed off.

I looked down at the glass in my hand. But did not take a sip. Much as I needed it now. More than ever. Who could predict what would happen with Wilby in this mood? Or was it only a mood? Worse? I went to set the glass on the bar. Trying to prove something to myself? Yes.

I turned to face him. "I'm not paying over a goddamned cent," I said, my voice harsh and loud.

Wilby's eyes snapped open. Then he blinked, peering across at me as if recalling me from some distant past. Then he started to move toward me, slowly, steps uncertain. When he was quite close, he squinted into my eyes.

"Dad, why y'go on fightin'?" His voice was sad. His eyes were sad —but baffled, too. "Level, pop. Willya? Y'love that limey wife that much? Honest?"

The appeal was so direct, so ingenuous and startling, that for a moment I could not reply.

" 'Cause that bugs me, man. I admit it. That really bugs me."

"I'm sorry," I said, surprised, "that you can't understand it." Wondering: what now, what next, where could *this* lead?

He shook his head. "Guts, man. Like Job. Way he took what they dished out, old Yahweh'n Satan. Both. Right up to end. End. Till he broke. Joke. Abhorred hisself, dust'n ashes, for askin' too many questions—" He paused and his lips curled into a grin. A glimmer returned to his eyes. "I don't hear you cursin' it, man—"

Curse what? Life? "I'm cursing it." I lied. And wondered in the instant whether it might not be the truth.

The sadness remained in his eyes even as the glimmer turned into that familiar cruel glint. "Man, one thing I ain't been able t'teach you—"

He saw through. He always saw through! Anger jolted through me. I was grateful, and the pity washed away, was gone. "You're getting what you want! Just tell me how to go about it!"

He laughed then, as earlier, and the antic mood returned. As I watched him swing away, brisk and buoyant again, it came to me that my foolish stubborn refusal to give ground on some deeper level—my failure to mask this refusal or to feign its opposite successfully—actually invigorated him: it was almost as if it drove him to push our conflict to its ultimate. And again I wondered: will the money satisfy? If not, what?

"Why, dad, it's like this! Y'put the bread in your check-check account, whole amount, an' y'make out a check, certified, certified and mortified, to this cat here on the card!" And, as if performing a feat of magic, he made a flourish with both arms, and one hand came up, a business card between two fingers. "Then y'go that address"—and he approached on his toes like a ballerina and waved the card in front of my face—"give the certified-beatified, holy-holy, slip paper, this cat, an' he hands over the painting!"

As soon as I took the card, he whirled about, then toppled full length, stiffly, to the floor, face down, and in the last instant his two arms came out to break the fall. Then, while I glanced at the card—name and address of an art gallery on Madison Avenue and a name, L. Neuenberg, in the lower right-hand corner—he began doing push-ups in slow rhythm as he talked.

"Bought in your name . . . plunked down a thousand this a.m.

. . . cold cash . . . make him hold it for you . . . hold it, sold it, cold, all yours . . . pay up balance . . . hundred-nineteen thou . . . thou shalt not steal . . . wheel-deal but not steal—"

"Then what?"

"Bring picture here . . . frame-up, man . . . frame-up or ship out . . . I buy picture . . . one dollar *and* . . . other considerations . . . no commiserations . . . legal mumbo-jumbo . . . bill of sale . . . type it y'rself . . . not even Phoebe-Phoebe . . she not the type . . . to type . . . but legal, man!" And he dropped and rolled over on the floor. "*Legal*, beginning to end! Admit-admit, ain't it beautiful? Ain't it the work of Jehovah hisself?"

"Beautiful," I said, pocketing the card. And legal. And diabolical.

"*Beautiful*!" he bellowed suddenly and sprang to his feet to do another cartwheel, landed upright, bouncing. "Wait'll I tell Jenny! Jenny-penny, always comes back! Wait'll you hear her laugh, man!" Then, assuming an exaggerated opera singer's pose, chest out, arms outflung, his voice bellowing, he burst into song. "Ohhh, do not blame me . . . there is no blame-issimo . . . blame me or tame or shame me or claim me or lame me . . . *because* . . . Sigmuuund . . . Isoldeee . . . Kierkegaard . . . S. Freud . . . Freud-Freud-Freud . . . has told us . . . no blame-issimooooo!" He ended on a deep note so loud that the walls seemed to shudder. Then he took a sweeping bow and straightened, twisting the ends of an imaginary mustache.

And while it went through my mind that Jenny and Donald, in bed just below, could not help but hear him, I watched him begin to pace up and down, fast, in a straight line.

"No guilt, guilt terrible, nobody's fault, nothing, trauma"—he was walking and speaking faster and faster—"complex, fixation, way y'are, can't help it, nobody, nothin' your own fault, *halt*!" And he came to an abrupt stop, stood at military attention.

Raving? Insane? How could I *know*?

"Lieutenant Adam Wyatt!" he shouted. "You have been wounded! Your right hand is bleeding! How, sir, do you explain that? Are you guilty, sir?"

I glanced at my hand. The blood had clotted somewhat. I placed it in my jacket pocket. It was burning hot. It rested on the cold metal of the gun. If he's gone completely mad, what will he do next?

"Are you *guilty*, sir?" He yelled again.

Guilty of what? Of helping him along the road? But how the hell could I be sure even now? I glanced at my watch. 12:13. Forty-seven minutes before lunch with Henry and his mysterious doctor friend. Plenty of time, but if I stayed here, what was there to be accomplished. If I left now, though, and Jenny did not return and if he discovered the cat—

"The court finds you guilty as charged!" He bellowed, then chuckled and relaxed. "Dad, y'didn't even finish your Scotch."

Did he want me to stay? I circled around him and went to the foyer. Was he again afraid to be alone?

"Looks like y'need it, why bleed it, make self home—"

The bastard. On target again. He knew I needed it, he took *joy* in knowing! But it would only blur my mind. Blur it *more*. My head threatened to explode. But I had lied to myself too many times: imagining whisky would clarify anything.

"No thanks," I said, "but don't let me stop *you*."

I was standing in the foyer, facing the front door, picturing the cat behind the closet door on my left, hostile and angry. If it made another noise and he found it—

"What's the hangup, man?" Still gently, quietly.

I turned around. His head was tilted to one side, eyes half closed but fixed on me. There was one question that clearly had to be answered. "How can you be so damned sure Jenny is coming back?"

Wilby rose on his toes and laughed. " 'Cause, man, what else can she do? Where else can the chick-chick go? Go-go, man, bitch can't get along without me, no pad, bad, starve. She's in the bag with some cat now, fuckin' or fruggin' or doin' the watusi, the monkey, swimmin' or jerkin' with some jerk!" He almost skipped across the room. "Who's sweatin'? Y'bettin' she won't, Jenny, bad-penny, always comes back. Gotta. Ours not t'reason why, ours but t'be'n fly, your fly's open, pop!" And he stood with his head back, roaring, the laughter continuing under the rush of words: "Jenny gonna get what always wanted, first-class all way, moonlight decks, captain's table, captain if he's able, what chick-chick always wanted!" Behind the mirth there had appeared an expression of exaltation on his face now, rapture. "Riviera. Sheiks'n dukes'n princes'n all the pricks hangin' with francs'n diamonds'n oil concessions, your taxes, Grace'n Onnaxis—" His laughter went high. He braced himself with one arm against the frame of archway. "Y'didn't ask 'bout me, though. Tell you, man, tell you anyway! The big-time, man! The vile, worst there is, open sesame, seeds of evil—" And now his words were rushing together. "Your little stake, only start, fart, peanuts for bellboys, only place test evil against evil is *hell itself,* push it all the way there, be saint that way, Saint Genet, flowers of evil, low man, low, *lowest,* go-go!"

No doubt now. None. Deranged.

Had he answered my question? Yes: Jenny would return because she had always returned before. But more: Jenny would return because Wilby *believed* she *had* to return! Yet, ironically, wasn't it more than likely that Wilby had arrived at this weird state of unreason largely because Jenny had *not* returned? The questions roared through my mind, roared and churned and intensified the splitting pain.

"What if she doesn't?" I asked because, the answer might—could! —bring everything into some kind of reasonable focus.

Instead of its triggering fury or panic, the question only caused him to cock his head to one side while he regarded me with a sad but unmocking half-smile. "Like I said on phone, man—Jenny don't come back, Wilby stays."

I had my answer. It made no sense, but in a world devoid of reason it did not need to.

His shoulders sagging slightly now, he strolled to the bar, slumped against it. "Don't sweat it," he said lazily. "Don't sweat. Sweat-yet. Jenny'll be walk-talkin' in here . . . one of these days—" With a somnolent weariness after the earlier frenzied exhilaration: "Or . . . night-nights. Takes some guys longer t'burn out . . . than it takes . . . other cats. Click?"

Cat! I thought for a second that, without will, I was going to throw open the closet door, pick up the cat, and hurl it at him across the room, as I had planned earlier.

But instead I went into the corridor, slamming the door behind me. Let him discover it himself, let it terrify him into hysteria, shock, total madness, into the void, sooner the better, get it over with!

I did not wait for the elevator. Along the hallway, plunging down the stairs—

What if I'm only imagining that he's begun to crack, is cracking? Convincing myself because I want to, need to, as he has to convince himself that Jenny's coming back!

Steps clattering, echoing madly in the stairwell, driving a thousand spikes into my brain—

What do I know about psychosis, insanity, any of it? Yet I've been playing with it, my only hope, plotting it—

Head bursting now. *Bursting.* Must stop, must get away alone, think, sort out—

Only hope? What hope? How could I know, predict, what he could do, would do, if he ever went completely—

Into the foyer, across the marble floor—

God, what have I been doing? Why did I even think of taking that damned cat in there? Or hiring Chenery's man.

Into the street—

"Taxi, Mr. Wyatt?"

No. No, Geoffrey, no, you blackmailing sonofabitch, you lying, limey, wifeless bastard, no taxi, nothing from you!

I walk toward corner. Don't run now: *walk*! Walk, Lieutenant Adam Wyatt, that is an order!

Hadn't I promised myself earlier to examine every decision coldly, ruthlessly, because of my own mind, not his, mine, *my* mind!

At corner I stand dazed and weaving on curb. Where? Which way? Lunch? A taxi slows. No. Have to have time to think, time to think it out, decide—

I walk.

Pat's Pub. One drink. Drink and think. Pat won't speak to me. After yesterday. Accusing Pat. Proves something, doesn't it? Pat and the cat. Proves something about myself. Hell yes—proves who's the one has delusions! Only one drink, though, please, just one, to bring everything into focus—

But I pass the door. Plunging on. Plenty of time before lunch. Too much time. Walked it before several times. Excellent exercise. Keep heart pumping. Thumping. Ask Arnold Wilder. But what if the danger's not in the heart?

"Everything under control, Mr. Wyatt?"

Chenery. Walking beside me. Again. Oh hell yes, Chenery—under perfect control, rigid control, how would you like to get slugged right here on the street—

"You have anything to report?"

Hell, yes, you want the full report? Wilby's going insane, Jenny's in bed with Donald doing the goddamned watusi, how long till Donald burns out, Wilby is staying, forever, not till Jenny comes back but forever, and how can you tell whether a man's going insane, Wilby or me or anyone, me for example, or what will happen afterward, is there a clear-cut line, *You Are Now Entering the State of Dementia, Speeding Means Loss of License,* slow down, if Wilby already over, then what, suicide, splash-splash, worse, wait for Lydia, what, *what*—

"You didn't notice them, of course, but I got two men on the door. One of them weighs two hundred and fifty-three. I asked him."

Fat man. Following. Why? To drive him over. Would it, could it, could I afford the risk now? But what else? What else is there?

"Did you check on the little lady, Mr. Wyatt? Is she still inside?"

I nod. "Man's name is Donald Abbott. If he comes out alone, I want to know." Why? Of what possible consequence or use—

"Oh, you'll get a rundown on all three sometime this afternoon. I have your home and office numbers in my book now. At the office, I'll use my own name, of course, but if I call you at home I'll say it's a Mr. Smith calling. Are you with me?"

I walk faster. Laughter like dust in my mouth. "Make it Jones."

"Jones? Well, if you say so—"

"He who pays the piper pays the sniper."

"If you say—Mr. Wyatt, do we have to walk this fast?"

Fast? *Hup,* two, three, four! What did you do during the war, daddy? Had a student deferment, studying with the Mafia—

"Mr. Wyatt"—huffing, puffing—"Mr. Wyatt . . . changed your mind?"

Mind? Wrong fellow, Chenery. Must be thinking of someone else. Someone who hasn't lost his mind.

"Anything *else* you want done?"

Anything else, like murder? Yes. Yes, Chenery—the only way. Have known all along. You are right! Only way!

I glance at Chenery. His thin face is turned on me as we walk. His forehead shows sweat. Behind spectacles his eyes water. He wants to kill Wilby. Has never seen him, has no feeling about my situation, has nothing against Wilby, yet wants to kill. For killing's own sweet sake?

"If it becomes necessary to kill anybody," I tell him, surprised at the perfectly normal tone of my voice, "I have a gun in my pock-et."

He frowns. "No cause to get controversial again. Here's my card.

If you need me or get any aspirations along the way, don't hesitate. Either number. Only if you call the house in Jersey, try to make it before eight at night unless it's a emergency. Telephone wakes the twins."

Must not wake the twins. Use silencer on gun? Or guns too messy? What alternatives? Spears, poisoned darts, machetes, any old jungle weapon in a jungle—

". . . can't keep up this pace"—puffing, panting, gasping— ". . . such a hurry, why not take a cab? Call you later—"

Good-by, Chenery. Good riddance. Home to Jersey now? Lunch? A little baseball with the boys? Put the twins down for their nap, beddy-bye. Then? Why then back to the job, of course. Family to support. Duties to be performed: mayhem, any size, shape, color, or price, how about a little permanent crippling, although homicide always simplest unless you find some fool with compunctions, some fool with illusion human life has meaning, revered. After kissing wife, back to the grind—herd them into the ovens, off with their ragged clothes, don't overlook the rings, gold fillings, how filthy those box-cars, how about a nice cyanide shower-bath? *Man is the cruelest animal.* Who said it? Too drunk to listen. Wilby quoting. Wilby should know. Does. Will prove. Man is the cruelest animal but who'd be cruel enough to tell him? Mercy. Pity! On all these faces. Noon-hour street. Sea of faces. Abstracted, unknowing, *confident*! Keep truth secret. Let him think he orders his life, holds his future in his own will. Free will. I do hereby bequeath my greatest possession, my freedom of choice, to those I love. If there is love. *Is* there love? Freud is the master of my fate and Darwin is the captain of my soul. Justice is my birthright, a strand of my umbilical cord. If not justice in this imperfect world, then certainly, by divine fiat and design, in the perfect world to come: the golden seats on the right hand, the infernal broiling floor, or rebirth as soaring bird, snarling tiger, royal prince of all India. For good is good and will be rewarded and evil is evil and will be punished and never the twain shall meet so long as Browning's in heaven and all is wrong with the world. Never breathe that Satan lost the battle but won the war and has been winning it ever since. For who is to say which is God and which Satan? Never, never shout this from any rooftop or pulpit or hilltop in the woods, Father, because you must consider what would happen if suddenly they did stop believing, all of them, at once, that there is anything, anyone, up there behind the star's million-year-old twinkle, start knowing there is not

even God in a devil's mask or Lucifer in a false beard playfully calling trick-or-treat, no omniscient intelligence looking into the billions
of antlike skulls that cling by illusion alone to this spinning cinder
lost in space on which even the sun's light is inevitably dying. You
must consider that truth is destructive, for what would happen, *think
about it*, what would happen if they ever got wise that eternity itself is
not even intended for them but exists, if it does, only as space so in-
termingled with time that neither can be calculated on Einstein's
drawing board or by any IBM computer yet computing—what would
happen? Imagine some diabolical instant of total illumination when
it's comprehended that meaninglessness and chaos cannot be divided
and subtracted by the expanding consciousness but can only be multi-
plied and squared by every illusory step toward final knowing! What
then, Father Job? If you ever realized that cosmic law itself is only
the distorted fantasy of fallible and groping men who prefer to agree
on their collective myopia rather than to acknowledge what would
make them go blind! What then, what then in that fierce instant of
universal truth? Would the accumulated howls of anguish and despair
detonate a cataclysmic holocaust not yet imaginable by even the
cruelest atomic scientist? Would the cinder, supposedly fixed in its
time-space path, shudder so that gravity itself would falter and all
things built and growing on its dark face would plunge outward into
the unknowable and uncaring nothingness? Or would the cinder itself
be shaken from its path and go trailing off like those other falling
stars we see streaking through the sky, their light dimming?

A blast of sound. A horn. A shriek of brakes. I stand staring down
at—what? Metal blinding in sun, car grille and glittering bumper
inches from my leg. I look up, over still-shuddering hood. Behind
windshield a shaken angry face in chauffeur's cap. I stumble toward
curb. Hear snarled anger, hear woman's laugh, hear more horns. I
step up, legs caving, I reach. Hand grabs, clutches green wood, newsstand, I lean. Clothes soaking, sweat cold down back, freezing in
armpits, but heat smothering, dank heavy cloud. Head splitting.
Heart thrashing. Nausea.

I lean, stunned and spent and breathing hard but—imagine it, imagine!—not even trembling! Waiting, though, waiting for this morning's merciful stupor to close over me again. Needing it now. Aching
for it. But instead: corner roars with intensity.

What happened? Where have I been? And how long have I been
there? Last night's world again: that's where I've been. But worse this

time, much worse! And without a drink. On a street, too—walking along a bustling street. Where have I *been*?

But I know. That's the hell of it. That hard sharp hypnotic clarity of reason—I know what it means. It is not reason. Reason's opposite. That brilliant sense of omniscience and godlike superiority—a private world of intensity and despair.

It's up to you in the final showdown. It always is. I know, Henry. I've always believed it. It's what we all said to Ernie Waite, remember? Remember, Henry? After the Messerschmidts got to us on the Hamburg run—or was it one of the Antwerp raids, or maybe Kassel?—Ernie locked to his tailgun, staring, not even wounded, mind blanked, while we all kept talking and explaining it was over, we were already over the Dutch Islands and safe, no more Messerschmidts, only it took three of us, remember, to pry those stricken hands loose, that deathlike grip, while we kept telling him he had to get hold of himself for God's sake because it was up to him now whether he'd recover or end up where . . . oh Christ, where he did end up, didn't he? *It's your job to keep yourself on the track. Agreed?* Agreed, Henry, but what if this isn't the same as Ernie's shock, what if this is something else altogether?

I look around in panic. Heads, faces, feet shuffling, bodies—not even a curious glance in my direction. Drugstore, tobacconist's, stationery, books, men's ties, flowers—

Not a bar in sight. And I can't seem to move. I don't have the strength to move. Has to be a bar. Bars on every street New York. One drink now. For strength. To clear my mind. And because I'm scared. Admit it. I've never been so scared. Not once, during the war or since. Never.

Because it might happen again, any second, who can tell, how can I know, ever be sure again that my mind won't snap back, or slip back, into that unreality, or reality, is it possible there's more truth in that unreality than in this, than in anything I can see or think or feel, that reality itself is—

Oh Christ, here I go again. Oh God, what does it mean, where will it lead, what's happening, I want to pray, I can't pray, I don't know how, I learned once but it's all gone, and with knowing, *knowing,* how can you pray, to whom, to what, who is there to listen, but there has to be some help, someone, there has to be—

A voice. Close. Speaking a language I do not comprehend. Do I imagine it?

I force my eyes open. When did I let my eyes close?

A face floats before me. Close. Sun shimmers behind. Face slowly, slowly swims into focus: a stranger, old, black-bearded, skin wrinkled deep, skin dark-hued beneath a pallor. He wears a stiff black hat squarely atop small head. And his dark eyes are filled with pain, a strange baffled personal concern which, almost at once, slows my pounding heart, quiets my raging blood, seems even to dry the cold sweat all over me.

He does not move. In the spell of the moment I cannot. The compassion in his eyes is depthless, the kindness almost desperate.

He speaks, but I cannot understand the words: the language could be German. I see helplessness flood his eyes. And he speaks again, this time lifting one hand as if he might touch me.

For an instant I feel tears stinging hot behind my eyes as some ancient solace reaches me. And I long to reassure him. "I'm all right," I hear myself say. I even straighten, still holding to the newsstand with one hand. "Thank you very much, but I'm . . . fine." I release my grip and smooth down my jacket, trying to smile. "*Danke schön.*"

But he is not convinced. He shakes his head, gaze still brimming with sympathy, an instinctive knowing—and a rebellious sense of futility.

And I know that, somehow, I must convince him. It's important —vital—that I make him understand that he *has* helped, that I *will* be all right, that I *am* fine now. "*Nein sprechen Deutsch,*" I say, wondering how I remembered and whether the words make any sense.

His lips open in the black beard. "Yiddish?" he asks, still hopeful.

Yiddish? My mind searches frantically for any word, any phrase that might convey to him the gratitude that has almost become a pain in me. Rosh Hashana, Yom Kippur, Bar Mitzvah. I feel a terrible shame—remorse—not that I cannot communicate in his language but that I should put this man through this. What right do I have to add to the centuries of suffering that he carries behind those eyes, carries with such dignity and yet is able to stop on a street corner, he out of all the hundreds heedlessly passing, to offer consolation to a total stranger who might, after all, be only drunk? But he knows better. Knows. And that wisdom itself soothes. I must tell him. I must make him understand if I have to clasp him in my arms—

"*Mazel tov*"—I hear my voice before I realize I have spoken. And I do not know precisely what the words mean.

His face looks baffled for a second. Then merriment lights it. The wrinkles deepen, yet at the same time, oddly enough, they seem to fade away; and I see him young, vigorous, in love perhaps and dancing on some village street in Europe. Gay music, reeds, strings, with sadness behind the joy. *"Mazel tov!"* he echoes, scoffing yet delighted. *"Mazel tov!"* And he laughs.

The laugh blots out all the indifferent frenzy of the street. Another face superimposes itself on his: Professor Kantor. Whom I had thought of several times in the last two days, but whom I had almost forgotten. Professor Bernard Kantor—those same eyes, that same joy and sadness in his face.

And then the laugh dies away. Our eyes are locked again. And it is this stranger, not Professor Kantor, to whom I extend my hand, realizing how very seldom in life the gesture holds any genuine meaning.

He looks down—does he see the claw-wound, the clotted blood? Then he looks into my eyes again and takes my hand. His is surprisingly strong and I have the strange impression that his grasp transmits some of that throbbing vigor from his hand into mine.

"Danke schön, sir." It is the best I can do. *"Danke schön."*

Releasing my hand, he steps back. Then he makes a courtly bow, as if himself relieved, a bow graceful and dignified and somehow, in spite of his frayed suit and worn shoes, not in the smallest degree incongruous, even on that rushing hectic street corner. As if satisfied now, he turns his back, and I feel a jolt of sorrow, loss: I shall never see this man again, or know him. I watch him walking away: just another shabby old Jew on the streets of New York, one of thousands, perhaps millions.

Seeing his form diminishing in the distance, I see also the history of a whole people: unwanted, century after century, trudging over desert-tracts, huddled under the slaver's whip, homeless, searching, straining under unimaginable burdens, the melancholy always mitigated by humor, some inherent dignity bred of pain and knowledge of men. And as the figure of the stranger loses itself in the press of the crowd, I can picture again the still incredible horrors of my own time: terrified families herded together like cattle, arms uplifted under pointed rifles, those never-to-be-forgotten photographs of the still breathing but corpselike skeletons with hollow cheeks and sunken eyes too stunned even to reflect relief or credulity at the sight of their liberators.

Yet . . . yet he had stopped. Man is the cruelest animal, but he had stopped. He had stopped and now it was possible for me to go on.

I glanced at my watch. Eleven minutes to get to the restaurant. I looked up at the street sign. Had I come this far? Only a few more blocks to go. With a sense of renewal and with the pain in my head now only a muted discomfort, gratitude flowing in my veins like some miraculous vital tonic, I started to walk.

I walked steadily now, slowly, and allowed my mind to drift back over the years. Professor Kantor. How many years? More than twenty-five, more than a quarter century. Yet I could still see his face: dark, soft eyes amused and ironical, with the same sadness that I had just glimpsed in the stranger's. And I could still recall his lectures: his relaxed manner as he goaded you into thinking, replying, making a fool of yourself; room 511 on the top floor dubbed Kantor's Cave, where in winter you could see the campus white with snow and ice; the scarred desk in the third row. It was Professor Kantor's idea that law was fundamentally an articulation of concepts that were themselves arrived at by human intelligence as part of the over-all evolutionary process; that prehistoric man's first grasp of the idea that there is and can be good as opposed to evil in the world was the step that had allowed all of us to inch forward out of the primordial slime or at least down out of the trees; that the first man who set down the rules of conduct that might allow his society to survive had performed his evolutionary duty and that we should be as grateful to him as to the one who developed the alphabet and more grateful to him than to the one who invented the wheel or discovered the laws of gravity or relativity. It was all coming back now, all that I had pondered on all those long years ago and had allowed to lie wasted and dead somewhere in my consciousness. Law traces the expanding moral consciousness of the race and if anyone doubted there was progress, let him consider the distance traveled even in very recent times between the divine right of kings and legal rights of the lowest individual on which American justice is at least theoretically based. *It is not a business then, gentlemen, or a way to get rich, but a sacred trust. And I use the word sacred in its best and strictly secular sense. No god has made it holy but men should.* It was his repeated contention that everyone, in his private as well as in his professional life, had an obligation to the process of human evolution: to edge mankind one small iota closer to its ultimate, but naturally unfulfillable, ideal. *What Christians, I believe, term the perfectibility of man. Even when we all know he is probably imperfectible. Still the irony does not seem to stop us. Remarkable creatures, aren't we?*

A plane passed overhead, glinting and immense in the strip of summer sky visible between the high buildings. What was it Professor Kantor had replied when some bewildered student, about to be drafted, had demanded to know how war could fit into *any* theory of law or progress? What? I strained to thrust my mind back through time. Professor Kantor's answer had stayed with me all through the war, and now I . . . yes, something about war itself being a breakdown of all law and civilization . . . yet . . . yet sometimes war appeared to be the only way to . . . to preserve what small progress had been achieved. The sad smile. *Ironic, gentlemen? Contradictory?* I could see his face in my mind clearly now, hear his voice. *Someone once wrote that the measure of a civilized man is the ability to suspend two diametrically opposed possibilities in the mind without going mad.* Now, crossing a busy street in midtown Manhattan half a lifetime later, I realized that it had been Professor Kantor's ideas that had sustained me through those twenty-five missions and were, in a sense, sustaining me now. *Bombs away!* Much as Wilby had tried to stir guilt, in that particular area he had failed. *Y'couldn't do it, man, 'less you was followin' orders'n got medals for it, click?* I became conscious of the gun in my pocket again. Don't be too sure, Wilby. But I felt no rage. I only felt now as I had felt on those damned raids: that sometimes there is a terrible and dirty job that has to be done. No particular dignity in it, certainly no glamour—a rotten job. I had done some of that job then—without remorse because there are now no gas chambers and the world, whatever else might be said against it, is not being run by a group of madmen. And if it came to it now, much as I hoped against it, I could probably do whatever had to be done again.

Destroy in order to preserve. Yes. And now I could handle that irony, too. Along with all the others. As Wilby's mind could not. As, last night and as recently as fifteen minutes ago, my mind could not.

Thank you, Professor Kantor. Dead or alive now. But probably dead. Yet never dead. So long as someone remembers, so long as your ideas influence a single human mind or act. A different kind of immortality, continuity—but a possible answer to the inevitability of death itself, the body, the consciousness. A strange calm had come over me. Professor Kantor, at least, must have died knowing that in

his own way he had fulfilled his sacred trust to evolution. Or he may
have died *not* knowing it—an irony he could also appreciate.

I was passing a familiar church: high steps rising to arched, open
doors. I could picture the cool interior, the quiet inviting dimness.
But I felt not the slightest inclination to go in. To go in now would be
tantamount to seeking help in any bar. Escape only. Like those moments of vivid lunacy when the mind, seeking to retreat from chaos,
embraces chaos. Like . . . yes, Father, forgive me, like that barren
tree in the woods.

I did not look back at the church with any sense of loss or anguish.
And I did not abhor myself for my questions. No dust and ashes because I do not have the answers to the riddles of the universe. Rather,
I was held in a kind of awe: no sense of loss or anguish now. Rather
a quiet pervasive astonishment at the ultimate mystery, without
dread. As if a hand that had clutched my heart since birth had slowly
relaxed its grip. And I knew that never in my life before had I known
the meaning of religious wonder—because, from birth, I had been
given the answers of myth and folk tale. And now, reverence removed, I knew a strange exaltation, and wondered whether this feeling in itself were not, in some small measure, my own personal fulfillment of my—of everyman's?—obligation to the evolutionary process. To have passed beyond that need for absolutes and final clarity
was to be able to embrace ultimate mystery without despair. With
hope then? Not the hope symbolized by human death leading to light
everlasting. I recalled standing gazing down on my father's dead,
masklike face and learning that he had taken his own life in the
woods, the same voice continuing with a woeful kind attempt at reassurance, *Remember, Adam, what the good book says—that we
should rejoice at a death and mourn at a birth.* I had then recoiled
instinctively, tearing my eyes from the beloved and hated stranger's
face, longing to put behind me all the questions and perplexities and
shock, to return to the more rational madness of war. But now, with
a knowing serenity, I recognized those words for what they were:
blasphemy, no matter who had uttered them or where they had been
recorded.

I gazed about me as I walked. If the world is not ordered, is it then
chaos? Or an imperfect order imposed by imperfect but aspiring men?
Consider these few miles of stone descending into the waters of the
sea below and rising as many miles into the sky above, this island
wrested from wilderness and obscurity by man himself. By his own

expanding concepts—mathematical and scientific and strictly human calculations beyond the imagination of even his own grandparents —he had constructed these cities within cities, hadn't he? Just as he was now his brother's keeper, not in his own village or state or even country but around the world: an extension of morality inconceivable even a hundred years ago. He *himself* had created this order that often appeared in the disturbing guise of chaos. And whatever meaning he would reach, or not reach—that, too, he would have to conceive of and then design for himself, rather than discover or blindly accept as ready-made and fixed. And why not? Why not, if he can throw off dread and terror and that deeper need for significance through his own personal immortality? Throw it off, as—how many million years ago?—he had thrown off the crustaceous protective and crippling sheath that had held him prisoner in the primordial swamp—

But—the irony, Professor Kantor—could he? *Would* he? Is he the master of his fate?

I was walking very slowly now, while my thoughts plunged ahead.

No, Father, no—he is not the master of his fate. He cannot predict or control the cooling of the sun or the always possible accident of colliding stars—any more than I can control the circumstance of my birth or my time on earth or the possible invasion of my body by the ruinous but accidental contamination of disease. But he *is* the captain of his ship. As . . . at last, Father, at last . . . as I am the captain of mine. I can't control the typhoon's fury but I can damned well make sure the hatches are closed, the sails are taut, the mast is fixed. Yes, Father, I am the captain of my soul, and without thanks to any gods, real or imagined. If that be arrogance, Father, arrogance is no sin, regardless of Job. It is time for arrogance. It is past time for man to be man.

I turned a corner. The restaurant sign loomed ahead. I glanced automatically at my watch: only two minutes late. Possibly the most important two minutes of a lifetime. Possibly.

Lunch with a doctor. I couldn't recall the name. Henry's idea of a way to recoup at least part of the money that I was losing. Losing? I felt no great sense of loss. The savings of a lifetime, yet somehow insignificant now in the perspective of what, at last, I had discovered.

And I slowed my steps. How could I feel this way? So quiet and certain, almost tranquil. How? Was this only the calm that lies in the eye of the storm? Or was this calm another trick of the mind—like

last night's detached observation, like this morning's stupor of indifference and despair, like those minutes of madness while I rushed
blindly along the street? The suspicion, however, stirred no terror; the
doubt clung to my mind, more question than fear, as I entered the
restaurant.

In the men's room I washed the blood off my hand: the cold water
cut into the gash, then exposed it. I bathed my face, conscious of the
perspiration all down my body, damp and warm now, no longer cold.
My collar looked wilted and the new tie was askew. I ran my left
hand over my cropped hair, again struck by the speckled silver all
through it and the concentration of gray over both ears. Then, quite
consciously, I looked into my eyes. They were still set deep in pockets
of shadow, but they stared back at me with a composed steadiness,
the pupils slightly enlarged. My face itself had lost some of its pallor;
it appeared to be flushed with heat or slightly reddened by the sun in
which I had been walking. But I had the impression that my entire
face had shrunk—did I imagine those hollow cheeks? And what was
it Henry had said about Lydia coming home to find me a shell of
myself?

Henry was seated at our usual corner table—business conversations strictly confidential, waiters hear no evil, speak no evil, expect
larger tips—and with him was a youngish man whom Henry, rising,
introduced as Dr. Crittenden.

After the handshake—his was firm but gentle and his smile was
unusually broad and flashing—and after we had settled into our
chairs, I discovered the highball at my place. And looked up to find
Henry's eyes on me, as he went on talking.

"Dr. Crittenden and I have been discussing this LSD drug that
we've all been reading so much about. He has some rather strong
convictions on the subject, I gather—"

Dr. Crittenden's voice was at once strong and consoling. "In the
first place, as I was about to explain, it's not precisely a drug. A de-
rivative of the fungus ergot, it's what is termed a psychochemical.
And it's said by its proponents to expand consciousness, at least tem-
porarily—"

*Grass . . . tea . . . goof-balls . . . religion . . . what's the big
diff, man?* I remembered passing Pat's Pub, the yearning in every fiber.

". . . been used with some success in psychotherapy, especially
with alcoholics, but it seems to have proliferated—"

Been watchin' you, man. Hooked. I picked up the glass, remembering also how I had lied to myself on the street: just one to clear my
mind, to prove I'm *not* hooked, the excuse of every alcoholic or incipient alcoholic, one and then another to make sure, then another.

". . . mostly young people who don't realize the dangers. For
what they call kicks—what is known as the psychedelic experience—"

I took a sip. It tasted fine. Cold and refreshing. I glanced up and
saw Henry's eyes flash away.

". . . amazing but the contents of a two-suiter piece of luggage
could incapacitate the entire population of the United States—"

Now that LSD kick, that's one bit I don't dig. I took another long
swallow. The calm remained, at once reassuring and just faintly disconcerting. *Tripped out, man . . . freakout . . . like I was gonna
flip. Off my . . . nut!*

". . . danger being that it's so readily available. Yes, I suppose
I do have strong feelings. But it's my opinion that it can fill the mental hospitals if something drastic isn't done to curb its use. When I
was a resident in Boston, I saw a girl brought in by ambulance who
couldn't distinguish between herself and her surroundings—"

And I was remembering the girl writhing in ecstasy on the floor.
Who wants children? Having children could never mean—

". . . one out of six patients admitted to one of the largest mental
institutions in Los Angeles have LSD-induced psychoses, many of
them permanent—"

I don't want your damn world!

". . . no actual knowledge of possible tissue-damage—"

"Doctor—"

"Yes, Mr. Wyatt?"

"By permanent psychosis, do you mean . . . insanity?"

Y'look it, man. Like you're gonna cop out. You flipped, dad?

"Insanity, as I'm sure you're aware, Mr. Wyatt, is the layman's
word. And a legal term, too, of course. But in the sense you mean it,
yes—LSD can and often does render a person incurably . . . as you
put it . . . insane, depending somewhat on—"

"On what?"

"Well, the average well-balanced person might be reasonably safe
from psychological damage—although even he could commit some
destructive or self-destructive act while under its influence—"

I am consuming the flame. Light. I can taste the flame. I can taste life!

". . . imagined he could fly, so jumped out of a window. A young man in California who imagined he had the strength to hold back a speeding truck—" His young face was flushed with disapproval. "Damn it, it's going to get out of hand!"

Conscious of Henry's eyes on me again, I said, "You started to say something about people who are *not* average and well-balanced—"

"Let's put it this way. It has been definitely established that for anyone with suicidal or homicidal tendencies or anyone who even suspects he has paranoid or schizophrenic inclinations, LSD, even in very small doses, could be tragic. Does that answer your question?"

Yes. It answered my question.

Henry cleared his throat, ran a hand over his head. "Just for the record—it's a felony to manufacture, sell or transport the stuff. It's considered, legally, a narcotic."

And then I knew: Henry had divined the drift of my questions, probably from the start. Now he was warning me.

"It makes me angry just talking about it," Dr. Crittenden was saying. "The ways people think of to destroy themselves just because they can't face things."

I looked at my glass. It was empty. I set it aside. And the food arrived.

"I took the liberty of ordering for you," Henry said. "How about another Scotch?"

"No, thanks," I said without thinking—and realized that I did not want another.

"Dr. Crittenden?"

"Oh no, thank you. I never drink at lunch in White Plains. It's only because I'm in the city. And to screw up courage, too, I suppose—" His smile flashed.

It was then that I remembered Henry's saying that he was going to get help for me, expert help. "Are you a psychiatrist, Doctor?" I asked.

"Me? Oh no. Just a GP."

I looked at Henry: he was frowning, fork poised, as if waiting for . . . what? For me to accuse the doctor of lying? For me to suspect Henry of plotting against me again? I smiled.

And then Henry grinned and said, "Eat your roast beef, you lucky bastard. You look as if you need it."

The beef was thick, pink, succulent. With the first taste hunger struck. But there was still something I had to know. "Doctor, there's no sharp line, is there, between . . . well, neurosis or psychotic tendencies and total insanity? I mean: very few people simply blow up and go mad, the way we think of it, do they?"

Dr. Crittenden glanced from me to Henry before he replied. "Well, as I told you, my experience is definitely limited. But, yes, there is a line—not one that an inexperienced layman or even someone such as myself might be able to recognize in most instances. However, a competent psychiatrist, after an examination and certain tests—"

"But a mind doesn't just go over a line and then explode in raving lunacy—"

Dr. Crittenden stopped chewing, stared. "But of course it *can* happen. Not necessarily raving lunacy, though." He cast another glance in Henry's direction. "There can be withdrawal, a refusal to deal with the real world, often a retreat into some fantasy that's more pleasant and satisfying to the deranged mind." He was looking at me again, frowning. "One can't conjecture, or predict."

Henry laughed then—and I caught the hollowness behind the sound. "I should have warned you about Adam. When he has a client he's concerned about, he gets terribly involved personally." He cleared his throat again. "One of the reasons I wanted Adam to hear the facts of your . . . predicament, Doctor. If there's anyone who can think of a way out for you, it's Adam. Shall I explain or do you want to?"

And he had adroitly changed the subject. But I had my information.

"I think you have all the facts—"

"Well, Adam, it's this way. Dr. Crittenden here"—and he lowered his voice—"is often paid by his patients in cash. And over the last several years he's fallen into the habit of putting the cash aside—"

"Not all of it—"

"Oh no, not all of it, of course, but a fairly substantial percentage—"

"It started out just so that my wife could have some extra spending money. She's not extravagant but she was brought up in such a way that—"

"Let's just say Dr. Crittenden has accumulated a large amount of cash—how much did you tell me, Doctor?"

"Well . . . upward of forty thousand."

"And he has it stowed away in a safe in the basement of his home."

"I wish I'd never gotten started! You don't dare buy anything in cash anyway, way the government keeps tabs on everybody. Secret police tactics—"

"The *point* is, Adam, that Dr. Crittenden has not reported this income to Internal Revenue and now he faces an audit—"

"No warning. You know how they do things! Suspect everyone, guilty or not!"

"The trouble is"—and Henry's voice, although not his carefully composed face, had begun to betray irritation—"the trouble is, you see, that his records in the office—name of patient, date of visit, how much charged, all that—won't tally with his income-tax returns. I told him I knew you'd be able to come up with a solution."

They both waited. While Professor Kantor's face flickered in my mind again. I ate the last bite and realized that neither of them had eaten half his lunch. Evasively, I said, "Why don't you go to a tax attorney, Dr. Crittenden? Why come to us?"

"My accountant referred me to one, but . . . but he—I forget his name—he phoned Mr. Brant here to see whether *he*'d handle the case."

I looked at Henry.

He began to eat again. "It was George Kimball and he told me frankly he couldn't afford to have anything to do with the case unless Dr. Crittenden—"

"He wanted me to confess. He advised—"

"Why," I interrupted, "did Kimball think of *you*, Henry?"

Henry's face hardened. "We were in law school together, that's all, and he thought someone who wasn't involved in tax law might handle the case . . . in an unofficial sort of way."

It is not a business then, gentlemen, or a way to get rich, but a sacred trust. The solution was transparently simple and it was not a legal one. It was, in fact, illegal. And Henry knew what it was as well as I did. But I waited.

"I've discussed it all with Dr. Crittenden, Adam, and we've tentatively agreed that if you can find a way out, you might be willing to help him—not as an attorney exactly, but on the side, in a *personal* way, having nothing to do with the firm." He paused and I recognized the technique. "Dr. Crittenden has agreed to pay twenty thousand dollars. In cash."

It all came perfectly clear then, of course. Henry had refused to handle it. Then, after I had told him about the hundred and twenty thousand dollars this morning—

"Which I think is outrageous," Dr. Crittenden was saying, sipping his coffee, "but I'm over a barrel and I know it. I certainly don't want to go to jail and I can't afford the disgrace."

"Do you think of any way to get this young man off the spot, Adam?"

Henry knew and had known from the beginning: go over the office files, remove a sufficient number of cash-payment cards to correspond to the amounts withheld, make certain the medical records of those same patients are put away for a while, adjust the appointment calendar to conform or, if necessary, make up a new one with those names removed, thus bringing the whole into mathematical conformance with the cash amounts reported on the tax returns—

"Perhaps you'd like some time to ponder it, Adam—"

Twenty thousand. In cash. Leaving only one hundred thousand to recoup after Wilby was gone. If Wilby ever left. A few more "cases" like this and I could recover within a year or so.

"Doctor," I said—and there was no anger in me, not even a sense of outrage, only that same somewhat disturbing calm—"Doctor, as a physician having sworn what some cynics call the hypocritical oath, would you commit euthanasia?"

Dr. Crittenden laid down his fork and his jaw set. "Certainly not. But I scarcely see how—"

"Recommend unnecessary surgery?"

"Of course not, but—"

"How about splitting fees?"

Now he was glaring. "Mr. Wyatt, my ethics as a doctor of medicine are unassailable."

"Well," I said, "my ethics as an attorney may not be. Up to now. But from now on they are going to be."

Silence. Henry's eyes were angry and baffled. A waiter poured more coffee.

When he withdrew, Dr. Crittenden said, "You're trying to make me feel like a criminal. For doing something everyone else does, one way or the other. It happens, Mr. Wyatt, that I do not agree with the way my tax money is being spent. Wild-eyed socialistic schemes, for political purposes. Poverty programs. Medicare!"

"It also happens," I said softly, "that I am not at all convinced about our policy in Vietnam. But that doesn't give me the moral right to break the law, does it?"

Henry sighed, still glaring at me, with puzzlement still there behind his eyes. "It appears, Dr. Crittenden, that Mr. Wyatt is refusing to accept your case. I'm sorry."

"So am I," Dr. Crittenden said, and he stood up, lips thin, nostrils flaring. "Mr. Wyatt, who are you to judge?"

I looked up at him. " 'He that is without sin among you, let him cast the first stone at her . . .'?"

"Something like that, yes."

"Doctor"—and I was listening to my words, which sounded soft and slow and wondering—"Doctor, if a man had to be innocent before he could judge others, or himself, there would be no justice and the whole fabric of law, *and* morality, and possibly civilization itself, would come completely apart at the seams."

Henry was frowning, his shaggy brows drawn together. And Dr. Crittenden looked bewildered. It was as if they were both trying to absorb something that was either too complex or too profoundly simple to comprehend—or that made no sense at all. And even as I heard the words echoing in my mind, I could not be sure, either.

Then Dr. Crittenden said, "Mr. Wyatt, you have a nasty cut on your right hand. I suggest you have it taken care of at once. It could infect and you'd find yourself in serious trouble. Good-by, and thank you for the lunch."

Henry watched him walk away. Then he ran his hand over his head, turning to face me across the table again. And he lifted an arm to signal a waiter.

"I think *I*'ll have a drink. Just to make sure my goddamned ulcer kicks up *more* than it's kicking!" To the waiter: "Scotch and water, high tide, no ice." Then to me: "How about you?"

I shook my head. Not because I was afraid to have a second— after all, I hadn't felt the first—but because I simply didn't want another drink at midday.

After the waiter had gone, Henry rubbed his craggy face. "Crittenden's an excellent doctor. I had him checked out. And before you came in, he was telling me—and not to set himself up, either—how he had stayed up two nights in a row with some kid because he didn't trust the nurses to give it the proper dosage of antibiotics every two hours. Saved it, too."

"I don't doubt that," I said, aware that yesterday, before I had by some mysterious process learned to juggle and accept opposites and contradictions, I might have doubted it.

Baffled, Henry had retreated into anger: his growl revealed it. "Harkness says he'll have your check at two-thirty, not one damned minute before and *probably* later." As I glanced at my watch—1:32 —he went on. "Did you talk with Chenery?"

"Mr. Chenery and I had a pleasant little stroll." Had he put the twins down for their nap now and was he checking to make sure his blowgun was loaded with poison darts? "Two of them, in fact. Chenery prefers murder but he'll supply me with anything available to civilized man."

Henry eyed me shrewdly. "Like LSD?"

Did he imagine that I hadn't guessed earlier that he had comprehended my questions? "We didn't discuss it by name, but your friend Chenery is omnipotent in the area of death and destruction."

The drink arrived and he lifted it to his lips at once. "He's not my friend, but you are. And you'd better give whatever you're considering some slow careful *rational* thought." I did not miss the emphasis. "You heard what Crittenden said about homicidal and suicidal tendencies. I don't give a damn what happens to that perverted sonofabitch, but I know you. You find some way to pull the bolt out of the nut-machine or you feed him something that makes him kill himself or anyone else, I know what'll happen to *you*. And I don't mean legally."

"I'm not so sure," I said. "Now."

He took a long gulp and set down the glass sharply. "Well, I *am*. And what's to be gained? How can you be *sure* it would work? You can't get him committed to someplace where they can hold him as criminally insane until *after* he commits a criminal act and is *adjudged* insane."

What he was saying was true, of course—and being true, ironic. But I said, "Hank, I just can't afford to pass up anything."

He leaned over the table. "It doesn't concern you, does it—being on this high moral plane you're on today—that anything you do now will probably be against the law?"

I considered this. Yes, it concerned me. As the idea of killing had concerned me when I joined the Air Force. "Sometimes," I said, "it's necessary to destroy in order to preserve."

"Yeh, I remember your saying something like that once in London." But he was still puzzled. "Then what about Crittenden? If you're willing to break the law yourself?"

I answered without hesitation. "I'm not saying that I don't respect the law, Hank. Even when it can't protect me. But I won't break it for money. Or for almost anything else."

His face was troubled, urgent. "You're seriously thinking of murdering a man or driving him insane!"

"I hope neither will be necessary. But you're right." For Lydia and Anne, yes—anything.

He straightened, he heaved a long sigh, then he said, "By God I think you scare me more now than you did this morning."

" 'Insanity,' " I quoted—and remembered now, as I had not been able to less than an hour ago, that it had been Oliver Wendell Holmes who had written it—" 'insanity is often the logic of an accurate mind overtaxed'?" It was a question.

"I don't know," Henry said, "I'm *damned* if I know."

"I don't know, either," I admitted—and felt no terror now in the simple acknowledgment.

He sat back, peering down at the glass in his hand. "Who was it who said that we should commit every act of our lives in such a way that, if everyone else behaved in exactly that way, we'd reach the millennium?"

I thought a moment, then recalled and said, "Whoever wrote it, it's not cant."

Henry lifted his gaze to me, and smiled. "I was wrong about you and Crittenden, Adam. I was only trying to get you a few tax-free bucks because I don't like to think of you and Lydia busted. After all, they taught legal ethics at the University of Virginia, too. I've been sore as the devil here because you turned him down. Or at least that's what I *thought* I was sore about." He sat up straight, frowning again. "But, hell, I guess I was just sore at myself for even considering it. Maybe, these days, a person's got to be a little nuts even to think about the rules."

I smiled then. "Maybe," I said, "but I hope not."

"Oh, shut up!" he growled. "You're not nuts." And he was leaning close again, studying me—again puzzled. "You know, I don't know how it's come about, but a lot's happened since this morning. I'm not even sure I know what I mean. You look twenty years older than you did two days ago and twenty years younger than you did this morning."

"That puts me right back where I started."

Henry laughed. "Do you realize, Adam, we haven't sat and talked like this in years?"

"If ever," I said.

"If ever." And now a sadness echoed in his tone. He let his eyes drift around the restaurant, avoiding mine, and finally said, "To hell with it. I'm going to give my ulcer another treat." He lifted an arm, caught a waiter's eye over my shoulder and pointed to his empty glass. "Adam?"

Again I shook my head. Almost an hour to kill before the check could possibly arrive from Harkness, yet I did not want a drink.

"I've been thinking about Lee Gray," Henry said finally, heavy brows lifting as he observed me. He waited.

"Well?"

"You don't want him in, do you?"

"Do you?"

"No. But I lied just now. I haven't been thinking about him at all. Until now. And I don't want him in, either."

The drink arrived.

"Adam—"

"Yes?"

"You got that monkey off your back yet?"

"Which particular monkey?"

And he smiled. "The one I mentioned this morning. Not that guilt doesn't have its place. Doubt we could get along without it. But it can gnaw your damn heart away if you let it. Reason somebody along the way dreamed up the idea of expiation. Penance or Yom Kippur, depending on your religion. Adam, haven't you put yourself through enough hell to be . . . what's the word? Purged?"

Had I? Would I ever be? Was hell large enough or long enough, hot enough or cruel enough? "I can't answer that, either," I said. Lydia, forgive me. Can you ever forgive me?

"Maybe you can answer this one then: how did you get that cut on your hand?"

"I was clawed by a cat."

Henry shrugged. "Well, you ask a foolish question—" He drank deeply, then said, "I'll ask another one—what now?"

"Nothing until I get the money. Then I'm going to buy a painting for one hundred and twenty thousand dollars and then I am going back to the apartment and sell it to him for one dollar. And what he calls other considerations."

Henry frowned, not speaking for a long moment. Then he whistled softly. "Other considerations being that go-go trollop, I suppose. Inflation's certainly hit the prostitution market." He shook his head, angry again. "Leave it to those perverted minds to dream up a scheme like—" Then he broke off and sat staring across at me. "You're going back to the apartment and then what? They'll just get up and walk out?"

"The girl's not there. And might not come back. He is, but if she doesn't come back, he says he plans to stay."

"Jesus H. Christ," Henry said under his breath and took another long swallow. "All right! What if he means it?"

"I'll have to face that when the time comes."

Henry nodded—but uncertainly. "You've been back there, haven't you?" And when I nodded: "And?"

"I can't be sure, but I think he's cracking up."

"Oh, you think he's cracking up!" he echoed with heavy irony, almost scorn. "And if he does?"

"I have no way of knowing."

He shifted in his chair, the anger returning to his voice. "Then how can you sit there as if—" But he stopped himself. "Adam . . . we've been discussing your . . . killing him. What if *he* kills *you*?"

"That thought simply hadn't occurred to me," I said, and realized, with only mild surprise, that I was telling the truth.

"Well, it *should* have!"

"I'll have to face that possibility when the time comes."

He slammed his palm onto the table. "No, you won't. You'll face it now!"

"Hank, I'll just do my best to see that doesn't happen."

He was leaning far over the table, so close now that I could see the small, fine lines of age spraying out from his eyes. "Listen! You don't have to convince me you've got guts. But you're missing my *point*! It's all well and good not to think about yourself—that's what you've been doing all along. But you're overlooking something!" He was whispering furiously. "What happens to Lydia if that bastard kills you?"

I stood up. The calm was shattered—but only inside because outwardly I was able to stand quite still, unshaking. I had overlooked it—how could I have overlooked it?

"Thanks, Hank." And I turned away.

"You want me to come with you?"

I could only shake my head.

"Call me if you need me. Anything."

I nodded and walked off.

There it was again: Henry as friend. This morning he had forced me to realize that I had not once considered suicide. Now, thanks to him, I knew that, of all the risks and potentials I had tried to imagine and calculate, my own death had not been one of them. Further evidence, if evidence were needed, that my composure of the last hour was illusory.

Still, as I strode more swiftly toward the office now, I felt in no danger of crumbling—or of my mind's veering off again into that no man's land of contradictions and ironies and wild logic as it had earlier on the street. Thanks also, at least in part, to Henry. To Henry who had been able to move outside himself just now, who had been able to think first of Lydia—whom he loved—but had been able to think of her in relation to me, whom he also loved, rather than in relation to himself. My gratitude touched a new depth. But not gratitude alone—rather, my growing certainty that love, love outside self, was not only a conceivable ideal but was possible. Existed. Even I, damn it, had not been thinking of my own death.

Now I had to consider my own death. *Y'couldn't do it, man, even if you had a gun. But I could. One kick I never had.* Yes, Wilby, I believe you: you could. Had I been laboring then under the most universal and irrational of misapprehensions, the same one that had carried me through those twenty-five missions—the unreasonable conviction that somehow I, being myself and therefore indestructible, must survive, that every bullet is marked by fate for the next fellow?

It's you or me now, dad. You or me!

I had read somewhere once, probably back in college, of someone condemned to death who had realized that if he had to live somewhere on a rock ledge so narrow that he had only room to stand, and around him and below only everlasting darkness and solitude and tempests and fathomless abysses, it was better to live so than to die. Whoever had written that was right: I could feel it myself. Death. Annihilation. Oblivion. Nothingness. Not twenty or thirty more years as I had imagined last night—the thought that had tortured me into what I knew now was only a shallow despair, the thought that seemed now only inconsequential—but quite possibly only a few more hours.

Lover, we're all gonna be dead. What's time?

And now I had the answer. It did not come to me. I simply knew it. Time, Wilby, is what we have. *All* we have. Time, whether it's years or hours or minutes or seconds, is eternity to each of us. And eternity is short: an hour is short, a lifetime is short, a millennium is short. But is that cause to weep and wail and gnash our teeth? This is the fact; these are the conditions. It's short for everyone else, too. Last night, Wilby, I nibbled at the poison-roots of your rebellion and the despair that drives you on to more cruelty—but, damn it, time is too short for that! Too brief and therefore—*therefore*, for that reason!—too valuable to waste in cursing what cannot be, what you feel should be but what in the nature of things never has been, cannot be, and never will be. But . . . but—and here's the point, Wilby, here's the whole stunning final point: life is not *less* valuable for being brief and mortal, but more valuable, more precious and important and potentially satisfying *because* of its very brevity! Because it *is* passing, because it *is* evanescent, because we *are* mortal. If I have two or three hours instead of twenty or thirty years or eternity, then those two or three *are* eternity to me. If all I have is consciousness, then a microsecond is infinity.

Which is not to say, Wilby, that I will not do everything in my power to extend that eternity of mine, even if it means cutting short *your* eternity. Because, Wilby, I am now the captain of my ship and my ship carries a precious cargo—as you know and have known from the start—although I still cannot comprehend how you *could* know. It carries those whom I love—how could you know if you cannot believe in love?—those who would suffer if I were to go overboard. Because they also love. How the hell could you—alienated and violently uncommitted—comprehend this commitment of which I have just become aware? Because if it were not for your cruel knowledge of it, you could never have brought me to this moment.

You may kill me, Wilby—possibly nothing short of that will satisfy you. Possibly nothing will ever satisfy you. *It's you or me now, dad.* I again became conscious of the heaviness in my right pocket. If it comes to that, it's going to be you, Wilby.

On the crowded elevator I recalled something I had heard smugly quoted and repeated all during the war: that there were no atheists in the fox-holes. During those years I had thought little of it—only that the statement did not correspond with some of the men I had seen in the cockpits, gun turrets, and bomb bays. Now, even though the word itself still held a vestigial distasteful note in my mind I had to be counted among them—and with no apology to anyone, with no regretful inclination to be anything else or to feel any differently.

Passing through the outer office, I realized why I had been hurrying. "Phoebe, get Mrs. Wyatt in London. You have the number. If she's not in find out when she's expected or where she can be reached." And hearing my voice, I could not detect even the dimmest suggestion of the trembling that was now deep inside me.

Standing at my desk, I feel the cigarette burn my fingers. I had not realized I was smoking. I squashed it out, tensed for the sound of the buzzer. I reached for another. Package empty. I opened the desk drawer: one package left in the carton. Nine packages since yesterday morning? Impossible. I tore off the cellophane. *Suppose those government reports are correct, as Arnold swears they are?* Lydia: several years ago when we had decided to stop smoking. *It only seems reasonable to me not to take the chance. I, for one, am going to try to get as many years as I can get—since what we have is all we can really be certain of.* So Lydia had known what I had only learned, or come to acknowledge. I stood in quiet amazement: if she knew, had known all along, then why hadn't we ever talked about it? Why were there so many things, important and vital subjects, that we had never discussed? *I really don't know why I occasionally get this impulse to go to church.* When had she said that? Some time when I was only half listening, too immersed in the day-to-day, year-to-year trivialities of the moment? *Perhaps it's only ingrained habit. Or perhaps some childhood reach for security.* And what had I said? *Or a hope for answers. In all the books today, no one really seems concerned in the slightest about the whys.* And I had not even read the books. Had not recognized or glimpsed the possibility that in her all along there might have been some hurtful and anguished hunger to know, to talk out, to find help, to reach clarity.

Astonishing. Amazing and awesome: so all that had been going on and I hadn't even been aware of it. Astonishing and . . . terrible, too.

The buzzer. At last.

"Yes?"

"The overseas operator says it will take at least ten minutes Mr. Wyatt. Because of the circuits."

Ten minutes. Forever. My watch read 2:02. Less than half an hour before the check.

"Thanks, Phoebe." And I wondered how she felt now, putting through the call to Lydia, how she had felt over the last three years: miserable, riddled with jealousy? It was odd, really, to think of all that had been going on around me, all that I had not been conscious of.

I dropped the fresh unopened pack of cigarettes into the wastebasket. He who is about to die refuses a blindfold and a cigarette. No, thanks—wouldn't want to get lung cancer.

Ten minutes and then—Lydia's voice. Why hadn't I phoned her before? *You may blame my Scottish grandfather, darling, but I don't fancy fattening the coffers of I.T. and T. This whole thing's costing us enough.* Not much, darling—only everything we've saved for more than twenty years. Only that.

I stepped to the window, gazed out. In one window across the street, a red-haired girl was sitting at a typewriter; in another three men leaned over a drawing board; and in another a stenographer was taking dictation from a man behind a desk. On the roof of a building down the street a huge billboard advertised, in blazing colors, a sleek-looking car; perched on the hood was a young woman wearing a bikini and smiling broadly. All part of a daily humdrum unremarkable pattern that I had seen, with variations, for years, so familiar that now I was blind to it.

As I had been blind to so many other things.

Leisurely Sunday mornings in the apartment, papers strewn across the floor after breakfast, Lydia in silken pajamas on the floor herself, chin propped on hands: *How would you like to be dragged to the Bolshoi Ballet this week? No, I thought not.* (Laughing and rolling onto her back, teasing.) *There's no foreign dialogue, you know.* Weekend drives to and from the country: summer with the lush green on all sides—*I hope summer never ends!*—and fall with the violent colors causing her to point out tree after lovely tree—*But September's always a trifle sad, isn't it?*—and winter with every trunk and branch wrapped in glistening ice, snow and hills rolling white in the misty distance—*Don't you sometimes wish winter could last-*

forever?—and spring bursting with greens and yellows, the air soften-
ing at last and the wind catching her fair hair—*I always forget:
May's the loveliest, after all!* The hurried five-days-a-week morning
meals, Lydia in housecoat, eyes still dim with sleep, skin clear and
fresh as a girl's: *I don't know why we take both morning papers when
you never have a chance to read even one of them.* Dinners with candles glowing on Lydia's pale loveliness across from me, silver gleaming, wine glasses catching the flame. Lydia teasing: *The French may
not know how to make love the way you do, darling, but I'll wager
you couldn't make wine like this if you tried.*

And what had I said? Where had I been while all this was going
on? What had I been doing, thinking? Of the day's appointments, a
hearing, a brief that had to be written.

I stood at the window lost in a trance of nostalgia at once painful
and strangely tender. And I wondered whether this was how a prisoner felt—a man sentenced to die in the morning—who could look
out across a countryside and see a light flickering in some strange
house across the hills, aching finally with the sense of loss and for the
first time, in anguished wonder, understanding freedom: what it
might mean to live in that house, to sit in the warmth and comfort of
that distant light. Was it invariably true that only a man confined
could comprehend freedom, that only a man condemned to death
could experience living? Can't we ever know what we have until we
have lost it?

The war came back again then. Lydia popping into the hotel unexpected as the air-raid was beginning: *Impulse. Well, what are you
going to do about it? What's a blitz compared to what you're going to
do about it?* We rarely spoke of those days now. Did Lydia remember? *What* did Lydia remember? I should know. I should *know*—

But how much did I know of her? Beyond her beauty and desir-
ability? What did I know of her as a person, an independent, separate, living individual? Is it possible that after all this time she's still a
mystery to me? A woman whose voice, whose slightest move can stir
me to desire, can always delight and satisfy *me*, but—

*I think it's a kind of miracle that we can still excite each other this
much after*—wrinkling her smooth brow and turning her head on the
pillow—*well, after quite a few years, what?* In love-making, her
varied moods: sometimes gay and playful, often intense and passionate, sometimes quietly, happily passive. But always unabashed, whole-

somely abandoned. *What I only hope*—her soft drowsy contented voice—*is that we can still enjoy each other like this when we're both seventy. And I don't see any reason why not, do you?*

Whatever I had answered then, now I could only hear Jenny's strident frustrated anger drowning out Lydia's voice in my mind: *Oh you are a bastard old man, not even a man!*

I had forgotten.

That Jenny, she takes it outta a man. Burns it out, click?

How could I have forgotten?

I did not turn from the window. I had not desired Jenny. I had not even been tempted to let Phoebe take me home, or to her apartment. I had not even been aware of any woman as a woman in the streets, in the windows across from me now.

Has Wilby won, then? On some mysterious level isn't this what he also—

The buzzer sounded. I could not move.

The buzzer sounded again.

In truth, Adam, I've begun to feel a trifle old—

No, Lydia, no! I was not shaking. I moved to the desk. No, Lydia, not you, ever, not old—

I touched the button. I uttered a sound.

"Mr. Wyatt . . . Mrs. Wyatt is on the line."

I picked up the telephone, bracing myself for the sound of her voice. In abrupt panic knowing: I can't bear to hear her voice. A humming on the line, a crackling in my ear.

Then: "Adam? Hallo. Adam?"

The musical tone, the precise words, low-keyed—her voice welled into my ear, flowed like some rare intoxicating wine through my whole body, flooded my mind with its familiarity and at the same time its strangeness.

"Adam, can you hear me? Are you there?"

Then I was able to speak. "Hello, Lydia." And my own voice sounded normal, perfectly casual and polite and natural, as I had no reason to hope it would. "Yes, I'm here. How *are* you?"

"I? Why, I'm splendid. Can you hear me? What a pleasant surprise. You know how I love surprises."

Did I? Yes, I knew, had always known—but how many times had I surprised her because she loved surprises?

"Adam, there's nothing wrong, is there? What I mean to say is: you're not phoning for any *reason,* are you?"

None, Lydia. None, my darling—except that I may never hear your voice again. "No reason," I lied—the first lie, the first of how many? "No reason, Lydia, except that I wanted to hear your voice." The truth now—not the whole truth, Lydia, but *true!*

"Well," she said, after a pause, "well, that's the nicest surprise of all."

Was there a note of caution in her tone? Why? Because I had not, at least in recent years, telephoned her simply to hear her voice? Or had I revealed something in my tone? My words? Or was it simply Lydia's intuition, what Anne always called her sixth sense?

"How . . . how's your mother?"

"Ohhh—you know Mother. Verge of death, then up and at them. Honestly, Adam, she's a war-horse. The pneumonia's left her weak, of course, but even weak she's almost her old self. Which I admit is not entirely to the good. How are *you*?"

How was I? I hoped she would never know. "Oh, a bit bored," I said—another lie. "A bit lonely—" Also a lie: *intensely* lonely, Lydia, I've never been so lonely in my life, I never knew what loneliness was! "I just wanted to say . . . hello."

I realized I was clutching the telephone, picturing her face across all those hundreds of miles while the line made odd spitting and thrumming noises: the delicate patrician clear-skinned face and bright blue eyes, soft, soft—

"Did you get my letter, Adam? The one I addressed to the office? I told you about going to the theater, remember?" I remembered: she would not go to the theater alone, someone must have taken her—oh Lydia, forgive me, can you ever forgive me! "It was really amusing. Here I was with Laurie—you remember Laurie? well, no matter—she's a dear, sweet old thing but a spinster to her toenails—and the play was all about these two sort of music-hall or vaudeville bums waiting for someone I believe was supposed to be God—who, fortunately for us, if not for them, didn't ever appear—and do you know what I was thinking?"

No, Lydia—I'm not sure I ever really knew what you were thinking. Tell me, tell me now, because I long to know, I ache to know.

"All I could think of was: I don't know who they're waiting for any more than they do, but isn't it pathetic that we all wait and wait and waste time, spend it as though we had forever—" She broke off.

. . . *Graceful and civilized thing to do is to demand less . . . and to settle for—whatever one has.*

No Lydia. My heart twisting. Not you. I don't want you to settle for less. I won't let you. I love you and I won't let you!

"Are you listening, Adam?"

"I'm listening." Now. How many times have I not listened? I'll always listen in the future, Lydia, if there can be a future, I want to know you, know all about you, know— "I'm listening, Lydia—"

"I was saying how sad it really is that we waste whole parts of our lives and our selves when—" Her voice drifted off again: why should she expect me to listen, understand or care or reply?

"When," I said, "time is all we have."

"What? I beg your—"

"When time," I said, firmly, knowing, "is all we have and no less valuable for being brief. Not meaningless, either, because it won't go on forever, the way we were promised. More precious because of that."

"Adam—" The startlement became a throb of excitement. "Adam, you don't even sound like yourself. You don't talk like—"

"And it's not pathetic that we all wait and hope for someone who won't come because he isn't there. Not sad or pathetic, but tragic."

"Adam!" It's a cry that turns into a sob—a sob across a thousand miles, across a sea, a sob sounding in its depths, in the electric current running through the cable in those depths, in the wail of wind, in the space and five-hours' time lapse between us.

Finally she said, "Adam . . . I'm coming home."

At first I was not sure I had heard the words; at first I thought perhaps I had heard the words only because they were the words I most dreaded hearing.

Then she said them again. "I've just decided, darling. This very instant. I'm coming home."

While I kept waiting for the shock to take over. Why wasn't I shouting that she couldn't come, that it was impossible, that she had to wait, give me time? Instead, I heard myself ask, "How soon?" and there was no mistaking the urgency in my tone, the need, the desperation to have her come at once, at *once,* damn it!

Then she was speaking in a rush. "As soon as possible. I'll phone Pan American. If there's no flight tonight—it's after seven over here, you know, I was just sitting down to dinner—I'm sure he'll get me something tomorrow. Even though I had hoped to take a ship. But I'll ignore my slight case of vertigo—" She paused as if for breath, and I realized that I had forgotten she rarely flew because of her aversion to high places. How could I love her and forget these things? Did I know her *at all*? I heard her laugh, low-throated and exciting, over the droning, snapping wire. "Darling, I'll be on the first plane that has a spare seat even if it has two wings and one propeller. It'll be only a matter of hours. Imagine!"

"Lydia—"

"Yes?"

"I love you."

I had to say it. It had to be said. A matter of hours could be forever. Tomorrow could be never. It had to be said. And, hearing the words, I wondered how long it had been since I used those actual words? Why? Why the hell hadn't I said them every day, every night?

At last she spoke, in a husky whisper. "Here now, here now, you can't do this to me with the whole Atlantic Ocean in between."

Then silence—only those faint sounds in which I imagined I could hear the sound of breakers, the crash of waves, the high Atlantic wind.

I closed my eyes, tears burning behind my lids. My throat was locked tight. *Hell is other people*. But I had been right then, that long eternity ago, Monday night, and Wilby had scoffed, but wondered. I had been right: *heaven* is other people, too. Or God. Or whatever word—

"Well," Lydia said then in her crisp, familiar down-to-business voice, "well, we don't have forever on long distance, that's one thing certain. Let's remember we don't own any I.T. and T. stock." She laughed. "I'll cable the flight number, all that rot. And Adam—"

"Yes, darling?"

"When I get off the plane"—and a frankly sensual anticipation came into her voice—"I'm going to say, 'Just in time! Well, what are you going to do about it? What's a blitz compared to what you're going to do about it?' "

Click. I stood holding the telephone.

She remembered. I was quivering all over. My blood was raging again. She remembered—as I had not, until yesterday, until today!

The tears were gone, but I kept my eyes closed. Picturing her, all of her, as I knew her, as no one else ever knew her, as I alone knew her: ever softer and more beautiful than that phantom in last night's dream, more desirable and incredible. And I longed to will myself across all those miles, that ocean, to find her, to hold her in my arms, to take and possess and hold that loveliness completely, utterly, to make love as we had never made love before, with exultancy, with joy, with savage abandon yet with tenderness, to bring her quickly to ecstasy, to savor the intensity of need and giving in her darkened eyes, in the side-to-side turning of her flushed and excited face, to satisfy myself through *her* gratification, knowing in the instant of mutual fulfillment that at least part of my own pleasure was the knowledge and certainty of hers. Then to lie with her, closely and loosely clinging, knowing that soon, very soon, the wildness will rekindle itself and the passion will rise brimming in both of us again. And then, slowly this time, with ineffable gentleness and now without urgency, to stir the deeper depths in both so that this time, this time, this time we come together, we merge, our minds dissolve, ourselves lost one in the other, as of light exchanged, as of light exploding in darkness, all strangeness gone, all singleness lost in total and profound accord.

I opened my eyes. I stared, transfixed, at the familiar office: the furniture and bookshelves and windows, the cluttered neglected desk. Like a traveler returning from a long journey and staring with fresh and astounded clarity at all he had known before. Sun dazzling. All angles sharper, surfaces smoother, reflections bright and hurtful to the eye. The moment was suspended, quivering and in itself infinite. To hell with Wilby and his gibes, Jenny and her taunts. Lydia is coming and we'll make love as long as we live, damn you both, and I'm going to live to do it, too!

I realized that I still held the phone in my hand. Slowly I replaced it.

. . . *demand less and settle for—what we have.* No, Lydia, you won't have to settle for that alone. Magnificent as that has always been, the beauty and satisfaction of that can now be only a part of a greater, deeper magnificence.

I took the gun and placed it on the desk. *You don't know who you are, dad.* No, Wilby, I don't. No one knows who he is because he is only what he is becoming. He is whatever he decides he will be. I took the six bullets from my other pocket. I know that now, Wilby, thanks at least in part to you. I picked up the gun and broke it open. I am going to get to know Lydia—more for her sake than for mine. I inserted the bullets into the chamber, twirled it, snapped the gun shut. To explore the richness and complexity that I now know exists, I have to live—*also* more for her sake than for mine. I replaced the gun in my pocket. I intend to salvage what is left of Lydia's bit of eternity. What I am becoming, Wilby, thanks in part to you, might cut short *your* eternity. I don't want to kill you, you or anyone, because I do have what you scornfully call a reverence for life. But a new reverence now: a certainty of life's intrinsic value simply because it exists, not because it has been created to fulfill some greater meaning outside its own consciousness. Isn't it ironic, Wilby, that now that I am ready to live, I am much more ready, and able, to kill?

And you, lad, are trapped. For life. All or nothing. All now, Lydia, all.

Yet . . . irony on irony: that damned dark road that had carried me to this point of knowing—where the road ahead now lay open and radiant with promise and fulfillment—had begun with that physical animal act that, if Lydia ever learned or sensed, would shatter all promise, all radiance, all future. For both of us. Yet if that road ahead, no matter how bright, is paved with lies—

I looked at my watch: eight minutes until two-thirty. I sat down at the small typewriter that I rarely used, inserted a sheet of plain white paper, and typed: "Bill of Sale." When I had finished typing there were two underlined blank spaces—for the name of the painter and the title of the painting—and otherwise it was a perfectly legitimate and legal document representing one hundred and twenty thousand dollars. Once it was signed it would stand up in any court in the country.

I ripped it out of the typewriter, folded it, and placed it in the inside pocket of my jacket. Six minutes to kill now. But minutes cannot be killed. They are too precious.

I walked to the window again, my step firm and solid. In the windows the pretty red-haired typist was making an erasure, her arms bare and brilliant and soft, her hair catching the light, and the secretary was now sitting back and chatting with the man behind the desk, her short skirt high on her legs, which flashed golden when she crossed them; and the model in the bikini still perched, outsize and voluptuous, atop the car in the billboard photograph. And I knew now, of course, why none of these sights—or Jenny's attempts at further seduction or Phoebe's invitation—had any meaning for me: not because I was impotent but because I had learned what Lydia had always known. *I keep remembering what Mummy always said— about sex and love being one thing. Or that they should be.* I remembered Donald watching the go-go dancers. I thought of Donald with Jenny. *It's the best night I ever lived.* Sex as kicks. Women as toys,

toys of flesh—not people at all. Unreal, not women, much as they imagined themselves desired as individuals—rather, projections of erotic male reverie so that, in reality, each sex act in itself amounts to no more than adolescent masturbation. *But temptation can't exist unless we make a free conscious choice.* True, Father, but what if a man could pass beyond temptation, so that temptation could not exist simply because, by loving, he somehow has moved closer to fulfilling Professor Kantor's concept of evolution, has fulfilled his own small particular obligation to it? After all, in terms of evolution, sex in savage tribes was always rape. Rape. *The only way it comes off is if you rip it off.* I remembered—with revulsion and that harrowing sense of guilt that had tortured me for two days and two nights. Forgive me, Lydia, it was not love, only brute fury and hate, love's opposite. Before I had learned that sex of itself is meaningless. Worse: ludicrous, absurd—not proof of manhood but betrayal of man, denial of his potential.

I heard the buzzer sound, but I did not move at once because I was savoring another bitter but invigorating irony: if Wilby was the grit that had invaded the oyster, the pearl was mine. And now, if necessary, I was ready to kill for it. To kill *him* for it.

Unless he killed me first.

The buzzer again. I walked to the desk.

"Yes, Phoebe?"

"I'm sorry to bother you, Mr. Wyatt, but—"

"Has the envelope come from Mr. Harkness?"

"Not yet. But there's a lady here to see you. A Mrs. Corbin. I've told her you can't possibly see anyone today, but she's terribly distressed and she insists on seeing either you or Mr. Brant." As I shot a glance at my watch: 2:27. "If you could spare a few minutes, Mr. Wyatt, I do think it might relieve her mind."

It was the first time Phoebe had ever made such a suggestion. Compassion. Again. And sharply, quickly, I remembered Mr. Corbin in the apartment Monday evening. *I don't know. I just don't know what'd become of them if they lost the house, the car—* And myself standing and shouting at the hearing yesterday. *And what percentage of the judgment do you collect, Doctor, in the name of justice and your goddamned hypocritical oath?*

"Phoebe, call Mr. Harkness. Ask him whether he wants you to pick up my check or whether he's sending it by messenger. And . . . send Mrs. Corbin in."

"Yes, Adam." Adam again. "And thank you."

Phoebe cared. About Mrs. Corbin? A stranger. I thought of the bearded old man on the street.

"Phoebe . . . when the check comes from Mr. Harkness, bring it in at once, please."

"Yes, Adam."

I remained standing until Mrs. Corbin entered: a heavy-set woman, plainly dressed, only in her thirties yet matronly and unprepossessing. We did not shake hands. When I had spoken with her several times before, I had found her nervousness and defensive illogic somewhat disconcerting and irritating. As she settled into the chair, holding her purse in both hands on her lap, her eyes looked guarded and angry—and, as Phoebe had said, determined. But behind this expression was the distress Phoebe had also detected: a sort of trapped distraction verging on hysteria. At once I longed to be able to reassure her, as I had tried to reassure her husband.

Instead, I said, "Mrs. Corbin, I owe you an apology."

"Yes," she said, her chin setting, "yes, I think you do." Then her eyes met mine directly—and almost imperceptibly changed. She frowned. "I know you're busy. Your secretary said you had an important appointment at two-thirty, but—"

"Take your time, Mrs. Corbin," I said, remembering that the bank closed at three. "Try to relax."

"Relax? I haven't relaxed in . . . I don't know when. Since the accident, I suppose. No—before."

But she's a fine woman, she's worked hard, she takes care of the children—

Mrs. Corbin crossed her legs, again, moved about in the chair, tried to compose herself, then sat up stiffly. "Now I know Mr. Corbin . . . my husband shouldn't have gone to your home night before last. I told him that. And I know that a person's personal life doesn't have any bearing on . . . their business and such—"

I remembered Mr. Corbin in the living room staring at Wilby's dark glasses, beard, clothes, boots. *I'm kinda Mr. Wyatt's legal adviser.*

"I don't think I agree with you, Mrs. Corbin," I said and watched her thick brows arch in surprise. "I doubt that it's even possible to divide a man's personal and business life." Had I always believed that? Had I even given it any thought? Or had I learned this, too?

"Oh. Well, I'm surprised to hear you say it. Considering what

Leonard told me. About your friends. And the way you were drinking." Her lips thinned. "Were you drinking before the hearing yesterday, too?"

Who had told her of that? "I'm not sure," I said. "In all honesty I can't remember. But I *was* drinking on Monday evening. To be absolutely truthful, I've been under a terrific strain these last few days. But that's no excuse and I don't intend it to be. I'm terribly sorry about what happened and I'll try to make sure it doesn't prejudice your case."

Mrs. Corbin was frowning. Bewildered. Her grip on the purse tightened. "Well . . . we all have our personal . . . worries. Don't we?" She was peering at me. "You . . . you don't look so good, really. You—" But then she squirmed in the chair again. "Mr. Wyatt, I'm going to be honest, too. I liked you when we talked before. And Leonard . . . he said he liked you very much, which was more than he could say for your friend. We both feel . . . felt that you were on our side and didn't want to see us taken advantage of by Lucy Sloane and those other lawyers. With Mr. Gray—well, he wants to win, I suppose, but it's only kind of his job." She paused and I waited, glancing at my watch surreptitiously. 2:29. "But I have to think about my husband. He's worked hard. Nobody but me knows how hard that man has—" She broke off, turned away slightly, biting her lip. "I worry about him more than anything."

She's so worked up about this, it's awful. I can't stand to look in her face.

"Mrs. Corbin," I said, "all your husband is disturbed about is what will happen to you and the children."

"Me?" she asked sharply, her face swinging around, chin lifting. "Why should he worry about me? Why, I can get a job tomorrow! Even if they take everything we own, I can always—" But the momentary anger flickered out. "It's only . . . Leonard and I decided, right from the start, we'd rather have just one car, maybe not so many luxuries, so I could be home with the kids. Neighbors all think we're . . . well, not like everybody else. But I can't see leaving kids with strangers just to have two cars and maybe a freezer in the basement, can you?"

I had never thought about it. "No," I said, knowing that I did agree. "No, I can't."

Her eyes had narrowed—puzzlement again. "You sure Leonard was worried about *me*?"

I saw it then, saw it whole. And said, "Yes, I'm positive."

"Well, isn't that remarkable? I mean . . . because he's always criticizing. Asking why I should be so nervous. Like I could help being—" She stared away. "So Leonard said that—"

I saw it and, while it pained me to see it, I felt another spurt of exhilaration, another small jolt of hope and renewal.

"He said it because he loves you, Mrs. Corbin." I had never said anything remotely like it to anyone before.

Her head came about again: the plain flat face, the prematurely graying hair, the bewilderment in her eyes clearing. "That Leonard. Here all I been thinking about all this time was him." The fondness in her tone and eyes was unmistakable, unabashed. "Isn't that remarkable?"

"I don't think so," I said. "It happens more often than we imagine." I was thinking of Colin Welch. *You can believe it or not, but I'm one of those men who loves his wife.*

Mrs. Corbin stared a long moment before she seemed to make up her mind. "Mr. Wyatt, I came here to tell you that Leonard and I have decided we don't want you to handle our case."

"I'm sorry," I said then, unsurprised. "I'll tell my partner and he'll probably assign the case to Mr. Gray or take it over himself. If I were in your place, I'm sure I'd feel just as you do."

Mrs. Corbin stood up, clutching her purse with both hands again. "I've changed my mind. I only hope I'm not making a mistake."

At first I said nothing. A certain joy and relief flowed through me and I was amazed at how important the case had become in my mind. Even though I might not even be alive tomorrow. But then, who can say with any certainty that he will be alive tomorrow? "Thank you, Mrs. Corbin."

"Frankly, I didn't like the way Mr. Gray told me about what happened at that hearing yesterday. Like he didn't care about my feelings at all. Or for yours, either, Mr. Wyatt, if you really want the truth."

"Then it was Mr. Gray who suggested that he take over the case?" But the question was superfluous. The only significant question was why I had gone along for five years without recognizing Lee Gray for what I now knew him to be.

"Mr. Gray said he'd already spoken with the insurance company and they'd approved—" She appeared to be watching me.

"Mr. Gray," I told her, "is not going to be with this firm for very long. What he did was unethical and unforgivable. He was probably hoping to take away one of our clients." Or as Lee Gray would put it, *grabbing while the grabbing's good.*

"Isn't it awful," Mrs. Corbin asked, head tilted to one side, "isn't it just awful the way people are?"

I stood up. "*Some* people. Not all. Or we wouldn't be able to survive, would we?"

Mrs. Corbin looked bewildered again. "Yes. Well. I really don't have time to think about those things." She walked heavily to the door. "But I guess that's true, what you just said."

Lee Gray's voice remained in my mind: *The Corbins are not our clients.*

"One thing more, Mrs. Corbin." And when she stopped and turned at the door: "I am certain we can win this case and I would advise against your accepting any settlement amounting to more than the insurance coverage you have."

Now she was completely confused. "Even if the insurance company thinks we should?"

"Even then."

She was shaking her head. And then she went out.

I looked at my watch again. 2:33. I touched the button.

"Phoebe, did you get hold of Mr. Harkness?"

"The messenger's here now. I'm signing the receipt."

It would soon be over. One way or the other. Finally. It had to be over today. Because incredibly—Lydia was coming. Should I have phoned her? She had decided to come because I had phoned her. Curiously, though, I was not sure I could face what I now had to face if I had not talked with her.

Phoebe came in. She handed the envelope across the desk and I tore it open, glanced at the amount. After I had paid a hundred and nineteen thousand for the painting, there would be a balance of about eleven hundred dollars. Plus ten thousand in the savings account and whatever was left in the checking, probably not more than a couple of thousand—if that much after the three-thousand-dollar check I'd cashed Monday. I placed the check in my inside pocket along with the bill of sale. Life insurance: about a hundred and fifty thousand. Lydia would be better off if Wilby killed me. I walked around the end of the desk. Not true, not true—as Henry, loving her in his own way, knew. As I, loving her as I had never loved her before, now knew, too.

And I had forgotten Phoebe's presence. She stood watching me as I halted.

"Make a note for me to discuss the Corbin case with Mr. Brant first thing in the morning, will you, Phoebe?" Just as if tomorrow would be an ordinary morning. Just as if there would *be* a tomorrow morning. "If I'm not here, tell Mr. Brant I'm opposed to any settlement that would cost the Corbins one cent."

"If you're not here?"

I stepped to the door, avoiding her face, where her question was reflected: composed but fearful. "I'm expecting Mrs. Wyatt home some time tomorrow, and I may have to meet the plane." A lie? Well, a distortion of the truth. A half-truth. Sometimes necessary, sometimes not evil at all—when had I accepted that casual known fact? Or was I only preparing myself for the larger lie that I would have to tell by living it?

"Adam—"

"Yes?" And it was necessary to look into her face: she looked older somehow, tired, and delicate lines came through her make-up.

"My home telephone number's in your . . . in Mrs. Wyatt's address book. In the drawer of the table in your front hall. Just in case there's anything I—"

Y'mean Phoebe? Good old Phoebe Waldron? And another small piece of the puzzle fell into place. Wilby had searched the place down on Sunday before I had come in. Afterward, he had not missed a trick, not overlooked any smallest opportunity to torment, to plant doubts, fears. *Knew it, dad. Had my report. That secretary of yours.*

"I'm sorry, Phoebe," I said before I realized I had spoken.

Her brows lifted. "For what, Adam?"

I could not tell her. Dared not. Not this late.

"Do you think I even imagine you'd call me?" she asked, and the bitterness was laced with soft self-mockery. "For any other reason than—" But she stopped and turned to the window. In its ruthless light I could see the roots of her dyed hair again: dark, a suggestion of gray.

Let me take you home. I'll take care of you. No demands. Just to be there.

I stood gripped in a pain that was not mine. What could I say? If I were some other person, some other kind of person, perhaps I could go to her now, reach out, take her into my arms, even if only for a moment or two. But I could not be that cruel. Could not do it.

"Go on, Adam," she said quietly, with her back to me, "go on, wherever you're going, whatever you're going to do." Then she whirled about and I saw a glisten in her eyes and they looked angry and rebellious. "I'm only sorry you had to find out. That's all I'm sorry about, *the only thing*! If it hadn't been for this . . . whatever it is . . . you'd never have known and we could have gone on the way it was until we were both old and—" But her voice ran down and she took a deep breath that shuddered so that it became almost a sob. Then she smiled, faintly, and the sardonic softness returned. "Until we were both old or until that shining knight in silver armor came charging down Fifth Avenue to carry me off to his castle in Bronxville."

I would never have known because she would have made sure— and I thought of Henry loving Lydia over the years with the same pride and dignity and restraint. Phoebe, like Henry, would never have flirted or betrayed by a single glance or act.

"But there's a bright side, too, Adam. That shining knight just might come, or might have a chance, if I'm not around you at all—"

Again she stopped. And it was then that I knew we were in fact saying good-by. No matter what happened to me now, she would give notice, saying she had had a better offer or that she had decided to go back to her home town in—even now I didn't know where she had come from.

"I'm sorry, Phoebe." It was the best I could do. I meant it with sadness and loss and intensity.

Her chin came up. "Good luck, Adam."

And I went into the outer office aware that, although she had no idea what I was going into or what it might mean, she was thinking of me now, not of her own quiet despondency and loneliness.

The telephone rang.

I hesitated in the door to the corridor. What now? Wilby?

Phoebe appeared, crossed to her desk, punched a button, and picked up the telephone. "Mr. Wyatt's office."

Still I waited. Wilby? Or Lydia's cable? Anne?

"He was just leaving. I'll see if I can catch him if you'll hold on—" Phoebe lifted her face; her whole manner now was efficient, impersonal. "It's a Mr. Chenery. If you don't want to—"

But I was already returning to my own office. Nine minutes left to get to the bank. I took up the phone without sitting down.

"Hello."

"Mr. Wyatt?"

"Yes, this is Wyatt. And I'm in a hurry."

"Is anyone else on the line?"

"No."

"Are you sure?"

"Yes, I'm sure. What do you want?"

A slight pause. Then in an injured tone: "Mr. Wyatt, I told you I'd give you a run-down—"

"If it's important, Chenery—"

"Only you can adjudicate that, since I don't know all the surrounding circumstances. The subject, the *male* subject, left the building at twelve-thirty-four. Alone. And by the way, Mr. Wyatt, he didn't have a beard, but my man decided he must be the one because of the way he was dressed. You did say a beard, didn't you?"

"Yes." Yes, I had said it, but Wilby had shaved it and I had slipped up. I should have told Chenery when I saw him on the street. I'd slipped up *again*! "Your man was right. Go on."

"First, he went to an art gallery on Madison. Would you like the name?"

"I have it. Go on."

"Then he went all over hell's half-acre. Mostly the go-go joints and bars, like he was looking for someone. My man made sure he was seen, like you said. But that was a kind of mistake because he lost the trail. The subject went into a men's room of one of those joints and never came out."

"Is that all?"

"There's the female subject. If you're interested."

"Quick." Eight minutes to get to the bank.

"She left the apartment building at twelve-forty with a gentleman answering the description you gave me—"

Twelve-forty—six minutes after Wilby had gone out. What if the three of them had met in the downstairs foyer, or on the street? Would it have changed everything that was now going to happen?

". . . proceeded by taxi to the United States Passport Agency, 630 Fifth Avenue. They stayed there approximately twenty minutes, and then went out drinking together. One of the same joints where the male subject had been looking. No lunch—just dancing, laughing and helling it up and having a ball. Then they returned to the apartment building—two-twelve, to be exact—and they haven't come out. They're in apartment 607."

"Is that all?" At least two minutes wasted.

"My men doubled back. The male subject gave his name as Wilbur Smith in the art gallery and said he was representing you in some transaction. The female subject, who gave her name as Jenny Smith, was told she couldn't get a passport without her birth certificate. And the heavy-set gentleman is named Donald Abbott, like you said."

"Is that all?"

"Mr. Wyatt," Chenery remonstrated, "I think my men did an excessive job considering—"

But I replaced the telephone. Six minutes.

When I went through Phoebe's office, it was empty. *Adam-baby, where're your manners? My name's Smith. Wilbur Smith, Mr. Monoxide.* What if Wilby had not been lying to Mr. Corbin on Monday night? But had known that I would *assume* he was lying. Especially if his name actually *was* Smith. Even Jenny wouldn't be stupid enough to give a false name to the passport office. And I had been having the country searched for a Wilbur Birchard. And now it was too late to make any difference. Jenny's joke. Hilarious.

Waiting for the elevator, I became conscious of someone standing nearby. The beatnik type with the goatee. He stood observing me and when my eyes met his, the stare turned into a hostile scowl. He stepped into the elevator with me, and, descending, I looked at the package he was carrying: printed on it was the name and address of a photographic laboratory that, I knew, occupied space on the nineteenth floor. *Whazzamattah wit' yah, yah some kinda nut'r sumpin'?* He stood well away from me, avoiding my eyes now. A delivery boy. Yes, I had been some kind of a nut—or something. Had been, was no more. One gamble you lost, Wilby.

Three minutes. I walked swiftly. The street was quivering with heat, but I was no longer aware of it except as a fact—an observation. The crowd had thinned somewhat but the atmosphere of rush-hurry-bustle was the same. In all this brightness and color and ineffable loveliness, these people were walking blindly, living without living. If only there was some way to say to them that, if dust and nothingness are to come, as certain as the fall of night, then not to savor the sun's brilliance, not to drain each second of its total content, is criminal—a crime against themselves and a crime against . . .

nature. Yet they are all innocent. As I had been innocent. And I began to wonder whether I could possibly have reached this certainty of life's ultimate and only value if I had not been thrust into Wilby's bleak netherworld of despair and bitter wretchedness—and if I were not now pierced with this premonitory sense of loss and death.

I turned into the bank. An enormous clock on the wall read 3:01. The high stone room was cool and hushed. Like a cathedral, or a tomb. Ignoring the elderly uniformed guard who nodded politely, I went directly to Mr. Harper's desk behind the wooden, churchlike railing. Mr. Harper looked up, his bland, pale face professionally friendly. "Oh, Mr. Wyatt. I'm sorry, I didn't recognize you at first." He motioned me into a chair alongside his gleaming, empty desk. "Well, it's been some time since I've had this pleasure, Mr. Wyatt." And then, while I apologized automatically for arriving at closing time, a part of my mind recalled a film I'd seen on television not too long ago: the story of a young man who, having been corrupted over a period of time, remained still youthful and handsome while a painting of him deteriorated and withered into a horrible image of depravity, degradation, decay. *The Picture of Dorian Gray.*

After I had explained to him what I wanted, he studied the check and the engraved art-gallery card I had laid on his desk, then said, judiciously, "Well, that doesn't sound very complicated. You wish to deposit this amount in your personal account and you would like a cashier's or certified check for one hundred and nineteen thousand dollars made out to this art dealer." He sat back: a trim, pleasant, balding man who had probably never known violence, or fear, or despair or the glimmerings of madness; who had in all likelihood also never known joy or recognized the ironies and complexities of reality. "And you are not inconveniencing me in the slightest, Mr. Wyatt. We're on a new schedule this summer. We don't close till four on Wednesdays."

Yesterday, or the day before, I might have burst into hysterical laughter, or tears. Now I sat staring into those mild, reassuring, unknowing eyes and waited.

"Is it essential that you complete this . . . uh, transaction today, Mr. Wyatt?"

"Yes," I said. "You see, the picture's to be a gift for my wife and I've just learned she's arriving home from Europe tomorrow, possibly tonight. I want to surprise her." Where had the lie sprung from?

"I see. Well, it's a generous gift, isn't it? Hm." He was tapping short, manicured fingers on the desk while I remembered: *That money's as much Lydia's as yours. And you can't pay out her own money to keep her from being hurt, or even in the hope of protecting her life, unless she can share in the decision.* "Well, the normal procedure here is to clear a deposited check before issuing—" Mr. Harper leaned a bit closer. "Mr. Wyatt, before we go any further, I feel it's my obligation to ask you a question."

"Yes, Mr. Harper?" Whether I have the right to use my wife's money to purchase a gift for her, even if the gift might be her life?

"For all I know you might be an art connoisseur, an expert in these matters, but an investment this substantial . . . I feel it's my duty to ask whether you are absolutely confident of this investment."

"It's not an investment, Mr. Harper." But it is, of course: an investment in the future, a gamble that there will be a future. And I am not confident in it at all. It's a long, long shot, Mr. Harper, but I don't have any short ones in sight.

"Yes. Well." Then he decided to smile. "May I ask who the painting is by?"

Wilby hadn't told me. Had I asked?

"Van Gogh," I said—the first name to drop into my head. I looked at the clock. No great urgency now, just to get out of here, just to get it over with, just to *know*.

"Oh, yes. He's excellent. An original Van Gogh." He stood up. "I've always been a great admirer of his pictures of Toledo, haven't you?"

"Always," I said. Even I knew who painted Toledo.

"He's the one who cut off his ear, isn't he?"

"No," I said, "I think it was El Greco who cut off his ear. And gave it to a prostitute."

Mr. Harper, frowning, glanced around. And I had the impression that the word "prostitute" whispered in this atmosphere was like shouting "God is dead" in Saint Patrick's Cathedral.

I recalled Lydia's teasing me once—when? how long ago?—about what she called my *insufficiently developed sense of humor*.

"One thing more, Mr. Harper—"

"Anything, Mr. Wyatt." He seemed eager to edge away. "Anything."

"I'd like to transfer all the remaining funds in both my joint checking account and my joint savings account to a new account in my wife's name alone—"

Mr. Harper had a little difficulty with this one. "You wish to close out both those accounts and to—"

"Consolidate is the word, Mr. Harper. Into one checking account, in my wife's name alone."

"Hmm. Well, of course, we'll be delighted to follow whatever instructions—"

He withdrew to some mysterious sacristy where world-shaking decisions are made in hushed, reverent whispers, and I sat thinking of Lydia. And wondering: is gaiety, or a sense of fun, or wit itself, not what I had always imagined—the spontaneous effusion of a blithe and carefree spirit—but rather defiance thrown into the teeth of the gods, man's joyful answer to his own bitter and anguished awareness of the dark threatening depths? Is it possible that this consciousness —for Lydia had her dark mysterious moods, too, which I lazily ascribed to physical causes—is the very source of her recurrent and amusing sense of fun? Will I ever know now?

Mr. Harper returned. "I believe everything's in order, Mr. Wyatt. Now if you'll endorse this check—" Only for an absurd instant was I tempted to make an X, wondering what would happen if Mr. Harper, or one of the armed but genial guards, discovered the suspicious bulge in my right-hand pocket. "*There* we are! And"—with only the mildest of flourishes—"here is our cashier's check in the amount of one hundred and nineteen thousand dollars. Mr. Houston—he's our second vice-president—and I decided that in view of the reputation of the investment house that issued your check and"—with a conciliatory, joyless laugh—"considering *you,* Mr. Wyatt—"

I folded the check and placed it in my pocket.

"And now again, if you please." And while I again signed, with a steady hand: "Mr. Houston and I agreed the simplest method would be simply to remove your name from both accounts. If that's agreeable, of course—"

"Mr. Harper," I said, "everything you do is agreeable with me."

And as I left the inner sanctum, passed the altar rail, and then walked through the nave, I was conscious of Mr. Harper's eyes following me. Wondering whether the poor man's competent to handle his financial affairs? Or whether Mr. Wyatt is seriously ill? Or does he contemplate suicide? And what is that odd protuberance in the man's right pocket?

Soon I was passing window after window displaying paintings. A few geometric patterns. Mostly wild and violent splashes of paint.

*Y'want it t'mean somethin'? I'll explain what it means. It means it
don't mean 'cause it can't mean 'cause nothin' does. Y'dig that?* No, I
do not dig, Wilby. That because there is incongruity and absurdity,
then *all* is absurd and nonsensical? *Is it possible all those men are
working that hard only to celebrate chaos? Some of them are no
doubt wallowing in it. I've been to three shows in one day and, darling, I do need a martini. But you know what? I think I've been trying
too hard. Today I just sat and stared at several of them and didn't
really try, or think. And the most curious thing happened: I began to
feel something for the first time. I'm not sure just what, yet. But
something . . . very strange. I can't wait to try again.* And what had
I done then, that evening? Had I tried to comprehend, to explore? Or
had I simply mixed her a martini and moved on to some other less
confusing subject? But now I knew, knew as a certainty, that unless
those artists are attempting to impose some new dimension of order
and feeling and significance, which *I* am incapable of comprehending,
then they, like Wilby, have given up. As I turned into the gallery, I
made up my mind: if such an unlikely possibility as a future existed
for me I would go on exploring this. Because the search was also a
vital part of living and one simply doesn't give up.

"Mr. Neuenberg?"

"Yes."

"I'm Adam Wyatt."

"Oh, but how do you do, Mr. Wyeth?"

"Wyatt."

"Of course, sir, of course. A natural slip of the language in our—"
He held a chair. "Won't you sit, please?" And when I sat, he sighed,
two hands together reverently as in prayer. "You have come to obtain
your purchase, no?"

"Yes," I said.

"But naturally. Now I have all the papers here, which I shall explain to you—" And while he talked, I glanced around. If the bank
had been a cathedral, this was a temple. If Mr. Harper had been pon-
tifical, Mr. Neuenberg was downright Buddhist: tranquil, overstuffed,
and superior. Whereas Mr. Harper's suit had been bleakly Madison
Avenue, Mr. Neuenberg's was elegantly Park. ". . . certification, bill
of sale, insurance. You understand that this insurance covers only
natural disasters, or mishaps. Fire, of course, storm. Not theft or
. . . well, other damage. But I am sure that Mr. Smith will take excellent care of it. He asked me to have it wrapped, not crated." Mr

Neuenberg did not approve. "Normally we arrange for delivery by van, with bonded—well, no matter now. He is an endearing boy, your young Mr. Smith, and a most fortunate young man to have such a generous . . . friend."

I almost smiled. Another of Wilby's *endearing* jokes, gratuitous cruelties. What pleasure he'd get imagining me trying to deny the relationship he'd so carefully and wantonly implanted in Mr. Neuenberg's mind. What satisfaction picturing me cringing in shame, stuttering futile denials, explanations.

"Mr. Smith," I said, "is the kind of boy for whom any red-blooded American male would do *anything*."

Mr. Neuenberg's dark brows became a straight line and he seemed to lose just a mite of his Buddhist composure. "I daresay." He cleared his throat. "And you do have the check?"

"Would I come without the bread?"

Blinking, Mr. Neuenberg reached a pudgy hand, took the check, studied it, turned it over. "Yes." Then he became expansive, as with relief. "Well, that completes the transaction, does it not, no?" He stood, hands clasped over abdominal protrusion. "It is always a joy to sell a masterpiece to someone who will appreciate it for its artistic beauty rather than for its commercial value."

I stood, too. "It's always a joy to pay a hundred and twenty thousand dollars to someone who appreciates its commercial value rather than its artistic significance."

Mr. Neuenberg's hands dropped from his belly. He shrugged. "One moment, please, sir." And he disappeared briefly into the rear room, or white marble shrine, then returned holding a wrapped frame with reverence. "If you wish to examine it to make certain—"

"Mr. Neuenberg," I said, "I wouldn't know a Van Gogh from an El Greco." I relieved him of the picture. "But that Mr. Smith, he can spot the difference between a Manet and a Monet at fifty yards in a dim light. That dear boy's also the kind who would punch a gift horse right in the teeth."

Mr. Neuenberg tugged at his cravat and took a single step backward. "He. . . he's very fond of *you*, I know."

"Fond?" I said, turning to leave. "Fond? That little bastard's in love with me. That's how Rome fell, you know."

The first taxi I hailed was empty. And it was air-conditioned. Luck. I'm going to need it. I gave the address and sat back, placing the wrapped painting on the seat beside me.

"What you got there, pal?" the driver asked. "You buy one of them things? I sometimes wonder: does anybody really *buy* them things?"

"I didn't buy it," I said. "I painted it myself."

"Yeh? You some kind of artist or something?"

"No," I said. "I'm some kind of a nut or something."

"I get 'em all."

He drove. After a while, he said, "How much is it worth, no bull?"

"One hundred and twenty thousand."

"Dollars?"

"Dollars."

"No shit?"

"No bull."

He shook his head. "I'm in the wrong business."

"Who isn't? But you've still got two ears."

When the taxi stopped for a red light, the driver turned around: broad beefy face. He studied me. "Pal, when I get soused, I buy maybe a tweed jacket I can't afford, but you go all the way, don't you?"

"All the way, pal."

But I was not thinking of the money alone. I had, in some strange and mysterious way, moved . . . all the way. Toward what? *You don't know who you are. Nobody does.* True, Wilby, because no one is something fixed and discoverable. We are all, always, in the state of becoming—which is living. And what I am becoming, whether aware of it or not, is what I decide to become. If I am allowed by the ironic nature of things the days and years in which to continue my becoming, I have within reach and sight now a fortune so staggering and fantastic that the largest sum of money imaginable fades into insignificance. Hell, Wilby, anyone can make money. You thought you were hitting me where I lived—but, Wilby, I've moved. The joke this time is on you.

The cab was passing Pat's Pub. I remembered the men sitting and standing along the bar, the young woman in shorts, all the jokes and boasts of sexual conquest—as if a man's summer freedom returned him automatically to the forest of prowl-and-fornicate-at-random. But if so, if all those summer bachelors were *having a ball while the wife's away,* as Pat put it, then what the hell were they doing at Pat's Pub all evening, drinking and killing time with one another? They were doing what I had done in the last month: having a few drinks in order to face the empty apartment, the frozen dinner or the delicatessen sandwich, the ball game on television, the eleven o'clock news, the empty damned bed. And why did they live this way for two or three months every year? So that their wives and their children, whom they loved, could enjoy the leisure and fresh air and pleasures of the seashore, the mountains, or a farmhouse in Vermont.

The taxi turned the familiar corner and then Geoffrey was holding its door open.

"Thank you, pal," the driver said when he looked at his tip. "You must be the last of the big spenders."

"I can spare it, *pal*," I said. "I'm broke." Then: "Good afternoon, Geoffrey. Yes, I *am* home early today. Yes, it *is* a hot one, but it's the humidity, really, although not as humidified as yesterday, as a friend of mine says." I crossed the marble-floored foyer. "And how *is* that wife of yours?"

Geoffrey's long narrow face was staring at me across the lobby as the elevator door closed.

As I ascended, I wondered whether I could possibly sustain this strange mood, at once quiet exaltation at the precious brevity of time and keen awareness of the absurdities that were in themselves, for the first time, exciting as well as amusing. There was, of course, the larger irony: that now that I had come to realize life, to cherish it at a level deeper than any I had known before, I might lose it. Would that prove Wilby's point—that all is meaningless? Might he, if he knew now what had happened to me, make certain that he proved *his* point by killing me?

But there is an irony beyond that one, Wilby: you yourself have forced me to view fate as accident and chance and I, having done so, have arrived at an acceptance that, instead of rendering my death meaningless and absurd, has given it deeper significance. If the end is the blotting out of my most prized possession, my own consciousness —and if now I *know* this and will yet risk it—then even its loss has meaning.

What happens to Lydia if that bastard kills you? I placed my hand in my right pocket as the elevator slowed. I'm going to do everything in my power, anything, to prevent his killing me, Hank—because I have learned the value of living but mostly because Lydia would suffer. I closed my fingers over the gun, with my index finger on the trigger. Pain from the gash spread through my hand and leaped hotly

up my arm. But, Hank, even Lydia's suffering, if it becomes necessary, is a form of living. I've done all I could do to prevent her anguish of any sort, but I'll do more to make certain *her* consciousness,
even if in suffering, continues to exist. Because *her* eternity is all *she*
has, too.

Approaching the door along the corridor, holding the painting by
its frame in my left hand while my right remained in my pocket, I
forced my mind to the immediate moment. Who was behind the
door? Had Wilby come back? Had Jenny? And if Jenny had not?

Setting the painting against the door frame and then using my left
hand, I let myself in. The havoc was so total that it was impossible to
decide whether it had been added to while I had been gone. The living room was empty. I glanced up at the balcony: the guest room
door was ajar, my bedroom door closed. I moved through the debris
toward the library, edged to the door, looked in. There was no one
there, but this time I felt a faint surprise: the screen of the television
set had been bashed in, or kicked in, and the resultant explosion, or
implosion, had spread fragments and rubble everywhere. I was reminded of those flats in London after the all-clear had sounded.
Home, sweet home. And how could it conceivably be put into order
by the time Lydia arrived? What had driven him to this? Jenny's failure to return, some infuriating bit of news, or some inner psychological catastrophe? Using every means as they came to hand, had I actually been successful in driving Wilby off the deep end? And if so,
might I have at least helped to create a monster that could only turn,
in madness, on me?

I returned to the living room, crossed it slowly, with caution,
reached into the hall for the painting, propped it against the telephone
table, and was about to open the closet door—had Wilby even discovered the cat?—when I heard a sound, upstairs: water gurgling
through a drain.

Jenny? Without removing my hand from my pocket, I turned and
passed the painting and mounted the stairs in slow careful silent
steps. I looked into the guest room.

Jenny—it could be no one but Jenny—stood before a long mirror,
her back to me. She wore nothing and she was gazing at herself in the
mirror. Her body glistened with water and her dark hair streamed
wetly down her back. *Go-go, man, bitch can't get along without me,
no pad, bad, starve*— Looking at her, I felt nothing but an instantaneous flare of hope: would they take the painting now and go?

Jenny must have seen me in the mirror, because she turned. She held the cat in her arms, against her breasts, and she was stroking it. For the first time, in spite of the gurgling in the tub beyond, I heard its soft, steady purring.

Jenny smiled. "You get your kicks peeking now? Well, go ahead."

I did. And felt nothing but a pang of regret that I had ever felt anything.

"You get any ideas, man, I got ways of helping what ails you."

I turned away and went down the stairs and heard her laughing, then calling after me, "Only way you got left, honey? *Lookin'!*"

But her words had no meaning. I had felt no quiver of desire. And knew as a certainty now that I would never feel it again for anyone but Lydia. If I was ever to see Lydia again and if—

"I heard something in the closet—" she must have come out onto the balcony—"and I thought it was a mouse. Then Cheetah must've got the idea it was me 'cause he meowed. Didn't you, Cheetah-baby?"

But I was no longer listening. I was staring at Lydia's portrait. Someone had painted a heavy, black mustache on the delicate upper lip and had blackened her smooth fair hair. More waste. More gratuitous and senseless destruction.

"*You* brought Cheetah up here, didn't you? Get down now, baby, just for a sec-sec." Her voice withdrew into the bedroom. "You stole him from Sam's and brought him up here to bug Wilby." She giggled, returning. "I only wish he'd found it. I wish I could have seen him when he found it!" Then she must have seen me staring at the portrait. "You like? Not bad. No art lessons, neither. Only I modeled once." She giggled again. "Caught the flu."

I turned then. On the balcony she was slithering snakelike into a slip of a dress.

My anger was surprisingly weak. But after all, it was only an image of Lydia. So far, nothing had happened to Lydia herself.

"Where's Wilby?"

She leaned over, bare elbows on the railing, face cupped in hands, eyes still merry. "Don't ask me. Hell, maybe. I just hope he *stays,* don't you?" Even her tone was different: gay, no personal resentment or bitterness.

It's all for you. Everything I'm doin', baby. All for you, Jenny.

"You like my dress, honey?" She straightened, whirled around—as if, even now, she could not resist flirting, taunting, hoping to torment.

"And Hallowe'en's a long way off!" She laughed and ran her two hands sensuously down the lines of her body. "Well, Sam does. Shorter the better. Tighter the better. He likes to see 'em looking. Think"—and she sniggered—"think it gives him an extra kick." Then she turned and swooped up the cat and held it as before. "Mix me a drink, will you, honey?" She purred as she stroked the cat. "Jenny-baby wants another drink-drink. *Please.*"

Instead—a tactic to persuade her or because I had to know more of what she had in mind?—I crossed to the foyer, knelt down, and tore the wrapping from the painting, using both hands.

When I had exposed it, I picked it up and carried it into the living room and propped it against the cocktail table, facing the balcony: a female figure, native girl in brown rich hues, bare from the waist up, Polynesian or Tahitian face, a suggestion of a mountain or red-rimmed volcano in the background.

"What's that ugly thing?" Jenny asked.

"That ugly thing," I said, "is an original painting by a man named, I think, Gauguin."

She eyed it. "Yugh. I got better bobbins than that."

I looked at the picture. The girl's face was not attractive, her breasts were not lovely—but the picture in itself was beautiful. No way of explaining why or how, but I wondered whether, even a few days ago, I would have felt this, or made the distinction.

"Don't I, honey? Don't I have better bobbins'n those?"

"Jenny," I said, "it is worth one hundred and twenty thousand dollars."

She whistled softly. "That, man, is a lot of bread."

. . . *first class all the way, moonlight decks, captain's table, captain if he's able—*

"One hundred and twenty thousand dollars and all for you, Jenny."

"All for me?" Her voice sounded awed.

"Anywhere you want to go—"

"Cheetah-baby, hear that? Anywhere I want to go!" The mockery was distinct. "With Wilby? With Wilby, honey? Oh you bastard, oh you bastard old man, you are full of crap, you are full of new wrinkles every time! And, honey, you been took! Oh, how you been *took!*" Then she laughed. "Do you know what a hundred and twenty thousand dollars *is,* man?" The laughter was gone and her eyes had

narrowed, but the excitement still streamed through her voice. "It
. . . is . . . chickenshit. It is bread for the birds, honey. Sam's
rich. Really stinkin'! Why, man, my Sam's so stinkin' he don't even
have to work if he don't want to! And he don't want to *now*. He's
going to learn me to speak French and then we're going to the French
Riviera!"

So there it was. I had known for hours, really. What now, when
Wilby stops searching and comes back? And what could I possibly
do?

"I thought," I said, "I thought you didn't put out for money."

"Oh, you are such on a stick, man!" No anger, though—only elation. "But you don't even get through. You don't get through, honey,
'cause you got it all screwed. All screwed." Smiling now—sweetly,
"Sam and me, we're going to get married."

Married? This time I was startled. Donald, how can you even consider it?

"I guess all us girls are the same. Inside. I guess we all want to fall
in love, really in love, and get married someday—"

Love? I thought of her trying to seduce me only a few minutes ago
upstairs. Donald, you damned fool, how long do you think it can possibly last? *That Jenny, she takes it outta a man. Burns it out, click?*
And she'll have the money by then, too, before she moves on to find
another Sam.

"Well, honey, *you* get the pleasure of telling Wilby. I only wish I
could see his goddam face!" She turned to the door.

What was I doing standing here worrying about Donald?

"I wouldn't want to spoil your honeymoon, Jenny," I said, "but
don't be surprised if you're arrested as soon as you get off the ship."

That did it. All the buoyancy and superiority left her. "Arrested?"

"As a material witness."

"Witness? Witness to what?"

"To whatever happens here when Wilby finds out you've gone."

She stepped to the railing to lean over it, panic in her eyes. "You
mean rotten sonofabitch old man—what, what's going to happen
here?"

Quietly, very quietly, I said, "It's more than likely that I am going
to murder Wilby or that Wilby is going to murder me."

Her mouth opened. Then she straightened. "Wilby!" She spat the
word in disgust. "*Wilby*! I hope you do. I hope you do kill the bas-

tard. Everything bad ever happened to me, he did it!" Her voice rose. "I hope he dies, I hope I never have to see him again, he turned me into a whore, I *don't* put out for money—*he* did it, he did it *all*!"

She hurled the cat down into the room—where it lit on its feet on the floor and arched its back—as she went into the guest room and slammed the door.

I stood watching the cat shake itself, then move in long lithe strides, hesitating a split second, then leap onto the sofa, where it curled, burrowing in. *Like I said on phone, man—Jenny don't come back, Wilby stays.* But it was Jenny's whimper of self-pity that lingered in my mind: she had become what she had become because of someone or something else, someone or something outside herself. Like Wilby. Victims, always victims.

And suddenly I was sick of all of it: the whining, the complaining, the grumbling and wailing! I felt the angry disgust rise like a choking tide in me. "If you're a whore or a bitch," I shouted up the stairs, "you can blame nobody but yourself!"

"You stay away from me, old man, old man!" Her voice was blurred behind the door. "You done enough to me, too!" The door flew open and she stood there, a small suitcase in hand—one of Lydia's. "You leave me alone. I'm free, white, and twenty-three and I'm on my way to the Riviera!"

I was looking up the stairs at her. "If you're twenty-three, I didn't rape you."

She smiled, her face contorting. "I'm twenty-three, honey, and you didn't rape me. You didn't have a choice."

"I had a choice," I said. "You always have a choice."

She laughed, her eyes bright and mean. "You never even had a chance, man. Like believing Wilby's name was—what was it you swallowed?"

"Birchard," I said.

She giggled. "Birchard. I only said it because it sounded like bastard. Bastard to go with Wilby." She looked pleased, proud of herself—still the delighted, amoral little girl, conscience forever free, years of destruction stretching ahead.

"But it's Smith," I said, and watched her mouth open slightly.

"How'd you know that?"

"Wilby told me." Which was only a fact—not true, but a fact. And for how many years had I believed facts to be the same as truth? "And it will be Smith when you are arrested, with Donald, in

France." Why was I still struggling? "And thrown into a French jail, and then sent back on a plane, *handcuffed*."

"Oh, you bastard, you are! Sam can take care of that." She was coming down the stairs. "He's going to take care of me, he says. And he has all the bread in the world. C'mon, Cheetah-baby, c'mon, time to split—"

The door buzzer sounded when she was halfway down.

Jenny's eyes narrowed, darkened, darted over my head to the foyer. "If it's Wilby," she whispered tensely, "he's not going to stop me!" But the panic was there.

The buzzer sounded again, in two quick spurts.

"Wilby," I said, "has a key."

And at that moment a key was inserted into the lock.

"It's your fault!" Jenny hissed. "You kept me here!" She whirled about and ran up the stairs. "It's all your goddamned fault!" She was in the bedroom.

As I heard the front door open, I turned, slipping my right hand into the pocket that held the gun.

But it was not Wilby. For a long moment the shock didn't reach me.

It was Anne.

"Oh, hello, Daddy. You didn't answer so I used my old key. Lucky I had it in my bag. I thought perhaps I could do a little—"

Anne's voice fell away as her gaze left me and roamed the room.

"—I was going to say . . . housecleaning."

She was standing on the foyer step: eyes bewildered, several packages in her arms, summer dress, no hat. I could only watch, throat closed, while that paralyzing sense of nightmarish inevitability closed over me again. It was happening now. Finally happening.

"It does need it, doesn't it?" I heard myself say, with a laugh that rang hollow in my ears. "I guess I'll never get accustomed to the bachelor life, Anne."

She was no longer staring at the room. She set down her packages on the telephone table, then came down the step. She was looking at me, with those direct, candid blue eyes that now appeared only baffled and concerned. "It looks as if someone had a party here. And what a party!"

"What a party!" I said. And then I slurred my words. "How about a drink, Anne? A good stiff one to catch up with me." I walked to the bar, not staggering but holding myself carefully erect as I did a slow broken-field side-step over the candles, the cups, the broken glasses, the ashtrays and saucers. "Only for God's sake," I said—what was I doing? why was I still trying this?—"don't tell your mother I've been drinking like this. You guessed it, Anne. Your old man's been on one long jag. For days. Vodka?"

"Oh, Daddy, how dreadful! I knew. I knew *something* was—" She came toward me, frowning, sympathetic. "What can I do? What—"

"What you can do, Anne," I said—and my voice did sound drunk, very convincingly drunk—"what you can best do for me is to clear out." And when she stopped in the middle of the strewn floor: "You asked. All I want is to be left alone. So I can sleep it off." Then I forced a hardness into my tone. "I don't want to see you, or anyone. I'm sozzled, as you call it, and I *like* being sozzled, and I'm going to go on getting sozzled and there's not a goddamned thing you can do about it!"

It was like a blow across her face. As I had intended. But, seeing the pain leap into her eyes, I went weak all over, knew I couldn't go on with it.

"Please, Anne," I said in a whisper, "please, if you want to help, just go home. Go away."

"But . . . but you look so—"

Old, Anne? Finally, abruptly old? *Oh, Mr. Wyatt. I'm sorry. I didn't recognize you at first.*

"I don't want you here, Anne!"

She nodded then, turned, stumbled once. "If . . . whatever you say, Daddy—" She moved into the foyer, her back stiff with hurt and bewilderment and helplessness. She was stooping to gather up her packages.

"When are you coming back up, Adam-honey?"

I saw Anne freeze. A flash of rage went down my frame—helpless rage. And I had the distinct impression that, in some other time, I had stood before like this, seeing Anne, hearing Jenny's plaintive voice, that it had all happened exactly like this once before and that all I could do now was to stand in hypnotic fascination and watch and hear it play itself out.

"Come on, honey. You can do it again."

Anne straightened, her gaze moving to the empty balcony.

"How many times today, Sam? That's nothing for *you*. How many times last night?"

Even the impulse that went through me—violent, murderous: get up the stairs, close her mouth, strangle the words back into her throat!—was somehow familiar. But I was helpless to move.

"Adam-baby, what are you *doing* down there?"

I heard the door open. I saw Anne's face and could almost see Jenny reflected in Anne's wide shocked dazzled eyes.

"Oh, Adam-honey, why didn't you tell me we had company?"

Anne's face had begun to distort only slightly. Only her lower lip curled and trembled.

It was over now. It had gone on too long. Now it was over.

"Who is *she*?"

But it was Jenny who asked it, not Anne. Anne looked too stricken, too dumfounded, to speak.

"I told you I'm the jealous type, honey."

It was then that I recognized the playful quality behind Jenny's tone—that same pleased gaiety that seemed a part of her today. But my eyes remained riveted on Anne's face—which had now gone slack and pale. Only her eyes held life: a glittering astonishment and revulsion that I watched intensify.

"That . . . that's my négligée," Anne finally spoke—but it was not Anne's voice. It was a whispered foreign echo of Anne's voice. She stepped down from the foyer. "That . . . isn't *yours*." She sounded like a perplexed child.

"You must be Anne then. She's pretty, Adam. Like the limey wife. Adam-baby told me all about you. And—what was the funny name? —Glenn-Glenn. And the little house-house in the suburbs. With split-level beds. That's where Adam told me all about you. Last night. In bed."

Anne uttered a small strangled sound deep in her throat. Her hands went to her face, both hands, fluttering there. Then she turned to look across the devastation at me.

I saw hate leap, bright and terrible, into her eyes. Intense, burning. Final. And abruptly it was not Anne's face, but Lydia's.

For the first time, for the first time, I wished in that instant that I were dead. That I could die. Now.

"Anne," I said, and moved from behind the bar, kicking my way through the rubbish, "Anne, let's go. I have to talk to—"

But when I reached her, she stepped back, eyes flinching, her stranger's stricken eyes opening wide.

I reached out. "Anne, darling, if we can go some place where—"

But as my hand touched her bare cold arm, it shivered, and her whole body heaved convulsively, and she stepped back, quickly, feeling for the step with her heel, desperation in her face. And I let my hand fall.

"She even *looks* like the limey wife," Jenny said from above.

Anne was in the foyer now. She tore her gaze from me and looked over my shoulder—but not toward the stairs. Toward the portrait.

Suddenly she screamed. It was so abrupt, so shrill, that it was like a single cold knife-plunge directly into the heart.

Then she was backing away again, face misshapen, twisting into ugliness, becoming old and sad and knowing and bitter as she reached frantically for her packages on the chair, knocked one to the floor, abandoned it, then turned to tug at the door, as the sobs began, tugged again, wild, with the sobs mounting. The door flew open, she stumbled backward, then plunged out.

I followed—to the open door, where I saw her running, saw her disappear under the EXIT sign over the stairway, heard her heels on the concrete steps before the half-glass door swung slowly, heavily shut after her.

Then I whipped about, went into the foyer, down the step, up the stairs. Devoid of thought. Only moving. Not even knowing what I intended to do.

On the balcony Jenny watched me approach, her face girlishly mischievous, even gleeful. More teasing than taunting. Delighted.

When I was facing her, she tilted her head. "Don't you want to rip it off? Last chance."

Then I realized why I had come back, why I had climbed the stairs. I swung.

My open palm caught her solidly, so hard that the pain in my hand exploded and shot up my arm, and the sound of flesh-against-flesh sent a shudder of cruel pleasure and satisfaction down my spine. She wobbled sideways, toward the stairs, eyes wide and wild and astonished, gasping. Her hands reached, clutched frantically for the railing; one hand caught, held a second, then slid along the railing to the banister of the stairway, then slipped—and then she was tottering at the top, upright, before she collapsed completely and went tumbling down the stairs, sprawling, head thumping against steps, wall, banister-posts, body clumping, legs flying, arms outspread and useless.

Until she lay in a crumpled heap on the floor below.

What was I doing here? I could picture Anne blindly crossing the marble foyer, rushing past Geoffrey, sobbing now, onto the street.

What was I doing here when Anne needed me?

I went down the stairs.

Jenny was whimpering now, almost moaning.

I stepped around her.

Was she really hurt?

I had reached the door when I heard her cry out. "Wilby." It was a plaintive cry for help. "Wilby."

I slammed the door behind me.

On the way down the seven flights I realized what I had done: I had given into irrational, atavistic impulse and allowed Anne to get away.

"Mr. Wyatt—"

Geoffrey again. He followed me to the sidewalk.

". . . something we must talk about, sir—"

"Where's my daughter?"

". . . only a misunderstanding, I'm sure, if you're willing to—"

"Geoffrey, didn't my daughter come out here just now?"

He frowned down on me. "Why, yes, Mr. Wyatt. She did. I had her little car parked here for her and she just bounced in and drove off before I could even open the—"

It took twenty minutes less than the usual two hours to reach the cottage in Newtown. If minutes and hours had any meaning. But they did not: the trip took ten years, more. Metallic glare, merciless sun, glimmering oppressive heat, snarl and hoot and speed and exhaust of a thousand cars. The cat's-claw gash reddened with my grip on the wheel; I watched it intensify, felt the pain spreading hotly over my hand and up my arm—and relished the pain. Relished it, gripped the wheel more tightly to increase it. *You got that monkey off your back yet?* No, Hank, and now never will, never. Anne knows. Worse than knows. Knows less than the truth and imagines more. And now Lydia will know. Or Anne will live a lie, too. As I shall. As I hope I shall be able. Alive to live it. Anne's face hovering just beyond the glare of windshield: that stricken look of shock and pain and incredulity. Horror. That flash of hate, the way she shuddered away from my touch. Shrank away, shivering. Cold flesh flinching. Drive carefully now, Anne, please, be careful, watch where you're going, don't cry, please stop crying, dear, keep your eyes on the road, don't speed, please, Anne, please—

Anne's face becoming Lydia's. Hate? Lydia on her way. Possibly in air by now. Many night flights this time of year. Eight hours, leave at four arrive midnight, leave at five arrive one in morning. Heavy tourist season, not much chance, especially east-to-west. But I know Lydia, once she makes up mind, I know Lydia, but I never knew Lydia, never did but will, never did but now never will, now cannot. Purged? Enough? Never enough. But what of others? Jenny? Wilby? They never suffer, atone. No justice if no pattern, if no God, no ulti- mate reward and punishment. No universal justice then, only man's. Law. And what we do to assure justice. Revenge? Yes, revenge, too. Jenny sprawled whimpering at foot of stairs. Hope she still there, hope bones broken, she lying there with only that damned cat and Wilby walking in. Never struck a woman before. No remorse. Sup- pose Jenny really injured, moaning on floor when Wilby finds her. What then? Chenery: take over. Only way. Don't tell me what you do or how you do it. But no traces. Just send me the bill. But I passed phone booth after phone booth without stopping.

I was approaching the last crest of hill, then around the last famil- iar curve, and there was the driveway. Cool between the trees, always cool, inviting. And Anne's car was not there. Glenn's little VW in the open garage, not Anne's. It had been the one possibility that my mind had refused to consider all the way: that Anne might not go home. I climbed out of the car and went up the flagstone walk that I myself had laid years ago—with what now-forgotten pleasure or irritation and sweat? Or joy unrecognized and so not realized? Satisfaction lost in preoccupation. In the slanting sun the cottage had a hurtful beauty: the weathered timbers, simple lines against high trees. Anne had been five years old, 1951, five years old when we bought it, five years old, and where had the years gone? How had they come to this? I lifted my hand to knock—I never knew whether to knock on the door or simply to walk in as I had always done up to a year ago—and then I saw the angry slash running in a red, flaring ridge from thumb to wrist, and realized that the hand was swollen and stiff, a yellow cast to the skin, and the pain now reached my armpit. But it was nothing compared to the ache that swelled emptily in my heart.

I heard Glenn's voice calling pleasantly from the side yard. "I'm out here. Who is it?"

Then he appeared around the corner of the house: tall, trim, athletic, blond crew cut, the smile ready to spring into place even before he recognized me. Bright sports shirt, crumpled, stained slacks.

"Well, this is a surprise! How are you?" That youthful heartiness

—which, when he saw me more closely as he offered his hand, faded from his face. "Is anything wrong?"

Should I tell him? Just blurt it out, get it over with, then get back to the apartment? No. For how could I trust him to explain it to Anne in perspective?

"Yes," I admitted, "there is."

"Well, come on around to the fireplace. Anne's in the city but I expect her any—" Then, moving across the lawn, he stopped and turned. "Does . . . has it anything to do with Anne?"

It kills me to see her suffer, that's all. I can't bear it.

"Yes, in a way, it does."

And I remembered, with ironic bitterness now, my year-long conviction, ever since the wedding, that Glenn could not take proper care of her. Too young, too immature. And of course I knew, as I sat down in one of the familiar wooden chairs drawn under the shade of the high-spread maple by the old stone fireplace, that in that same single year Glenn himself had resented me equally, or more so. *Oh no, I won't tell you, Daddy. Because then you'll buy it and send it up to the country and then Glenn and I will quarrel—*

"Can I get you a drink? You look—"

"No, thank you." And with faint surprise I realized that, in the long drive, I had not once thought of stopping for a drink before facing Anne. Anne, who was not here. Where could she—

"Do you want to tell me or do you want to wait for Anne? She should be here any minute."

How could I wait? With Lydia possibly on her way, with Jenny leaving, with Wilby returning to the apartment.

Then I had to rely on this boy to understand and then to relate it to Anne in such a way that *she* would understand. How could I possibly trust him? A young man who, in these days of so-called liberated youth, was concerned about his wife's virginity. Not only would I shock him, I would put into his hands a weapon that he just conceivably might use against me in his telling.

I calculated the risks and made up my mind: I had to get back to the apartment, get it over with in one way or the other. "I can't wait," I said.

He nodded, moving to the fireplace that I had built. "Do you mind if I go on with this? We like to eat out here in the summer and I know how tired Anne can be when she gets back from the city, so I thought I'd play chef tonight. Hamburgers and salad if you'd like to stay—"

If he loved Anne, he would not hurt her. *That* is what I had to rely on.

Sitting there, looking beyond him at the gentle slope of browned-out lawn, looking beyond the croquet court, I could see the top of the screening around the tennis court in the grove. And this morning's dream returned. I had to force my mind away from its lurid, unreal details, abruptly understanding them and acknowledging their significance for the first time.

"It all started," I said, "on Sunday night after I left here—"

I attempted to capsule what had happened on Sunday night, leaving out whatever I considered unessential to comprehension of it all, some part of my mind straining to hear the sound of a motor in the driveway. Glenn was not looking at me, but he was listening, sober and thoughtful, occasionally fanning the charcoal.

When I arrived at Wilby's demand for money on Monday morning, he did turn to stare at me. "But once you *knew* it was a shakedown, why didn't you go to the police?"

"It may have been cowardice," I said. "I thought at the time—no, damn it, I still believe it was principally to protect Lydia and Anne."

"But if you were innocent?"

"I just told you: by that time I wasn't exactly innocent."

"Because you slept with her? Anybody would have understood that."

"Not Lydia. And for that matter, not Anne." It was a warning, a fatherly warning—the first I'd ever offered. "And what about the scandal? How would you and Anne have fared up here? Your business?"

"Go on."

"I did go to the police, in a sense."

And then I told him of my visit to Stanley Ephron, followed by my lunch with Anne.

"She came home a bit tipsy," Glenn said. "I gave her hell for driving in that condition, I remember."

Driving. Where was she now? How was she driving now? She was worse than tipsy now.

But I described Tuesday morning. *These parts, rape in the second degree, click, law-man?* And explained that I had learned since that Jenny was twenty-three. Quickly I moved into last night: the party, Wilby's growing wildness, my own recklessness and violence.

"As it turns out, it might have been better if I'd gone through with it then."

He was forming the hamburgers in his hands, then placing them aside on a sheet of wax paper. "But if there was no abortion and you knew it, why didn't you call the police then?"

That young, uncomprehending logical mind! I hesitated to give him the answer, but he had to understand. And it might be up to him to protect Anne later. "He said that if he was arrested, he'd wait, wherever they put him, he didn't care how many years—" We were looking at each other over the glowing coals, the heat shimmering between our eyes. "He said he'd kill Lydia, or Anne, or both. And if you knew him, you'd believe it, as I did and as I do." I did not mention, *Lotsa things worse'n death, man. I don't care how I get my kicks.* But I did say, "He also threatened Anne's child, if and when she has one."

I saw Glenn's face tighten, saw his eyes contract, his body go taut. After a moment, he said, "You were right. It would have been better if you'd gone through with it when you had the chance."

And then another thought dropped into my mind: what if Anne had stayed in the city and had decided to go back to the apartment to face it out with me?

"I might have to go through with it as soon as I leave here," I said —and knew it to be true, the decision already reached inside me. Anne walking in there to face Wilby—

"Why not?" Glenn growled and turned to hurl a ball of meat high into the trees. "Why *not*? They're going to teach me how to kill men I don't even know, men who haven't done a damned thing to me! People who haven't even threatened me!"

Vietnam again. Regardless, I said, "Maybe they haven't, Glenn. I don't honestly know. But if Johnson's right, we do have something to fear. All of us. You and Anne and your children later on."

Frowning: "You believe that?"

"I said I don't know. I haven't thought enough about it. Or a lot of other things."

Glenn was standing with legs apart, regarding me, his eyes troubled and young and asking—and suddenly I realized that we'd never talked before, really talked, the two of us. "Go on," he said, and I had the curious impression that he wanted, or needed, to hear whatever I had to say.

"If Johnson's wrong, we're a nation of murderers and he's a criminal. But what if he just happens to be right?"

"What about the scum we play along with? Not just there, all over
the world."

I shook my head. "Glenn, you've played football—"

"Not All-American, like you—"

"I guess it comes to this: trying to live a decent life is like running
broken-field in a meadow covered with dung heaps." And Glenn
smiled faintly. "If Johnson's right in this, then it's just another rotten
damn job that has to be done by somebody. Again."

Glenn's smile faded away. "Like getting rid of this Wilby character?"

And I knew then that if I had been able to find a way to deal with
Wilby on Sunday night, I wouldn't be here now. No sound of a motor
or the crunching of gravel on the driveway. "There's a man named
Chenery," I said—and then I told Glenn of his proposals.

"I'd use him," he said flatly when I'd finished. "Chenery looks to
me like your best bet. And a hell of a lot cheaper than a hundred and
twenty thousand dollars."

"That's one way of looking at it," I said, thinking of the Gauguin
painting and the papers in my pocket. Why not? Do I even have the
right to moral considerations? Could I afford the luxury? *Y'live in the
jungle, dad, y'gotta survive.*

"Glenn," I said, and my mind flinched away from the words,
"Anne came to the apartment this afternoon. That's why I'm here."

He stood quite still. "Yes?"

Then I tried to describe the scene: how Jenny had behaved, even
though she was leaving, how Anne had left in hysterics. But I could
never describe Anne's face.

"I told her," Glenn said, angry and sad at the same time. "I told
her to stay away from there. I knew something was up, I didn't know
what, but I tried to—" He broke off.

What he had tried to do was to spare her. Himself suspecting—
Ain't it terrible how people always believe the worst?—Glenn had
tried in his own way to keep Anne from that appalling disillusion-
ment. About me: that was the strange, astonishing part.

"Now," Glenn said, "you want me to tell her what you've just
told me?"

"In any way you want to. Yes."

He shot a glance toward the driveway, tensing as if he had heard, or hoped to hear, or had imagined, the sound of Anne's car. Then he fixed his eyes on me, coming closer. "I'll tell it as straight as I can," he said and I realized he had understood what I had not meant to say so bluntly. "You can trust me to tell it straight."

In those words and in that gaze a great many things cleared between us. A year. He had always felt, or silently believed, that Anne and I had been too close—and now I knew, or admitted, without words, that he had been right. As Lydia had been right. And both he and Lydia had, in separate and different ways, suffered by it. While Anne and I had either not acknowledged, or ignored, or—in our own separate and different ways—even resented their feelings as an intrusion on ours. I had always looked upon my relationship with Anne as rare and uncomplicated and especially satisfying; now, seeing it in the sharp light of its loss, I recognized it as the complex source of a corrosive alienation among the four of us.

In spite of all this, there was not the slightest hint of triumph or sly satisfaction in Glenn's direct blue stare—which was really a pledge. "I'm sorry," he said, and stepped closer. "You *could* use a drink, couldn't you?" The gentleness in his tone was new. "Let me mix it." It was almost a plea.

I could use it all right. One. The tiredness had caught up. Suddenly I was bone-weary, shot. My hand and arm throbbed with each heartbeat. And I was damned if I was going to run from alcohol the rest of my life. If there was such a thing now as the rest of my life. "A short one," I said.

"Look," Glenn said suddenly. "Look: it must have been a hell of a shock for Anne, considering how she feels about you. But Anne's a big girl now, and she can take it. And nobody, *nobody* can blame you! I'll make that clear to her if it takes all night!" He turned and strode toward the house.

I watched him disappear and knew that he was going in now to pour out the last few drops of Scotch I had seen in the bottle on Sunday. My heart contracted. No wonder I had wanted to give them things. But for the first time I realized his pride—and respected it. Poor kids. Then I remembered Lydia and myself in those first uncertain years in New York after the war. And my pity turned to a warm envy. What I'd give to have those years back.

Tires crunched on gravel. Then a horn sounded, once.

I was tempted to leap up. Anne had *not* gone back to the apartment! Thank God. Or fate. Or chance. Or her own character.

But now I had to look into that face again, that beloved wounded face, and see there the anguish and—what? Hate?

I heard a car door slam and I stood up. Anne was walking toward me over the seared grass. She held herself somewhat stiffly, her gait slow and steady. She came closer, into the shadow of trees, before she stopped. No hysteria in her eyes, only a direct, unquestioning calmness. There was something masklike about her entire face. "I knew somehow you'd come here." And her voice was tranquil, too—intensely quiet. "You must have sped."

Glenn appeared then, a glass in either hand. He set them down on the arm of a chair and went straight to Anne and took her into his arms and held her. I watched. I watched with an odd sensation of satisfaction. Relief. I saw him kiss her, gently, on the lips, saw him stand back and study her. And I saw her eyes meet his and saw a smile flicker along her lips, quickly and faintly, before it disappeared.

"Yes," she said, "I think I will have one, dear. I'm sorry I'm late." She moved to the two glasses, picked up both of them, and then moved toward me. That masklike quality remained on her face. "Father?"

I took the glass. I could say nothing. She had never called me Father before.

"We've been worried," Glenn said. It was not a rebuke. And I realized that everything that had been going through my mind in the last half-hour had also been going through his, possibly with even greater intensity and pain. "I'm just ready to start grilling." He moved a chair. "Why don't you sit down? I've asked Dad to stay but he can't."

Dad: another shock. But a pleasant one this time.

But Anne did not sit: she continued to look at me—not puzzled so much as pleading. A trace of that earlier incredulity shone in her eyes. "I drove slowly, because I had to have time to think. To sort things out." And it was then that I recognized a sort of tensile uncertainty behind her composure. "She's even younger than I am, isn't she, Father?"

"Anne—" Glenn said, behind the chair.

"Yes, dear?" Her voice sounded like the reverberation of thin glass. "Yes? Oh, I see. You two have been talking. Male to male." She took a sip. "How odd. I suppose you explained everything, Father. To Glenn."

"Yes, he did." Glenn came to stand between us. "As best he could.

Anne, believe me, I have an inkling as to how you feel, but he's been under a strain, too."

Anne was frowning now. She took her eyes from mine. "Poor fellow," she said ironically, thinly. She took another swallow, longer this time. Then she pivoted slowly to face me again. "Only don't fret, Father. I have no intention of telephoning Mummy. Or cabling. Or writing." It became a challenge. "That's up to you."

Anne was waiting. So I managed to say, "Thank you, daughter."

Anne said, "Glenn, I have something to tell you later. Not about Father. About . . . me. Something that I think might be important." Her eyes, on me, inquired whether I knew to what she referred. "I've decided there's only one way to live."

I knew she was right. But looking at her, sensing the cruel ache in her, hearing the hurt bafflement in her high-pitched tone, I saw not Anne but Lydia standing there staring at me. And I knew with renewed certainty, that I could never tell Lydia the truth.

"One way to live, Father"—and Anne's tone quavered dangerously—"the way you *taught* me. Not the way you *live*."

"Anne!" This time Glenn took her arms in his hands, firmly, and edged her backward to the chair, where her legs seemed to give way and she sank into it, still staring bleakly at me. "Now sit there and finish your drink." His tone was husky with love and gentleness, concern backed by a firmness I had never heard before. "Dad's leaving I'm going to walk down to the car with him and then I'm going to come back. I have something to tell you, too. Do you understand?"

She finally took her eyes from me. She looked up at Glenn as if something in him had taken her by surprise as well. She frowned. And then I saw flash over her face that familiar, quick expression of rebellion.

"I'll be right back," Glenn said, "and you are going to listen."

His promise was directed at me, I knew, but his strength caused the rebellion to turn into a strange small smile on Anne's face: bewilderment mingling with satisfaction.

"Aye, aye, captain," she said—but behind the mockery was a woman's gratitude. She sipped at her drink. Then she said, "Darling, I've decided something else, too."

"Later," Glenn said and started to move off.

"Glenn—" And when he stopped: "Wherever they send you, for basic or whatever it's called, I'm going with you."

"We can discuss all that—"

"I think it might be fun. Some little room in some funny little town."

Glenn turned to look at me, as if he sensed what I might be feeling. But he was wrong this time.

"Anne," I said, "if you care what I think, I think that's a very wise decision."

"I didn't ask *you!*" Her eyes were too bright, too pointed. "I'll make my own decisions, thank you."

I nodded. We both knew: we were saying good-by to something between us that was gone and could never be there again. We were both aware that a knot had been severed, or unraveled, and that now, in some incongruous and contradictory way, in spite of our pain, we had both been set free.

There was sadness, too, in her tone when she said, without moving, "I'm not going to ask what happened to your hand. But I want you to promise to see Dr. Wilder. Tonight."

And at once I remembered Arnold saying, *That girl of yours is a real woman.* Meaning Lydia. The night Anne was born.

"I promise," I said.

She stood up then, nodded, made no move toward me, simply turned and walked toward the cottage—not running, as she usually did, but walking with a poised womanly dignity.

When she disappeared through the door, I walked toward the driveway, Glenn following.

"You're going back in there, aren't you?" he asked.

"Lydia's coming home. Tomorrow. Possibly tonight."

"Jesus." It was the first time I had ever heard him swear. He opened the door of the car. "Do you want me to go with you?"

I climbed in and slipped under the wheel, then looked up into his face.

He shook his head. "I couldn't leave Anne now."

I started the motor, satisfaction stabbing again.

"Listen—"

"Yes, Glenn?"

"It's—I know it's not the time to tell you. It might make you feel better. Or it might—" He hesitated, then made up his mind. "The reason Anne was so miffed when you didn't show for her birthday dinner yesterday is that she had looked forward to telling you herself. She's pregnant."

I looked around him, toward the house: Anne was nowhere in sight.

Glenn laughed softly. "It's sort of an odd time. I mean the way it works: my going off to kill and Anne—"

But he only let the unfinished thought hang there between us. And I remembered when Lydia had first told me: *Now that all the shooting's finally over, it does seem a good time, what?*

And then I felt a jolt of that strange wonder and joy that I had believed, since Anne's birth, I would never know again. I felt it and let it warm me, spreading all through my body and mind—another and totally different kind of renewal.

"Don't worry about Anne," Glenn was saying then. "I'll make her understand. I'll *make* her."

And I looked up at him again and knew that he would. He was smiling again, but now the smile seemed genuine, full of life and hope, and it was reassuring.

"I think you will," I said.

"You going to call that man Chenery?"

"I haven't decided." I didn't want to think about it, any of that or what was coming, just for a few minutes now.

"Well"—and his hand reached through the window—"well, good luck, sir. And call me later, will you?"

I nodded and shook his hand while pain shot up my arm even though he clasped it gently, and then I felt his other hand on my left elbow in the window, grasping it hard, very hard. And I remembered for the first time in years that the only disappointment I had ever known over Anne's birth had been that, because of its complications, Lydia could never have another child and I would never have a son.

"If you kill him," Glenn said in a harsh whisper, "there's not a jury in the country would convict you."

He let go and I threw the car into reverse, backed up, and turned around, and then I was driving along the narrow curving drive between the trees. In the rear-view mirror I saw Glenn stand a moment before he turned and started toward the cottage.

And it came to me then, in that unlikeliest of moments, that his generation—his and Anne's and Wilby's and Jenny's—was the first in the history of man to face what they faced: not the bomb alone, not only the possibility of the total annihilation of your own species, but at the same time the awesome likelihood, if not certainty, that your species has no meaning anyway, that the sky is empty and that no

ultimate significance exists. To face both at the same time—how to
live with that? What to do? Destroy before being destroyed, torture
while there's still time to torture, avenge yourself by turning on your
fellows? Or, like Glenn and Anne, accept the conditions as they exist,
and find, or try to create, some new vision of order?

The joy remained, throbbing and expanding. Born in pain. Out of
despair, hope. Out of sorrow and bitterness and disillusion, this sense
of glory and continuity! A kind of immortality in itself. Through love.
Through love, the only bridge.

*Y'gotta make sure y'don't start seein' what's real, 'cause if y'ever
start really seein'—* What, Wilby? What then? I'm looking. *This* is
real. More real than you'll ever know.

Level, pop, willya? Y'love that limey wife that much? Honest?
You'll never know, Wilby, but you suspect, don't you? You suspect it
is love that's brought us to tonight. *'Cause that bugs me, man. I admit
it. That really bugs me.* Even you, Wilby, in some strange way you
sense it—or long for it. But you'll never know it. You'll never know
it, Wilby, and I know why now, I've just learned, something you will
never even understand, something I have just come to understand
myself. Your love thrives on its own hungers and needs—*yours.*
Whatever warped satisfactions, or joy in pain, you get from Jenny's
bitter scorn, her spitting contempt, *you* need those satisfactions for
yourself. You take care of her, Wilby, but not for her sake. *Her* de-
pendence feeds *your* tyranny. Even your wild dream of giving her
what she's always wanted is not for her, but to hold her, to hold her
for yourself. Why? Beyond the pleasure of your own cruelty and the
unnatural enjoyment of your own pain? Because you can't even be
certain you're as depraved or worthless as you have to believe you are
without Jenny—someone, *anyone!*—as audience. How else can you
be sure of reality unless you see it reflected in someone else? How
else can you prove to yourself your own corruption and degeneracy?
What *you* need!

But there is another kind of love, Wilby—outside self, beyond self.
And, suspecting its reality, you have to test it, destroy it if possible.
That's why you've been pushing, reaching for new ways to probe it,
because if you ever acknowledge it, if *you* ever start really seeing
what *is* real—

*An' who knows, lover—maybe by time I'm out Shakespearean
Anne'll have a kid y'wouldn't want t'see anything happen to. Kinda
things I got in mind.*

I froze at the wheel. I had to grip it to keep the car on the road. The pain leaped up my arm, plunged into my shoulder and chest. The cold clamped over me suddenly, a chill, intense, consuming, so that I was shuddering inside. And all the triumph and joy flooded out. Instead of that bright vision of human possibility that had opened like some promising vista, a view into the very heart and meaning of life itself, I stared through the windshield into the depths of utter blackness, not even seeing the parkway stretching ahead.

I knew then what had to be done. All doubt and hesitation and reluctance gone. A cold primeval passion took over. And I gave myself to it.

Miles later—half an hour, an hour?—a siren sounded behind, a red light flared in my mirror. I slowed automatically, thinking of the gun in my pocket. No permit. Law. The patrol car, wailing, passed, speeding on. I felt no relief—as I had felt no fear. Law? Professor Kantor knew: there are times—

It was then that I saw the sign: EXIT—WHITE PLAINS.

Dr. Crittenden and I have been discussing this LSD drug that we've all been reading so much about—

Now that LSD kick, that's one bit I don't dig. Hiroshima, Nagasaki—way it must've been. Like I was goin' off it. Off my nut. Allllll the . . . way—

I have anything you might need, any time. Or one of your clients maybe. Poison, dope, knockout drops. Any kind of weapon you can name.

I'd use him. Chenery looks to me like your best bet.

It has been definitely established that anyone with suicidal or homicidal tendencies . . . paranoid or schizophrenic inclinations . . . could be tragic.

You going to call that man Chenery?

"Hello. May I speak with Mr. Chenery, please?"

"Pop? Just a minute. Hey, Pop!"

I could picture the house in my mind: pleasant, modest, on a tree-shaded street in a small town in New Jersey. I could picture Chenery coming to the phone now, in a living room with flowered wallpaper or in a front hall cluttered with children's toys and clothes.

"Yes?"

"Mr. Chenery?"

"That's my name, yes. I recognize your voice so I'd prefer you not state yours on the telephone." His tone was anything but cordial.

"Mr. Chenery—"

"One moment. Chuckie, run your train in the dining room for a while, like a good boy, will you? Your father has business. . . . Hello again. Now, as I might of mentioned, we can't discuss on the telephone. Are you with me?"

"I'm with you, but how the hell—"

"Now let's not get that way again. You hung up in my face this afternoon, you know."

"I'd forgotten. I'm sorry, but—"

"He who pays the piper—"

"Mr. Chenery, I want to know whether—"

"Let's be circumspectual—" he warned.

Back into the nightmare. The other face of reality. Alice through the looking glass. One of Chenery's men stalking Wilby: laughable, sinister—absurd. Jungle world of paranoia: phone tapped. Chenery and Wilby living in adjoining caves on the same cliff.

"Are you still there?"

"I'm thinking," I growled, "how the hell I can be circumspectual!" Then it came to me. "Mr. Chenery, I'm on a *trip*. A *freak* trip, Mr. Chenery. I'm waaaay out, man."

"Where are you calling from?"

"A service station near White Plains. On the Merritt Parkway."

"The Hutchinson River, I believe," Chenery corrected. "About an hour from the city? Well, so am I. I'll meet you in the lobby of your apartment building—eight forty-five."

"But Mr. Chenery—"

"I'll have what you want, but I can't even speculate what you want it for."

"He who pays the piper—"

"And thanks for remembering not to call after eight. Be with you forthrightly."

"Forthrightly," I said weakly and replaced the phone. I leaned against the side of the booth for a long moment wondering whether he had understood me.

"I'll take care of the motor-car, Mr. Wyatt. Very good care, sir. I'll have the garage chap around to pick it up. But Mr. Wyatt, there's something on my conscience. I—"

"I'm to meet a gentleman here. A Mr. Chenery. Has he arrived?"

"Not yet, sir . . . Mr. Wyatt, I have a most abject apology to make to you. I've been taken in, as it were. You see, the young chap said they were your cousins from—well, sir, I thought he said Iowa but I realize now he must have said Ohio. Still being something of a foreigner, I invariably get those two particular states confused. But, of course, he was only having his little jest, anyway, saying he was your cousin. But I did leap to the improper conclusion, you might say—all due, I might add, sir, to my own state of mind these past weeks. Why, the girl even told me herself, when they first came on Sunday, that she was a guest of Mr. Abbott's. And now—"

"Now what, Geoffrey?"

"Well, now with what's happened, I know she was telling the truth, you might say. But I'm also terribly afraid *you* misjudged *me,* too, Mr. Wyatt. You still don't believe I have a wife, do you, sir? Well, I do, and I wish I could say it differently but she *is* ill. And . . . and I've been half balmy, you might say, thinking of her being put away in some state institution. We all know what those places are, it's even in the papers now how inhuman—"

Helped 'em kill the looneys . . . old looney wets his pants . . . old woman dirties hers . . . white coats beat 'em up . . . worse . . . leave 'em by window . . . winter . . . pneumonia—

Looking up into Geoffrey's troubled, even pleading, eyes, I said, "Yes, Geoffrey, I suppose we do know what those places can be."

"That relieves me greatly, sir. It really does. Because I'm going to be entirely candid and throw myself on your mercy, as they say. On top of worrying about her, I've been terrified you'd report me, sir, and then I'd lose my position—and then I don't know what I could do. I couldn't even *visit* her. Mr. Wyatt, it's God's truth: putting everything together and thinking of what I tried to do, too, I've been worried at times I might be round the bend myself. I'm not a blackmailer. Honestly, sir, I'm not. But . . . well, you live with a woman so long, something grows between you. I doubt I'm making myself clear, sir—"

Even Geoffrey. "You're making yourself perfectly clear," I said. Even Geoffrey, who would break the law out of love; who could fear for his own sanity because of his concern for someone he loves. "I have no intention of reporting you, Geoffrey. Whatever's happened is strictly between the two of us."

He was shaking his head from side to side. "How I could ever have imagined a man like you could—it's a fact, sir, a man doesn't know what he'll do or think when he gets desperate!"

"I know, Geoffrey. I agree."

"I've as much respect for the law as the next man—"

I interrupted. "Geoffrey, how did you learn all this? About those two—"

"Oh, didn't I tell you? The girl and Mr. Abbott took off this afternoon in that sporty little Porsche of his. *She* said something about going to Ohio—yes, I'm correct this time, *Ohio*—to get a birth certificate to prove she's alive. They were very gay, sir, both of them, laughing and making merry. Although I must say, her face did appear rather blue and swollen on one side. They left within the hour after you did, Mr. Wyatt. And Mr. Abbott said they were also going to France and he had no idea when they'd be back, but keep the home fires burning. Only one thing did seem to perturb him a mite: he asked me to keep an eye out for that cat of his. Said he'd pay me to take care of it for him if I found it."

"I see," I said, as Chenery appeared in the door and stood waiting. And I did see: fond as she was of Cheetah, Jenny—angry at the world and at having been knocked down the stairs—could not resist leaving the cat for Wilby to discover. A final cruelty: her farewell to Wilby, who had taught her everything she knew and then had taken care of her. "And what about her brother?"

"The young man is her brother? Well, that explains *that* then, doesn't it? Mr. Abbott didn't think to mention that anyone would be using his apartment while he was gone. But the young man—her brother, is he?—he came in . . . oh, possibly two hours ago now and went upstairs. And frankly, sir, he seemed to be . . . well, inebriated or not himself at any rate. He didn't even say good evening and normally he couldn't be more polite."

"He's a very polite young man," I said, and went to the door, where Chenery nodded, curtly, and allowed me to go out first.

"There's a bar they call a Pub around the corner," Chenery said. "Not that I want to drink."

We turned the corner and walked together. It was almost nine but a faint light lingered in the street. The windows were lighted. Wilby was in the apartment. Alone. Alone with the cat. Jenny gone.

"Mr. Wyatt, I know you got a lot on your mind, but I'm not accustomed to having my clients hang up on me on the telephone."

"I've already apologized, Mr. Chenery. I apologize again."

"Well, that's more like it." He was unwrapping a stick of gum. "Heard something on the radio in the car? You happen to have your radio going?"

"No."

Chenery might be, as Glenn had said, my best bet, but there was something more than distasteful, something disgusting, in being forced to deal with him. *What about the scum we play along with?*

". . . little boy, Union Beach, tortured and stabbed—"

. . . *like running broken-field in a meadow covered with dung heaps—*

"Nude, of course, when they found the body. Twelve cigarette burns, beaten with a stick so hard it broke off, stabbed with a marlin spike—"

What did this recitation of horrors have to do with me, with the horror that I faced?

"Medical examiner said the stabbing came at the end of what had been done to him. Sexual rage. That's my point, Mr. Wyatt—these sexual deviators don't deserve to live in a civilized society."

And what was it Henry had said this morning? *When I read some of the things these perverts are capable of, I'm damned if it makes sense to let them run around loose!*

How can y'push it . . . how can y'find new crimes . . . how y'gonna carry it to the goddam limit, like murder—

What was I trying to do—justify whatever I now had to do?

We turned into Pat's Pub. Not crowded now. Empty booth in corner. Have to get this over with. Soon.

"The usual, Mr. Wyatt?" Pat asked, standing at my elbow, broad swarthy face looking down.

"Pat," I said, wondering why, with this cold urgency in me, I bothered, "Pat, I'm surprised you'll even speak to me."

Pat waved a beefy hand. "Aww, everybody takes on too much once inna while, huh? Them things you accused me of, Mr. Wyatt—they just didn't add. But way I figure: everybody's a-got his troubles. Am I right? Some people—donna know why it is—some people, they gotta take 'em out on others. Hell, Mr. Wyatt, people gotta troubles, they gotta drink, am I right? Keep my bambinos in shoes!" Pat laughed. "What'll it be?"

"Coffee, Pat."

"That," Chenery said, "is a superlative idea. Make it two."

"It's a-my pleasure, Mr. Wyatt. Honest-a-God."

And when Pat had gone, Chenery propped his elbows on the table. "Well, Mr. Wyatt, here we are and I wait your orders, like they say. I'm at your disposition."

"Did you understand what I was asking about on the telephone?"

"Mr. Wyatt," Chenery said, ready to be insulted again, but long-suffering. "Of course I got the drift. You was sub-tle, but I wasn't born day before yesterday." His eyes, behind the rimless spectacles, appeared reluctant, as if, since the idea was not his, he couldn't really approve of it. "But I do think it's my duty to—"

He broke off when Pat appeared and set two steaming cups on the table. "Two coffees, gentlemen, sugar-a-cream onna table. Anything else, holla."

Chenery reached into his pocket and tossed to the table, like a couple of dice, two ordinary white sugar cubes. "This what you had in mind, Mr. Wyatt?"

I stared down at them.

"Enough for a long long trip. I don't recommend your putting them in your coffee, Mr. Wyatt." He was smiling slightly as he took a sip. "Hmm, they do make good coffee here, don't they?" He scooped up the two cubes, shook them in his fist like dice, then rolled them across the table. "No smell, no taste. Two hundred and fifty micrograms each. Reason I was a little late is: I had to drop by upper Broadway to pick these up on a street corner up there." His voice took on a meditative quality as he sipped his coffee. "Did you ever think what could happen if someone dumped . . . oh, maybe only a few pounds of this stuff in those reservoors up around Croton Falls? Why few hours later, whole city'd be just a mass of zombies. You'd think you was in a insane asylum. Unless you happened to have a glass of water yourself. Then maybe you'd think you slipped a cog yourself. Are you with me, Mr. Wyatt? Don't that edify you?"

"Mr. Chenery," I said, "it edifies the hell out of me." I picked up the two sugar cubes and put them into the small pocket-within-a-pocket of my jacket—and felt the gun. My hand, now, seemed unnaturally large and numb. "Thank you."

By permanent psychosis, do you mean . . . insanity?

"Now, now," Chenery said, "let's not be so hasteful. In this business I've found it's always best to examine the grease in the frying-pan before jumping into the fire. Are you with me?" He leaned closer. "How do you plan to use these?"

"I'm going to mix an old-fashioned for a friend of mine," I said. "In the hope that it'll make him slip a cog, as you say."

Chenery shook his narrow head. "Risky, risky."

"What isn't? How long does it take for these to take effect?"

"Both of them?"

"One or both—how the hell should I know?"

"One of those alone is a—well, there's no such thing as a normal dose. But five hundred micrograms, they tell me it could be lethal." He drank the dregs of his coffee, noisily, with his little finger crooked delicately. "But since you're paying for my advice, Mr. Wyatt—even if you don't take it—I brought along something else." Again hand to pocket. Again he tossed something to the table: a long yellow capsule. "Now with that LSD you could have a raving maniac or a stiff on your hands. With this, it's just a dead man. And it takes about a hour, so you got plenty of time to get this faggot out of the apartment."

I considered: a gun, two LSD cubes, Chenery's slow-acting poison —an armory. I picked up the capsule and slipped it into the change-pocket with the sugar cubes. Who could say what I might need? Should I thank him?

"Capsule pulls apart in two pieces. Use the powder. Clean, Mr. Wyatt. Don't even leave much trace in the blood and who's going to bother anyway just another beatnik addict passed out in the gutter. Are you with me?"

I stood up. But before I could turn away, he spoke again.

"I know it's a opportune time, all you got on your mind like this, and I apologize for mentioning the subject—"

"If he kills me," I said, "Mr. Brant will pay your bill."

"Oh no, nothing like that. I always consider money secondarily. No, it's like this: if anything goes haywire and anyone happens to inquire, like in a police station, where you obtained these things, you better forget my name utterly. Are you with me?"

"That goes without saying, doesn't it?"

"Well," he said judiciously, pursing his lips, "well, it does and then again it don't. In my business you can't be too conscientious." One hand smoothed his thin gray hair. "Whatever that kooky fag threatened you with, you and your loved ones, why that wouldn't hold a candle to what I'd have to have done. I'd just have to, Mr. Wyatt. My whole business depends on it. Are you with me?"

I turned away without answering and went to the bar. "What do I

owe you Pat? Two sandwiches yesterday, how many drinks, the
coffees—"

"Onna the house, Mr. Wyatt. Lemme buy you a couple a sandwiches, huh? Y'got other worries. Take it easy, huh?"

What can I say? He wants to do it. For some reason. I know the
reason: a compassionate man. Which is to say—civilized. Like the
old Jew on the street.

"Thanks, Pat."

"I'm bettin' on you," he calls after me. "I got my whole wad onna
you, Mr. Wyatt. Straight across the board!"

Luck. Those take-offs years ago: the roaring speed on the runway,
the slow straining heavy ascent. Hands waving. Luck. If I'm cap-
tured, Chenery, I'll give only my name, and rank, and serial number
—which I have forgotten.

The street. Darkness above. Glow in sky. Lights. Windows. Radiance, really. Like the cottage. Oddly enchanted. At once lovely and
harrowing. As if I might be seeing it for the last time. Seeing it, seeing
this. Years ago, looking down on those patterned farmlands before
reaching the Channel: stone fences, hedgerows, houses, barns, people
cycling on roads, working in fields—ordinary routine tasks. Same
stab of nostalgia now. A warm envy. How lucky. If they only knew.

Jenny gone now. Wilby alone with cat. Task at hand. Hands on
controls. Lydia on her way. After nine now. Nine to midnight: three
hours. Keep mind on job. That letter in his pocket. If Hank's right,
another letter by now. Make sure. Get it from pocket, all costs.

Panic now. What if I'm wrong? Know nothing about insanity,
symptoms, signs, and portents. Only how I felt on street at noon, last
night in bed. How could I judge Wilby's state, considering state *I* was
in? State I might still be in. What if symptoms only another Wilby's
fiendish jokes? *They didn't send me, dad. I chose . . . such great
performance that courtroom . . . judge convinced . . . foxed 'em,
click?*

Or, if I'm wrong, if only Wilby-joke, do I have *better* chance?
Against a *sane* mind?

Police car, cruising slowly. Stops across street. Will pass before me
when light changes. Two uniformed officers. My last opportunity?
Hand of fate?

Two years, five, ten. I don't care how long, click?

You won't have a second's peace . . . rest of life . . . thousand deaths every time she goes marketing . . . hairdresser's . . . matinee—

Light flashes. Police car approaching across wide street, passing, slowly. Officer idly glancing, guarded but curious. How do I look?

Just for the record—it's a felony to manufacture, sell or transport the stuff . . . legally a narcotic—

The gun. Sullivan law. How many laws broken? How many more to break?

Only one way to not break the law—that's not to break the law.

Tail-lights red down street. Gone.

You're a lawyer, ain't you? What you think of people don't honor their contracts? Like the U. S. of A.?

Light flashes again. With click. Across street. No hurry now. No delay.

Who was it said . . . every act of lives in such way . . . if everyone else behaved in exactly that way—

Turning corner. Familiar awning ahead. Familiar number on awning. How many times?

. . . termed a psychochemical . . . said by its proponents to expand consciousness—

Mine already expanded. No drug necessary. Never more alive. Never wanted more desperately to stay alive. Years ahead. Only fifty. Last night, too few years left—appalling. Tonight, those years seem forever, *are* forever. For me. For me and Lydia. So much to do. To know. Lydia—

Knot of people on street. In front of building. What? In small circle. Some staring down. At what? Others looking up side of building. I stop. Others come running. Heart stops.

Cop out. You'n me—off the terrace. Splash-splash.

No breath. But no one screaming. No backing away in horror. Only a murmuring curiosity. No police.

I move. Hear my steps, firm, and steady. So this is it. It ends like this. All for this?

"I don't get it. I always thought cats could land on their feet—"

"Yeh, they land on their feet like they got nine lives."

I stop on curb. Breathing again.

Cheetah in gutter. Blood. Crushed. Crumpled. Geoffrey stooping alongside. Lifts cat's head. Lets it fall. Cat's eyes stare. At nothing. No hostility now.

"Some people don't deserve to have pets."

"Ahh, only a cat for gossake!"

Geoffrey looks up. At me. Then stands. "I don't know how I can tell Mr. Abbott."

Mr. Abbott has another cat now. One that will claw him to bits.

"How far yah think she fell?"

"Cats don't fall."

"This cat sure as hell fell!"

"It didn't fall. Somebody up there ought to be ashamed of theirself."

"Here, let me open it, Mr. Wyatt. Curious, isn't it? That its neck should be broken. Do you supppose that's only an old wives' tale, that a cat always lands on its feet?"

No. Live cat lands on its feet. If neck broken, broken first. Then thrown over balustrade—

"Mr. Abbott's certainly going to be crushed."

Like Cheetah. No doubt about it. Crushed. By Jenny.

"Geoffrey—"

"Yes, Mr. Wyatt?"

"If you hear anything unusual from my apartment, summon the police."

"Unusual? The—"

"Or if I call you on the house phone, no matter what I say or who I seem to be talking to, do the same."

"Certainly, sir, but if there's anything—"

"If you don't do this, exactly as I've told you—or if you speak of it to anyone—you're going to lose your job and be arrested for attempted extortion."

Elevator. Seven. Door slides.

No remorse. None. No pity. Reduced to legendary beast protecting his own? Cave on cliff with Chenery and Wilby? If necessary, yes.

Thou shalt not kill. Distance from swamp to law. Fish to philosopher. Evolution. Obligation. Regression.

All in same boat. Mysterious sea. Where are we going? No one knows. But time all we have. Brief for all. If someone insists on blasting holes in hull—because he hates self, because he hates boat, because he doesn't have guts to jump overboard, whatever sad, tangled reason! —he must be eliminated. To save boat. Simple. Fundamental.

If you kill him no jury in the country would convict you—
Off elevator. Down corridor. Last time?

Hand in pocket again. Flesh of hand taut, sore. Pain of grip harrowing, piercing. Finger stiff and throbbing on trigger.

Quiet inside. Key in left hand.

No pause now. No hesitation! Throw open the door, what are you waiting for, take gun from pocket, unlock door, push it open, fast, locate him, take aim, blast, fire point-blank, get it over with, think of Anne's face, Lydia on way, *her* face, blast again, fast, hear explosions, watch body stiffen, crumble, lie twitching, life ebbing away, what matter, hates life anyway, stand gazing down pitiless with primitive primeval satisfaction—

How did you happen to kill him, Mr. Wyatt? I came into my apartment, surprised him, ransacking, look at it, so I shot him. How'd you happen to have a gun? Took it away from him. How? Jumped the bastard, *took* it! Doorman tells us you knew this boy, tells us you instructed him to phone us if—

I insert key in lock with left hand. Twist it. Right hand still in pocket. Gun clasped, pointed. Pain intense.

Apartment dark. Cavelike. Only light from hall in slash across foyer.

Inside, I reach for switch. No sound. Has he gone?

I flip switch.

In light I glance around quickly. Room comes into focus. Desolate. Strange.

Wilby sits in the center of the living-room floor, his back to me. He does not move. A trick?

I speak his name.

Then I step, cautiously, in a wide semicircle through the debris on the floor until I can see his face.

It is almost unrecognizable: scratched, clawed, torn, bleeding still —a red-streaked mask, horrible, pitiful, grotesque. His eyes are flat, withdrawn. Opaque.

He still does not stir, eyes do not blink. But, closer now, I see tears. They do not fall, only further glaze and obscure the already dazed blankness.

Is this what I had hoped for, or not dared hope for but nevertheless worked toward?

But beneath my shock pity gnaws. I fight it down.

Now what?

Get him out of the apartment. But how? And what if I'm wrong? What if, even now—

I speak his name again.

He seems not to hear.

I see his bare arms now: red-streaked, raw, the flesh torn ragged.

Then, carefully, I allow myself to glance around the room. Mute and terrible evidence of cataclysmic violence. Wilby and Cheetah—to Cheetah's death. Could I ever have imagined this? And as he fought, as he held the cat and broke its neck while it hissed and flailed in final desperation, had he wondered whether the cat was even real?

But I can feel no relief. Only horror. And caution.

"Wilby," I say—and for some obscure reason I whisper, as in a sickroom, or place of death, as if a raised voice might mysteriously shatter this cataleptic stupor and return us to some other, more treacherous plane—"Wilby, Jenny's waiting." Closer, bending down, but hand still grasping pointed gun: "Jenny, Wilby—*Jenny*."

He does lift his head, does not turn it, does not seem to move a muscle or a nerve.

And I feel a chill, a chill unlike the cold fury, the fixed determination—a chill that goes deep and is more than a shudder. Still, what must be done—

"I've found Jenny. She *needs* you."

His head twists now, but as if in annoyance—as if a fly is buzzing near his ear and interfering with the sound of some music that only he can hear.

"Jenny is waiting."

And now his eyes seem, ever so slightly, to clear. But again in pique at the intrusion.

I stand before him now, above him. "I'll take you to Jenny."

Out of here, onto the street—then what?

But he does not hear, does not recognize me.

Along with the frustration, hope flares, wild and dazzling, even while I debate whether I should touch him, perhaps shake him— anything to stir him from this, to make him *move*!—even while I feel an overwhelming, weary sadness at all the waste, loss, futility that have finally brought us only to this.

I reach a hand—my left hand—to his shoulder. At my touch he leaps, his whole body recoiling. And his eyes widen.

Then he moves again, moves so fast, so expectedly and violently that, even before I can step away or pull the trigger, I feel his shoulders smashing against my shins.

My numb, swollen finger finally grips, a reflex not quick enough because, while the gun explodes, muffled only slightly by my pocket but shattering nonetheless, filling the room with its sharpness, I know at once, tumbling backward, that I have missed.

I know, falling, that it has all been a trick, another trick, I should have known, and then I'm flat on the floor, my head cracking behind, and he is somehow above me, his weight pinning me, his bloody, ugly face inches above mine, his eyes cruel and murderous as Cheetah's, but now I feel an immense, incredible release while I hold onto the gun and try, in the tangle of cloth, to direct it upward, knowing too late that I should have blasted when I first came in, should have given in to that jungle impulse, but the release is exploding into a blood-lust that swarms through my veins and I feel a burst of enormous animal strength, power, joy, even as I see his huge fist plunging down at my face, so that I twist my head aside and swing from the floor with my left, a wide blow that catches him on the ear, he groans, and then I hear him cry out sharply as his fist crashes into the floor, hear the cracking sound near my ear, I feel a savage exultancy and roll to one side as his weight falls from me and then I am standing, pulling the gun from the pocket in the same second that I whirl to face him, but even then I do not want to shoot but rather to slug in fanatic frenzy, to smash, to hear the sound of flesh splitting, bones splintering, to see blood spurting, but I pull the trigger again with that same thick awkward finger as his shoulders smash against my legs again, harder and higher this time, while his hand reaches up, fingers clawing into the sore, tight flesh of my right hand, talons sinking to the marrow so that my mind blanks with pain while it tenses for the shot that does not come, and then I am on my back again, knowing now that my hand has given up the gun in that instant of unbearable agony, hearing the thud of the gun on the carpet while my mind fights for consciousness against the sickening ferocity of pain.

Then Wilby is standing above me, but backing away, cowering slightly, the gun somehow in his hand.

And he is weeping. From pain? Weeping openly, not sobbing, all is quiet, tears streaming over the bloodied map of scars and scratches that is his face. While in his eyes now, in place of the frightening catatonic glaze, there is a red-streaked brilliance: mingled hate and a terrible, wild sadness as of someone who has been betrayed. The suffer-

ing is so naked and piercing that, instead of wondering whether he
will fire the gun, I can only think: he has not gone mad, it was only a
trick, he has not gone mad and now my only hope, if any, is that
someone heard the shot.

Only our heavy breathing sounds in the room and the acrid smell
of burned powder and cloth mingles with the other stenches.

Finally he whispers, "You tried to kill me, didn't you?" Swaying
above me, still half crouched, barefoot, hair over face, voice incredulous, grotesquely indignant. "You sonofabitch, you tried to kill me!"
He is trembling all over, the gun shaking in his left hand while his
right—the one he rammed at my face and crashed into the floor—
dangles loosely.

Did Geoffrey hear the shot? The muffled report still echoes in my
head. Did anyone hear it? No one in Donald's apartment below, but
surely someone upstairs, or next door.

Wilby's expression changes: his face twists into a grin and his eyes,
bleakly outraged one instant, sharpen into points of pleasure the next.
"I didn't think you had it in you!" His tone is shrill with joy all of a
sudden. Delight. "You tried to do it!"

What he has asked for, begged for. And I missed. Missed because
the bastard tricked me. Again. Slowly, every muscle and nerve
screaming, I manage to stand, rage burrowing into my marrow. Did
Geoffrey follow my orders? How soon can I expect to hear a siren
below?

Already aware of the hopelessness of what I'm doing— *Bread, it
don't mean nothin' t'me. Green shit!*—I turn my back on him and
step to where the painting lies facedown in the rubble of the floor.
With my left hand—my right is as useless as his now—I lift it by the
frame and prop it against the cocktail table, facing him. A stellated
crack zigzags down the center of the heavy glass top of the table, and
the picture frame looks nicked and cracked, but the painting itself is
intact.

I face him. "Take it and get out." But I hear hollow futility in the
words.

Wilby's face holds a trace of mockery. He doesn't even glance at
the painting. "Are you ready to curse it now?" And for the first time I
realize that he no longer speaks in that slurred argot which I had always suspected was imposed or acquired. "Ready to curse life
now?"

What he has demanded all along. What he has to have. More than the money, the painting, Jenny. What by God he won't get from me. "I'm ready to curse *you,* you bastard." My voice is a low growl. "But you're not life."

If the police come, everything I've tried, everything I've done will be wasted, total loss: back where it all started Sunday night. The questions, scandal, his arrest—and, worse now, what he will do when he gets out.

"You hate me, don't you!" A shrill cry, sharp and unexpected, wild. "You've hated me from the start!" His eyes have changed again: pupils enormous and dark, a bruised and blurred look. "*You* did this to me! *All* of it!"

The gun no longer shakes in his hand. And suddenly I know what can be done. Very simple. Very final. As soon as I hear the police in the hall, I'll rush him, he will fire the gun, they will arrest him for murder or shoot him. If they arrest him, Ephron and Henry know what's been going on: they'll make sure he doesn't get out of it. And Lydia and Anne will be safe. Suddenly very simple.

He takes a single step toward me, face contorted in fury. "Jenny's gone! You know that? She took all her clothes! Jenny's gone and it's your fault!"

Whatever is to come, it can't happen until the police arrive. "I had nothing to do with it."

"Calling her a whore! Making her *feel* like a whore! Filling her with your phony ideas!" He comes still closer—but not so close that I can risk reaching for the gun. "If you hadn't refused her, she'd still be here! You only did it to get at *me.*"

Always back to the sick stalk of self. "The whole world's set up for one reason alone—to get at you."

"You brought that cat in here, too, didn't you?"

What if no one heard? What if the police aren't coming at all?

"Answer me, damn you! *You* brought that cat in here, didn't you?"

If no one heard, it's up to me. But how? The only way I know, the only hope, if it is a hope— "What the hell cat are you talking about?"

Uncertainty leaps like fire into his face. His eyes flinch, his chin sags, and he lifts his swollen, injured hand as if to stroke his torn face, but the pain is too much and he winces. "What cat?" A whisper —a whisper of utter terrified incredulity. Then he shouts, "*What cat!* Look! *Look* at me." He steps back and extends his arms—and the temptation to go for the gun hardens in me even as I tense for the sound of the siren. "It tried to kill me!" He is near tears again. "Look what it *did* to me!" Beseeching, piteous. "Just *look*."

I stare coldly at his ripped, blood-smeared arms. "I don't know what you're talking about."

Then I wait.

He turns his arms over, frowning. A wild bewilderment gathers in his face. Then he whirls away and runs to the terrace, disappears.

Is it my chance? Dial Geoffrey. Make *sure* the police come. Make sure he shoots at the right moment. *What happens to Lydia if that bastard kills you?* Yes, but damn it, what happens if he *doesn't*, if he's still here when Lydia walks in?

"Somebody took it away." Too late: I waited too long. He's back. But something in his voice now, something in the way he stands slouched and uncertain and befuddled, sends hope through me. "I killed it. I strangled the"—a shudder—"I choked the life out of it. Felt it going out. Only that was a cat. Not like the *soul* leaving the body. Cats don't have souls, do they?" His voice is distant, almost faint. "Felt it going out, *seeping* away." He moves into the room, but only a few blind steps—and I feel a chill down my spine, a shock too deep and profound for terror or panic. "If you jumped, would you know, going down? It's the knowing. Did the cat *know* when I was choking it?" He is not speaking to me, to anyone. "Guillotine. Or John the Baptist. That's the way, though." Head lifted, eyes unnaturally bright. "Is there one instant, just one, but long as a lifetime, *all* lifetimes, when you know you're dying, *know* it in your head because you can see your own body flopping, see your own blood and know it's yours? Do you know the secret then? Too late, but do you *know* it? What life *is*. What it really is—" His voice trails off.

He's close. I don't know much about these things but Crittenden said there was a line. He's close now. And what if he goes over it with a loaded gun in his hand?

Silence. No sound of siren or commotion below. Nothing. Even Wilby's breathing is silent now. What if, while he's standing there with the gun lowered, I were to make a quick dive?

Abruptly Wilby turns and goes out to the terrace again.

Cop out. Both of us. Suicide pact. Splash-splash.

Let him. How can I stop him anyway? Cheetah: body crushed and crumpled in gutter. Geoffrey thinks he's staying in Donald's apartment. Let him jump! They'll assume he did it from the terrace below.

What about the love note he burned up? You think he hasn't written another one by now? Terror does strike now. Scalding, urgent, fierce, sending me to the terrace door, fast . . . *one thing worse than your death . . . rest of her life with that doubt—*

But I stop in the doorway. Because—what do I expect?—he stands at the balustrade, his back to me: shoulders slumped, whole body slack. I do not move closer, but not because I am afraid he will trick me. Staring across the dimness at him, I know now that he did not trick me earlier, when I came in. That was no ruse. Is it possible now, by some stratagem impossible to imagine, to thrust him back into that catatonic state so that his madness will be unmistakable to anyone?

"You do hate me, don't you?"

At first I cannot even be sure he has spoken: a whisper, faint, blurred. How has he sensed my presence? Or is he speaking to me?

Bleakly then, without turning, he repeats the words. "You do hate me, don't you?"

Hate: the fuel he thrives on, or wastes away on. But nevertheless needs. If I feed that need, will it only—

"We can't help what we are, you know—" His tone is again reasonable. Slowly, he turns, a shadow against the shadow of building beyond. A suggestion of whimper in his tone: "How can we help what we are, any of us?"

And I know that, if I am to play this out to the end, I must answer him. "You can help what you are," I growl. "And I know damn good and well you can help what you *do*."

"Do? What do we do?" Boyish innocence, unfeigned, and reminiscent of Jenny—but only this afternoon Wilby was boasting of the evil he did! "What do we do? We just want to live. Like everybody else."

"Like hell! You don't want to live like *anybody* else." If you want to live at all. "You want to live *your* way and smash any *other* way and *whine* about it into the bargain."

"Whine?"

"*Whine!*" And the anger surges through me even as I'm aware that I'm using it—although uncertain to what end. "It's all I've heard around here for days and I'm up to my neck in it. If you want to live, live. Admit you're sick and get some help. And in the meantime, leave the rest of us alone. Just because you're miserable, why the hell make sure everybody else is miserable, too?" As I take a breath and a step, I wonder whether my own rage has taken over or whether I am actually trying to reach whatever kernel of reason might be left in him. "Hell, you were born naked just like the rest of us. Nobody promised you a damn thing when they pulled you out of the womb. *Nothing*! These are the conditions. This is the way it is. They didn't invent the bomb just to get at *you*! If you don't like the way things are, change them. Start with yourself!"

He does not move. After a long moment—in which I decide that the silence in the street means that no one heard the shot and no one is coming—he cocks his head. "Y'preachin' t'me, dad?"

Recognizing the change in his speech—the more normal mockery and slur of words now—it occurs to me that I might have returned us both to more familiar ground. And potentially more treacherous ground? "I'm not preaching, I'm talking. You're always wailing that no one talks with you. It's because you don't *listen*! You're not listening now."

"I'm . . . listenin', man—"

"God isn't dead. He was never there. He didn't *die* just to bug *you*."

Silence. Then his head straightens.

"Sick? Y'said I was sick—" It is not quite a question. He is moving slowly toward me. "How can I be sick, man, when the whole goddam world's . . . sick?"

You're sick, Wilby, and if there's any way to do it, I'm going to make you sicker. But how?

"Even if the whole world's absolutely insane—and it's not—it's your job not to be."

His eyes flare. "My *job*! You *are* preachin' t'me!" His voice rises. "Like my old lady. Readin' her goddam Bible t'me! Prayin', prayin' and readin' it and preachin' to me, an' all the time fuckin' up the town!" He is so close now that the streaked map of face, contorting, turns into a red blotch, eyes frantic. "Liar! Like you!" His spittle sprays my face but I do not step back. "*Hypocrites*!"

Then he whirls about and stands upright at the balustrade, shoulders straight, arms outstretched. He shouts into the darkness, " 'Did not Moses give you the law, and yet none of you keepeth the law! Why go ye about to kill *me*?' "

I hear the inner cry, though, behind the quotation which he has distorted now to his own meaning. I hear the strain of the hunger, the yearning, the demand that the world be what the world cannot be.

" 'And the earth also was corrupt before God, and the earth was filled with violence!' "

Then he drops his arms and leans over the balustrade, pointing the gun toward the street below, crouching to sight along the barrel as if it were a rifle.

"Which one y'want dad?" A high-pitched excitement in his tone now. "Old lady walkin' the dog? Ol' moneybags gettin' outta the cab? Or the blond bitch with him? You name it! You play God this time!"

What now? I step closer. *Did your client see the morning papers? Some kid in Texas. Certain kind of mind. You never know when it's going to happen.*

"All evil!" he cries. "All guilty! Don't matter which one gets it, which one don't!"

"How can anyone be evil if there's no good?" I hear the harshness in my demand, see his face lift from the gun. How can I even hope to use reason against a mind already lost in reason's opposite? "How can anyone be guilty if there's no innocence?" What weapon but reason do I have?

For a long moment he does not stir. I hear a bus rumbling by on the avenue, a taxi-horn bleating, the whine of a television, in the distance a doorman's whistle.

Then Wilby laughs and, kneeling, he braces the gun with his distended right hand, sights along the barrel again. "You don't bug me, man." But I hear, or perhaps imagine, a kind of hysterical desperation in his tone and wonder whether I have not actually driven him to what he now intends. "How many'd that cat in Texas get yesterday? Seventeen, papers said. I only got five bullets. Five outta five, man. Any bets? Any bets, you bastard?"

"I'll bet," I tell him quietly, "that you won't get more than one."

Then I watch his head twist. He squints up at me. And I have to stifle an impulse to reach, to bring my fist down on the wrist holding the gun. Would he let go? Would it fall those seven flights? Then what?

"Then you'll get the second, pop—"

"I realize that."

Bafflement twists his face. "What do *you* care? They're strangers—"

I do not reply. I relish that note of boyish incredulity in his tone. I wait.

"What difference does it make to *you*?"

I hesitate. The answer is vital. Does he really want to know? Can I hope to confound him further? "We're all in the same boat. All they've got is what we've got. Time."

"An' . . . an' nothin' comin' after?"

"Nothing."

He stands up. "Then what difference does *anything* make?"

"Stop whining!" It's a shout now, angry and certain. "Everything makes more difference! If this is all there is, this is *more* important!"

He steps back. The gun is now pointed to the floor. "More? You . . . you crazy or—" He is blinking. "You must be *nuts*!" But the doubt is naked in his tone, bewilderment. "You don't believe that."

"If I didn't believe it, you'd have been dead two minutes after I walked in here tonight."

Then I turn and go inside, uncertainty gnawing at me. What if I have taken the wrong tack entirely? What if I only confound him into further violence, since violence is invariably his answer to confusion?

I move to the bar, lifting my heavy hand—pain forgotten until I move it—and force it into the pocket. The capsule and the sugar cubes. *LSD can and often does render a person incurably, as you put it, insane—* But what if that person has a loaded gun in his hand, a loaded gun and definite homicidal tendencies, as *you* put it, Dr. Crittenden?

Wilby comes in. Fast. He moves toward the stairs and starts blindly, swiftly up them. "Jenny, we're gonna split. Jenny-baby, this cat's nuts, this cat's—" But he stops at the head of the stairs, stops and stands there with one foot on the balcony, as if it has just come to him that for some reason which he must get straight in his mind Jenny is not there.

Then he turns to look down, and as he does so he swings the gun to aim it directly at me over the banister. "Christ, how you hate me!" It's a wail, forlorn and yet ferocious. "Only, man, y'don't know what that means. Y'don't dig that. 'Cause that only means y'love me! 'Cause, by cause, hate, straight, is love, by cause dove—" He takes a breath and then the words stumble over each other. "Reason y'sent Jenny away, stay away, play, you want me alone, 'cause hate means love an' y'want t'throw me out on the street, naked on street where they'll beat me, I know, as ye sow, so shall ye—" Then he is moving down the stairs. "You. You're only who y'think you are, only what *I* think you are, all I am to you, too, true-blue, only what *you* think *I* am, but I'm *not!*" He laughs—a high-pitched cackle. "That's the joke, biggest joke of all, nothing's what it is because it's not, it's just not *there*." Whether he is conscious of my presence or not, he moves toward me, his bare feet stepping heavily on the broken glass on the floor although he seems unaware of it. "That's the joke, don't you see, everything has to be its opposite or it's nothing at all, which it is, which-bitch it is anyway, now listen, now listen, if anyone could hold those in their hands, those opposites, imagine, *think,* like holding fire and ice in your hand same time, air and water, yesterday and tomorrow, space, space and time, or . . . or the beginning and the end, time divine, by cause, you see, don't you, by cause you'd be divine then, *he*'s the one holds it all in his mind, holds it, folds it, and has peace—" His eyes, which may or may not see me, seem to bore into mine with an eerie exaltation, some inner joy that is almost orgiastic. "Peace and nothingness, and glows, heaven and hell, and peace—" Then, with shocking abruptness, his tone changes to a wild insistence. "You understand, don't you? Tell me that, you do understand, oh Christ, someone has to understand somehow, brown cow, Christ, thrice-blessed, somehow, someday, doomsday—" Then he is yelling into my face. "Tell me you understand, damn you, don't let them get me on the street, don't let them beat me even if I deserve, observe, conserve, Christ, *tell me you understand!*"

I understand that if everything is its opposite, centuries of evolution are wiped out in a single swipe. I understand that regression is madness. I understand that you, Wilby, are insane. And I understand that, with luck now, I shall not have to use the capsule or the sugar cubes in my pocket because anyone can recognize now that you—

"Tell me. Do you, does anyone, will anyone, tell me you understand!"

I hear the despair bleak and terrible in his voice. I see it in his frenzied eyes. And sadness mingles with my hope.

"Of course I understand."

Silence. But only brief. For, before I realize that he is moving, he lifts the gun and brings it down with terrific and paralyzing force on my shoulder. I even hear it whizzing past my ear before I feel the blow and stagger sideways.

"*Liar!*" he howls. "Liar! No one understands, ever, clever, bastard liar!"

Wobbling lopsidedly I make it to the bar and behind and pick up a whisky bottle, grasping it by the neck in my left hand as the pain spreads over my right shoulder and shoots down into my chest and into the aching infected arm and hand, so that, even as I tense for further assault, my mind threatens to blank.

But Wilby has moved away, shuffling around the room, his bare feet trudging over the debris, walking in a ragged, aimless semicircle. Has he forgotten me already?

No choice now. None. Unless by some miracle I can get hold of the gun, I'll use the capsule. *It takes about a hour, so you got plenty of time to get the faggot out of the apartment.* If I can't get him out of the apartment, he can die here. No more compassion. No more mercy now. Circumstance narrows choice, but choice remains.

My numbed, thick fingers reach into the small change-pocket and separate the gritty cubes from the smooth capsule, grasp it and, the pain grinding, manipulate it into my palm as I lift my hand from the pocket. I set down the bottle, and with my left hand reach for two glasses and place them on the bar.

Across the room, though, Wilby whips about and starts toward me again, his jaunty, contemptuous swagger replacing the aimless, shambling gait. He stops before he speaks. "Man, y'don't know what's comin', do you?" I recognize the relish in his tone and know at once that cruelty will follow, as I splash whisky into both glasses. "You'n me, man, we're gonna stay right here'n wait for the limey wife. How's that grab you?" But his grin is faint and empty, the mockery hollow, the elation thin and somehow off key.

With his eyes on me, I fumble with stiff clumsy fingers, below the bar's surface, to separate the two parts of the capsule. He has returned to reality, or to his version of reality. Have I brought him back from that netherworld of unreason by saying that I understand? How, against a mind such as this, can you ever *know*?

"Stay right here together, pop, till the bitch walks in—" Standing off balance, both arms dangling, head tilted, legs apart: a ludicrous parody of himself. Then he steps to the bar in several long, swift strides. "Like this, man, like this. She comes in an' I let you choose. Which one gets it first? Which one watches the other one get it?" Eyes riveted on mine: glazed, but with a pleased wildness quivering in them. "Let *you* choose. You watch her or she watches you? Which one, man? Which one?" He laughs again—the cackle cracking and reverberating around the room.

The crowning cruelty. The ultimate torture conceivable. Nevertheless, conceived out of his own sense or knowledge of what love is, or should be; conceived out of his need to test it, to deny it utterly if possible.

"Which one watches?" A whisper, quavering with excitement. "*You* choose. You tell me—"

My mind flinches from the pictures erupting in it and I cannot separate the two parts of capsule without using both hands and risking that he will notice. I know he will insist on an answer. What can I say to befuddle him further, or to convince him? The truth? "If it comes to that," I say slowly, "I'll watch."

His face lights; triumph, glee. "You'll watch! *Why*?"

Doesn't he know—that, given a hopeless choice, I could not let Lydia suffer the agony of watching me die—and could not risk what Wilby might do to her afterward? Can I take the chance that, actually, he does know this by now, much as he longs to believe otherwise?

"Why, man?"

"You figure it out!"

"I *know*! 'Cause y'figure then you still got a chance. You, personal. *You*!"

"Naturally. First law of the jungle. Self-survival."

It's a risk and I'm aware of it. But what isn't a risk now?

He snorts a laugh again, but even as he does so, his face clouds. Doubt darkens his eyes—uncertainty. "*Love*!" He spits the word.

"What's love got to do with the jungle?"

He turns away then, face twisting, muttering, "Lies. You . . . you'd lie to *God*."

He has seen through—as I intended. And hope courses through me again, giving me the strength to bring my right hand to the surface, to break open the capsule while his back is turned, to shake the powder into one of the glasses, and then to stand watching him as he prowls the room, erratically again, stumbling this time, kicking aside whatever comes against his feet. Has he actually begun to believe what he cannot allow himself to believe?

"Only"—and as I see him shambling about, I have to strain to make out the words—"only, you don't *get* t'choose . . . Me . . . one who chooses, loses . . . make her watch, see, look . . . what you *don't* want . . . you no choice . . . I—" He stops at the fireplace and stands looking up at the portrait. "I take care you, limey-Lydia-bitch-slimey-limey . . . tear off goddam clothes . . . strip

naked . . . not shoot you, too, new . . . hang you off goddam terrace, ankle, one ankle, go ahead limey, scream, yell . . . too late,
might let go, might not, might—" Then, with a shadow of his old
grin, he faces me again. "Think she go nuts, man?" But his gaze is as
blurred as his words: does he even see me? "Nuts . . . way y'think
I am . . . way y'tried make *me* think I—" His voice sounds as limp
and exhausted as I feel. "Only now y'know I ain't, click?"

I am too weak even to pick up the glass from the bar. If there is
any rage left in me, it is too deep and profound for me even to feel it
now. Everything I try only seems to drive him to conceive new and
more unspeakable atrocities. All I know is that I must not let him kill
me. If no one heard the first shot, what chance that they would hear
another? Police not coming. No one coming. Only Lydia—

"Well, pop?" The taunt sounds empty—as the threat, I know, is
not.

"I'm going to have a drink." My voice is remarkably steady. I pick
up one of the glasses and place my hand around it to obscure its clarity in contrast to the slight muddiness of the whisky in the other.

"Drink?" He comes toward the bar. "Drink?"

I take a sip of the whisky without tasting it. "What else can I do?
It's going to be a long wait." I shove the other glass across the narrow
surface. "I need it if I have to listen to you."

He squints into my face, not even glancing at the glass. "Cool.
Still . . . cool—" But there is suspicion in his tone, in his glazed
eyes, and I remember that any detachment on my part has always disturbed and confused him. "Signifies, dignifies, got y'where it's shortest, click?"

"Click. Click."

"Clickety-click-click!"

The very sound seems to give him an idea. He steps away, nodding, as if I had myself made a suggestion. Then he lifts the revolver,
breaks it open, using his puffed yellowish-blue right hand as if he no
longer feels the pain in it. He shakes the bullets into his palm, intent
on what he is doing, and again I am tempted to try to make it around
the end of the bar. But he selects a single bullet, reinserts it quickly
into the chamber, and spins the cylinder as he tilts his head and listens to the clickety-clickety-clickety-click-click-click sound. When it
stops, he snaps the gun together, ignoring me, and strides, vigorous
again, swift and certain, to the terrace door and, placing the gun

under his right armpit, he hurls the remaining bullets across the terrace with his left arm.

He swings around to peer at me across the room. "Y'game, man? Y'cool enough?"

Then I remembered. Last night. *How 'bout game Russian roulette, dad? One chance in six. I'll even go first.*

He is standing very straight, eyes luminous. "Givin' you fair shake, man. Givin' you chance, prance, nance, click? Bullet's not for the limey-bitch if—"

He brings up the gun and places the end of barrel against his left temple. His eyes are wide.

One bullet. Not for Lydia if it kills Wilby. Or me.

"Y'think I ain't cool . . . cool as you—" He pulls back the hammer with his thumb and the cylinder whirs a single notch, hammer snapping into place—

"You say when, man—"

One chance in six: best odds I've had. Go ahead, Wilby. You poor sick cruel bastard, go ahead and get it over with.

"Say it—" A feverish breathlessness in his voice now. Does he enjoy the waiting? Is he thinking now of the falling guillotine? With some sick ecstatic torment and pleasure behind those fixed, blind eyes?

"You hate me, say when—"

What happens if I tell him to shoot? I open my mouth to speak —but say nothing. Who can predict that perverse mind? If I say the word, will he, instead, swing the gun to me and keep pulling the trigger until it fires? Leaving him alone here to wait for Lydia.

"If you hate me, say it!" His voice thins to a taut low cry, at once pitiful and pleading and desperate. "*Say it!*"

If I thought he'd do it, I wouldn't hesitate. But, instead, I say, "I don't hate you, Wilby." A lie: I have never hated anyone so much. "I feel sorry for you." The truth—the one truth that he cannot bear. Or that I now hope he cannot bear.

His eyes close.

A moment passes.

Then: *click.*

He has pulled the trigger.

He has pulled the trigger and the gun has not fired and he is still alive. And the gun still has one cartridge in it. And Lydia is coming.

No shadow passes over his face—of disappointment, or surprise, or relief. When he finally opens his eyes, they look stunned but also filled with an eerie exaltation that sends a cold shudder crawling over my flesh.

And when he lowers the gun—very slowly, almost as if the act held some ceremonial significance, as if it were part of some mysterious ritual—and speaks, I hear a new quality of wonder, of awe, in his voice. "I knew. I knew. So be it, Father." And his face now, despite the scars and ridges of blood and red smears, appears transported, even saintlike. "So be it, Father. Thy will be done."

With the shudder moving into my spine, I can only stare in silence, wondering: what does it mean, what next?

Then he is moving toward me, almost floating, eyes fixed on me and yet on some spot or vision beyond me.

I watch as his hand comes up, holding the gun. Then, in that same detached but exalted way, he says, "Your turn." And he places the gun on the bar and withdraws his hand.

Startled, I do not hesitate. In a single motion I set down the glass, pick up the gun, and step backward. And then the shock and realization reach me. And I feel relief welling hotly and slowly through me.

His eyes seem to focus then. He smiles, very faintly. "Your turn." He speaks now with a calmness and precision I have never heard before—almost with benevolence, as if he had just conferred some great benefaction. Gently, softly: "Your turn now."

The logic behind the gesture is clear. I know what he wants, of course. What he expects. "Game's over," I say, wondering whether he can hear me. I drop my eyes to the glass of whisky with the poison in it: is there any need for it now? "My life's all I've got. I'm not going to play games with it." Not that he expects me to: whether he's aware of it or not in his own mind, he wants me to use the gun on him.

"This life? But this life's only . . . what's this life compared to eternity?"

Eternity? The shock moves deeper in me. Who is this person watching me from across the bar now? Is it the boy who suffered such anguish and rebellion because he knew his life was not immortal? It is now as if another personality, or shadow of a personality, has entered that body.

Yet Wilby himself remains, too. Because now he says, "All for the limey wife—" And as I grasp the gun more tightly, ready, he goes on, with a rueful despair that does not sound like Wilby at all, "A whore and an abomination on the earth. Like all women. Like Eve. Whore of Babylon—" It flickers through my mind then that Wilby's view of women and the Bible's are, after all, not too dissimilar. Behind the words, Wilby himself is still goading, pressing. He lifts his voice and turns about to stare up at the portrait. " '. . . by means of a whorish woman a man is brought to a piece of bread; and the adulteress will hunt for the precious life.' "

I glance at my watch: eleven minutes after ten. Is he far enough gone so that now anyone, even a policeman on the street, can recognize—

"She has been selling her body on the streets of London!" he cries out—face lifted, eyes glittering, like some mad prophet out of the Old Testament. "The slut has betrayed you in a thousand beds, on a thousand dark nights!"

It is Wilby, yet it is not Wilby. Behind the prophet shouting fire and brimstone there remains the homosexual hater of women, the betrayed angry boy intent on driving me to kill him. A shadow behind a shadow. How long should I wait before taking action?

He whirls about and comes to the bar again. Now his face is grave but frowning. "You . . . I cannot make my words to sense for you." He speaks with great reasonableness and in a low earnest tone. "You must understand. You are the instigator, liquidator, you the instrument of *his* will, you have the power but only the power squared because of *him,* you do what he ordains, like me, like me, see, pee, piss, see?" He leans closer. No depth in his eyes, only a flat brilliance. Imploring: "You cannot spare me, care me, by cause of your feelings, because, by cause, by law, his law, you must do what you must do, even if you love me. Like Abraham. Only a double sacrifice squared becomes—" Then he straightens. "I am innocent yet I must be punished. You must see that, cat, pat, rat, not for evil but for—" But then he breaks off, and there flashes in his eyes for an instant a familiar cunning that causes him to step away, out of reach, with my left arm almost as stiff as my right from grasping the gun. He reaches behind himself and when his hand reappears it holds a folded sheet of paper. "Wrote you a letter-better-letter—" He smiles, placing his darkened, swollen hand, with the letter, on the bar. The mockery in his smile holds a strange sadness. "Every word true." He leans. "Love—"

I extend my hand. "Give it to me." I speak as if to a child, gently but firmly. "Wilby, give me the letter."

The smile widens but remains empty. He shakes his head. "Letter's for limey-slimey, love—"

A fresh fury sets in. Insane or not, he's not going to read it to Lydia. Insane or not, he is not going to force me to kill him.

"Wilby"—but can he even hear?—"Wilby, I'm not going to do your dirty work for you."

He stiffens. "Dirty?" Shocked. "His work, not *mine*." Then, crying out again: "You have no choice! You are the instigator, liquidator, you have been *chosen,* you—"

I make up my mind, fast. With my right hand I reach, quickly. I place it over his, feeling the pain leaping all through me at the contact, then watch as the two enormous and purple hands grapple, like two grotesque under-sea animals in a life-struggle. His grip on the letter is deathlike. I glance at his face: eyes on me, face composed, a half-smile quiet there, as if the pain that he must feel is not a part of him at all, as if that struggling hand, which now manages to curl the paper into its palm, is also not really a part of him.

Then his other arm comes up and, in a swift chopping stroke, he brings the heel of his hand stiffly and sharply down on mine. The pain is stunning. I lose my grip. I step back. I know what he's doing and he's not going to get away with it. He's not going to get what he wants and finish me off at the same time. I'm not going to shoot him here in my own living room. Not if he's as far gone as I think he is.

When my gaze clears, I see him standing there stiffly. Waiting for the shot? Braced? Hoping?

Twisting my wrist, I raise the gun, raise it high, and bring the barrel battering down sideways on the purple bulge of flesh still grasping the letter. Despite the pain in my own right hand and arm, I can feel the shocking spasm of pain in his as the steel crushes swollen flesh. I hear the ugly, crunching sound first, then his piercing, uncontrollable scream. The hand twists, falls open, flesh gushing blood, and the crumpled paper falls loose on the bar. I grab it quickly and crush it in my right palm, the gun once again ready. Then I watch as his right arm, twitching and leaping like an animal stabbed, sweeps down the bar, carrying with it the whisky bottle and both glasses. I hear the crash and watch him staggering backward, uttering unearthly howls as he automatically brings the hand up into his left armpit, bending forward at the waist, eyes blank and wet.

As the howls turn into prolonged wails, broken by gasps, I shove the paper into my pocket, take down an empty glass, stoop quickly to pick up the bottle that is gurgling whisky onto the stained and already ruined carpet. I splash whisky into the glass and look up. He has sunk to the floor on his knees and he is rocking back and forth, the keening sounds in rhythm with his actions.

It is then that I decide. I feel a terrible and shattering pity—but no regret, no remorse. None. For what I have done or for what it is necessary now to do. I take the two sugar cubes from my pocket, drop them without hesitation into the whisky, and then, holding the glass in my pulsing and distended hand—the gun clasped and ready in the other—I move around the end of bar and approach him.

His keening has subsided into breathless moans, and now he is sitting back on his haunches, eyes closed, head tilted back and to one side, face running tears and blood.

With some care I set the glass on the floor in front of him and step away. If he plunges at my legs again, will I shoot?

"Take a drink," I command him, my tone hard. His sobs work on my nerves and I somehow cannot control the gnawing pity.

He does not appear to hear me. *There can be withdrawal, a refusal to deal with the real world, often a retreat into some private fantasy—*

"Wilby!" Sharply. "Drink the whisky!"

My voice cuts through. His head straightens. His eyes drift glassily around the room, find me, stop. He is no longer sobbing: only an occasional hiccup-like gasp for breath.

"I . . . I was sent here . . . tears . . . to suffer—"

Hearing his words, I recall last night: Wilby lying on the floor waiting for the blows to fall. Now the blow has fallen—what he has demanded of me from the start.

" 'Father, forgive them; for they know not what they do—' "

Behind the quote and behind the shadow superimposed on him, Wilby remains. A double image. Which will speak next? Or are they one? It is like hearing one speaking through the other yet recognizing both, knowing both. And as I realize this, I recognize—without being able to define it—a certain strange logic in it all. An insane logic? Mysterious, yet observable. My own mind plunges, as if it too were about to drop into the abyss.

"They have punished me, Father . . . your sin . . . my sins . . . their sins—"

Slowly then I lower the gun. Even as Wilby stands up, I do not direct it. His bare foot, smeared with blood, touches the glass on the floor. He looks down, then half kneels, picks it up in one hand with a kind of awed curiosity. Will he drink it? *But five hundred micrograms —they tell me it could be lethal.* No need now for him to die. Unless he recovers, remembers—

He peers at me again. Then: "He tempts me, Father." But he is speaking to me. "He has brought me to the pinnacle and now—" He shakes his head. " 'Thou shalt not tempt the Lord thy—' "

And then in a wild action so abrupt that I automatically crouch, raising the gun, he hurls the glass across the room, whisky sloshing crazily toward the ceiling and over the furniture, the glass itself crashing against the wall, shattering, the remaining liquid splotching and then running darkly down the wallpaper.

Don't make me do it, Wilby. I don't want to have to do it now. Don't ask me why, either. Just don't make me do it.

Angrily he cries out, " 'And take heed to yourselves, lest at any time your hearts be overcharged with surfeiting and drunkenness!' "

Then, as if the explosion inside has reinvigorated him, he begins moving, fast, in a straight line, up and down, shouting. "I have come! My father's work, shirk, not shirk, thy will be done, son, I am the light, tight, bite, kite!" He stops, mutters, "All things are delivered to me of my father; and no man knoweth who the son is but the father; and who the father is but the son, and he to whom the son will reveal him—"

The words sound vaguely familiar, out of the past. Yet it is difficult to decide whether he is actually quoting scripture or murmuring more of his own irrational gibberish. And I realize, listening, that the distinction between the two is blurred—perhaps even undefinable.

For a brief instant—in which I know that I must take action now, soon, quickly—I recall my father tramping the Nebraska hills, himself half mad with grief and loss of meaning. And I think of all the millions of people, century after century, finding meaning in unreality. I thrust the thought and the memory aside.

His eyes are now fixed, narrowed and incandescent, on the painting, which is still propped against the cracked cocktail table. Quietly he speaks. "Shameless woman, blameless, vengeance, all things written, fulfilled, whore of Babylon, written, bitten, smitten—" The wildness erupts again, flares like fire through his eyes, and he steps to the painting.

Too late I realize what he intends.

"All women are whores!" he screeches.

And he plunges his bare foot through the canvas.

I hear it rip and feel my hand tighten on the gun. Savage fury explodes in me.

"Shameless tits! Evil, evil, vengeance is mine, saith—" He kicks the painting again and again. Then, when only a few fragments of canvas hang from the frame, he turns away and stands with his back to it, and to me, breathing heavily.

Even hell's something, even hell's better'n nothing—

My finger is stiff and cold on the trigger. I tried to spare you, Wilby, you bastard, I tried to save you, even insanity is something, death is nothing, your time is your eternity, something is always better than nothing, but not now, *not now*! One hundred and twenty thousand dollars. How many hours of work? How many thousands of hours in twenty-five years? I am sick and shaking with rage, choking on it.

Then he turns. When his eyes find mine, he does not glance at the gun but he grins. And in that instant he is himself again: wholly Wilby, cruel, taunting, full of hate, mocking and challenging. When he speaks, though, it is as before—softly and sadly. "What profit it a man if he gain the whole world—" He tilts his head. "Root of evil, root, boot, shoot—"

And, weak and spent, drained now, I know that he is still demanding death. Still insisting, even now.

But I have not come this far to have him win in the end. And while jungle-like revenge pulls at every nerve in me, I know that I must conquer it. Rigidly I lower my arm, and the gun.

Whatever you are moving into, Wilby, whatever it is you dread, you won't get out of it this way. I, too, believe now that even hell is something and that something is always better than nothing, but even if I didn't, I wouldn't kill you now. I won't do it because of myself, myself and Lydia and this apartment and our life and the suspicion, almost a certainty now, that it's no longer necessary to kill you in order to destroy your threat.

Whether he reads this, or part of it, in my face, I cannot know. But I watch him nod, as if acknowledging something—his defeat? His face is again serene. He moves slowly, in the same floating walk that I observed before, to the terrace door, and disappears.

Without hesitating this time I hurry after him. Not now, Wilby, too late, you had your chance. Not now, damn it!

But he is not climbing onto or standing on the balustrade. He is kneeling, half turned from me, head lowered, both arms at his sides. He is mumbling and, as I halt in the door, I strain to make out the words. "Soul . . . exceeding sorrowful . . . to death." His face is again streaked with tears, anguish and fear in his voice. "Father . . . be possible . . . this cup pass from me—" Then he seems to listen. Then: "I know, I know, I *know*." As if he has actually heard a voice explaining something to him. Slowly he stands up. "I will arise . . . to my father . . . say . . . Father, I have sinned . . . against heaven . . . before thee—" Again he listens—while I can only stand and stare, wondering why I feel neither relief nor shock. He nods his head, in sadness and resignation, and starts toward me, slows down, frowning, stops. "You see, you see"—in a rushed whisper, his eyes vivid with excitement, "way it has to be, true works or prove to have anything true, blue, by cause sinning takes blood to repent, sacrificed, double sacrifice only triples it, to be redeemed before he descends in wrath and glory—"

Is he speaking to me? I cannot be sure.

"He has not forsaken, I thought in my head he remembered, in his heart I am free, but he reads my head, he knows and he knows that's why I can't control people noticing—"

Incredulity grips me, quiet but powerful. Has he now gone completely over that line, so far over that I am finally safe? That Lydia is safe, that Anne is safe? But I recall, too, how he emerged from that catatonic state earlier, emerged and attacked. I do not place the gun in my pocket. I do not take my eyes from him. If he has gone over totally, it only remains for me to find a way to get him into competent hands, hands that will care for him. But even this decent and civilized consideration comes second. First, I must get him out and away from *here*!

" '. . . taketh him into an exceeding high mountain—' "

I search my mind for a stratagem to get him to move without shattering this mood, without jolting his mind back into—

" '. . . all kingdoms of the world . . . glory of them—' " His eyes are fixed glassily on me, penetrating. Then, abruptly, he shouts,

"I will not worship you! Thou shalt worship only the Lord thy—"
Then louder still, with violence and hate contorting his face: "Get
thee hence, Satan!"

Then he wheels about and returns to the balustrade, his back to
me. He lifts his arms and I see his right hand dangling at the wrist.
He extends his arms on both sides of his body. "They shall mock me
. . . scourge me . . . spit upon me . . . they shall *kill* me!"

And now I realize what it is he dreads: he actually believes he will
be crucified. He believes it and suffers from the certainty. Yet there is
that weird exaltation still in his tone, too.

How can I take advantage of it? How can I make use of it to get
him downstairs, onto the street, away?

". . . that the scriptures and the prophets might be fulfilled—"

His body sags. He stands limply, arms still outstretched, and his
head sinks to one side.

How can I enter his fantasy? Is it possible to—

I move closer. I speak softly, recalling now some of the words of
the Gospels I had heard Sunday after Sunday years ago. "The hour is
come—"

He does not move. Has he heard? I repeat the words and add, "Behold, the Son of man is betrayed into the hands of sinners."

I wait.

Nothing.

Hopeless.

Should I phone Arnold Wilder? He would at least know how to
proceed, whom to call. But what of his questions, what about the lies
I would then be forced into?

Wilby's head straightens. He moves. He turns to face me.

" 'Friend, wherefore art thou come?' "

Christ's words to Judas Iscariot at the moment of betrayal. What
next? What follows in the story? He stands waiting. And I remember:
Then came they, and laid hands on Jesus, and took him. Can I take
that chance?

I place the gun in my pocket, reach out my hand, and take his arm,
holding it tightly, pulling him toward the door. His face retains that
odd serenity as, submissively, he moves with me—through the door,
across the living room. I do not hurry him. My heart is hammering. I
am not breathing.

On the foyer step he halts and throws back his head. "Father, Father . . . why hast thou forsaken me?" A muted harrowing cry of despair, deep and terrible. But then he whispers, as if answering the voice that echoes only in his mind, "Not my will, but thine—" And he moves again. "Then did they spit in his face . . . buffeted him . . . smote him with palms of hands—"

I let go of his arm to throw open the door to the corridor. He passes into the corridor without pause. Does he have the vaguest idea where he is, or is he lost completely in that unreal world of myth and superstition handed down over the centuries?

As I follow, I feel at last a surge of relief, triumph. It is not his madness in which I rejoice, but my own deliverance. He is out of the apartment at last.

Now, in the hall on the way to the elevator, he is speaking again, this time with an earnestness that causes the words to trip over each other. "Alone, that's how he sits, all alone, always, ice all around, and wind, and nothingness, it's lonely, highest peak, which is why, by cause, justice cannot interfere with the instigator by cause he started it all, so he loses by causing, by cause is effect, which is why he sends his son, not to take on the sins of the world, no, not take on but *commit*, by cause it is ordained, commit the lowest, vilest, to *know*, why he has to suffer and be punished, that's only how it is, everyone knows that—"

The elevator door slides open before us. He does not appear to see it. Again I take the chance and take his arm. He shudders once in the grip of my hand, but—compliant, without protest—he allows me to guide him.

As the elevator goes down, he nods, speaks: "Your hand—"

At once I release his arm. But he is staring down at my other hand. Astonished—then he does see, after all!—I watch as he bends to examine it closely, his face touched by a strange compassion and concern.

"Withered hand . . . stretch forth thine hand—"

Bracing for the pain and ignoring it, I lift my arm. I watch as he closes his eyes. A long moment passes.

The elevator floats to a stop. He open his eyes, gazes down at my hand, and a fleeting satisfaction, not quite a smile, passes over his face. "It is restored whole, like as the other." And he drifts out and across the marble floor of the foyer.

I only glance at my hand: flesh puffed and dark, with fine lines of fiery red clear on the surface now, pain as intense as ever.

His voice floats back to me as I follow. "I will destroy this temple and build it again in three days—"

Geoffrey has the door open. His long lean face looks startled.

Wilby pauses in the door. "Roman soldier—" He is speaking to Geoffrey. "I forgive. You will cast lots for my vinegar and gall, you will feed me my garments, but in three days behold the skies will darken and there will be a great earthquake, which makes only six days left—"

Geoffrey only stares in silence as Wilby passes out into the street; then, still holding the door, he turns to me.

"Geoffrey, call the police. Send them to the corner." I nod after Wilby as I go through the door. "Mr. Abbott's friend needs medical attention."

"Yes, sir. Rely on me, sir."

And as I follow Wilby at a distance, I wonder whether Geoffrey has glimpsed in him some reflection of the illness that his own wife suffers.

Then I become conscious of the curious stares turned on Wilby, the sniggers, the nudges and muttered amusement. And I feel an angry protectiveness. What the hell do they know? Or care? All they see is a young man with a blood-and-tear-blurred face, raw arms, and bare feet, walking with a strange and graceful composure, dreamlike, his gaze fixed ahead of him at once serene and benevolent and un- earthly. What do they know?

And my mind flashes back in time, across the years, to the streets of Fort Perry: leading my father home, hating the smug, uncaring, contemptuous faces staring, half hating my father at the same time. Forgive me, Father. Forgive.

By the time I reach the corner, Wilby has moved toward a man who leans, sagging, against a store-front: bedraggled, unshaven, ob- viously drunk. As I approach, Wilby is speaking to him and, when I stop, the drunk squints up into Wilby's face, muttering something in- coherent and obsequious.

Wilby reaches his injured right hand into his pocket, draws out a snarl of bills, lifts them above his head and lets them flutter down to the sidewalk. "Render unto Caesar things that . . . profit a man gain if lose his immortal—"

Almost at once a small crowd gathers. The drunk is on his hands and knees snatching at the bills. A woman cries, "Here, you bum, that's mine!" And a man in shirt-sleeves knees the drunk aside and bends to pick up whatever bills he can lay his hands on. Another woman's voice shrills, "Well, why not, that's what I say, don't be that way, why *not* for gossake?" And in the center of the furor Wilby stands, imperturbable, meek and detached, head straight, lifted.

He speaks as to a listening multitude, only a few phrases clear above the excited voices and commotion. ". . . say unto you . . . live by sword . . . perish by eternal hope damnation . . . good them hate you—"

While I stand helplessly now on the perimeter of the growing crowd—

A man shouts, "Louder'n funnier!"

". . . bless them that curse, purse, nurse you—"

A woman hoots, cupping hands at mouth. "Music! Say it with music!"

But Wilby does not lift his voice. ". . . except that ye repent, relent . . . my father . . . come to redeem—"

A deep male voice grunts in disgust. "Ahhh, it was just a come-on—"

"Some kind of fanatic—"

". . . despitefully use and persecute, known as the sacrificers by cause the cause is known—"

"Look, his feet are bleeding—"

"A nut, that's what he is—"

"Somebody musta shut a door on his hand—"

". . . a while ye shall not see me, then again forty days and forty nights in the desert ye shall see me—"

"Come on, we're gonna be late—"

"Wait. What's he *saying*? It's *interesting*—"

Unable to go on watching and listening, I shoulder my way toward Wilby. I have almost reached him when I hear the low whir of a siren behind me, see a flash of red light, see the drunk slither away along the store fronts. I turn around with relief and yet with a sudden trepidation, almost panic.

A patrol car pulls up to the curb. A uniformed officer, heavy-set and sweating, steps out and starts bawling, "All right, break it up, move along, break it up!" He sounds disgusted, tired. "Move on, *move!*"

The driver opens his door and I make my way to the front of the car and place myself in his path as he is about to step to the curb.

"Officer—"

Young, extremely tall, with a heavy-jowled face and dull impatient eyes, he hesitates, looking over my shoulder toward Wilby and the uproar. "Outta my way, mister—"

"Listen. That boy's sick. He needs help."

Behind me I hear the crowd dispersing, muttering, and the other officer saying to Wilby, "All right, kid, okay, show's over for tonight. Knock it off."

"Redemption draweth nigh, there is still time, if the rhyme is right, bright—"

"Knock it off, I said!"

Hearing the threat in his tone, I explain to his partner, who is still peering beyond me, "He's not hurting anyone. He's not breaking any law. The boy's obviously a mental case. What he needs is—"

Now the officer's eyes are on me—cynical, suspicious. "Yeh? What you know about this odd-ball?"

While behind me his companion asks, "What's your name, pal?"

"I don't know anything except what I can see and hear." With urgency straining my voice: "It's obvious, isn't it, that he's been injured and it's your duty to treat him with—"

"Don't tell me my duty, mister. Everywhere I go, somebody's telling me my duty now they got this review board." He glares beneath a frown. "You happen to know this character's name?"

"No."

Behind me: "Just your name, pal. You know your own name, don't you?"

And Wilby's voice, unruffled: "I am the resurrection and the dark. I have spoken, broken, *enough*."

A few snickers, one outright laugh.

And the officer shakes his head, asking, "Ever seen this creep before, mister?"

Bleakly. "No." Hopelessly. "I don't know him, but what's that got to do with it?"

"Sure you're not his old man, something like that?"

"No."

He steps around me. "Then whyn't you stay outta things ain't your business in the first place?"

"He needs medical help, not jail!" But it's a desperate and futile plea, unheard or ignored.

I turn to watch the two policemen conferring in whispers and shrugs as Wilby, head lifted, asks mildly, "Are ye come as against a thief . . . brief . . . annihilators . . . to take me from Gethsemane to Golgotha?"

A man shouts, "Golgotha, New Jersey! I know it well!" And the young woman clinging to his arm sniggers, saying, "Shh, *listen!*"

Wilby hears none of it. "A place of a skull—"

The heavy-set officer wipes his brow. "Okay, okay, pal, we'll take you to Golgotha." He sounds bitter, unreasonably hostile, and grabs Wilby by the arm, the right arm, not gently, and leads him, submissive but proud, toward the car, through the few silent, curious stragglers who remain.

Wilby does not wince. With that same bemused and rapt exaltation on his face, with grotesque dignity, he allows himself to be conducted into the rear seat with the heavy-set patrolman following. I stare through the side window as the tall one climbs in and starts the motor. Wilby stares straight ahead—at what vision, of fulfillment, or terror, or both? The siren whirs once.

And Peter remembered the word of Jesus, which said unto him, Before the cock crow, thou shalt deny me thrice.

As the car draws away, Wilby turns his head. Our eyes meet. Does he even see me? There is no recognition in his gaze. Only . . . detachment. A profound and astounding peace. *Some, they got hell inside. Night'n day. Others, though . . . lucky ones . . . they got a kinda peace . . . faces kinda lit up . . . like they found nirvana . . . salvation—*

I turn and begin to walk back to the apartment building. But I cannot weep, Wilby. I'm sorry for you. I mean that. But I cannot weep. It was your choice, not mine, from the beginning. And in some awesome and mysterious way which I cannot fathom, what is happening now is your choice, too. I do not know how, but you yourself chose this way out. If I know nothing else, I know—have learned—that each of us chooses, minute by minute, year by year, chooses and becomes. I can feel sadness, Wilby, and compassion, but I cannot weep for you. It had to be you or me: you set up the rules. You pushed the game to its limits, Wilby, and you cracked. And if I had any of it to do again, I would not hesitate to do exactly what I have done today and tonight. I have no remorse, Wilby—no compunction, no guilt. What has happened tonight, or some form of it—whether suicide or madness or brutal destruction of others—has been in you all along. And self-willed. I have taken advantage of that, I know. And given the same alternatives, I would do so again. After the terror, I can feel only pity and sorrow. Not for what I have done, but that it must be so.

Passing Geoffrey, who watches me without nodding, I say nothing. Time for explanations tomorrow. Explanations and more lies. Time enough tomorrow to begin building that shaky foundation of lies on which the future must now be based.

I feel Geoffrey's eyes on me as I step into the elevator. . . . *half balmy, you might say, thinking of her being put away . . . state institution . . . all know what those places are—*

Yes, we know. And do nothing. A cruel and unjust world. Which Wilby could not accept. Instead of doing something, he opted out. As most of us do, one way or the other. As I will not do now. Never again. Curious and ironic that I have come to this through Wilby. The grit, invading the oyster shell, producing the pearl.

As the elevator rises, the sense of relief becomes intoxicating. I can feel it flowing through me, healing and quickening. It's over. It's really over. We're free again: Lydia, Anne, Glenn, all of us. Invaded, imprisoned, now liberated. Free.

I walk the familiar corridor as if seeing it for the first time—or in a new light. No longer blind, I see it as a path to a place where meaning and promise are concentrated.

I open the door slowly, at once hesitant and quivering with anticipation.

I go inside.

Again I am reminded of those towns and cities in Europe after the war. At first I am struck with dismay: how can such ugly and utter devastation ever be restored to civilized order and the safe, quiet beauty of which I was in the past only faintly and smugly aware? How can it be done?

Why, it can be done in the same way that all those plundered and ravaged and pillaged cities all through history were rebuilt, the way people everywhere have always restored their cities and their lives after any catastrophe, fire or flood or hurricane. It can be made whole and beautiful again by the will and energy and spirit of man. By commitment, and love.

I go about throwing open the windows, the terrace door. Then I turn the thermostat to its coldest extreme. Get the stench out first. The stench of the swamp and jungle.

I take off my jacket, the pain in my hand and arm flaring, and become conscious of the weight of the gun in the pocket. I take it out and look at it. Will the time ever come when any weapon will be as anarchronistic as those ancient altars on which human sacrifices were performed? I wrap the gun in my jacket and place it on the lower step. If Professor Kantor was right, that time will come; but meanwhile, in order to survive to that distant point in evolution, to survive against the enemies of the process—

I look at my watch. Five minutes until eleven. More than an hour before Lydia, with all the luck and determination and resourcefulness imaginable, can possibly arrive. It's more likely that I have the whole night and part, at least, of tomorrow. Even working with one hand, I can do it. I can do anything now, *anything*!

I pick up the cracked picture frame and look at the gaping emptiness that had once been beauty. Beauty that I had not been able to recognize but that Lydia would have grasped at once. More than twenty years of work; more than twenty years of my life. Still, I do not feel the loss. The savings of my entire adult life. Not true! I'm not yet fifty years old. The savings, then, of only *half* my adult life. And anyone can make money. A sense of power surges through me as I carry the frame to the incinerator chute in the kitchen and locate a broom and dustpan. If half my adult—and therefore meaningful—life is behind, then half lies ahead. If not another twenty years, then whatever part of those years I do have: my eternity. It's not the length of time that matters, but what happens in that time, however long or short!

Returning to the living room, I am aware of the strength, the buoyancy, of my step, the vitality pumping in my veins. It's over, *over*, and Lydia will soon be here!

I look up at the ruined, the desecrated portrait. Then I take it down from the wall over the fireplace. In the whole city of New York there has to be someone who can remove the paint or ink or whatever. If not, someone who can reproduce it as it was.

Lydia. The idea of her presence, her actual presence, flesh and blood and loveliness, makes me go hollow. She'll be here soon and I will possess her again and *know* for the first time that I am possessing more than the beauty of her body, know that I am possessing mystery, mystery that over the years I'll have the excitement and satisfaction of exploring and even possibly unraveling.

The joy is fierce in me now. The exhilaration and anticipation make me giddy. As I begin to work with the broom, swiftly and with certainty, a wild exultancy takes over so that, for a few concentrated and passionate moments, I feel that I will actually utter some ecstatic cry of relief and renewal and expectancy. And I know, too, that if everything that has happened had not happened, I would not be capable now of this depth and intensity of feeling and knowing.

The telephone rings.

❧ Postscript

Dear Lydia:

As soon as I heard your voice on the phone that night, I knew that it was not over. I realized at once that none of it could ever be over and put behind until there was truth between us. The future, if there is to be one, cannot be constructed on that foundation of lies and half-truths.

While I heard you explaining, tearlessly, of your mother's heart attack and death just as you were preparing to leave London, I kept wondering how I could find a way to tell you so that there would be some slight chance of your understanding. Then, when you said that you would have to stay there for at least three weeks to clear up all sorts of business matters having to do with her death and that you honestly hoped I wouldn't feel obliged to come over, it was as if fate —chance again—had intervened.

Three weeks. Arnold wanted to put me in the hospital but I convinced him my arm would heal at home. What you have read is what I dictated in the last three weeks, Lydia—dictated into a tape-recorder that Henry provided, dictated at all hours of day and night, always under the influence of antibiotics and almost always in intense and sometimes unendurable pain as the infection was driven from my hand and arm and bloodstream. Anne and Glenn and Henry, as well as Arnold, who was a stern and fatherly tyrant, made sure that I ate well and regularly, although I would not allow any of them to stay more than a few minutes at a time. I have not been able to read over the pages you have just read because Henry had them typed by a secretarial service, explaining that they were a novel by a friend of his, and I finished dictating only the day before you arrived. Henry offered to meet your plane and to give you the manuscript and to make some explanation: I can only hope he was gentle, but, knowing how he loves you, I am sure he was.

It was Henry, too, who followed through on Wilby. His case has been diagnosed as hopeless: he lives in a world of his own imagining and will never emerge into the real world again. He will be sent back to the hospital in Ohio because he did commit a particularly horrible crime there, for which he was committed. There is no danger now that he will escape or that, if he should, he will even remember what happened here. Henry also reports that the doctors told him that, no matter where Wilby exists physically, he will be happy inside himself until he dies. If there is an irony there, I have not yet been able to absorb it fully. That Wilby should, in the end, be the one to find peace—

I have received a card from Donald: a brilliant picture of the beach at Cannes. On the back he wrote only: *You were so right.* He did not mention Jenny.

Lydia, as I dictated—awkwardly, I know, and sometimes without coherence, I am sure—I was aware every second of the pain you would suffer as you read the words. But I knew, too, that if you yourself had a choice, regardless of your own anguish, or mine, you would demand truth. (I do know that much of you, Lydia, or have learned it.) And I was aware, too, that if I believe in anything in the Bible, it is only that the truth shall set you free. Not the Bible's truth, but truth itself. This, then, is the truth, Lydia—as unvarnished, as complete as I have been able to see it and to make it.

And now only the questions remain:

Will the truth really set us free?

Are we yet capable or ready for truth?

Is the world—all of us and what we have made the world and failed to make the world—at least somewhat responsible for Wilby's mind? What it hated and rebelled against and had to escape one way or the other?

Even though he is now lunatic, can we risk not examining his ideas? Can we dismiss his questions because those questions—to what degree?—drove him to madness?

Did Wilby ever have free will and did he himself choose? Or is that very idea only an illusion necessary to survival? Or at least to some inherent demand in us that somehow meaning must be imposed and we must be able either to recognize or to create that meaning?

What did I do that I should not have done? Or what did I do that I failed to do?

In placing those whom I love first, I moved a small stumbling step outside myself—but did I move far enough? Did I betray the process of evolution by protecting my family and acting ruthlessly toward those who threatened us? Will we ever be capable of moving further? Toward what?

If man is not ultimately perfectible, is the illusion that he is also vital so that we can go forward and yet live as civilized men, not savages, in the meantime?

Does man always realize too late what he has—what he is and what he might be?

Most important—more important than anything else, Lydia—is the question now: what will you do when you have finished reading this? I am not going to say I love you. What you have just read is a long and complex love letter. I can only hope. Has it come too late?

Henry knows where I am. I am waiting for your answer.

Ever,

ADAM